'Extraordinary ... a real sensory experience ... suffused with colours' — *The Bookshelf*, ABC Radio National

'Cadwallader's evocation of medieval London is vibrant. And her delineation of the crafting of the book is endlessly fascinating' — *The Australian*

'Masterfully handles an ensemble cast bursting with conundrums and secrets. Poetic, unpredictable, and totally immersive' — *Better Reading*

'Superb ... an ecstatic evocation of the skills of scribes and illuminators' — *Australian Women's Weekly*

'*Book of Colours* brings alive a harsh but rich past, filled with the fantasies, fears, sly wit and tender longings of the medieval imagination' — Sarah Dunant

Praise for *The Anchoress*

'Sarah's story is so beautiful, so rich, so strange, unexpected, and thoughtful — also suspenseful. The narrative examines the question of whether a woman can ever really retreat from the world, or whether the world will always find a way to come after you ... I loved this book' — Elizabeth Gilbert

'Affecting ... finely drawn ... a considerable achievement for a debut novel' — Sarah Dunant, *New York Times Book Review*

'Robyn Cadwallader does the real work of historical fiction, creating a detailed, sensuous and richly imagined shard of the past. She has successfully placed her narrator, the anchoress, in that tantalising, precarious, delicate realm: convincingly of her own distant era, yet emotionally engaging and vividly present to us in our own' — Geraldine Brooks

'An ambitious debut … [offers] pleasures of a subtle and delicate kind … Cadwallader plays gracefully with medieval ideas about gender, power and writing' — *The Guardian*

'A surprisingly gripping tale of faith, temptation, grief, defiance and self-acceptance' — *Daily Telegraph*

'Elegant and eloquent' — *Irish Mail*

Robyn Cadwallader lives in the country outside Canberra. She has published a non-fiction book about virginity and female agency in the Middle Ages (2008), a poetry collection, *i painted unafraid* (2010), and an edited collection of essays on asylum-seeker policy, *We Are Better Than This* (2015). Her first novel, *The Anchoress* (2015), was published in Australia, the UK, the United States and France; it won a Canberra Critics Award and the ACT Book of the Year People's Choice Award; it was also shortlisted for the Indie Book Awards and the Adelaide Festival Literary Awards, longlisted for the ABIA Awards and Highly Commended in the ACT Book of the Year Award.

Book of Colours

ROBYN CADWALLADER

FOURTH ESTATE

Fourth Estate

An imprint of HarperCollins*Publishers*

First published in Australia in 2018
This edition published in 2019
by HarperCollins*Publishers* Australia Pty Limited
ABN 36 009 913 517
harpercollins.com.au

HarperCollins*Publishers*
Level 13, 201 Elizabeth Street, Sydney NSW 2000, Australia
Unit D1, 63 Apollo Drive, Rosedale, Auckland 0632, New Zealand
A 53, Sector 57, Noida, UP, India
1 London Bridge Street, London, SE1 9GF, United Kingdom
Bay Adelaide Centre, East Tower, 22 Adelaide Street West, 41st floor,
  Toronto, Ontario M5H 4E3, Canada
195 Broadway, New York NY 10007, USA

A catalogue record for this book is available from the National Library of Australia.

ISBN 978 1 4607 5797 0 (paperback)
ISBN 978 1 4607 0705 0 (ebook)

Cover design © Sandy Cull, gogoGingko
Cover illustration © Sandy Cull, based on image by shutterstock.com
Author photo by Alan Cadwallader
Epigraph quoted by kind permission of Dover Publications Inc., New York, from Cennino d'Andrea Cennini, *The Craftsman's Handbook: the Italian "Il Libro dell'Arte"*, translated by Daniel V. Thompson, Jr.
Typeset in Sabon LT Std by Kirby Jones

19 20 21 22 23 LSCC 10 9 8 7 6 5 4 3 2 1

For my children, Jessica, Myfanwy,
Daniel and Demelza

Painting ... calls for imagination, and skill of hand, in order to discover things not seen, hiding themselves under the shadow of natural objects, and to fix them with the hand, presenting to plain sight what does not actually exist.

Cennino d'Andrea Cennini (b. 1360),

Il Libro dell'Arte

Mathilda

Wain Wood Manor, Welwyn, Hertfordshire
May 3, 1322

It is wrapped in soft yellow cloth that shines with the light and falls into rich shadows in the folds. Untouched in the centre of the table, the bundle seems abandoned.

Roger de Southflete, stationer of London Bridge, stands behind a chair. 'I hope the book will be suitable to your needs, Lady Mathilda,' he says, and nods toward the package he has delivered.

Mathilda frowns. She is standing on the other side of the table, a chair pulled out as if she has been about to sit but changed her mind. 'I'm sure the book will bring me comfort, even as it is. Master Dancaster's work is bound to speak to me of God. That will be enough.'

She lifts a hand toward the bundle, but lets it drop again. Anticipation is a strange creature. For nearly two years she has waited for this moment, and now it is here, she doesn't want to unwrap the parcel. How long she has imagined the illuminators with brush and quill, bent at their desks day after day, choosing colour and gold leaf. How long she has waited to see their work. But now she doesn't want to look inside.

She reaches out and touches the cloth. It's soft and shifts beneath her fingers; someone took care to wrap the book beautifully, whatever they thought of it. Was it William, or was he too angry? Dancaster, perhaps; did he send his wife to buy a small piece of silk? Mathilda's eyes prickle with tears when she thinks of a woman laying out the cloth, folding it over the book, handing it to Southflete. That silk, it's such a kind thing to do. She wipes her eyes. Only weeks ago, the awkward bundle wrapped in cloth was Robert's body.

I

London
October 1320

Flaying the Skin

If you touch the page, it's smooth and fine. Up close, you can see the pores where hairs once grew. It's no easy task to turn animal skin to this. Goat or sheep, maybe calf. The slaughter, then the flaying, hide stripped from body.

The parchmenter chooses his skin carefully and his work begins: the soaking, scraping, stretching and shaving. Hard labour it is. Nothing fine is made without it be broken down first. You can't have delicate illuminations on a rough page. The lady will forget this was once a beast, too coarse for her, but only because the parchmenter does his job. And does it well enough to be forgotten.

But don't you forget. Flesh made ready for the word. Our Lord, who came as a man of flesh, is called the Word of God, his body stretched on the cross as tight as skin on a frame.

The Art of Illumination

Unaware of the cold, he followed the icy road, turning again and again to look behind him. Felt the crawl of eyes on his back, heard whispers in the rustle of trees, saw shadows creep and dart. Each time, a shock ran through his limbs, had him ready to run. And each time, when he realised he was mistaken, the relief emptied him out, left him ragged. Still, he was sure they were behind him somewhere, following, demanding justice.

At night a black river ran through his dreams, coiling and twisting beneath a moonless sky. He slept and woke, slept and woke, exhausted by the effort, and walked on. He wanted to cry, his chest ached with the need, but that was allowed only to the innocent. Grief was forbidden him.

One morning, a fresh fall of snow hushed the world like a blanket. A companion that asked no questions, it gathered him in. All was whiteness and he wanted only this, to go on walking, thoughtless. At first it seemed reprieve, but it was the chill, settling into his bones and his mind, lulling its danger. As much a threat to his life as his faceless pursuers. On he walked, step by step, thinking he could walk forever.

Gradually, the white turned muddy, ground into slush by feet and hooves and cartwheels. His boots leaked, then soaked through. The road filled with travellers riding horses and farmers driving their loaded carts and reluctant animals. Sound and smell drew him on, tugged at his raw and aching body, reminded him he was a man, fleeing.

It was almost dark when he walked through Bishopsgate, moving slowly on numb feet. His fingers had lost all feeling and had fixed themselves tight into a fist. The new smells, some of them not even food, awoke his need to eat. He bent over, then stooped further as a cramp twisted and dragged his innards, threatened to topple him completely. But this was not the place to stop, and one, two, three people passing by knocked him, not seeing him or not caring, until he lost his balance and fell. He winced at the shock of it. Pulling himself to his feet, he stumbled into a passing woman.

'You watch yourself, you,' she shouted.

He flinched and stumbled back, fear flaring again.

'You need to be indoors, you do,' the woman scolded. 'If you've nowhere to go, try St Mary's.'

He said nothing.

'St Mary's,' she said more slowly. 'St Mary Spital, y'know? The hospital. Back out the gate you came in, walk a little way and it's on the right. You'll see it easy enough.'

He stared at her, eyes wide, as if the words meant nothing, so she pushed him back through the gate, onto the road he never wanted to see again. 'That way. I'd say you've come a ways. In this weather, only fools or desperate men travel on foot. You gotta name?' she asked.

He could manage that. 'Will.'

He woke with a start at the ringing of a bell and peered around, instantly afraid, though he couldn't remember why. The call to prayer rang on and, as he sat up, his body returned to him: his legs ached, his hands and feet throbbed, the skin tender. God before food, he thought, as he mumbled some words. He took the bread being handed out; that, and some ale, made the morning seem possible. The last days came back to him and he peered around, the familiar fear returning. The men nearby seemed barely alive, most of them mere bumps in their beds, others limping or bent. He must look just like them. He noticed two monks talking, heads together, one nodding in his direction. His belly clenched. Had men been here, swords drawn, demanding to claim him? He needed to move, hide himself in the crowds of London.

He pulled himself upright and drew in a sharp breath as needles of pain shot through his feet and into his legs. A fitting penance, he mused, though there would never be shrift enough for what he had done. The weight hung above him, stifling and close, shutting off air. But he hadn't wanted to go; it had been Simon's idea, after all, and— He stopped the thought there, refused to rehearse it all again.

Outside, the sky was clear, and the early sun bounced off the frost like a demon, straight into his eyes. It was strange to see blue in the sky, though it did nothing to change the piercing cold of the air. He felt again for his money purse, checked for the hard edges of coins, still there, wrapped a hand around it as tightly as his bandages would allow him, and threw his pack over his shoulder: a few clothes, a roll of parchment, his precious brushes and knives wrapped in cloth. He tried to be alert to eyes watching him too closely, or a body pressing too near, but it was hopeless; the morning travellers carried him back inside Bishopsgate, a tangle of people, shops, stalls, carts, baskets and animals, dead and alive.

He looked around to see if others were alarmed, but they were all too busy, too familiar with it. Bundled through the tumult, he came out into an open space, the junction of four streets. Ahead of him was the widest, longest street he had ever seen, lined with shops and houses, some three storeys high and leaning across to each other as if in greeting. He stopped, caught by the spectacle. A hand on his arm, the grip of fingers. He pulled away, turned, ready to punch and run, but it was only a woman with a basket of foul-smelling herrings. She clutched at his arm again, croaked something about the price, but he wrenched himself loose and pushed her so hard that she fell. Panting, he stumbled on without looking back.

The ground rose toward the far end of the street, and now and then between the shops he could see a cross. It must be St Paul's Cathedral with its new spire that he had heard talk of. He kept on, step by painful step, up the incline. It was slow walking, but in time he reached a second open area where five streets ran together into a broad space large enough, he thought, for football, or even a joust. At one end, set atop a base of octagonal steps, was a sculpted tower about the height of the shops nearby and decorated with tiers of arches, figures carved in fine detail and a crucifix at the very top. Will climbed the steps, drawn by the beauty of the sculpture, and ran his fingers along the word carved into the stone. Eleanor. So this was one of the crosses he had heard about. Overwhelmed with grief at the death of his wife, King Edward I had commanded a cross be erected at every place the funeral procession had paused on its way from Oxford to London. It seemed like a story, a romance recited at a market, pictures sketched in the air, but there it stood, tall and elegant.

Above the general clamour, Will realised one voice was louder than the rest. The man was standing in front of a church, his clothes black and ragged.

'What more warning does our Lord need to give us? For years now, he has sent flood and he has sent famine to make us turn from our sins. Seven years we have suffered, and this is not the first time. Only three generations past, eighty years by man's measure, the sky was covered with a black cloud, blocking out the sun for the seasons of a year or more. Once again, God pours out his wrath. As the prophet Jeremiah declares, the Lord has a strong arm and a mighty anger. He brings justice with a sword. Did he not destroy Sodom and Gomorrah? Did he not drive his people into Egypt?' With each question, he raised his fist into the air and brought it down into the palm of his other hand. 'Did he not destroy the world in a flood? As he promised, he will not let the waters swallow up the world, but he reminds us, with rain and frost and ruined crops that bring hunger and death, that he is a vengeful God.'

'There'd be food enough if the rich didn't hoard their grain!' an onlooker shouted.

'Do not speak as the fool does. The rich don't bring the rain or the harsh grip of frost. Hoard they might, but in their greed they only serve God's justice. Even so, they will be judged, as we all will be. Admit your sin. Turn from wrongdoing. Do not think that God hasn't seen you in the darkness of your misdeeds. Nothing will cover over your evil.'

Will stepped back, stumbled against the cross behind him, and grabbed onto it for balance. Had the preacher looked at him? Did he know, even here in London, what he was running from?

'Where's God's mercy then, for the little ones?' a woman shouted, a baby in her arms. 'My boy ain't no sinner.'

'We are all born into sin, born of fornication and lust, the desires of the body,' the preacher answered.

'Yeah? I bet you know all about lust, eh? I bet you're still preaching sin when you give it to the harlots,' someone else shouted, a hand at his groin. The crowd jeered, relieved at the joke.

At this, Will was released from the grip of the preacher's attack, and he turned away.

The cross had just enough lacework and carving to give space for his hands and feet, and despite his aching clumsiness he climbed up as far as he could for a better view of the city; the churches and the river, centre of any settlement, would give him his bearings. Behind and to his right was St Paul's Cathedral, its huge grounds filled with buildings and edged by a high wall. Beyond, down the length of a street, he could see the river shining white with ice, the docked boats now trapped in its cold grip. He climbed a little higher, hoping to see London Bridge and the Tower of London, but his view was blocked by buildings. Instead of the rough map he had hoped for, he gazed across the mix of order and confusion, a mass of shops, houses, markets and churches all held inside a great wall. The city crawling, curling and bumping into itself.

Slowly, holding on where he could, he shuffled around the cross until he faced the other direction, toward the sounds of men yelling above the bellowing of animals. From this height, if he looked carefully, he could see carcasses streaked with white swinging from hooks, piles of bloody, shapeless skins, and offal, green and pink and brown and black. The Shambles, a street seething with slaughter. A breeze blew its smells toward him: the shit of terrified animals, the sharp iron of blood. Will's belly heaved and he looked away to his left, toward the magnificence of St Paul's, its coloured rose window, its tall spire and the cross on top almost touching the few patches of cloud hovering above.

At the base of the roof was an army of gargoyles, stone-grown and weather-worn, each one distinct, all reaching out beyond the gutters, spout-mouths open. Creatures dragged from some netherworld and put to work guarding the holy ground beneath. Such proud ugliness, so assured of their right to be there, as if directing water away from the building was merely a foil for their true status. Will was entranced. What minds the masons had, to carve from solid stone such creatures that seemed at once of air and earth. Hybrid beasts: bird beak, wolf mouth, monkey snout, ox hoof; ravaging teeth and horns; flapping ears and wings; howl and snuffle, snicker and growl. He had seen the like before many times, on smaller churches, but here, on the edges of the cathedral's magnificence, they were at once more grotesque and more impressive. Here and there the sun flared on a shingle, then faded as the clouds shifted.

Will startled at a movement, looked again. One of the gargoyles began to stir. A trick of sun and shadow, surely. He focused more closely. The creature's nose was flattened apelike to its face, two horns protruded from the top of its head, bulbous eyes peered around. Slowly, as slowly as stone moves, it closed its mouth, pulled in its long neck and turned its head. Their eyes met. Will's belly turned to liquid. He lurched, slipped from his awkward perch, grabbed onto a curl of stone tracery to save himself from falling, gasped in pain. When he looked up again, the creature was gone.

He climbed down from the cross, caught at the arm of a young boy running past and asked him what street this was. Cheap, the boy shouted as he pulled away. So this was Cheapside; Will had heard talk of it. He walked on.

Will was determined to avoid the river, so he couldn't understand how he found himself at its edge, staring down with it staring back. The sun lit up its frozen ripples. As Will stood, mesmerised, a young lad chased his ball toward the middle, held up his hands in victory, waved to his friends, and though one boy cheered, the others looked on, silent, uneasy. Held their breath like Will.

'Get off the ice, you brat,' he shouted. 'Now. It's not thick enough to walk on. Get off.'

The boy tried to make his way back to the edge, slipped and slid, fell over twice. Then a single 'Oh!' Had he heard something? Was there a movement in the ice? Will couldn't tell, but the boy's face collapsed from triumph into fear, his mouth wide in fright. Will closed his eyes, felt the heaviness creep up into his throat, choking his breath, waited for the crack and the splash. But there was nothing more, only the boy on land, boasting that he was never scared, no he wasn't, God's bones he wasn't. He didn't argue, though, when one of the group suggested they play on the moors instead of the Thames.

Will wondered: would he have run onto the ice, stretched out a hand, dived in? Was that how forgiveness worked? Days turning back like the pages of a book, Cambridge and London folding one on top of the other. The water, the ice, the faint 'Oh!' of shock. The clouds opening, the deep voice of God proclaiming, Here, take this moment, William Asshe. Redemption, they would call it. But there was no crack, no splash, and the chance was gone to find out how sorry he really was.

The dock nearby was empty now but for the gargoyle which squatted, watching him, arms crossed on its knees, penis dangling loose between its legs and a wide grin cracking its ugly face. The round eyes blinked slowly, its throat gurgled with the green slime that lined it.

2

London
October 1320

The Limner

Truly, God the Creator is an artisan, measuring the earth and the heavens, dividing light from dark, land from water, shaping trees and mountains, moulding with his hands sea creatures, animals, birds and all crawling things. And finally, bringing forth humans from clay.

One who paints is an artisan humbly following the Great Artisan. As a limner, you must have an eye that observes carefully all of God's creation. You must have imagination that sees visions of what might be, of all that God has created that is not yet known to us. You must have a heart that encompasses order and disorder, the serious and the playful, so that you can understand the delicate dance between word and picture. But these things, important as they are, are not enough. Above all, you must love your work, listen to all it asks of you, let colour and shape, light and shadow, lead your brush.

The Art of Illumination

Gemma was on her way home from the bakehouse when she noticed a man climbing Eleanor's Cross. Usually it was children, who'd get a whack from whoever nearby cared enough about the sanctity of a carved tower, and could reach them. That wasn't her on either score. There it was, set in the middle of this open space, on high ground, and if it wasn't so awkward to climb, you'd swear it was made as a lookout. A few people glanced up, but no one disturbed this climber; he was probably too big for anyone to dare.

Turning left down Old Change and past St Paul's, she paused at Godric's cart to buy leeks. How he'd coaxed them to grow in this weather, she'd no idea; those in her back garden were short, stumpy things that had to be boiled and boiled, and even so they tasted bitter. The mud in front of the cart was worse than in other places, the overnight freeze softening in the sun, making the ice give up its rich mixture of rotten fruit and vegetables, and the human shit that Godric tipped from the bucket before he left at dusk. It wasn't allowed, and he could have walked the short way to the river or used a public privy, but it was quicker and easier to use a bucket then throw it toward the river, hoping the incline, the rain or the dung carters would take it away. Bad business, Gemma thought, because the stench made the vegetables themselves seem rotten. It was always the same, and though she had often vowed never to buy from the vegetable seller again, he was old and sick, and he grew better vegetables than anyone else, so she gave him whatever custom she could.

Behind his cart, Godric seemed to be disappearing, day by day, shorter and thinner.

'This'll be the end of me,' he said. 'I been cold, but never like this. Nothing'll warm me. It's death in me bones.'

He was always dismal, but this time it seemed he was right: his chest was sunken and his face was sharp and angular. Gemma handed over coins, murmured some words of hope she didn't believe, and turned. Light caught her eye and she looked up at St Paul's, stopped to absorb the lines of its spire and rooflines, its arches, pillars and coloured glass. Most days, the cathedral was a shadow that loomed over Paternoster Row, so close and so familiar that she never really saw it, but this morning it was glittering in the sun, its colours dancing as if the world had just begun, fresh and unsullied, as if the cold and famine were nothing. Well, to a building they would be;

all it had to do was stand in its glory and bear the preaching and indulgence of those who looked after it, and the smell and chatter of those who crowded inside. Cold, hunger, sickness, it had no idea, built to last forever.

'Gemma! Oy!'

A tug at her shoulder thrust Gemma back into the cold world, ready for an argument. It was Annie, laughing.

'Ooh, your face, Gemma Dancaster. Good thing you don't have a knife.' Annie stepped back in mock fear. 'You don't, do you?'

'Not in the mood for laughing, that's all, Annie.' Gemma hoisted her basket higher on her arm.

'Ah, Alice, is it? She's gone then? I saw her leave with her bag.' Annie's smile dropped and her face softened. 'It's the best thing. It's a good position with the bishop, and she's close by. I'd go into service too, if I could live on the Strand in a grand house.'

'You sound like John, you do,' Gemma said. 'The girl has an eye for colour and line. Why waste it cleaning the sheets of a fat bishop?'

'No, Gem, you're wrong there. That bishop's not fat. Old and thin, he is.'

'Don't mock me. I mean it.'

Annie laughed. 'Come on, Gemma. We gotta laugh, don't we?'

'Why laugh, Annie? My only girl, she is. The house is full of men now. I'd always thought we could give her good work in the shop.'

'What, John's shop? Painting on books?'

'Why not? Look at Mabel, Mary's girl, she's just begun work as a silk maker.'

'That's making silk though. Not so hard to do once you learn. Different from a limner, ain't it? Making books with prayers, you know, about God, it's—'

'Don't say it, Annie. Don't you say those words to me.'

'Oh, well ...' Annie began, not knowing what to say, then 'Watch it, you!' as someone bumped into her. It was a tall man with bandaged hands, walking unsteadily toward the Thames.

'Just saw him climbing Eleanor's Cross,' Gemma said.

It was only a short way back up Old Change and left into the Row. Gemma pushed through the door at the left of the shop and into the narrow space that led to the hall, then through another door, past the kitchen and into the wide yard. The chickens squawked when they saw her and she wondered if Alice had collected the eggs. And realised again, as if she hadn't just been talking about it: Alice will be collecting eggs from the Bishop of Llandaff's hens from now on.

She turned, walked back into the hall. All the way up the stairs she rehearsed the argument she'd had with John, over and over. Work as a limner would suit Alice. 'Life as a maid is hard work for little pay, and after twenty years she's an old woman with a bad back and no money. And still a maid.'

'She'll marry. You see. It'll work out. You know the situation: no girl in London's ever been apprentice to a limner, and if Southflete has his way, none will ever be.'

'Southflete. Again. Why should Southflete have—'

'You know as well as me. We can't afford to cross him. How would we get work then? What little work there is these days.'

'But it makes no sense. Nuns have been doing the work for years, and I don't think it's their praying makes them any more suited than Alice. She has the eye for it. They say there's a woman in Paris works with her husband decorating all manner of books.'

'It's Southflete you'll have to argue with, not me. But it's no point telling him about the French woman. You know how he feels about the French.'

'Don't pass all the blame to him. You've position enough to argue as well, John Dancaster. Where would you be if my

pa hadn't taught me how to gild and paint? Apprentice or
no, Alice should be taught. Take her on in the shop, show
Southflete what she can do. Make a decision.'

'I have made a decision. We can't afford two new
apprentices and Nick's of age now. Why do I have to say all
this again?'

'Because Alice is older than Nick and you should have
started her in the shop two years ago.'

'Doing what? What work, Gemma? I have to start Nick
now, and you know we don't have any work, apart from what
Benedict and I can do, and then time enough to scratch our
arses whenever we want.'

Gemma dumped the basket on the floor. What was she
doing upstairs? The food belonged in the buttery downstairs.
Sighing, basket on her arm, she headed downstairs again,
step by heavy step. It was always the same, and the argument
always travelled that familiar street with a wall at the end.
Not enough work. The day had been when John would turn
folks away for all the work he had. The court, bishops, nobles.
But not now. Everyone in London was struggling since the
famine, but there was something more to it with John. He no
longer sought out commissions the way he once had. It seemed
almost that he didn't want to work. The reason lingered at the
edges of her mind, a thought too awful to turn and face.

Mathilda

Wain Wood Manor
May 4, 1322

Mathilda sits in the tiny closet she must now use if she wants some time alone. The book of hours is on the shelf, still untouched. For all her unease about it, she lifts it down and unwraps the cloth. The cover is plain, as she had asked, though she would have liked studs, perhaps some embossing. She turns the pages, careful of them, as if they might do her some damage. William would have worked on these pages, and Master Dancaster, each day adding a little more decoration.

She passes quickly through the first few calendar pages, pauses at the page for March, knowing that Robert's death will be added next to the number sixteen, and keeps turning without looking closely. There's a story, it seems, with a fox; some saints, though she doesn't linger to check which ones; Christ enthroned, the Virgin and Child; a juggler with balls; a head with legs but no body; a collection of pots. Like images in a dream, they pass by her eyes.

She stops, finally, at a page showing the chapel in Aspenhill, the manor that is lost to her. The carved grapes on the wall behind the altar are touched with light, and Robert, painted in profile, is kneeling in prayer across from her. The forehead is wrong; she remembers how his eyebrows pushed out like a ledge above his eyes, those dark lights tucked into a casement. Not that it's meant to look like him; it's only the family coat of arms, the antelope springing, that makes it Sir Robert Fitzjohn. She touches the face with her fingertip. Robert, gone now.

What would he have thought of his portrait in the book? Would he have studied the coat of arms to see if it was accurate, even as small as it is? She'd never thought of the book as frippery, as Robert said. It was beauty and prayer together. But now she wonders. Perhaps it is, after all, a judgement on her and her longing for pictures. What were the words of William's friend, that scholar from Cambridge? A sinful luxury to close up the pictures inside a book. Father Jacobi always said the desire to look was dangerous. 'Eve, after all …' he would begin, and Mathilda would stop listening. She knew it so well: the apple, the gaze, desire entering Eve. Even looking upon beauty was a sin. Mathilda touches her belly, the slight swell that only she can sense.

Should she have used the money for her tenants? Given John and Thea Beecroft more help? Given more to Lettie Carter, her Reggie's body carried home the day after Robert's? Even so, it's not the book she had imagined. But so much is not as she'd planned: Robert, the lands, the inheritance. Her life. She doesn't need another reminder of so much that is lost, and closes it.

Robert had been sceptical about the book, but for different reasons.

'Need? You say your prayers well enough. As did my mother, and without a decorated book.'

'It's not enough for me to go to chapel, or rely on Father Jacobi's prayers. He says it's one of my duties to pray the hours. For the family, the children.'

'Praying the hours like a nun? Next you'll be demanding one of those "spiritual marriages": all prayer and no duty to the family. We need an heir, Mattie.'

Mathilda looked stonily at her husband. 'Don't be cruel. The memories are everywhere in this manor. I live with them every day. You don't. And I pray for another child. I pray.' She stood and walked a few paces, tugged her gown smooth, tried to push down the pain, the memory of Gavin; it would never leave, but she didn't need it right now.

Robert bent his head, looked at his boots, then spoke quietly. 'Prayers yes, but decorations? Pictures? You're always warning me about buying what we don't need.'

'Don't pretend you can't understand,' Mathilda could hear the hardness in her voice, grief and anger combined. 'You've seen Lady Warren show her book to visitors, opening at the family heraldry, announcing their lineage to everyone. She may as well say it: "This is who we are, and this is what we can afford. This magnificent book." Well, we could do the same. Ask for the family heraldry to be painted on important pages. We show others who we are, who we intend to be.'

Robert laughed. 'People without enough money to pay for what we fancy, that's who we'll be.'

'This isn't fancy. It's strategy.'

'Strategy?' Robert's smile faded. 'And what do you think I'm doing? It's almost certain now I'll be appointed keeper of the peace here in Hertfordshire. That's not a fancy. Nor is battle. The Scots are animals. And there's more to come. Unrest in the Marches, Despenser building his influence. I thought Lancaster was the one to help control the king, but now I doubt it.'

Mathilda knew what he was thinking. A small, womanish object: what had it to do with men and swords? All the money and effort Robert and his men spent on horses and arms, the bluster and noise of riding out to battle, the wounds and weariness, the endless arguments, the plans and complicated strategies. All of that seemed so important, and she was asking for a book scarcely bigger than Robert's hand. But she liked to think that something so small and beautiful could have some use even in that world.

'You decorate your horses, carry shields and banners. They're all ways of declaring power, even before the armies fight. A book like this would be the same, help build alliances. If we order the illuminators to paint the heraldic devices of those around us — the Warrens, de Laceys, de Nevilles — the book becomes our pledge to them of our support.' Mathilda was matter-of-fact, but she watched her husband's face; her words were beginning to shift him.

'Well, I suppose when I inherit from Edmund, a grand book like this would be a statement,' Robert said.

'Edmund? Is it so bad? Is he …?'

'He's been worse since the freeze. I can't see he'll last long.'

Mathilda's face was suddenly hot, as if she had been exposed. Despite her pity for Edmund's lingering sickness, it was the prospect of Robert inheriting his lands in the Marches that made a book like this affordable. 'It still seems wrong to me, inheriting from a man younger than you. And your nephew, too.' She meant the words, though she had often thought of what Edmund's death would give them.

'That's how it works. He has no heirs, so I'm the next in line. And it's not as if I'm sitting back waiting for it. I'm the one who's fighting in his place, remember. Fighting for him to keep his lands. Inheritance isn't the simple gift you think it.'

'Then we need to start soon. You know how long it takes to make a book like that. Scribes, limners, binders — who knows what else? If we begin the commission now …' Mathilda hesitated, suddenly aware of her words. How easily her discomfort at waiting for Edmund to die had been smoothed over by the prospect of beginning the book.

'Ma, are you in there?'

The door opens.

'What's that? Is it what that man brought yesterday? Ooh, is it the book that Will drew?' Joan reaches out to it.

'Leave it, Joan.'

'But Ma, I want to have a look. You said we would just have to be patient until Will and Master Dancaster finished painting the pictures in it. And we have been.'

'Not now, I said. Leave me alone.'

As Joan stamps out of the tiny room, Mathilda hugs the bundle to her chest. It is as if the book accuses her. All her strategies for their advancement after Edmund's death and, as far as she knows, the man is still alive. And here she is, alone and hiding, Robert cold in the ground.

They brought him home wrapped in the caparison he was so proud of, though she'd always thought it too rich to be thrown onto a horse, dirtied beneath a saddle. And beautiful, the green of newly budded leaves. She touched the edge of it while the body was still on the cart and thought, stupidly, how hard it would be to clean the blood and dirt from it. Now a shroud, of sorts.

She told the men to carry Robert into the hall, but they began to murmur, and Fraden, the steward, said quietly, 'They've come all the way from Boroughbridge, my lady. It's near three days and the body ... well, the body has begun to seep. The barn, I think, would be best.'

He was right; the smell was foul.

Cornell, Robert's page, struggled under his master's weight, but insisted that he would help the men carry him, though he collapsed as they lowered the body onto the workbench in the barn, hastily cleared of tools.

'Give the lad some ale and food, find him a place where he can sleep. Put clean hay in a stable,' Mathilda said to no one in particular.

'I washed him as best I could, but that was the day before yesterday. Or maybe the day before that,' Cornell said. 'There wasn't time.' He bent his head and as Godwin the stable boy led him away, he muttered, 'Devil take Despenser. If only the king hadn't brought him back. If only ... Sir Robert might ...'

Angmar, Mathilda's lady-in-waiting, offered to prepare the body for burial, to save the lady from its stench and sight, but Mathilda had enough wits, beyond her shock, to know that she must do it herself. Ysmay, the cook, disappeared into the kitchen and returned to the barn with her arms full.

'To keep us safe from demons,' she said, and set candles at each end of the body, then salt and earth next to Robert's head, saying, 'You might put them in his mouth, my lady. For protection. And I'll open these big doors so my lord's soul can escape.'

I hope it's done that by now, Mathilda thought, and heaven knows we need the fresh air. But she saw how frightened the cook was of this body, the dead among the living, and as Ysmay rushed out, crossing herself once more, Mathilda realised what a comfort it was to have those rituals of protection.

She sent away everyone save Angmar, telling them they could keep vigil later. She had seen the dead before, had prepared bodies before; she would do this. Father Jacobi had followed the short procession from house to barn with the body, praying continually, and at first it was a comfort to think of Robert's soul, wherever it was, being cared for. But now the words sounded like flies buzzing round rotten meat, and Mathilda asked him to pray in the chapel. He left, unhappily.

Rotten meat it was when they pulled away the caparison, the stench creeping inside their noses and mouths, taking over every part of the barn, thick and heavy, with an odd sweetness that made it worse. The women gasped, covered their noses, crossed themselves, and though they wouldn't admit their fear, it was a plea for protection. Angmar ran to the corner, vomited and apologised, crossed herself again. Mathilda's stomach pushed into her throat, bile in her mouth, but she held it down.

She had feared this moment for years, but had never imagined it would be like this. She looked at Robert's face, though it didn't look like him at all, the skin tight, the cheeks sunken as if suddenly his teeth had grown too big for his mouth. Perhaps this really isn't him; perhaps he's riding home now, she thought wildly. She crossed herself again.

They set aside the sword laid on top of his body and began. The clothes had hardened with mud and dried blood, but were now sodden with foul, seeping liquid. The women cut and tugged at the cloth, gasped and retched. Angmar asked pardon each time. It seemed more fighting than caring.

The effort over, Mathilda told Angmar to take the clothes and burn them, and to leave her alone. It wasn't that she wanted to cling to Robert, but she was hoping that this final moment with him, with the body, would help her understand.

She had seen death many times before, but never in the man who knew her body so well. And she had known his, until this day. It seemed an ugly creature now, collapsed over its bones, the skin purple-red with tinges of green, livid where the sword had cut: once on his right thigh, twice on his left arm, and most brutally upwards into his belly. As she washed away the smears and clots of blood, the wounds leered at her, stark and raised like lips.

Her hand slid across his cold chest, the skin hard, repelling her, the whole body resisting her touch. What was this? Something unknown to her, monstrous in its refusal to live and breathe. She wanted to cry, to know that he was gone and wail out her pain, but there was only a tangle of confusion. She couldn't understand what this was. Death, they called it.

Without realising, Mathilda has opened the book again and turned the pages. A defence against the memory, perhaps. Along the bottom right border of one page is a man in armour, his visor closed and sword drawn. He urges his horse onward toward the left side of the page, where a giant snail waits, more than twice the size of the knight. Its shell spirals from the centre in shades of brown, the ridges marked in black. It could be lying still or it could be moving slowly along the stem of its vine; nothing about it suggests action, though its antennae are up and forward. How does a snail ever appear to be moving? For a moment she is ten, plucking a snail from a stone wall, feeling its slimy body suck as it holds on then lets go and shrinks away, tucking inside the shell, smooth and slightly rippled, like fine bone. She looks again at the picture and smiles, though she doesn't find this massive snail funny. Implacable, that's what it is, whatever the priests say. For all Robert's planning and his money, his years of training to fight, his casing of armour and his sword, there was always this massive creature slowly creeping toward him. The hulk of its shell, its satisfied smile, certain of victory. The quiet creep of it. And now it is coming after her. She doesn't need to ride out to meet it, with sword and in armour; it has come to her. Fear, shame, debt. Uncertainty.

3

London
October 1320 – January 1321

Creation

Proverbs tells us that when the world was created, Wisdom played before God, forming all things. In the same way, the artisan at work plays between the realms of the real world and the world of imagination. Neither realm should dominate his work. The mind and the hand must be free to wander, finding creation in that space, the tension between the real and the imagined.

The Art of Illumination

Will rented a room and slept, venturing out only to buy food. He stayed away from busy places like Cheapside and the markets, keeping instead to the maze of back streets, learning their doorways and shadows, which alleys led to a hiding place, which ones to avoid because of their dead ends. He didn't even know who might be chasing him, but every stranger's face seemed to be watching. A push, a sharp word, even the crawl of unease, and he would turn, alert, ready to run or fight.

His small stash of coin wouldn't last long, he knew, and he used each one carefully. There was no work, not even on the docks, now the river had frozen. The streets were crowded with people just like him, poor, sick and hungry. Except that they were innocent. Day by day he grew more desperate, saw himself as one of the half dead slumped against a wall.

One morning he noticed a baker turn from his stall so he took his chance, leaped forward, snatched a loaf and ran.

When the baker shouted, a few arms reached out to grab him, but Will stuffed the loaf inside his tunic, swung with clenched fists, felt the shudder of skin and bone, and kept running; he knew how to escape. When he stopped, finally, panting and coughing at the end of a dark lane, he pulled out the bread and broke it apart, his belly rumbling at the prospect of food. But someone was there, watching, ready to haul him away. He peered into the gloom of damp brick and wood. A glimmer, then gone, like the blink of an eye; a soft gurgle that he'd heard somewhere before. A rat, he thought. That's all. Slowly, slowly, the shape formed from the stone of the doorstep. The gargoyle watched, nothing more, its eyelids closing and opening unevenly, first one and then the other. Will gagged, threw away the bread and retreated to his room.

After that, he gathered with the crowds at hospitals and almshouses, stretching his arms up to take whatever food they handed out. He'd never thought of himself as one of the desperate ones, but there was safety in being one of the faceless many.

The strumpets called out to him as he passed the lanes where they worked, but he told them he had barely enough money to keep himself alive. One lonely night, though, he swapped some coins for a few moments of Eva's time. He was surprised to discover he wasn't really interested, too concerned with surviving to enjoy the touch of another. His cock did what she asked of it, but he felt a bit like a performing bear obeying its master. Still, he enjoyed her unquestioning company, and sometimes he'd stop by Gropecunt Lane to chat with her and Bea when their business was quiet; he wanted no more.

Though he rarely gave thought to such rituals, the festivities of the Yule season and then the turning of the old year into the new, hoary though they were, seemed to invite him out of the shadows. He had left Cambridge just after Michaelmas; surely he was forgotten by now.

He began to drop in to taverns and alehouses, listening and watching for news of work on a book, nursing one drink all night, being careful not to stare, to listen without looking, making himself the weary drinker seeking only oblivion. Even though the sense of danger had lessened, shame kept him in the shadows. In Cambridge, he knew and was known by most of the shopkeepers, many of the students and just about every child in the town: his big hands, his love of singing, his loud laugh. How long was it since he had laughed?

Sabine's alehouse on Watling Street was where he felt most at ease, and he visited whenever her broom was set outside, advertising she'd made a brew and had some to sell. It wasn't especially tasty, but it was cheap, and she was content with his vague answers to questions. She was tall, her face flushed, her sleeves pushed up over a large patch of molten skin on her forearm, the result of an accident with hot water, Will thought, but others told him that it was her man, now long gone, who had done it.

Sabine loved a conversation about local politics: gossip about Nicholas de Farndone, the mayor; revelations about John de Wengrave's abuses of power when he'd been mayor three years earlier; the chancellor's plans for tax rises. 'Mark you what I say, Will, he'll make his move soon enough,' she would say most nights, whatever the subject. She was canny about the ways of the city, and when Will asked about the book trade, she suggested he try Le Petre et Paule on Paternoster Row, the tavern where some of the illuminators and scribes gathered.

'So's I hear, it's where those in the trade do their drinking. Not all of 'em, mark you. There are those on London Bridge as well are in the trade, and some wouldn't raise a pot with the likes of any in "Peter and Paul".' Sabine had no time for Frenchified words. 'No doubt they're all happier that way.'

And so Will visited Paternoster Row once or twice, but it was in an alehouse on London Bridge that he met Osmund, the panel painter, a man as tall as Will, but with the fine features everyone seemed to consider essential for a painter. His nose was so pointy it could pierce skin, and his chin not much safer.

With no money and almost starving, Will gladly took the work he offered, though only a season ago he would have thought grinding pigment all day was drudgery, and beneath his skills and experience: seven years of training and two years working as a limner.

'That vermilion ready yet, Asshe?' Osmund yelled, without looking up from the banner.

Osmund was gruff and impatient, but Will was surprised to discover anew the simple pleasure of milling the stone then grinding it down. Vermilion, especially, had be be ground until it was like silk to touch, its grains so tiny they were almost impossible to see. How many times his master, Edgar, had made him do it over again when he was an apprentice: 'You'll grind until you do it in your sleep, lad. Grind and mix, because it's what God put you on this earth for. Grind until the only thing that has any meaning is the paint, the purest colour.'

Will stirred the egg yolk into the red powder, watching it thicken, the colour intensify.

'God's teeth, Asshe!' Osmund shouted. 'You said it was ready, so where is it?'

Will wanted to throw it, watch it dribble down the man's thin face and drip off his pointy nose, but he'd worked too hard to see it wasted, and he needed the job. He carried the red paint safely across to Osmund's desk and paused, in spite of himself, to look at the banners he was decorating for the parliament at Westminster. The outline of St George was finished, the tempera applied, and the red — it was a beautiful colour that Will had created — would be used for the cross on his shield and the hauberk draping down to his knees. But it was the saint's face that caught Will's attention, the fine detail of his eyes, the slight dip in his eyebrows that suggested humility and piety. That technique was something to remember. If he had to be here, at least he could learn.

The prospect of working on a large painting, and on silk especially, had seemed an intriguing alternative to the detailed and meticulous work of decorating capitals and creating foliate borders that he was trained for, but it soon became clear that Osmund was not likely to give him the chance. Will told himself he didn't care, that he didn't want to waste his skills on decorating grand displays for the powerful. Why strew their way with roses? Still, with each passing day he became restless to use the colours he made and to paint with the brushes he washed.

It was some weeks later, just as work with Osmund was becoming unbearable, that the words 'grand book' made their way to him through the gloom of Le Petre et Paule.

The air was fuggy with the smell of sweat, fatty beef and the thick, bitter waft of ale that had soaked into wood and straw and cloth. The tabletops were lacquered and sticky with it, swollen and oiled with it. Will had been standing near the door, cradling a single pot of ale for over an hour; he wasn't there for the drink. Patient and still, he watched and listened. Lingering at the edges had become second nature. In one corner a group was gathered around a table, talking in snatches, laughing now and then, weary from the day's work. Complaints about the tariff on fish, news of threats to the chancellor, curses about a neighbour's leaking privy. Will took a long swig and was just deciding to give up on his vigil when some words stopped him.

'A book it is. A big one.' The speaker put down his ale, looked around. 'Folk from Hertfordshire, they are. Sir Robert Fitzjohn. Grand houses, estates. The book's for his wife,

Lady Mathilda, eldest daughter of the de Saunfords; it's her father's old manor, Aspenhill, that they live in. She asked for my workshop to decorate her book, and for me, specific, so Southflete told it. Said it had to be me and no one else.' He sat back on his stool.

Will moved forward a few steps, trying to stay in the shadows. The man who had spoken was square faced, his cheeks beginning to sag into jowls. ·

'Pulling at my balls you are, John Dancaster,' a second man said, spraying ale and spit as he spoke. 'The lady asked for you? What'd make her do that? You've said yourself, sitting in this here tavern, that lately your workshop ain't had more'n a call to decorate a breviary with a sprig of leaves.'

That was John Dancaster? Will took another step forward, but stopped short, sidled into the shadow again.

'What do you know of the book trade, Jack? What empty words are those?' Dancaster slammed his hand flat on the tabletop and his friends looked up suddenly at the noise, surprise on their faces.

Jack seemed abashed, but still he blustered on. 'Steady there, Dancaster. Why such choler of late? You say it's welcome news, so tell us then, man! Get on with it. Tell us what they want.'

'A book of hours it is. Illuminations, miniatures, decoration, gold leaf,' Dancaster said quietly, traces of venom still in his voice. He paused to let the words find their target, scanned the faces.

So it *is* Dancaster, Will thought, the man he had heard so much about. He was very different from Edgar, his serious and lordly master in Cambridge.

'Southflete says they asked for me. Specific,' Dancaster said. Now there's a word he likes, Will thought. Specific.

'"Only John Dancaster." That's what Southflete said.' Dancaster raised his eyebrows and looked one by one at the men. Waited for the words to settle.

'Wanted you, John?' Jack was smirking. 'They wanted you as they know you need the work. Did you get a good price then? Come on, tell us.'

'Not telling you my business, Jack Tyler.' Dancaster's anger had passed, his voice defensive now. 'They're used to making deals, aren't they, the rich? Used to getting what they want for a good price. How else d'ye think they make all that money?'

'Thought so.' Jack crossed his arms, satisfied. 'Been done, you have. Done right and good. Lady Whoever-she-is would never know what work you've done.'

'Aye and she did. Saw the rose I always draw. In every book I do, I draw a rose. The Dancaster rose, it is, the one on the sign outside my atelier.' He paused. 'So, Jack Tyler, that's how Lady Mathilda knew.'

'Maybe so ...' Jack was still ready to argue.

'Think I'll call Hugh of Oxford to come and work with us again.' Dancaster looked away from Jack to the other men. 'Grand book like this. Last time he was here, he was looking for work, said there's not much in Oxford. Not much anywhere, 'cept now.'

'That's well and good, John, but take a care you get your money.' All the faces turned to the voice, serious, authoritative. 'I'm amazed at Fitzjohn ordering a book like that. He might have land in Hertfordshire, but that's from his wife. From all I hear, he hopes to inherit family land near the Welsh Marches.' When there was no response, he went on. 'Well, think about it. The Despensers, father and son, have been claiming land for themselves ... surely you've all heard that? Now Despenser the Younger has Tewkesbury and the manor of Hanley, so that's a lot of influence in the Midlands. That, along with the land he's already claimed, puts pressure on all the Marcher lords. He could claim an earldom there, especially as he's king's favourite.'

'Aye, Wat, you're right.' Jack nodded, serious now, obviously pleased to have some support. 'Despenser's son's a crafty bugger, knows how to play for power. It's not for naught they call him the king's right eye. Keeps the king warm at night, I hear. More'n the queen is welcome to do.'

'Who's to know, Jack? Nobles at court say that, but they're jealous the king takes advice only from Despenser,' Wat said. He looked at Dancaster. 'All I'm saying is that the Fitzjohn lands might be under threat, John. Unless Mortimer and the other barons can rid us of the Despensers somehow.'

'Well, Southflete spoke to Fitzjohn. He knows what's what with the aristocracy, and he thinks he has the money.' Dancaster was subdued now. 'And you know how the gentry climb, specially those on the lower rungs.'

Grunts and mutters swirled in the thick air. Dancaster pressed on.

'A book like this is a sign you've got money. Or expect to have it. Status, not wealth in your hand, that's what the nobility's all about. I'm not so dull that I'd believe the woman only wants to pray and glorify God with her book. She wants status, influence. That's why she's asked for the coats of arms of all the nobility nearby to be painted in the margins, so she can show 'em. That's what it's for.'

Wat lifted his hands, palms out. 'Good luck to you, John. All I'm saying is that nothing's certain. War's brewing, mark me. And civil war, I mean: the king and his barons.'

With the talk of war and the machinations of nobility, the conversation collapsed into unhappy mumbling and calls for more ale. Jack found someone else to argue with, and Dancaster sat quietly. Will waited in the shadow. He wondered at this man with such important work to do, sitting here, drinking. Perhaps he hadn't begun yet; perhaps this was a celebration of recent news. As some of the men began to move away, Will bought two pots of ale, sat down next to Dancaster and pushed one in front of him.

'Sounds like you've made good business whatever they threaten of the king and war,' he said. 'What's that to do with a beautiful book, eh? It's a grand commission. Thought I'd celebrate with you.'

'Well, why not? Very kind, sir. At last, a man who sees a good deal,' Dancaster said. He smiled at his new companion and threw down the drink. 'John Dancaster, master limner, I am.'

'And another pot, John? The name's William Asshe.'

4

London

January 1321

Gathering

To understand the process, watch the scribes at work in their shop. See the strange, nesting arithmetic of their work: four sheets of parchment folded and cut to make eight pages, each tucked inside the next. A quire, a gathering. For now, it is a tiny book of sixteen sides, unbound and awaiting colour.

The scribe writes side after side, in order, as word must follow word. Yet the limner must unmake this order, let the sheets lie flat upon his desk. And so, that strange arithmetic is revealed once more: the first page lying alongside the sixteenth, the second sharing parchment with the fifteenth. Consider this as the model for all that we do, not only the pages. In your work, learn that order is unravelled, but only so that it may be enhanced and then restored as something new.

The Art of Illumination

Will stood in the open space where five ways met, where, on his first day in London, he'd climbed Eleanor's Cross to see the city. He looked down Paternoster Row. In the early morning drizzle, the shops, the same as most others in London, seemed grey and misty, and he imagined a huge hand pressing the buildings together from the sides until they were tall and thin, squashing them close to keep them from teetering. Will knew the Row now. He had drunk in the Peter and Paul many times, and had wandered the lanes that ran off the Row toward the Shambles and its bloody trade. He loved the selds off Ivy Lane, the way its narrow entry opened out like the pages of a book into courtyards full of stalls: fishmongers, egglers, cobblers, haberdashers, fruiterers. There were shops near his small room on Bread Street, but the Ivy Lane selds, enclosed as they were, felt safer from eyes hunting for a tall man with large hands. Even though he had nowhere to cook, he always visited Floria the eggler who, with her thin face and big nose, seemed to be turning, day by day, into one of the hens she owned.

About thirty of his large strides from Eleanor's Cross took him to the swinging wooden sign painted with John Dancaster's red rose. Will paused under the overhang of the upstairs jetty. On the other side of the street, a man was pissing against the wall of a house, one hand to his breeches, the other arm bent to cradle his forehead; he could have been leaning, or he could have been holding up the wall. Will waited, but the man didn't move. Perhaps he was asleep, mid-piss, after a long night on the ale. Perhaps he was composing a song or devising a new theology.

Through the mist, the buildings softened, wavered; the Row became Cambridge High Street, the grey winter morning became a warm summer night. Students were staggering home from the tavern, laughing at Simon collapsed against the wall of Peterhouse. Turning to them, he had lifted a wavering hand in protest, then managed a few slurred words, insisting it was ideas, not vomit, that poured out of his mouth. Will shook his head, as if the memory would fly loose into the drizzle, but instead a movement at the rounded top of St Paul's wall caught his eye. It was nothing but a stone, surely. But no, there was a head, tilted to one side, water trickling from its open mouth, one round eye winking at him. Will shuddered, stumbled, shook the water from his back and hood, and bent his head to step through the door. He paused in the narrow hallway, took a breath to settle his shaking, and opened the second door into the shop.

In the doorway he breathed in; the mingled smell of parchment, pigment and ink carried him back to Cambridge and Master Edgar's shop. The lamps were alight, and the warmth, probably from a stove in the hall, made the golden air humid. He looked around. It was a simple room, like most of the other shops on the street, with a large front shutter, a small window at the side and four desks, enough space for all of them to work. At the back a door led into a tiny chamber, more closet than storeroom.

'Ah Will, there you are,' Dancaster said. 'Pull off that coat and meet the others. This is my wife, Gemma.'

Will was surprised. He hadn't expected a woman in Dancaster's shop. Most likely there to help out with this and that. But if she was only helping out, why take the desk with the best light? He smiled and tipped forward from the waist, not a complete bow, that would look foolish, but women liked the gesture. 'Gemma. A delight to meet you.' As was his habit, he followed the lines of her face. Neat, her nose small but rounded at the end, her eyes hooded. Such brilliant blue. Lapis.

Gemma nodded but didn't speak and looked away.

'And Benedict, my apprentice.' Dancaster took the few steps to the next desk. 'But not for much longer, eh Benedict?'

Strong nose and chin, simple, bold lines, eyes hiding, mouth drawn tight. Benedict shook Will's hand weakly and muttered something he didn't understand.

'And Nick, my son. Our new apprentice,' Dancaster said as a young lad peered from the storeroom and disappeared again.

Dancaster pointed out his desk, and Will retreated to it, wondering if there really was enough space, given the cramp of resentment and unease that filled the air; after the way he had crept into this work, under cover of ale and jokes, he decided it was wise to keep his peace.

Gemma avoided looking at him. She didn't like the man. It was that simple. John had planned to write to Hugh of

Oxford, last she had heard, and then there was his drunken rambling after the tavern about a new man and his skill, the beauty of his painting. Now this stranger had arrived, tall and confident, as if they'd sent all the way to Cambridge asking for him. John said he was new to London, hadn't set up his own shop, so he'd nowhere to work but here in the atelier. She'd have to see him every day. She glanced up. Why should he be so tall? Irritating, the way he looked down and smiled. He was chatting to Nick, the boy looking at him as if he was the Lord Jesus himself, golden rays radiating from his head, a beatific glow to his cheeks and eyes. That'd be trouble, and the kind that John wouldn't deal with. By God, he'd better be competent, and more. With John's problems of late, she didn't have time to deal with anyone who couldn't get the work done.

Nick was laughing, his hands carrying out a nervous dance against his thighs the way they always did when he was excited. Gemma smiled to think of what this day meant for him. For years he had played around her feet in the shop, spilt pigment and gesso, then as he grew older asked questions, peering over her shoulder, always impatient to turn fourteen so he could officially begin. Gemma felt the struggle, a pain in her chest. She loved her son and wanted him to take up the craft; he showed real ability. But it was Alice who should have been apprenticed first.

Will was joking and laughing too, a sound that seemed to roll around in his chest before it emerged. Benedict, only two or three paces away, was leafing through the model book, pretending he didn't hear. He loves that model book, Gemma thought; it's how he spends his spare time, memorising the things he should copy, leaf by leaf, curl by curl, worrying he'll paint something out of place. Something different, Mary save us. Stroke by stroke, his work was his own faithful version of the drawings in that book. As John always said, there was nothing wrong with that, and as she said back to

him, there was only so much that was good about it. It wasn't
even the copying, but the worry Benedict put into everything
he drew and painted; you could see it, worry burrowed into
the parchment, bleeding through the colours. John said it was
only her fancy, but that was John, refusing to see it. He knew
as well as she that even though they needed to be faithful
to tradition, they had to be prepared to change. Whatever
Manekyn the scribe and Southflete said, that's what would
attract customers: new ways of drawing and painting. It was
happening already in France; there were rumours of a young
illuminator in Paris with new techniques, though she hadn't
seen any of his work yet. And in Italy too, no doubt.

Gemma sighed. Even though they wouldn't let her have the
title 'limner', she knew the job was so much more than being
accurate. She had no words for what it was; others had tried,
but hadn't managed it either. Some said it was God, inspiration.
After all, God the artisan hadn't bothered making copies when
he created men and women, dogs and cows, trees and beetles,
each one different. Look at Benedict, that roman nose, the
wrinkles over his eyes, though God didn't make them, that
was just fretting over getting things right. Does God think he
got Benedict right? she wondered. No doubt this man Asshe
would think the creator pleased with how *he* came out.

John was sitting at his desk, his eyes vacant, his hand resting
gently on a small bundle wrapped in cloth, as if it were
the head of a child. The first gatherings of the manuscript
ready for painting. As the door opened he stood up, quietly
groaning. A figure stepped in, looked around briefly, took off
his cape and shook it, brushing down the velvet trim. His hair
was fair, the colour of straw, but his eyebrows were darker,
almost burnt umber.

It seemed to Will that the visitor took up all the space,
even though he was thinner than John and only a little taller.
He carried himself with an air of authority and control.

'Master Southflete.' John nodded. 'You know Gemma, of course, and Nick. Come and say good morning, Nick. He begins today as our new apprentice. He's very keen.' The lad stepped out of the storeroom, looked at the stationer and down at his feet.

'And this is the new man, William Asshe,' John continued. 'Did his time in Cambridge with Master Edgar Gerard.'

Will stepped forward a few paces as Southflete scrutinised him, head to toe, his eyes lingering finally on his hands. Always the hands, Will thought. He uncurled his fingers from their tight ball and flexed them lightly. 'I'm two years a journeyman. I apprenticed with Master Edgar then continued with him, working for the most part on treatises, some herbals and once or twice a breviary.'

'So. Why leave good work? What made you think London would want you?'

Gemma looked on. For once, she thought, I agree with the man. For Asshe to leave a man as highly respected as Gerard, he has to be in some kind of trouble.

Will hesitated, looked around as if for help. 'I needed to leave, is all.' He felt the air around him move, a whisper in his ear, sticky feet on his back. Southflete simply waited. 'And I've always wanted to come to London, to seek out some kind of grander book.' As Southflete slowly raised an eyebrow, Will wished he hadn't said that, and scrambled for safety. 'For some time I helped Claude of Paris, you see, who worked with Jean de Floret.'

The stationer raised both eyebrows now, but slightly. A query. Those eyebrows seem capable of speaking, Will thought. He didn't want to admit it, but he felt like his twelve-year-old self, that uncomfortable mix of nervousness and defiance; it would be dangerous to challenge this man.

'Master Claude was in Cambridge for a time, come all the way from Paris to work on a book of hours, and at night, in exchange for me mixing his paints, he'd teach me: how to draw many figures in one room and show its depth as well as its width, how to draw figures and drapery with fluid line, the new ways they're using in Paris. It was him that helped me design the piece I was painting to become a master.'

'You have letters from these men? Recommendations? You've checked this, John, no doubt.' Southflete turned to John who made a slight move of his head. Noncommittal.

'Well, I ...' Will began. 'I have here the page I was working on for my master's piece.' He reached over to where his bag was hanging on a hook by the door and carefully pulled out a roll of parchment.

John smiled and nodded to Will as Southflete unrolled it on the nearest desk and bent to examine it. Gemma looked across; the desks were so close that she could see the painting without showing how interested she really was. She tried to hide her surprise at the graceful lines, the way the gathered figures seemed to run like ripples down the page. So this was the new Paris style.

'Ah, the Beatus page,' Southflete murmured.

Will knew enough to say nothing more, but to let the images do their work. Ever since he'd seen his first Beatus page, he had wanted to paint one himself. He was eleven, maybe twelve, years old that first time, hiding behind the sacks of dried beans in the kitchen at home. Inside a large letter *B*, David was playing his harp, and along the margins scampered all manner of animals. Close to David's feet, a lion with a lamb nestled between its legs was mesmerised by the sound of his music, and beneath it, an elephant with a blackbird on its back, a dog chasing a deer, two peacocks, a wolf, and a goat surrounded by twining foliage.

'The first psalm is most often decorated with a full-page letter *B*. You have not followed the tradition,' Southflete said.

'No. I use the animals to show the beauty of King David's music, and to remind the reader of the creation of the world. The most masterful music has the power to conjure worlds in our mind.' Will paused a moment, choosing his words. 'And some readers will be reminded of Orpheus and his power to tame all animals. In that, some scholars say, he is a type of Christ.'

'So you learned a bit of scholarship in your copying of treatises,' Southflete said, a slight lift at the edges of his mouth. 'Show me your hands.'

Will lifted his hands, but wouldn't stretch out his arms.

'These aren't the hands of a limner.'

'So everyone tells me. They're hands made for working with my father hauling wood and shaping cartwheels, they say. But for all that, they have my mother's gentle touch and feeling for line and curve, and I have her eye for colour. *Alis grave nil.* Nothing is heavy if you have wings.'

Southflete's eyes had been drawn back to the page, but at the sound of the Latin words he looked up quickly. 'Mmm,' is all he would admit. Then, 'He'll need to be enfranchised, John. We can't employ men who aren't citizens of London. You have that in hand?' And to Will: 'You'll join the fraternity of St Michael. Now, we have to get on. We don't have time to stand chatting in Latin.'

Gemma sat back and let out a quiet breath, not sure whether she was relieved or cross that this new man had skill.

Southflete stepped away from the desk, cleared his throat and addressed them all. 'You understand, I'm sure, the importance of this commission, the honour bestowed upon you all to be engaged to work on a book of such magnificence.' It was as if they were his students, being lectured, thought Will. 'The de Saunford family is a well-established and distinguished line, Lady Mathilda an heiress. Sir Robert, though from a lesser family and only the youngest son of George Fitzjohn, has claims to inherit from an ailing nephew. No doubt the king will soon notice him.' He looked toward the bundle John was still protecting. 'Manekyn and his scribes have completed about one half of the script. That's enough for you to begin. The next pages will be ready as needed. Some of it's in French, as the lady requested, but the prayers are in Latin.' He glanced at Will. 'The lady has asked for the book to celebrate the future prosperity of the family. They want to establish their prospects and position in the county. And soon, as I said, at court.'

The rich and their ambitions, Will thought. Never content with all they have.

'Now, I'll explain the schema of decoration.'

Nick had been leaning against the doorway of the storeroom, but at those words, he slid slowly to the floor. Beneath the dark eyebrows, Southflete's eyes shone. He's enjoying this, Will thought.

'The main illuminations tell the story of the Holy Family through to the Passion and Resurrection. We've chosen subjects that best suit this theme, but you are to use the marginal decorations to weave in the history and prospects of the family. Their coat of arms, as well as those of influential neighbours, some portraits of Lady Mathilda at prayer, pictures of the Fitzjohn estates, that manner of thing. Status, prosperity, the future for their heir. Keep that in mind. This is to be the sacred history, the story of our Lord ...' Southflete paused a moment, giving the words a respectful weight, '... interwoven with the Fitzjohn–de Saunford history.'

Will wished he had some parchment and a plummet to pass the time. Instead, he began scratching a curved line in the desktop with his fingernail.

'The two main duties of a noblewoman are to live a godly life and to continue the family line,' Southflete continued. 'Lady Mathilda has two daughters. A son died while young, so I hear, and they no doubt pray for an heir.' He gestured at the bundle of pages. 'An heir and a book, this book, that's what they want.'

John began to stand as if the stationer had finished, but Southflete continued, his voice a little louder now.

'You know we don't reward invention, especially not in images of our Lord and the blessed Virgin. And the saints, too, must be depicted in the traditional way.' At this he looked directly at Will. 'You have model books to show you. Who is an ordinary limner to decide on the image of our Lord? Or of the blessed Virgin? Remember that you are artisans, craftsmen. Your duty is to maintain the tradition of illuminations to the best of your ability. Leave behind invention, whatever the French might try to tell us. It is blasphemous and dishonourable to meddle with traditions, but that has always been the French way.'

Will uncrossed and recrossed his arms, shifted his feet so that they banged against a desk.

The door closed behind the stationer. A silent, communal exhalation. Shoulders dropped, legs stretched out.

John stood. 'It's not often we get to work on such a book. This is the Dancaster workshop, and it's known for fine work. I expect everyone to work to that reputation. If not, you'll be scrubbing Nick's pots for him.' He paused. 'As Southflete says, it's all marked up with the subjects written in, given as Manekyn knows more Latin than any of us. For the rest, he leaves it to us.'

Will could no longer resist. 'I know Latin, or a fair bit. I learned in Cambridge from a student there, a friend. He …' His words faded. 'I practised reading the works I decorated, so I can help with words if you don't know them.'

John glanced at Will and continued. 'We need to keep in mind the schema, the weaving of the sacred story with the story of the book owners. This is more than pictures on a romance or a herbal. It's prayers to God we decorate and a holy duty we have.'

'Pa, come on. That's words enough. Let's begin,' Nick cut in.

'Quiet lad. These are things you need to know,' John said. He looked down at the bundle of pages. 'We'll each of us take a gathering of eight folded pages. I'll be doing the calendar. There's to be a few portraits of Lady Mathilda at prayer, of course, and she wants me to go and paint her in her chapel at their manor house.'

'But isn't the chapel always painted the same in these books: an altar, some carved wood, some drapery? Why do you need to go there?' Benedict asked.

'I know, I know. But in a book that's painted for one person's devotion, it's important to give her the idea that the book is her world, that it shows her praying in the places she's familiar with: chapel, church, manor house. It's a long way to go, Hertfordshire, but they're the ones paying for the book, so that's what we do.'

Will clenched his teeth on the words he wanted to say. Why agree to such foolish demands? As if their payment gave them such rights over a skilled illuminator.

'Will, you begin the next quire,' John went on. 'Our Gemma has the training of young Nick to look to, mostly on making the colour, and whatever they can do on the book together.'

Training the lad, Will thought. That explains why she's here.

'And Benedict, you take the next quire, though I'll have to talk to you about the capitals. Begin with the borders for now and—'

'The borders? But …' the apprentice began. Will could see his jaw tighten.

'Yes, the borders. I've told you before how important they are. A border alongside the text is a frame. We have to keep them similar, even though we've different hands on it. Together we'll decide on colours and a design so's the book looks whole.'

'But I've been here more than six years now, and come Michaelmas I'll be done my time, so I don't see why I can't do some large capitals instead of—' He cut short his sentence, but the word *Will* hung in the air.

'I won't be signing off on your seven years if you think decorating a book is all about what you fancy. Just you think a moment about Hugh of Oxford's work. He makes a page alive with no more than a border, and why? Because he sees the value of it. If you don't value what you paint, it'll always be inferior, and I'll have none of that on my book. I was about to say that you could do some of the large capitals later on, but now I don't know. You'll have to convince me that you're capable.' His voice was no louder, but there was an unmistakable sting in the words.

The room was still, uncomfortable.

'Do the work, or I'll have you back grinding pigments and pissing for the lead white as I said,' the master finished, iron in his voice.

5

London
January 1321

The Book of Light

This is a book about light, about finding light and painting with it. Illuminating. That is why the one who does this work is called an illuminator, a limner. Worker with light. Do not assume that this refers only to the gleam and glitter of gold leaf. The limner brings the light of understanding and awareness; with line and colour and gold he illuminates the words he decorates.

What is colour itself if not light in all its forms?

The Art of Illumination

Upstairs, Gemma looked through the window of their solar, the room that jutted over the street. The moon was almost full and shone white on the oiled parchment, lighting up the tiny whorls and pores that were once the skin of a living animal. Through it, she could see only the shape of the spire of St Paul's, so she opened the window briefly and looked out. The cold rushed in.

She resented the dark shadow of the cathedral looking down over them like a frowning cleric, disapproving of the row of shops at its feet, most of them busy writing and decorating and binding books that told of its God. Were they never good enough for him? If he cared at all, God had not shone on them of late. But tonight, the moon glowed onto the cathedral's roof and the tower seemed slender and delicate, as if the deity had changed his mind. Downstairs in the atelier, pages of words and blank spaces waited to be filled with colour and shape. Perhaps the wheel was turning.

Later, in bed, she and John whispered to one another about the day's work.

'Our Nick is more than ready to start,' John said. 'He wanted to mix paint and make gesso before Southflete had even arrived.'

'I know. Just to mix something,' Gemma laughed. 'And did you see the look on his face when Southflete went on and on about the schema for the decoration? He's right, though. The man is a bore.'

'But think of it, Gem. A grand book like this. Things have changed for us, at last. The chance to do beautiful work, show what we can do.'

'I was just thinking about that. I only hope we can—'

'Don't, love. Don't doubt what's given. This is a blessing. We can do this.'

Gemma closed her mouth on the words she wanted to say. How long was it since John had talked like this, about the work he'd do, and not the lack of it? Early on, they'd worked on everything from herbals and breviaries to psalters, sometimes for bishops or nobility at court. Years of decorating small books, of painting capitals as fine and beautiful as they could manage; the pleasure of watching John touch with colour and then with light and shadow, of seeing the work emerge and illumine the pages of words. And then the lean times, John's work not quite what it had been, though it was difficult to say just what was wrong. A bad year or two, was all.

'The new man,' she said. 'He seems to know what he's doing. Don't like him, but he has skill.'

'You'll see, love. It'll be all right. Just think, a grand book.'

When he ran his hand down her hip and between her legs, she kissed him. This, she thought, this loving the illuminations, the making of something beautiful, that's what we are. She couldn't remember the last time they had been like this, together.

John pulled her closer and she felt him rise against her: his chest, his mouth, his cock. 'Did you see Southflete's shoes, how long they are?' she giggled. 'How does he even walk in them? Suppose he has to make up for his tiny prick somehow.'

'Gem,' John warned, but went on: 'Roger de Tinyprick Southflete.'

They both fell to laughing.

'Seems you don't have that trouble,' Gemma said, and straddled John. As she lifted herself onto him, she tried to suppress a groan, conscious even after six years of Benedict sleeping not far away. Might do the lad good, she had often thought, but still. As she began to rock, John pulled her face down to his, kissed her and whispered, 'Tomorrow you'll have to confess this, swyving like animals do, you wicked woman.' He laughed into her neck.

She smiled, enjoying the thought, sat upright again and pulled off her chemise. Her skin puckered at the cold, but as she warmed, she watched his limner's hands explore her breasts, and noticed the way the moon slid across her as she moved. Animal. Swyving like animals. The shadow of the spire and its cross on top.

While John slept, she lay awake planning the next day's work and trying not to think about the woman who had ordered the book, probably asleep in a soft bed with hangings. Interweave the sacred story and the lady's story, that's what Southflete had said. Birth, childhood, watching a child grow into an adult: that's what women do, the lady as much as any other woman, Gemma mused. Watching a child suffer and die — they do that too. Clarissa's pain had lasted almost longer than Gemma could bear before she'd fallen into the sleep she wouldn't wake from. John had held her when she'd sobbed, but he could only say it wasn't for them to understand the will of God. He'd shushed her as she'd cursed Christ for his thirty-three years when he'd given Clarissa less than two. 'He sees my heart, they say, so it doesn't matter whether my mouth says the words or not,' she had thrown back at him. Then a year later, when Ella had been allowed barely a breath in the world, Gemma hadn't even bothered to curse God. She had done with him. And she hadn't even tried to talk to John about it. Annie had told her he probably couldn't bear to speak the words. 'Men do their grieving different from us,' she had said, and no doubt she was right. But Gemma needed more than his reassurance that it would be all right, that line he used whenever life was tough. And now Alice was gone as well. John hadn't even told her that he was looking for a position for their daughter. He'd walked into the shop, going on and on about a conversation with the Bishop of Llandaff, so pleased was he that at first she'd thought it was a new commission.

She pushed back the blankets and stood on the cold floor, searching for her chemise and something for her feet; there was real danger, she knew, in those night thoughts, those demons that played around her heart.

Downstairs, a blanket around her shoulders, she pulled the small bundle from the bottom of a chest in the hall, collected her ink and quill and sat at her desk. There was no noise except for the sound of parchment sheets slipping against one another. She had already ruled up the first page and marked enough space for a decorated capital and the title above it. 'The Art of Illumination', that might be best, she thought, but there was time to decide; it was simply important to begin.

Looking over the notes on her wax tablet — *flaying the skin, the limner, patience* — she sighed. When she wrote those, she'd had Alice in mind: a book on the arts and skills of illumination to help with Alice's training as an apprentice. Everything she had learned from her years in the shop gathered onto parchment. Now it would be Nick's book, and perhaps she would copy it later, for Alice. What would John say? No doubt he would think it unnecessary, a whim, like the foolish idea of hers that Alice should become a limner.

She would write it by herself, while others slept. A time she preferred, the deep quiet that darkness brings.

Now she had to begin, mark words on parchment, commit herself to ink, state her purpose and give her name. That's why she had scrawled her thoughts into wax that could be easily smoothed away, had hesitated to name herself as author. Authority. She looked at the words sunk into the yellow wax:

You will ask who it is that spends so many words to instruct others in the art of illumination. A master, surely! Someone whose name is known across great cities from London to Paris to Genoa and beyond. Tell us your name, you cry.

Let this be enough for you: know that experience, observation and work have been my teachers, and that we are all apprentices to the Great Illuminator. In the light of his works, there need be no names or boasting of skill, only desire to learn with humility and love.

Gemma put down her quill and sat back, relieved that the first words were finally in ink. Now she could continue. Did she believe them? She must, or she would never have begun this, but that was not enough. She could hear the voices of men like Southflete, Hugh of Oxford, and even John, who would laugh at her: she was a creature of the margins, a monkey with quill and vellum composing its babbling. The new man, Asshe, would paint her that way. She had seen how he looked at her, the same way as the stationer. She could hear her mother now; she wouldn't have understood why this seemed so important, but she'd have told Gemma to stop fussing about the men. *You've made a beginning, lass. Forget them and get on with it.*

Gemma worked into the night. Outside, apart from the wardens and the rakers gathering up the city's daily muck, London was sleeping.

Mathilda

Mathilda's dread slides in and out of sleep and waking. Fleeing, always fleeing. It was weeks ago that they took flight. Her body has stopped but in her mind she is still running, holding Maggie and Joan close, looking behind her, always looking behind. She wakes in bed, feels her daughters beside her, their even breath, and tries to match their rhythm with her own. But the darkness is freighted with the past. She gets up. Downstairs the hall is full of slumbering bodies, and this house has no chapel, so there is only one place to go. She lights a lamp and steps into her closet. Taking down the book, she hugs it, runs her fingers over the yellow cloth, a defence against the memories. She opens it without looking at the pages, and breathes in the smell, a strange mixture that she thinks of as sharp and thick, that must be paint and ink and parchment. In the glow of the lamp, it feels as if it could spiral into the room. Strange, middle-of-the-night thoughts.

It was Fraden's white face, more than the steward's words, that frightened her. He wasn't a man given to fear.

'If we leave behind some things of value, that'd probably be enough for the soldiers. Looting the house should keep 'em happy, at least so as to leave us alone,' he said, his voice almost steady. 'Lancaster's been tried and executed, though it was a trial in name only, they say. And those that fought under his banner treated the same. Word is Mowbray, Clifford and Eyvill were hung, drawn and quartered. Now they're tracking down any that tried to escape, nobles disguising themselves as peasants. They're charged with treason. The man has no mercy.' He paused, went on more quietly. 'There's talk of recriminations against the families as well.'

'Recriminations? But Robert's dead. What sort?'

'Like I said, victory's made Despenser even more brutal.'

'Fraden, what recriminations?'

'Some wives imprisoned, property taken. All to stock the king's coffers, I'd say. Mostly wives of the leaders, from what I can tell. I know it's rushed, and with Sir Robert's funeral only days past, but I think it best to leave here, go to your manor in the hills. It's small and out of the way, not easy to reach. The soldiers likely won't bother you there.'

'It's that serious then?'

'Those thugs need only a thumbnail's excuse to rampage. They'll turn their orders into whatever they want them to be. But like I said, they might be content with looting. As for your other lands, including the estates belonging to Sir Robert's nephew, it's too early to tell. We'll have to wait.'

That's all Fraden would say, but Ysmay was overflowing with news of men castrated before they were drawn and beheaded, others thrown into the Tower of London, even small children dragged away screaming with their mothers. 'Lord only knows what they did to the poor women as well,' she said, then stopped.

Mathilda had seen the Tower, its high walls and narrow windows, but not inside, though she could imagine well enough from stories what it would be like: the dank cells, the smell, the rats. Perhaps they kept the noblewomen and their children somewhere more comfortable than where they threw ordinary ruffians. But she *was* a ruffian, it seemed, and of the worst kind. Wife of a traitor, bearer of his seed.

For the first time in years, she wished her father was alive to tell her what to do. And Robert would have known. But the dead don't give counsel. Mathilda closed her eyes, drew in a shaky breath. 'Ysmay, go and help pack what we need before they're beating down our door.'

Ysmay stared at her, drama frozen on her face. If she wants me to soothe her, Mathilda thought, she'll be disappointed, and watched the cook rush away. She wouldn't think about the captured wives and children of the nobles who'd fought against the king, though there was a faint screaming at the edges of her mind. It was the girls she worried about the most. Maggie was too young to understand the threat, but her face showed the rasp of agitation at the rush around her. Godwin, the stable boy, distracted her by asking her to help pack the horses' brushes. Joan, just turned twelve, became very quiet. How much had she heard?

'We need to leave here, Joanie, and spend some time at Wain Wood. Just until the skirmishes with the king are over. So many soldiers roaming around, it's safer. We'll tell Maggie it's a holiday.'

Joan nodded, unconvinced.

Agreeing to leave, Mathilda realised, was just the first of many hard decisions. She couldn't take everyone with her, but she couldn't leave them behind for the soldiers. One of the grooms and the cook's help she sent back to their families nearby, telling them they would be safer there; the rest would travel with her, though it would slow everyone down. It was an odd kind of mercy — for her, if not for them — that some of their men had ridden to battle with Robert. Where were they now? Dead, in prison, hiding in forests? But the village was another matter. Some of the men had been forced to ride with the king, to boost his forces, so the village was without the young and strong. How many of them would come home eventually? She told Fraden to arrange for the tenants to share the stocks of grain and food her retinue couldn't carry. That was an easy decision; the alternative would be Despenser's men getting their hands on it.

They packed a few clothes and some food. There wasn't time for more than that. Mathilda hesitated in the hall beneath the tapestry she loved more than anything in the manor: an enclosed garden, it showed, with a man and woman standing beneath a tree in the centre, its leaves a soft blue-grey, its boughs laden with oranges.

'They're apples,' Robert had said, as he gave it to her, 'but they can be oranges if you like. It's yours, after all.' He'd smiled; she had expected him to argue.

Beneath the tree, two rabbits played among violets, daisies and lilies. Mathilda knew the rabbits were symbols of fertility, the heirs she would bear, but it was the play of line and shape that she'd noticed: the scalloped edges of leaves set against the simple branches, the globes of oranges, the detail of the tiny flowers. It was the only thing in the house that she wanted to take. But the horses were ready, Maggie was pulling at her arm, scared and crying. There was no time. She swept her hand across the texture of its stitches and walked away. Now she wonders if she should have made time. At least she still has her mother's breviary.

She can barely remember the ride away from Aspenhill, the manor she was leaving to the king's soldiers, up through the hills, trying not to look back. Would the soldiers lie in wait behind the trees, or ride openly against her little party? Were there rules for this kind of thing?

Most of the silver plate and the linen she left, and some of Robert's belongings. It was practical, and necessary, and Robert would have demanded she do the same, but Mathilda feels she has abandoned them. Abandoned him, more like. Any day, he'll come walking in the door and ask for his best velvet coat. Or for that ugly decorated bridle.

Sitting in the dull lamplight, she wonders. Whose horse is weighed down by it now? What thug of a soldier, or courtier, has snatched it from its hook, perhaps even swung it in the face of anyone who challenged him, stuffed it into his bag? What chipped teeth, bad breath, misshapen nose was now wearing Robert's velvet coat?

* * *

It's a strange creature, this captivity. The weather is warmer, and though she has prayed for the freeze to end, Mathilda now wishes it would return to make riding a hardship, the roads impassable. There's a strain in the house, a siege mind.

For the first few days they spoke quietly, glancing at the door, expecting it to burst open. She imagined the soldiers, the struggle, calling to the children to run, run, out the back and away. Feeling the arms hard around her, the ropes tight on her wrists, the screams, tears. Raw soldier stench, jokes about tasting gentry cunt, being thrown over whatever was close. This table, this one here.

Mathilda has always loved this house for being so quiet, away from the rounds of visits demanded by noble etiquette. When she was Joan's age she played by the river and built tiny houses from its rocks. She always thought Wain Wood cosy, so much warmer for being so small. Even the hangings on the walls, dusty and faded, are comfortable rather than grand. She expected that the feeling of captivity would lessen with the days, but it drags on, becoming at once deeper and more familiar. The manner of her life. Now any noise outside is louder, suddenly frightening. Childhood monsters, she thinks. Demons in the cupboard, dragons behind the hedge, giants at the door.

The girls sit quietly, peering at her face, knowing something is wrong. She warns Angmar, and especially Ysmay, to say nothing to them of the reprisals taken against the families of the king's fallen enemies, but the cook's voice is laced with drama, even when she's telling the girls to eat their dinner. Still, she gives them things to do, has them helping in the kitchen. And, as children do, they begin to play and laugh again, though as if someone is watching, waiting to scold them for their noise.

* * *

As day follows day, siege turns to a tense boredom. It's impossible to remain terrified every moment, especially when the threat has no real shape, though a sudden sound, a spider-touch of something on her skin, and it springs out from the shadow. Fraden has gone to find news, whatever kind there may be out there, and Mathilda waits, anxious to know something, anything, from the world outside.

She closes the closet door and picks up the book. She rubs her fingers across the ridges of binding on its spine. My companion. A waste, you are, but you're all I have. She touches the first page. Where there is no paint, the animal hide is smooth, and though it should be a comfort, it makes a kind of jangle in her mind, like the sound of Maggie's practice on the vielle. The last time she touched Robert's skin, it resisted her fingertips. She needs to find a drawing that will be safe: not her own portrait, not Robert's, not even Mary or Christ, and not the play of monsters.

She decides to look for the Dancaster rose; it will be on every page that the master limner has painted himself. She knows from Lady Margaret's psalter, where she first saw Dancaster's work, that the rose will not be easy to find; a limner's identifying mark, if there is one at all, ought not draw attention to itself. As she turns the pages, she realises that this means she must look closely at page after page, the one thing she doesn't want to do. Still she hunts, keeping her mind away from the detail, resisting the colour.

It takes some time to find, but here is the rose, in the border near the illumination of Mary with Christ; she's excited to find it tucked in among daisies and trefoil-shaped leaves. It's not like the roses in the garden, exactly, its petals more regular, forming a thick nest that curls around its deep centre. As she looks closer, she sees how the red darkens a little to make shadows, and touches of white show where light falls on it. Who is this man with such a gift? She presses a finger against it lightly.

Matins of the Virgin. The prayers are in French, and easy to read. Although she has vowed not to look at the illuminations and get caught up in the beauty of the book, her eyes slip away from the rose to the picture of the Virgin and Child cradled inside the large circle of a capital *D*. She knows it so well, mother and child held inside that sphere of love that seems strong enough to keep the baby safe forever. Mary looks down at her son and he looks out to his future; whatever he sees, Mathilda thinks, Mary is smelling the myrrh of her son's death. And here am I with my daughters, cowering against the threat of prison, hoping this small house will be a shelter. Living with the shadow; in that we are alike. It's a comfort.

Beneath the picture of Mary and Child is her own portrait. Mathilda touches the face. Simple lines for eyebrows, nose and mouth, a few fine lines for the criss-cross of her braid. Untroubled, a face at prayer. Perhaps that's how she looks to other people, just eyes, nose and mouth, the skin still smooth enough. She's no longer that woman: heiress of a noble family, mother of a continuing noble line, wife of a gentry man with great prospects.

Underneath, in another layer, like the parchment before the final layer of paint has been applied, that woman is frowning, crying, screaming. Has she always been this, a traitor's widow, the shame just waiting to emerge?

But she knows that's only a small part of why she wants to stay away from her portraits in the book. Though she couldn't choose whose wife she was, she had chosen what kind of wife to be. She remembers the night the portrait was drawn, so much she hadn't expected and wants to forget. Or doesn't.

Days pass, each one the same as the last. Fraden returns and says that the reprisals are slowing, and other matters occupy the king, but still the talk is of traitors. Robert's need to defend the lands he would have inherited; which lord he was sworn to ride with; which side he fought on in the battle — it wasn't as simple as a choice between fighting for or against the king. But the word 'traitor' doesn't allow for subtlety. Traitor, the one who betrays. Judas betraying Christ with a simple kiss, his thirty pieces of silver. Having followed him, loved him and learned from him, still it was not enough for Judas, and he led the soldiers to his Lord. But there was the kiss, that sign of intimacy. It seems blasphemy to say the words out loud. Could Judas have loved Jesus all the same? Could he have seen the picture with different eyes from Christ? Confused, but loving? Robert loving his king and heading out to fight him. But the soldiers wouldn't care what he had felt, given the chance for violence. All they would see is a traitor.

6

London
February 1321

Sketching

Begin your decoration with a leadpoint, also called a plummet. It is here, in the simple sketch, that the life of the decoration begins. Although it will be painted over and hidden from sight, take care. Your painting cannot be finely shaped if the sketch is hurried and unconsidered.

The uncaring limner will say the sketch is a shadow only, a ghost of what has been and is soon gone. That limner looks only to the ferment of colour. But consider: the sketch is like a simple framework that will be covered to carry wood and stone and glass, all that we see of a grand house. Or it is like the pot that fell into the cesspit, never to be seen again, or bones buried in the churchyard. Though now unseen, they were once the life of the city on which we now stand. Learn to look at a painting with the eyes of an artisan, to see where and how it began. Everything we form, be it a cathedral, a book, or a life, carries hidden traces of its beginning.

The Art of Illumination

The page was bare but for its neat rectangle of words, a corner left blank, space for a capital. *T with Christ enthroned* was the simple scrawled instruction. Will picked up the plummet and a rule, all he would need to draw the capital and its frame. And put them down again. He knew how to do this, he had drawn many capitals before, and he could see in his mind the finished picture of Christ, his hand raised in blessing, light radiating around his head. Edgar had shown him the order of the many steps: how to draw the outline, apply gesso and gold leaf, paint the layers of colour, and build the richness of the image. He had learned it all, step by step.

But Claude, the French master, had touched his hand to his chest. 'Most of all, William, you must feel it. All this knowing about pigment and line, it is worth …' He had flicked his fingers and opened his hand as if letting dust or a feather fly from it. 'It is worth nothing if you do not feel in your bones what it is you do.'

Edgar had laughed at Claude's extravagant French ways of speaking, and reminded him of the long history of painting sacred subjects. 'We can't overturn the wisdom of tradition because you *feel* something. The illuminators of our country do not have your French ways,' he'd said.

Unaware, Will touched his own chest. How much had he lost on the road from Cambridge? The snow and ice had felt like punishment, but they hadn't made him clean. His bones had rattled like a dead man's, feeling nothing. What would Claude say to him now? He could see him leaning over the parchment, a slight smile, his eyes wide, a furrow on his forehead. Begin, William. Begin and let your hand and arm take you where you need to go. He would begin.

Still he sat, twisting the plummet in his fingers. For eleven years he had imagined a moment like this, beginning a grand book, a chance to show his skills. He knew he had them. Or once had. He thought of Lady Mathilda, and perhaps Sir Robert, turning the pages, admiring the detail and the rich colour, bringing the book out to show visitors. Was that why he painted? Wouldn't they see only the money behind the gold leaf and lapis?

For a moment, he panicked, searching for what his yearning had been. Had his desire led him to a shadow, a ghost of what he had thought it was, his work no more than a fancy for the nobility? Simon, leaning over his shoulder, breathing in his ear.

'You about to start then?' Nick was peering over his arm at the pages. 'You'll be drawing first, won't you? Sketching out everything before you'll need me to mix for you.'

'I will.'

'Ma says this isn't what any other new apprentice gets, to work on a book like this, for such an important man as Sir Robert, with all his lands and money. I can't even imagine what it's like to be him. He's a knight, with his own men, Pa says, and they'll be riding off to the war soon. Think on it. Horses and swords and battle. And our book will be in his house, on his estate!'

'No better people than us, they are, Nick. Probably not even as good as us.'

'But he has manors, and he's in charge of men. Knights and—'

'Doesn't make them good. It means they're powerful, that's all.'

'But—'

'Enough about the rich. Not worth you thinking about. And now it's time to work.' Will was sharp. 'Rearrange the shelves of the storeroom, if there's nothing else to do.'

Nick hadn't finished. 'You not singing today, Will? I like it when you sing, even if I don't know what the words mean.'

'Go!' Will almost shouted.

'You want to shut up those riches inside two covers where only a few see it. And they learn nothing from it. Does admiring a rich illumination cause the gentry to treat people better?' Simon's eyes looked black sometimes, as hard as his words.

They argued, night after night, in an alehouse or in Simon's tiny student room. But in a book of prayers, Will said, the noble folk see Christ, and the Virgin, and saints; they read prayers and the images help them understand what they are saying. The book, and its pictures, teaches them how to live.

'They see the paintings on church walls along with the rest of the faithful, grand murals calling them to live godly lives. If they don't heed the call there in church, why would they notice it in the comfort of their grand houses, reclining on their soft cushions?' Simon asked.

'But beauty is important to us all,' Will argued. 'How else can beautiful art be made? It must be the wealthy who pay for the pigment and the labour; that's the order of the world. We need patrons.'

'What's the point of great beauty if only the privileged see it? Better to offer simple work if it means that more folk can see and use it. Does the king, surrounded by sumptuous tapestries and sleeping under his rich coverlets, dream of ways to protect the poor? Do lords learn of ways to care for the folk on their lands? Bishops wear lavish robes embroidered with gold and silver and preach God's love to those who barely have enough to cover themselves.'

Will couldn't argue with the logic, but he was sure there was more to say. 'Line and colour matter, even for those who are poor. Maybe more.'

'Exactly. So paint for them, not for the rich.'

Will had heard the argument before and he had no other answers. Finally, worn down, he declared his own truth. 'For me, making pictures is like you reading or arguing, or my pa shaping a fine wheel with the right balance. It has always mattered to me, above all else. Father Michael called my talent a blessing, a gift from God. That's why I began.'

Simon waved his hand. 'How can it be a blessing from God if you want to give his beauty only to the rich?'

Will felt winded by the blow, as sharply as if Simon had thrown him to the ground.

He shook his head, looked around the shop. Gemma and Benedict were bent over their pages, but John was watching him.

'You right there, Asshe? Know what to do? What are you working on?'

'Christ enthroned,' Will said as John walked across to his desk.

'Christ enthroned? That should be clear enough. Have you not done one before? I thought you—'

'Of course I have. I showed you, didn't I? I'm thinking, planning. And I can't do that with people peering at me, asking questions.'

Benedict and Gemma looked up at the jagged words, but John put a hand on Will's shoulder and said quietly, 'Course you know what to do, Asshe,' and walked back to his desk.

Will kept his head down, ashamed. He barely recognised this young man with doubts. Edgar would have had him back to scrubbing for months on end if he'd spoken to him that way; it was wrong, and he would have to apologise. Later. For now, John's hand had settled him, drawn him back from Cambridge so he could begin. He'd try something small in the margin. Plummet in his hand, without thought, he let it guide the way.

From a single point, the lead circled, small then larger, opening out into a spiral. He began to hum. The curved nub of a head, the short tail behind, and two long feelers stretching out at the front. He sat back and looked, but something was missing. The snails he had watched as a boy, taunting them to pull back their feelers, had a second, shorter pair as well.

'Is that a snail you're drawing?' Nick had returned, peering closely, his head blocking Will's view.

Benedict raised his head. 'A snail? I thought you said it was Christ enthroned. You said you were planning it. All your good ideas, keen to begin, so you said.'

'Just getting started,' Will said. The man was right, though. All he could manage was a snail. 'But I'm glad you asked, Benedict. How are your borders?' One day, he thought, he'll be in my margin. He smiled widely at him. There was something about Benedict's jealousy and nervousness that made Will feel he could do anything. 'And Nick, if you want to watch me begin you can, but stay back, and don't bump my arm.'

'But why a snail anyway?' asked Nick.

'To entertain the Lady Mathilda,' Will said. 'To make her think about God's creation.' My hand drew what it wanted, he thought.

'The snail's a sign of humility, isn't it?' Benedict said. 'Can't imagine why *you'd* be drawing one, Will.'

Will laughed. The joking helped, even if Benedict didn't mean it. He began working on a vine, bent over like a wave beneath the snail's weight. His hand knew the way, as it always had; it remembered.

He was eleven or twelve, a boy scratching around behind the jars of grain and the sacks of dried beans in the corner of the kitchen, digging where he had seen his mother smoothing over the earth then dragging back the sacks to cover whatever she had been doing. Thinking no one had seen her. The next day, while she was outside pruning the apple trees, he crept to the hiding place. It was easy to shift away the dirt, soft and lightly turned; it must have been often disturbed. Beneath, two pieces of wood covering a hole roughly lined with stones, and tucked inside it, a small sack. He thought it would be some salted meat set aside, or maybe a small purse of coins, so he was surprised to feel something hard with square edges beneath the sacking. At first, he couldn't tell what it was. A black fan that splayed and crackled as he pulled it free of the sack, it smelled smoky, but not like the fire they burned each day. He turned it over and realised. It was parchment, a book, burned at the edges and so crinkled that the covers wouldn't close. But when he separated two of the charcoaled leaves his breath stopped. Inside, the blocks of words were surrounded by pictures such as he had never seen: flowers, vines, hares, foxes, bees and snails curling and crawling along the margins.

He turned the pages, wondered at the colours of this new world. Some had only a creature or two, and others had only words and a little bit of red decoration; most were broken and crumbled at the edges. And, on a few pages that he knew must be special, the pictures shone with gold, touches of sun, bright against the blackened edges.

Suddenly, the pictures shifted and his head rang. He'd forgotten where he was: in the kitchen, at the secret place, holding the thing that must be forbidden. His mother bent and scooped up the book, lifted it into her arms as she would a baby or a wounded animal. Then she looked down at him, her face serious, and stretched out one hand to him.

'This will be our secret now, Will. You understand? Tell no one.' Her hand was tight on his shoulder and he twisted, but she gripped harder. 'No one. Not your brother or your sister or your father. Specially not your father.'

'I won't, Ma. But can I look at it? Just look? Not to hurt it. At the pictures. That snail bigger than a hare. And the dragon. Can I look again?'

Her hand loosened and she looked down at the book, touched the edge of its pages. 'Only if you keep the secret. If not, your pa'll take it away.' She paused, beginning to smile. 'Did you see King David playing his harp? It's near the front.'

That was the day it began. Perhaps the need to keep it secret made the book more special. He loved the anticipation of digging for it, the creeping into the kitchen, then hiding behind the sacks or sneaking it outside to his favourite spot in the hollow of an old oak. Years later, though, after he had seen more books and illuminations, he recognised that it was the burning that set the book apart for him, like a dog with three legs or their hen with one eye stuck closed after a fight. The pages had the scent of smoke and crackled as he turned them, as if they were still on fire.

7

London
February 1321

Pigment

A book is about earth as much as skin. For earth, nothing is too worn out, threadbare or mouldy. She takes it all, gathers it in. Grinds, liquefies, bakes, compresses. Quietly, slowly, making her treasures of colour. Hacked from cliff and mountain rock, or dug from dry ground, the stone is crushed and milled, then the colour separated from the dross and ground to fine powder. Some colour you will make yourself, squeezing juice from berries and leaves, or placing together elements that react to form a third substance and hue.

Think of the unknown people, women and men, and children too, who first gathered soil into the small basins of their palms, spat on it and painted with fingertips. Who then crushed stone with another stone. Remember that they were curious, questioning, asking what might next be found and transformed in the service of beauty. That, too, is your duty as an alchemist of colour.

The Art of Illumination

Heads down against the drizzle, Gemma and Nick turned into Distaff Lane. A hand reached out, a pleading sound from the bundle collapsed near the shop corner, but they kept going. It wasn't difficult any more; the sick and dying were so familiar, like the muck on the street, that Gemma barely noticed them. From time to time she would wonder who might have known them, given birth to them, laughed at their jokes or scolded them, but that was a miserable game with no answers. If she let herself dwell on it, she'd sink down too.

The apothecary's shop was busy, as usual, the street outside crowded with the ailing who could stand and, more importantly, pay for Sewale's ministration. Huddled under the jetty of the overhanging storey above, they were all so wet it made little difference; they stood as one, backs to the weather, heads bent, arms crossed against the cold, moving only to cough or spit. Gemma watched as a man on crutches dragged himself toward the shelter and tried to shuffle in among the crowd. A few heads looked around and cursed, a few people pushed back with elbows or shoulders, and the man gave up, drooping where he stopped. In this weather, he'd be lucky to last a week, Gemma thought, whatever tea or tincture Sewale might give him.

She and Nick joined the gathering to wait their turn at the counter, though Gemma was wary and stayed back a pace or two. It was only last Yule that more than fifty beggars had been crushed to death at the Friars Preachers, waiting for alms. Hoping for a chunk of bread, squashed by those around them, gasping for air. She shuddered and looked up sharply as the crowd pushed, some shouting.

'Gerroutavit, you! Wait your turn.'

'What you doing? I was here first.'

She and Nick stepped further away from the jostling.

'I'm here for Bishop Laurence. He needs medicine urgently.' It was a man in livery, his voice certain. 'I have no time to wait.' He waved his hand. 'Sewale, I need to speak,' he shouted. 'Bishop Laurence's business.'

The apothecary opened his door and peered out. 'Aye, step up then. Make way, you ugly louts. Let the man through, else I'll see none of you.'

The crowd parted before the servant, but as he passed, one, then another, and another, bumped his shoulder, nudged his elbow, put out a foot. Sewale opened his door and let him in just as hands reached out to grab and punch. The apothecary frowned, growled and slammed the door.

Gemma shepherded Nick back into line as those around them cursed. She knew she didn't need to be there. She hadn't brought Benedict when he began as an apprentice, but she wanted to bring her son, relive her own visits with her father. He had taught her so much, and smiled whenever she'd talked about becoming a limner, but there had been fewer lessons for her once John arrived as apprentice.

The apothecary's shop had seemed a place of wonder, so much horror, mundanity and magic gathered under one roof. Back then, standing among the crowd, holding onto her pa's sleeve, she had seen with different eyes, recognising not people and illnesses, but something akin to the dead in a picture her pa had painted. It had haunted her for years. In a garden stood three rich people arrayed in gold and velvet, their eyes vacant with contentment, and next to them three skeletons, their eye sockets empty, worms crawling through their stark bones. Her pa had read out to her the words inscribed beneath the dead — *What you are I once was; what I am you will surely become* — then told her to close the book and feed the chickens.

She knew now, though, that none of those standing with her were rich, and few of them needed to be reminded of their frailty. These last few years, as winter refused to move on, Death had stalked the streets breathing ice and snatching food from the starving. Those who clustered at the apothecary's counter were worn out with the effort of surviving; the dead were simply dead.

She and Nick shuffled forward, the lad gradually insinuating himself among the press of bodies to peer through the opening in the shopfront, the wooden shutter folded down to become a counter. Only customers who needed the apothecary's ministrations could go through the door.

Her pa had taken Gemma inside a few times, into what had always seemed to her another world. Glass bottles, brass instruments of all shapes, pots, bowls and flasks, the smell of spices, herbs and God knows what else, liquids bubbling and steaming over flame, dust from powder ground and mixed, stuffed objects of all sizes, dried fungus, rocks, bark and moss. The air itself had seemed different, thicker, almost as if she could have touched it, gathered a handful and taken it home. Those chunks of bone, her pa had told her, were from a unicorn's horn, to ward off poison. And hanging above their heads, a long, flat creature with a huge mouth. It was a crocodile, Sewale the apothecary had told her, but a baby one. In strange hot countries, they grew to ten times its size, big enough to swallow her whole, he'd said, and laughed so much with his wide, awkward mouth and big teeth that she had been terrified. That had been years ago, but still, each time she visited, she looked for the crocodile, now brown with dust and part of its tail broken off, and remembered the thrill of imagining the little beast growing so huge that the shop wouldn't hold it.

Finally at the counter, she told Harry, the assistant, that she'd come to pick up the order for the shop.

'It's a big one,' Nick added. 'On account of it's an important commission. A book of hours for Sir Robert Fitzjohn.'

Harry probably knew that, and if he cared at all would have been surprised when the order was placed. Longer than usual, and the first in quite a while. Whatever he thought, he only grunted and piled the jars of pigment and bags of stone and wood onto the counter, ticking them off the order: red ochre, brazil wood, turnsole berries, umber, limestone, yellow ochre, gum arabic, Armenian bole, woad and lapis lazuli. Nick looked around to see if others were watching, impressed.

'No malachite,' Harry said, his voice flat.

'What? None?' Gemma said. 'When will it be in?'

'Can't say, can I? Nothin' on the boat.'

'There's never been a problem before,' Gemma said. 'We gave you the list in good time, Harry. Have you forgotten to order it?'

Harry looked at her under his eyebrows. 'You got problems, you get John to come speak to me. I'm not arguing with a woman and a lad.'

'But it's for the book. I have to mix it,' Nick cut in.

'Make verdigris. That's green,' Harry muttered, packing the order into a sack.

'It's not just any green ...' Nick began.

His words trailed off as Gemma stepped closer to the counter and put a hand on the sack, making Harry stop and look up. 'Three seasons until your apprenticeship is done, is it Harry? Nothing's certain, though, is it? Now, you order the malachite. Because we need it. Soon. Else I'll have words with Sewale about your lazy ways.' She waited until he nodded, then turned away.

Nick picked up the sack and ran after her, but he could barely keep up.

Gemma stalked to her desk, leaving Nick to unload the sack and sort out the storeroom. Benedict was bent deep over his work and Will was humming as he drew, here and there adding a snatch of words.

'No malachite,' Nick announced. 'No idea when it's coming.'

Will glanced at him and nodded, though he kept up his song. '*Dira vi amoris teror, et venereo* ... mmm, hhmmm, hhmmm. I'll need malachite.'

'What I told Harry,' Nick said. 'He didn't listen.'

'We'll talk to Southflete. He'll know how to get some,' Will said, and began the song again. '*Igne ferventi suffocatus ...*'

'No, we won't ask Southflete,' Gemma cut in, glaring at Will, who stopped singing but said nothing.

Will met her eyes. Who was she, making decisions like that? And if she was meant to be training Nick, why did she insist on sitting at that desk, tinkering with paint?

'What were those words you were singing?' Nick asked.

Will looked away. 'All about the torments of love, boy. About being torn on the wheel of desire.' He smiled. 'Very painful.'

'It's we who suffer.' Benedict's eyes didn't move from his parchment. 'Torn on the wheel of your noise.'

Will laughed and turned to Benedict, delighted with his joke, but perhaps it wasn't meant to be funny. For some moments, Will studied the apprentice's profile and realised for the first time, how ... What was the word? Dignified? Yes, dignified, it was. He didn't know anything about Benedict: whether he had always lived in London; why he wanted to be a limner; how he'd met John. He should go for an ale with him one night. 'Not going well there, Ben?' he asked.

Benedict ignored him, and the moment of fellow feeling faded quickly.

Will looked toward Nick and shrugged. 'How about I help you with that sack? I'm almost finished here.'

In the storeroom, barely a closet with a bench and some shelves above it, Will and Nick unloaded the sack. Nick was excited, asking about the pigments, wondering when he would begin grinding or mixing each one.

The chance to begin an apprenticeship with a grand book, Will thought, to see it emerge from pages of script, watch it take on colours and shapes. What if he, young William Asshe, had been made apprentice to John Dancaster nine or ten years ago, instead of to Edgar with his particular ways and rules, making him wait a full year before he was even allowed to put brush to parchment? He wanted to be resentful, but knew there was no force in it; he had been an arrogant boy, so convinced that his talent needed no guidance. He frowned at the memory. One night, only a few months after he'd arrived in Cambridge, he'd crept into the workshop, mixed some red and blue paint, and begun work on a decorated capital *W*, heart pounding in his throat. He'd wanted to show Edgar what he could do. Excitement, guilt, pride, simple clumsiness, probably all of those, and he'd spilled paint across the page. Fortunately, he'd had enough sense to mix only small amounts of paint, knowing time was short, but there it was, red streaked across five lines of script. Then, to make it worse, he'd tried to blot it away.

But it was Gemma, not John, who was giving Nick instruction. A woman, though she seemed to know what she was doing.

'So, where's your pa today?' he asked Nick.

'Dunno,' Nick said.

'I just wondered, thought he'd be working hardest of all of us. Is he sick, then?' Will tried to sound like it didn't really matter.

'Ask me ma. She'll know.'

Will knew he wouldn't do that. Instead, he grabbed Nick around the shoulders, knocked his legs out from beneath him and wrestled him easily to the floor, pinning him down with one large hand on his chest.

Nick kicked his legs, struggled to move then gave up and looked at Will, his eyes large, his breath fast.

'This, young Nicholas Dancaster, apprentice limner of Paternoster Row, London,' said Will, 'this is the best organised storeroom in all of Christendom.' He patted Nick on the chest, smiled and walked, humming, back to his desk.

8

London
March 1321

Fraternity

A limner never works alone. Even if, in time, you become a master and run your own shop, you are connected to those in the book trade: the parchmenter, the scribe, the scrivener, the binder and the stationer. A book cannot be made otherwise. Those in the trade must gather together to form standards of quality and orderly business, but the connection is more than practical. Even those who vie with you for business are your companions. Your trade relies on commissions and work will be uncertain. The fraternity, or the guild, where one has been formed, will offer support, as you will in turn give support.

The Art of Illumination

The fraternity of scribes, scriveners, illuminators and binders met in the church of St Michael le Querne in Westcheap, near the end of Paternoster Row. On his first morning in London, Will had noticed the church jutting into the junction of streets, though he hadn't taken much notice of it then. Now, as Father Paul prayed, the limner peered around. In the arch above the altar, St Michael stood defiant in armour and boots, his spear outstretched, almost touching the vulnerable neck of the dragon that flew from the right side of the arch, its mouth belching flame. The saint's tunic and hair rippled, his head was thrust forward; the dragon's wings curved above, following the topmost line of the arch. Will shivered, held his breath, wanted to thank whoever the artist was. Next to him, John was still, head bent in prayer.

'The fraternity just happened, without much planning as far as I can tell,' John said, the service over. The two men ambled through the church, Will gazing at the saints depicted on the side walls. 'St Michael's was the parish church for most in Paternoster Row. Still is, of course. Gemma could tell you more than me about the fraternity. Her pa was a master limner, and she'd go along with the family to meetings. Numbers were small to begin with, local folks gathering for support. A fair few were in the book trade in some way, so it grew from there.

'When I joined, there still weren't many rules; they weren't needed. Just had to make sure the fees that we paid were properly handled, and that wasn't a problem until Frederick Cook made off with most of it. We never did get it back. Made it hard when John the Bookbinder died, and his widow had none of the support she was entitled to. So, things changed.'

At a door at the side of the sanctuary, he stopped. 'We meet in the undercroft now, but there's talk of paying for a chapel to be built. Don't know how. No one has money, even for the church, after the famine and this bad weather. You'll be expected to join. We need six men to vouch for you to buy freedom of the city. If you don't do that, Southflete'll make it hard for us.'

'Yes, yes, I will. That's what I want, to be a citizen of London. And join the fraternity. But I don't understand. Southflete's not in this fraternity, is he? His shop isn't hereabouts. It's on the bridge.'

'Ssshh, not so loud. It's not that he has many friends among us, but power, you know, there's no saying what a man'll tell him if he overhears us. Southflete's not a member here, but he has connections everywhere: the court, Oxford, York, Peterborough, Ely. He knows those with money enough to commission books and he can tell them which scribe or limner they should go to. And it's his influence will persuade the aldermen to agree to us forming a guild, not that it's likely for a time yet. Manekyn's the head of this fraternity. I think you met him, the scribe in charge of copying the book, and Wat Scrivener helps him. But Southflete has Manekyn's ear, and gets what he wants. You'll see soon enough how it works.'

John reached out for the door handle, fumbled, lost his balance until Will put out a hand to hold him up. 'So dull in here it's hard to see,' John muttered.

Will pushed open the door and they stepped down the stairs into a mingled smell of ale and damp, the stone whispering with loose grit beneath their feet.

Will immediately liked the room. The low ceiling was a clever design of arched spans projecting upwards from a single point at waist height on each of the two long side walls. Both points were decorated with a corbel, a simple carved head: a man on the left side, a woman on the right. He studied the lines above him, a combination of single pointed arches and double angled arches, the spans meeting at a midpoint to create a dome. This design was for strength, he knew, and he had seen it many times before, but he noted anew the pattern the arches created, their clean and elegant lines. For all that the room was crowded, it was welcoming after the tall, straight lines of the church above. He knew most of the people gathered on benches drinking, talking and arguing, and smiled when he thought how much it was like the Peter and Paul; it was Paternoster Row relaxing. John handed Will a pot of ale.

'Idla's brew,' he said. 'You're in luck. Truth is that Hawisia Archer makes the ale at her house, but Idla helps from time to time, and it's always better. We don't tell Hawisia, of course. Idla just smiles and says she has a secret way.' He looked toward a woman sitting quietly on the end of a bench, arms crossed over her chest. Shadows seemed to have taken up a home in her cheeks, as if no amount of light would shift them. 'She's not well of late, though they need her to keep brewing when she can, and she weaves baskets, too. You must have seen her Tom coming and going. They live upstairs next to us. He sells her baskets, and the belts he makes, in those stalls near the end of the Row. Barely enough to get by.'

'And they're in the fraternity?' Will asked.

'Well, they're in the parish, and they live in the Row, just next door to us, but they're foreigns. Don't have the money to buy their freedom like they should. Some here say we shouldn't let them in, that it's time Tom joined with other girdlers, but this is their church and times are tough. And besides,' he smiled, 'Idla makes the kind of brew that keeps the naysayers happy.'

'So not everyone is in the book trade?'

'Most of us, and some here say that everyone should be.' John sighed. 'There'll be rules about that soon enough, especially when we're a proper guild.'

As was his habit, Will looked around the room studying faces. They all had two eyes, two ears, a nose, mouth and chin, so what made each one so different? Manekyn was standing at the far end of the undercroft, ready to begin the meeting. His skin was like hide, smooth and thick, marked with two deep lines running down the sides of his face; when he smiled, a crescent formed on either side of his mouth. Next to him stood Wat Scrivener. Will had met him a few times in the Peter and Paul, a man almost the same height as him, but thin, with black hair springy as an urchin's, eyes, nose and chin all neat and round. But something saved him from looking like a child: his bearing, perhaps, or the two straight lines of a frown above his nose. All of this Will tucked away for his pen.

As he began to focus on conversations, Will realised the air was swirling with talk of the Iter, the inquisition into London's illegal confederacies. Underway for less than a season, and its impact was brutal.

'Inquisition? It's more of a blood bath,' Henry Archer said. 'Only last week, John Baker took sick after they kept him there all day checking his books, asking questions, accusing him of fixing prices with the other bakers. John Baker. Can you imagine? He can make bread, but he couldn't scheme and cheat if he tried.'

'Baker? God's holy bones!' Rowley Buxton, the parchmenter, growled. 'Devil take those men and their Iter! Cursed Stanton and his devil companion Scrope. Doing Despenser's work, that's what it is. Plenty of coin in payment they get, no doubt — the money they take from us folk. Keep us weak while he takes over. That's Despenser's plan.'

'And what's the king do? Kisses Despenser's sweet white arse, that's what.'

'Ah, things might be turning.' It was Wat.

The group of men looked toward him. He always speaks as a man who knows, Will thought, even if only to ask for a fish pie.

'I hear Hamo de Chigwell and his men plan to bring a petition to the king, asking him to end the inquisition,' Wat continued. 'And they might have success, you know.'

'But why? Despenser's busy seizing any land he can in the Marches. No mere mayor of London can stop him doing as he likes.'

'True, he's been wresting whatever land he could. But he's not as strong as he was; Hereford and Mortimer are pushing back, taking up arms. And,' Wat said, his voice rising, 'they've demanded Despenser be handed over to Lancaster.'

'Well, Lancaster's hiding up north,' Henry said. 'I'll eat my balls for dinner on the day he takes Despenser.'

'Now that'll be something to see,' Rowley said.

Wat smiled. 'Awful as that sounds, Henry, let's hope you have to. Maybe Lancaster will surprise us all. But if the king lets Despenser go on as he is, and doesn't sort out this problem in the Marches, it'll come to our gates. You'll see.'

The muttering turned to a gloomy silence. Wat was usually right in his predictions.

Nearby, another group was raking over more bad news. 'I hear Leon's dead,' said a man Will hadn't met. 'Argument over a cock fight, it was. Perkin refused to pay up what he owed.'

'Ah, he should never have trusted that Perkin,' Peter Binder sighed.

'Yes, but he should have let this one go, should have known Perkin would always get the better of him. Pulled out a knife, he did. Stuck him in the belly. Lasted till morning, but there was no chance.'

'It's the Iter, the worry. Raises a man's choler,' Peter replied.

'Maybe so. But Perkin was always one for a brawl, Iter or no.'

Content to simply look on, Will watched the anger and frustration rise and fall like dark waves among the gathered clusters of locals.

The meeting began then with a debate about the planned chapel that, as expected, was over before it really began; Manekyn pointed out that there was little spare money. Rowley Buxton's apprentice, Maynard, had been accused of affray, and needed someone to stand mainpernor for his appearance in court; Luanda de Biville was still waiting for her property to be settled after her John's death, eight weeks ago now, and needed a loan to see her through; Leon's children would need some help, with no mother and now no father to look after them. Southflete sent a message through Manekyn to remind them all that the quality of their work must be maintained at the highest standard. Those gathered groaned almost as one, but Manekyn frowned (creating a series of deep lines in his forehead, Will noticed) and shouted that it was the duty of each master to be sure that the London book trade took good care of its growing reputation.

And then it was the turn of William Asshe, limner and journeyman. John spoke, recommending his new employee to the fraternity, and asking for five men, along with him, to stand surety for Will so that he might buy his freedom of the city. The response was a general murmur of agreement and two men immediately stood up to offer their support.

'He has a fine voice for a tune or two, as well,' Henry said.

'Aye, and he knows some Cambridge words to drinking songs. Those that students sing,' Rowley added.

The gathering cheered, but before others could join in support of Will, Manekyn began again.

'Wait! We—'

'Leave it be, Manekyn,' Henry cut in. 'We've had enough for one night, and we all know Will.'

'No, there's a question or two we should be clear about first. A man's voice for bawdy tunes isn't enough. As Southflete reminds us, our trade depends on us being thorough.'

He's enjoying this, Will thought, but he nodded with what he hoped was a smile.

'Tell us your background, William Asshe, and how you come to be in London,' Manekyn said.

Will told the story: his father the wheelwright; his own interest in drawing; the parish priest finding him a place in Cambridge as apprentice to Edgar Gerard; his work there on treatises; his leaving to find work in London. He hoped it was all they'd want to hear

'There,' Peter said. 'Good enough for me.'

'Wait!' said Manekyn again, and the gathering groaned. 'Edgar Gerard, as we know, is a fine stationer and limner. Why would you leave such a position?'

'It was ... I've wanted to see London, to work here, since I was a lad.'

'Yes, but why now? Why, when you know work is scarce and you'd almost finished your master's piece with Gerard?'

Will realised then that Southflete had told the scribe of the
Beatus piece, and instructed him to dig further. His palms
were damp. 'It was a sadness. A tragedy.'

'A tragedy? That sounds like something we might see at
Smithfield, declaimed from the stage.'

Will was studying the ceiling, following the curved line
of the arch, trying to settle his panic, when John called out.

'Give it up, Manekyn. A tragedy he says, and a tragedy it
is. What's wrong with the word?'

'Details. A word can hide details. Wat and I know that
more than any of you.'

'It's the man's private business,' someone shouted.

Will didn't see who it was because the carved head on the
left wall, at the base of the arches, had turned to look at him.
Surely it had been only a man's face. Had it changed? The
nose had spread, the eyes were larger. And those bumps …
Were they horns beginning to grow? Slowly, with strangely
delicate care, it withdrew one leg from the solid stone beneath
its head, then another, and another, its eyes focused on Will.
The meeting argued on, but he heard nothing. He watched
the creature creep along the stones of the arch until it reached
the peak.

'Will? Will?' John shook his arm.

Will glanced at John as if he hadn't seen him, then looked
up again at the gargoyle, which had turned its body upside
down and was hanging from the arch's apex, its eyes never
leaving him.

'Will,' John said more loudly. He shook Will's arm again
and looked round at the gathered faces. 'A tragedy you say.
We've all known affliction, one way or another. Surely that's
enough for us. Not something to talk about, is it?'

Will, his face white, gathered himself enough to nod. 'Yes.
Not something I talk about.'

Amid the gathering's murmurs of sympathy and mutterings
of their own sorrows, Manekyn was forced to submit. Three

more men declared themselves prepared to support the new limner's claim for citizenship and the meeting ended with a rough cheer. Will thanked them all, and when he looked again, the ceiling was empty, the head at the base of the arches that of a benign man gazing at the woman on the other side of the undercroft. Always there, and always out of reach.

'Now, William Asshe, a drink for you to celebrate, and a song for us!' Tom shouted. 'Give us the one about the friar and the bishop's woman.'

Will took a gulp of the ale Rowley handed to him, though his hands were unsteady, and began to sing. The deep vibrato of his voice rolled up from his chest, strong enough to cover the wavering of his nerves. He realised that he could do this — perform, be loud, tell jokes — and cover over the haunting. Singing, he discovered, kept the memories away.

9
London
April 1321

Composition

The page before you will have words arranged according to the needs of reading, in lines where word follows word, else the reader would find no sense or way through. Imagine a city where all streets ended suddenly in walls, or wandered with no purpose, as in a maze. It would be abandoned by its people. Likewise, words must have the order that words demand.

But the requirements of decoration are not so simple. The page needs shape and order, but not so much order that life withers. Consider the beauty of curve and curl. And, as with a breathing city, let all of life be there in the book, from high to low, animal and monster, story and joke, devotion and dance, for God the Great Artisan made it all. On some pages, simple vines and flowers may be enough. On others, let decoration be lush and bountiful.

The Art of Illumination

It was early morning, the chimes of the bell for Prime fading. John handed Gemma the calendar pages. 'What about you get on with them for now, Gem? You know what to do as well as me. I'll be back soon,' he said.

'But you told the shop that my job was to help train Nick, and that's what I've been doing. And you said I could help just a little with the colour. I was there, John.'

'It was for Southflete's ears, that's all. You know we need you to paint as well, but we can't stir Southflete's pot. You know how he goes on, that everyone who works on the book has to be recognised by the fraternity.'

'Of course I know. But don't tell me there's nothing to be done. You're recognised everywhere in the trade. You could argue for changes.'

'When it's done and the Fitzjohns are happy, we'll have more position to argue with.' He walked to the door. 'Just let it be for now. Don't keep on about it, especially now we have this commission and so much to do.'

'I know how much work there is. And how will we manage? We have Benedict, still an apprentice, and this man we don't know, who arrives and thinks he should be employed. We had agreed to ask Hugh.'

'Don't go over it all again, Gem. Will was here, ready to start. And he knows what he's doing. You said so yourself. And I saw your face when you looked at his Beatus page. You know he can do the work. So, with Benedict, and you, and me—'

'You, John? You're going out again on some message. You know that's for Nick to do.'

'And I'll be back.'

'And then? You'll find something else to do. What's wrong, John?'

'Leave me be, woman.' John slammed through the door.

Gemma sighed, and turned to see Nick watching from the doorway. 'It's Pa, isn't it? It's—'

'Leave it, Nick. Don't worry about him. Do your work.' She had asked the question, but she was afraid John would answer.

Gemma sat at her desk and looked down at John's sketches on the pages. The decoration was to be simple flourishes of vine, but the lines of leadpoint were rough and uncertain, far beneath the work of a master. She traced a wavering line with her finger. The thought that had been stalking her, the fear she hoped was only her anxious fancy, drew closer. It was time she faced it. But she shook her head, wouldn't let it in.

When they had first met, she had loved John almost as much for his painting ability as for his laugh and his certainty that all would be well. Back then, he'd had every reason to think so; the Dancaster rose, painted at first on a whim, became the mark of his talent, and Gemma had learned to trust in it. As a child she had lived between two worlds. She loved the mystery and beauty of her pa's pigments and painting, his lessons about grinding and mixing, his stories of the illuminations and the strange creatures he drew in the margins. Helping out, she would imagine herself doing this fine work one day. But her ma taught her that life was too uncertain to risk trusting in such flimsy things, things that couldn't be eaten or worn or used to keep the family dry and warm. Illuminating was well and good, she'd say, but only if there were folks willing to pay for such a luxury. Day after day she would drag the young girl back into the kitchen or the garden to teach her the next lesson in frugality. When John arrived as apprentice, it was almost impossible to keep her out of the shop.

Benedict and Will walked in and went to their desks. Gemma didn't look up, though she put an arm around her work to shield it from view. When they had settled to work, she glanced up and rubbed her fingers together. Sunlight ventured through the open shutters, but despite that, and the stove's best efforts at warming the room, it was cold. The two limners were bent to their work, their shapes softened in the early light. For a moment the scene was a painting, the two desks and curved backs echoing one another and framed as if by the decorated borders of a page. Limners at work. That picture would not tell all the truth there is, she thought: the ambition, fear and tension that lingered in the gently golden air above them. What was this beautiful book they were decorating? The truth of what might be, a shining moment? Or a deception?

Clouds scudded across the sun, and the room sank into its usual dull state. Will was humming as he worked and

Benedict was drawing, peering at the model book after every few lines. He looked miserable, anxiety heavy like a hump on his back. She wondered what had happened to the lad who had been so eager six years ago, wanting to learn, desperate to put lines of ink and paint on the page. It had been her job to train him, and she had him begin, as with Nick, grinding and mixing pigments, and cleaning the little clam shells that held the paint for each illuminator.

'So little sea animals lived in here?' he'd asked her. 'They remind me of ears. See? The shape and the curves, the way they're uneven and indented. And the way the shell is wavy in places and smooth in others.'

Gemma had smiled. 'Looking closely like that is important for a limner, Ben.'

He'd looked pleased, but said, 'I'm always called Benedict. Not plain Ben.'

And so Benedict it had been.

She hadn't needed to remind him to keep the storeroom tidy, or to clean up, or even to grind the pigment more and more finely, and there were times when she'd had to warn him to stop making something 'even better', as he called it, and to move on with the next job.

'It's what you tell me to do,' he'd say. '"Do it as well as you can," you say.'

It had been hard to argue with that, but Gemma had slowly realised that she should have done something sooner. 'Only God is perfect,' she had said a few times, but his answer was always the same.

'And we do all we can to honour that perfection in our work.'

He'd listened to all Gemma taught him, attentive and earnest, but continued to copy. 'He doesn't exactly refuse,' Gemma had said to John. 'I just don't think he can do more.'

As Benedict grew older, he'd decided that a woman wouldn't really know about painting, and barely listened to her. She'd asked John to talk to the lad but he'd waved it off, as he did most awkward issues. 'The lad's growing, is all. And you've always said you want some more — what is it, spirit? — in him. Well there it is. You can't complain now.'

But that was where the 'spirit' — had she really used that word? — had ended. Now it was all worry about getting things perfect. Gemma had even wished he'd do what all apprentices did, and go out at night, find trouble in cock fights or wrestling, even bear baiting. She'd never dreamed that he might do something violent, but drinking, dice games, bowls, maybe even football would help. Or Gropecunt Lane. That was probably what he needed, but she couldn't suggest that. Break the rules, Ben, she'd wanted to say. Just once. We'd curse you and punish you, but I'd rest more easy. Because then you would paint with your body, not just from the model book.

Gemma shook her head and tried to focus. Dates of saints' feast days, dates of local markets, dates of birth, marriage, death, the Fitzjohn and de Saunford families. Lives made into a list of sacred history, family history, the ordinary days of buying and selling. So much wrapped up and bundled into each line.

Two roundels: one of the season, one of the Zodiac symbol, the scribe had written. John had made some hurried sketches and it wasn't clear what he had intended, so she would start again. It was always a strange moment, this beginning. Stepping through a door, as if feeling her way downstairs in the dark, waiting to recognise the steps under her feet, the wood and plaster beneath her fingers. She would mark the circles out first.

'Nick, I need compasses,' she called. No answer, so she looked up; there he was, leaning over Will's shoulder, laughing. That man! 'Nicholas, do your job.'

Nick straightened and looked toward his mother. She was peering again at the page, and didn't need to see his look of guilt.

'And Will,' she said, 'stop singing that song.'

Will looked up and frowned. Who was she to tell him what to do? Master's wife, was all. 'Why, Gemma?' he coaxed. 'It's only a love song to …' His voice trailed off at Gemma's face, daring him to go on. He hummed a bar or two and stopped, went back to his work.

Nick placed a pair of compasses on her desk and stood nearby to watch.

'One of the roundels will be here.' She indicated halfway down the right margin. 'And one here.' She pointed to the bottom right corner. 'When you plan, think about the complete page, not just parts of it. There are so many words on a calendar page, but in the form of a list, so it doesn't have the neat edges that most pages have. And then there are the rubricated capitals as well, so you need to keep the decoration simple, uncluttered. Elegant. See?'

Nick nodded.

Once she had drawn the two circles, Gemma began with the capital and the border; she'd feel her way toward the rest. It was only leadpoint at this stage, but the first sketches were important. At the top of the page she drew a *J* inside the large space the scribe had left empty before *anuaris,* a word without its head. Obedient to her plummet, a thin vine began to grow from the large capital, trailing across the top of the page and down the margin to loop around the first empty circle, then continued its way to the bottom, where it circled the second one. Some heart-shaped leaves curled away in the corners.

'I'll need gesso for the gold leaf,' she said to Nick. 'Make it just like I showed you, then mix it up with some Armenian bole. But that batch is dark, so be careful not to use too much. Add and mix, little by little, just enough to make a skin colour.'

She noticed Will look up suddenly at her mention of gold leaf. 'I'll paint on the gesso, get the simple work done so it's ready for your pa.' She would have to be careful of this new man and his ambition. What favours would he earn for telling

Southflete about a woman who painted? She shook her head, went back to the page.

The first roundel would be Aquarius, pouring out the water of the old year from his urn into the simple waves in the bottom half of the circle, the river of life that kept on flowing. Blue. Turnsole blue would be enough. But her jaw was tight, resisting a decision about the second picture. Southflete had told them that the early pages were to be demonstrations of Fitzjohn wealth and status.

'The calendar pages must be beautiful scenes of life on the demesne, you understand. Of course, you will have painted these before, Dancaster. Chubby infants, well-fed peasants, colour, beauty, you know well what is needed; the bounty of the Fitzjohns must be shown.'

Beautiful. How, in a village farmer's life, would January be beautiful? Snow if the weather was kind, ice if it was not. And this past year, colder than ever. Frost that rarely lifted, and then only to snow or rain. London had clenched its teeth, frozen to the marrow, too cold to move. At least the cramped lanes and houses blocked some of the wind; what it was like in the country, she couldn't bear to think.

Had Lady Mathilda left her fire, chanced a look outside her door at the freezing, starving children? Did she step a foot on the hard, frozen ground? But beauty, the lady wanted beauty, and beautiful it would be. Stories. Romances among the prayers, nothing to disturb the Lady Mathilda.

Perhaps she and Sir Robert were kind enough to roast a pig or two for Yule and bring their people into their wide hall, a moment's ease from the village's suffering. So, feasting it would be, as was the custom, peasant and lord alike standing before a fire, ale in their hands and meat on their plates. It was, after all, easier to paint beauty.

A gust of icy wind from the doorway lifted the parchment, and before she could pull away the quill it had left a black line across the page.

'By all that's holy, what are you—' she shouted, then she saw the long, pointed leather shoes of the visitor. She looked up.

'Yes, by all that's holy, Gemma. Foul weather it is.' Southflete looked her in the face, as if daring her to finish her sentence.

'It is indeed,' she agreed.

'It's your husband I'm seeking. I thought to find him here, at work.'

'You're moments too late, I'm afraid. I was tidying away John's work as you walked in. Said he has to follow up his order for vine leaves. He knows a man who says he can bring some when next—'

'Moments? I'm surprised I didn't see him on the street.'

Gemma stood, pages in her hand. 'Ah, he walked down to Old Dean's Lane, to pass by the pepperer as he went ...' There was a danger in embroidering the truth, and even more a lie, she knew. 'I'm coming, Nicholas. Don't add too much bole to the gesso, remember. I'll check it in a moment,' she called toward the storeroom.

Nick looked through the doorway, bobbed his head at Southflete, and mumbled something.

The stationer glanced at Benedict then walked toward Will's desk. 'Good to see the work progresses, Asshe. You're settled in? Making your way? I expect beautiful work from you. None of that French style, though. I wonder, have you seen Dancaster today?'

Will was aware of Gemma frowning. 'As the mistress says, he stepped through the door just short moments past,' he answered. 'And I'm well settled in the work. The parchment is good quality and Nicholas there a fine assistant.'

At the positive mention of his name, Nick ventured into the room and stood near Will. Southflete nodded. 'I've just visited Manekyn. Tell John the next quires are finished and ready to collect.' He pulled the door shut behind him.

Gemma looked at Will and nodded, without smiling. 'I'll come and have a look now, Nick.'

Will bent again to his page. He knew by instinct when to dissemble, though he wasn't interested in rescuing Gemma. Maybe the stationer should know that she was fiddling with compasses and leadpoint on the calendar pages. But it was strange, John away from the shop so often. Just what was he helping to cover?

At the bench, Nick was blending a pale pink mixture of chalk and bole on his slab.

'I'm just heating the hide glue, and I'll have to soften the honey as well,' he said.

'Good, Nick, this colour is just right. I'll help you get the right consistency.' She would need a section on gesso in the 'The Art of Illumination'.

'Why did you remind me about the colour just then?'

'To be rid of that man and his questions. He was at Manekyn's shop, so why didn't he bring the finished quires himself?' She took the muller from him and slid it in circles over the mixture, testing for any grittiness. She was back in her pa's shop, feeling the dry chalk and bole powder gradually transform to a paste with water and gum. It was akin to flour taking up the thickness of egg, but she had always felt the magic of gesso, forming a kind of pillow for the gold leaf, lifting it from the page to shine, its pink colour giving the gold another, richer tone.

'Ma?' Nick said. 'Is Pa in trouble with Southflete? The way you wouldn't say where he is …'

Gemma grunted, brought back to the troubles of the shop. 'I don't know where your pa is, Nick. But even if I did, I wouldn't tell Southflete. We're doing this work, not him. He's a stationer, that's all, talking to customers, organising for parchmenters, scribes, binders, us. But it's our work decorating the book. Our work, however much he likes to parade.'

* * *

She continued tracing over her sketches with black ink; the slash across the page, thanks to Southflete, she would have to scrape away later. The first line had the stutters of her anger and her nerves, the second one no better. She was holding back, resisting what she knew she could do. Devil take that man Southflete!

Shouts outside in the street, the sound of a horse's hooves in the mud. That was Annie's voice cursing, and though Gemma couldn't make out the words, she could imagine the scene. The horse's legs looming large in the narrow street as Annie drags little Drew back to her side with one arm, making a fist in the air with the other. The rider taking no heed, mud splatters.

It didn't take much to earn Annie's curses, but it seemed that everyone in the city was ready for a brawl, resentful of the Iter, nervous of what the justices might do to them. She had seen the gatherings near St Paul's Cross, heard the fear and frustration in the voices of the crowd. It was strange to think that all that was happening out there, while inside the shop the talk was mostly of line and hue. Still, as John said, even a book of prayers has its politics.

Gemma could still hear Annie, probably now complaining to the hucksters in the Row about the preening thug and his arrogant ways, Drew's near escape from death, her timely rescue. Another line, a new breath out, the curved line taking her with it. Her hand settled into the familiar rhythm and she forgot the world.

When St Paul's rang its bells for Sext, Gemma looked up, surprised that the morning had passed already. Once she had finished the sketches for January, she had moved on to the other months, absorbed in ideas for the roundels of the seasons, especially the summer months of harvesting, haymaking and threshing. Drawing inside the tiny circles needed a fine hand,

and the concentration helped her to ignore the thought that
there had been little to harvest in past years, despite the wheat
and corn turning golden beneath her brush.

Manekyn's shop was crowded and dusty. This was Nick's job,
picking up pages, but Gemma had always enjoyed visiting
the scribe, his shop's smell not quite the same as their own,
but still full of suggestion. The shelves at the back held some
small finished books, most of them sold back to Manekyn by
those who'd commissioned or bought them, and waiting for
the next buyer. One wall displayed fading sheets of parchment
showing rows and rows of neat lines, all the same words, but
each in a different script. Manekyn was proud of the range
he could offer to customers, and the quality of his work was
widely known.

'Ah, Gemma,' the scribe said, 'you've come for the pages.'

'Yes. You've finished a few more quires, I hear.'

Manekyn nodded and stood up, stretching his back
carefully. How old must he be? She had first visited him with
her pa when she was no more than ten and he had seemed
old then, as if he'd been covered with dust. Gemma knew
he was chary of her, a woman meddling in paints, but he
also knew she could read and write well. She had even done
some work for him when he was busy. He showed grudging
respect, Gemma had once thought, but it was more than that,
especially after her pa died. Manekyn had helped with the
legal demands, transferring the shop to John, and had visited
often, pretending business, reminiscing. He missed her pa as
well.

'How's the new man, then?' the scribe asked as he leafed
through piles of parchment, hunting for the quires.

Gemma winced, wondering if they would be bent or
dirty, but there they were, wrapped neatly in a thin bundle.
Two quires at most. Why ask to have them picked up? 'I don't
have much to do with him,' she said.

Manekyn widened his eyes, a question. 'But he's working in the shop, isn't he?'

'Yes, he is. Crowded, it is. And he's such a big man.'

'Big hands, too. And a past that makes me worry. John's such a trusting soul. What's that story of a tragedy? Has he told you any more?'

Gemma's scalp tightened. 'No, nothing,' she said evenly.

'Did he really work with Gerard?'

'Seems so. I've seen his—'

'I wouldn't trust to his words, Gemma.'

'His master's piece. A Beatus page. It's very fine.'

'Is it?' Manekyn's voice was full of doubt.

Gemma stepped toward the door. 'John is very pleased with him.' She touched the door handle. 'And so am I. Thank you for the quires, Manekyn.'

'Of course, Gemma.'

It was only a few steps along the Row and across to the atelier, but Gemma stopped outside Rayner the pepperer's shop to ponder the scribe's words. She'd thought the fraternity's acceptance of Will would have been enough for Manekyn, but apparently not. And he was thick with Southflete.

Mathilda

Wain Wood Manor
May 12, 1322

Life is arranged for mourning, Mathilda thinks, but not for grief. There are no rituals for these moments in the night when everyone else sleeps and the deeper darkness opens up. She slides from beneath Maggie's arm, lights a candle and creeps into the tiny closet. The girls don't stir.

Grief: she has known it before, but not like this. She sat by Gavin's bedside watching his sweet face, the slight rise and fall of his chest, gathering it in; she knew this was all she would have of him. When his breath stopped, she wailed her despair, too exhausted and bereft to care when Robert hushed her. The pain is lodged still in her chest, a constant ache, a presence that she would miss if it left her.

But Robert's death is so different. It's two months since he died and she's surprised at this grief that is more a shadow, or a haunting, than loss. She gropes for the pain in her heart, hopes for tears and sobbing, but they're not there. Perhaps it was the running and fear, listening to every new noise, planning everyone's safety, and not just her own. So much to think about that there was no room for crying. But now she has so much time.

That day, Cornell walked only a few paces into the hall, his clothes ragged, his words by turns falling over each other, then refusing to come. She knew by his white face what he was trying to say; for years, every time Robert rode out to fight, she had expected this. 'I understand,' she said. 'Where is his body, Cornell?'

She had wanted to argue every time Robert was called to

arms, but there'd been nothing to say. It was the way their lives were set; no amount of protest would change that. She wanted to obey God, didn't she? She understood the threat to their position, didn't she? She wanted their lands protected, didn't she? Mathilda could argue with herself just as well as Robert would have, so she'd kept silent. He was away so often, on parks and estate business, if not to battle, that his absence seemed normal. What does she miss, exactly?

For a moment, after Cornell pointed to the door, mumbled something about the cart outside, and the shock of the news passed, she felt a shiver of — what was it? Not anticipation, there was too much loss for that, but a sense of something new at the thought of being set loose from a husband.

'You know already, I think, that a third part of the property comes to you. That's the law.' Oliver, her lawyer, shuffled his way through documents as he spoke. He had arrived only days after the news of Robert's death, and waited until the funeral was over to talk of business with Mathilda. 'But first there are debts to be paid: the arming of Sir Robert's men, losses on the estate, money owed. Then there is the application for probate. In time, it would be wise to remarry for financial reasons—' He would have continued had Mathilda not walked out.

Now, so much of whatever was left, that widow's inheritance, is gone. Surely the soldiers won't bother to come to Wain Wood. She picks up the book of hours, and settles it in her lap; just the touch of it, small and solid, is a solace. It's as if, whatever else happens, its neat pages will be with her.

It is objects, she realises, things that she can hold and feel, that have marked her way through these past weeks. She insisted she would do the inventory of Robert's goods herself, even though Fraden was more than capable. Seeing and listing everything her husband had owned suddenly seemed important. They began in the solar, then the kitchen and dining hall: clothes and boots, furniture, linen, silver

and plate, then moved to the stables to record the horses and
equipment. She felt a brief pang when she handled the cup
that Robert had used most often, and when she touched the
back of his chair at the table, but allowed herself to drift into
the brief comfort of naming and listing.

It was in the stables, when Fraden held up Robert's bridle
studded with silver, that she began to unravel. Two, maybe
three years earlier, Robert had ordered extravagant new tack
for his horse, and Mathilda had felt only disgust at the waste.
All that display, and it was too grand to take into battle, it
seemed. The leather straps gleamed and the silver decoration
flashed when Fraden lifted the bridle from its hook, but all
Mathilda could see was Robert's face the day he'd brought it
home and she had scoffed and turned away. Now she sees the
moment again. He had looked toward her, his face as open
and delighted as a child's, wanting her to enjoy with him this
thing he found so beautiful. She hadn't been ready to see it.

Her chest hurts; now it's too late. Why does love, if that's
what it is, come only in his absence?

Mathilda watches the girls, wondering how much they
understand. They don't seem to miss Robert. Joan cried at
the funeral, but Maggie seemed more curious than upset. She
nodded silently when they told her that the shape wrapped in
a white shroud was her pa, but she asked later when he would
be coming home. Mathilda understands; even now she thinks
the sound of a horse's hooves or a jingle of tack might be him.
Joan says very little, and it's hard to tell if it's grief or this
waiting, trapped inside; she peers at her embroidery, pulls out
stitches then puts it down to gaze blankly at some spot on the
floor. Perhaps she is thinking of her father.

As if she knows that Mathilda is watching her, Joan looks
up.

'Joanie, come and look at my book with me.' A few
days past, Mathilda noticed the pictures of Jesus as a child

and realised that the limners must have painted them for the children. They sit on the bed together and Mathilda turns the pages until she finds the picture that might make Joan smile.

The sun shines down from inside a cloud, its beams marked by long, thin lines of gold that stretch across the page to the opposite corner. Jesus, his curly hair surrounded by a halo, stands in the air, supported only by sunbeams, and below him are the friends who have fallen down, trying to do the same thing, some on their heads, as if they're doing handsprings, some on their hands and knees. One small child looks up, palms open, in awe of Jesus hovering above him in mid-air.

Joan laughs and points to the tumble of bodies. 'Look at that boy. His head is flat on top as if it's been squashed.' But then she becomes serious. 'I think that I'd be cross at a boy showing off like that, doing things that he knows nobody else can do.'

Mathilda smiles; it's hard to think of Jesus being five, or seven, and always behaving. Wouldn't that make him not really a child?

Joan examines the painting carefully. 'I like the way the sun's smiling. And all the flowers around the edge. It's very pretty. Did Will paint this? I wish he'd visit again. He was fun.'

Mathilda looks at it again. 'I don't know who did this one. There's no rose, so it's not Master Dancaster. Perhaps Will did it, especially for you. Or one of the other limners.'

'So will he visit again? I could ask him then. Could we write and invite him to come here? Or when we go back to the old house? He liked your tapestries and the dovecote so much he'd want to come again. He drew them both. And this house is so small and plain.'

Mathilda touches her daughter's head. 'I don't know whether we'll be going back there, Joanie. We need to wait and see.'

Joan turns the pages, pointing out little animals and odd-shaped people in the margins, reaching out now and then to touch her mother's knee, make her look. And Mathilda laughs or gasps, but it's the past she remembers, barely more than a season ago in the big manor house, when her skin felt as new and soft as Maggie's.

When Oliver arrives a few days later, Mathilda takes him to a corner of the hall, hoping no one will overhear them. The lawyer has the papers he's spirited out of Aspenhill, bundled together, and now safe from thieving.

'I've bribed my way into having probate passed quickly,' he says, 'though that could be overturned by the king, if he rules that Robert died a traitor's death.' Those two blunt words hang in the air for a moment, then Oliver rushes on with legal details, terms like *laesa maiestas*, *seditio* and *proditio*. As if they could soften it.

Mathilda is immediately angry. She starts sentences and stops, trying to find an accusation to throw at him; she opens documents and doesn't read them; she fights back tears. Finally she says, 'Robert's dead and gone, however many masses he might have ordered for the sake of his soul. I have girls to look after. Tell me in plain words what all this means for me.'

'It's too soon to say, Lady Mathilda. As you know, the families of some of the leaders have been imprisoned, their lands confiscated. But the court might be too occupied with the living to take notice of those who died.'

'You think Despenser's spite will run its course quickly?' she says.

'He and the king are determined to show the people how betrayal is repaid, that's true. But it seems it wasn't simply his opposition at Boroughbridge that condemned Lancaster. His trial listed felonies, burnings and depredations, as well as a long history of undermining parliament. He was considered a traitor even before he marched on Boroughbridge. They can't accuse Sir Robert of those crimes.' He pauses. 'Others, though, seemed only to be defending their land against Despenser, as Sir Robert was, but the ruling is that they and their families must be punished. Their status makes them an example.'

'So we wait to see the extent of the king's anger? And to see whether or not the soldiers want to ride this far to find us?'

Oliver nods and takes refuge in the documents Mathilda must sign.

The illumination is Christ enthroned. He sits, majestic, surrounded by gold, looking outward, his face serious and still, one hand raised in blessing. His legs are slightly apart, and his robe drapes from his knees in the kind of graceful folds that Mathilda recognises from the sketch William made of her. An angel at each corner blows a trumpet declaring Christ's glory.

Her eyes shift to the lower left of the painting, to her portrait in profile, kneeling in prayer and adoration, her hands raised toward Christ. Behind her, Joan kneels, a smaller version of her mother. It's not intended to be a likeness of Mathilda, to look like her in particular. It's to be the figure of the devoted owner of the book, Lady Mathilda, with her elder daughter; the shield design on her cote-hardie makes that clear.

But when Robert ordered the book, she wasn't a widow. That changes the way she looks at the picture, but how, she can't understand. Perhaps she would have felt like this even were Robert alive and looking at the book with her; perhaps the idea that a widow's eyes are different from those of a wife is as fanciful as the drawing of a rabbit on horseback, jousting. A woman straying outside her station.

Whenever Robert was at court, or on campaign, she picked up the running of the estate as easily as she put it down when he returned, a cape she pulled on and later let slip from her shoulders. That's what she thought, but now that

she knows he won't come back she is beginning to discover
room for other feelings. She remembers how furious Robert
was when he returned home during the freeze, absent from
Yule to Harvest, to find a third of the sheep flock had died of
murrain, and accused Fraden of mishandling their care. He
hadn't seen the weather, or the toil to save them; he wasn't
there when Fraden warmed the lambs, fed them by hand,
then all but wept in frustration when they died. All Robert
could see were numbers and failure. At the time she felt the
unfairness but said nothing; now the memory makes her jaw
clench.

She looks again at the illumination, the gradual shading of
colour, the fine beams of gold around Christ's head. He looks
straight ahead, but he isn't looking at her. The glazed look of
a man distracted by many concerns. Of course, she doesn't
expect God to look at her. It's Mary who gazes at people with
loving eyes. But this is different, because Mathilda is painted
there; she can see herself gazing up, giving her full attention
to a man who doesn't see her, isn't interested.

She closes the book, stands, then kneels, wants to confess
that ingratitude. Why should Christ look on her, a sinner?
Christ enthroned. She doesn't expect the king to look on her,
so why should Christ? Perhaps Father Jacobi is right about
these decorations — not only frivolous, but dangerous. But
she knows it isn't really Christ she has been thinking about.

In the darkness of night she lies, sightless and sleepless in the
black. She gets out of bed and walks to a window, cold flaring
through her legs as her feet touch the floor.

She wants the book to help her pray, and nothing more.
All her plans of letting it show the prospects of the family
have slipped away, but it refuses to let her be, reminds her
of all that is lost. Robert, their land, her safety, her tapestry.
It's a strange thing, this gradual movement from being two
people brought together as a means of advancing family

connections to becoming something more, to whatever it is that grows over fifteen years. She'd like to give it a name, but it's not worth wondering about; it simply was. That's what her mother would have said. And now it is no more.

She wants all those thoughts to disappear; she wants Robert to leave her free to deal with all that his treason has given her — fear, loss, uncertainty — but he lingers, even here in the small manor house that he never liked. As if he has more to say to her.

10

London
May 1321

Borders

Think of the border decoration of your page as a wall. It keeps out and it keeps in; it welcomes or defends. Let your border be a way of defining the page, but do not make it so strong a fortress that images cannot wander beyond it. It may be the loop of a vine, a drooping flower, a monkey with bagpipes. Let them roam, sometimes, to give your page commerce with the world outside. The lady who holds a prayer book may not understand this, but she will know, without thinking of it, that her prayers are offered not only inside her chapel, but in the world of all creatures.

The Art of Illumination

Will could tell that Benedict was unsure and he nudged him forward, through the workshop door. 'Come on, Ben, we both need to stretch our shoulders. Painting's hard on the eyes, hard on the back, because it's long and slow. Men build a house faster than we decorate a book, but that's because our work won't get knocked down or burned.' He paused as he shut the door and added, 'Well, it might get burned a bit, on the edges sometimes, but that would only make it more valuable, eh?'

'What are you talking about? And it's Benedict. Benedict.'

'I know who you are, Ben, course I do. Why else would I be taking you out?' Will slapped him on the back, and that was nearly the end of the night before it had begun. 'At least it's not so cold tonight.'

'Gemma made you do this, didn't she?'

'Made me do what?'

'She was always telling me to go out. Go to the tavern, the market, play football. She's made you do it.'

'Gemma? She barely even looks at me. She probably thinks I'm a fool, or a wastrel, or a thief. I don't know what she thinks, save she wouldn't be trusting me with you.' Will put an arm on Benedict's shoulder, leaned toward him. 'Look, Ben, we sit next to each other all day and we hardly speak. What's wrong with going out for an ale? I asked Tom too. Thought we'd show him around, give him the city, as he's new. And you must know the city better than me. Come on, he's waiting for us.'

'Tom? But he's a foreign. There's already anger in the Row about him setting up his stall opposite the shops. Peter Binder says he shouldn't be there, taking up space. He says it makes it hard for his customers to get past.'

Benedict was walking slowly, resisting the outing, so Will linked arms with him to encourage him along.

'What's a man to do? He's only been in London a few months, not much longer than me, and doesn't have the money to buy his freedom of the city. I had some coin when I arrived, but even then I had to work for weeks to save enough. It's hard on someone like him coming here without money to spare.'

'Even so ...'

Will could feel the heat running down to his fingers. 'Have you seen what life's been like in the country these past years? Yes, it's been tough here, but those on the land have been flooded and frozen and flooded again. What do you think they should do? Starve?'

Benedict's arm in his was pulling away; Will took a breath to calm himself. 'But tonight we forget hard work. Come on, he's waiting for us down by Old Change. Where'll we go?'

The apprentice shrugged, so Will went on, 'Likely there's a game of dice at Sabine's house. That might be the place to start.'

'Sabine? Who's that?'

Will regretted this excursion already, but he couldn't bear spending every day next to Benedict's stony face and hunched shoulders. A pot or two might loosen him up. A short spell with a strumpet was probably the best way to get the boy's blood moving. Perhaps later tonight, after a few pots, they could take him to Cock's Lane. He looked at the face next to him, at the clench of eyebrows, the tight mouth. No, it would take more than Sabine's ale to persuade Benedict to unbutton for a rough woman in a dark lane. The stews, perhaps, on another night; they'd have a better chance in a brothel house, however slovenly.

'Tom!' he called.

The man was hunched over, stamping his feet, shivering. Will gave him a bear hug, as much to warm him as to greet him. 'Ah Tom, the weather's warming. Can you feel it?'

But Tom was more cloth and bones than body and his face was grey, almost the colour of parchment.

'You know Ben? He's come to show us the dark and seedy corners of the city.'

'I hope your seedy corners are warm, Ben.' Tom smiled. He wrapped his cloak tighter, but it was so worn, it could do little to protect him.

Benedict murmured something about knowing nothing of corners, but he shook Tom's hand.

'Sabine has a stove just for you. And we can buy pies on the way,' Will said, and tugged again at Benedict's arm.

Sabine's front room was hot and crowded, the air a yellowy haze, as if the smells of ale, sweat and the street's foul mud, now drying on the clothes and boots of the drinkers, had taken on colour. When the three men walked in, Sabine was arguing with a customer, politics no doubt, Will thought. Catching sight of him, she turned, stepped closer and pushed him in the chest.

'Where you been these weeks, Asshe? I thought you'd had

enough of us lowlifes once you got work on that fancy book. And here I was the one as told you where you'd find work. Did I not, Asshe?'

'Leave a man be, Sabine,' Will said. ''Twas my talent and charm got me labour, nothing more. And I've come back, haven't I, though only our Lord knows why. Not for the looks of the ale-mistress or her customers, that's sure. But instead of the thanks and gentle touch a woman should give a man, you offer me violence.'

'Devil take gentle touch, William Asshe. My fist's the only gentle touch you'll get from me.'

Will laughed. 'And here, my lady, are your new customers: Tom Herfelde, new to London, and Ben Broune, apprentice with Dancaster.'

'You men should choose your friends better,' Sabine said to them, and smiled. 'Ale all round?' As she worked, she chatted with Tom, asking him how villages were faring in the freezing weather, then moved on to her favourite subject. 'You heard the news then, Will? Barons from the Marches have attacked Despenser's castles in Wales. Newport, Cardiff … even Gower has been captured. Near to destroyed, some say.'

'You know me, Sabine. I stay clear of all that talk.'

'Then you're more of a fool than you look. Aren't you in the pay of a lord from the Marches?'

'Not quite,' Benedict said. 'He has lands in Hertfordshire, from his wife, but expects to inherit from his nephew in the Marches. He'd be there now, I suppose, fighting.'

Will looked at him in surprise; so he had been listening while his head was buried in the model book.

'And Lancaster?' Tom asked. 'Has he finally ventured south to join the fighting? He has land in Wales as well. Surely he's protecting it?'

'Well, as I hear it,' Sabine said, 'he sent troops, but he stayed in the north. He's a funny one, he is. Hot and cold. Can't be trusted, if you ask me.'

'But the king's worried, must be,' Benedict said. 'Word around Guildhall is that Hamo de Chigwell is to be mayor again. The king knows he needs the people onside.'

'That right, Ben? So he'll drag us common folk into his arguments.' Sabine sighed. 'Civil war is coming, sure enough. The Marcher barons will make their move.'

Will laughed. 'I should have put money on you saying that. Someone's always making their move, eh Sabine?'

In one corner, three men crowded around the only table in the room.

'Ah, dice. Let's see if there's the chance of a game,' Will said.

'Not me.' Benedict took a swig.

'No, none of that, Ben. We came out for a game. You have to play.'

'I'll none of gambling, Will.' As Will laughed and grabbed at his arm, the apprentice batted his hand away. 'I said, I'll none of gambling, Asshe. Leave me.'

Will was aware, in a vague way, that his easy manner combined with his size and his love of song won most people over. He had become used to having his own way, so he wasn't about to be denied by this stuck-up lad, especially now that he had struck him.

'Wouldn't hit a fellow, would you? That's churlish, Ben. Now come and play.'

'Don't think you can push me further, Asshe. I told you I'd not—'

'Will, enough.' Tom put his hand on Will's arm. 'Listen. The man doesn't want it. Let him be.'

Denied now by two men, and surprised by Tom's quiet authority, Will was embarrassed. He turned and pushed a path through the crowd, away, away. His mouth wouldn't sit properly in his face, his eyes had nothing to look at. No one noticed him, except the men he shoved too hard in his haste to get past them, but he felt himself the object of scrutiny.

Seeing a familiar face, he went to stand behind the man shaking the cubes of bone between his palms. 'Winning, Adam?'

The man, olive-skinned and dark-eyed, looked up at him. 'Nah. You better bring me luck, Asshe.'

Will patted him on the shoulder and said nothing. The dice tumbled onto the table, and heads crowded in to see them settle.

'Nah. Eight it is,' another man said. 'You lose again, Hoddeson.'

'I'm out then,' Adam said, pushing his few coins across the table. 'I never did trust your dice, Hugh.'

It could have been a joke, but the tone was sharp, and Hugh stood up, knocking over his stool. 'You calling me a cheat, Adam Hoddeson? Are you?'

'No, no, he means naught.' The third player at the table stood too, his voice soothing. ''Tis the pain of his empty purse talking, that's all. That's right, Adam, isn't it? Let's play. If Adam's out, let Asshe here see if he can take back your coins then, Hugh.'

The rumblings of men denied their fight subsided into murmurs about bets and rules and Adam pushed away from the table as Will squeezed onto the free stool.

He wasn't interested in gambling, but he loved the dice, the small, neat cubes and the simple markings. These ones were bone, the six sides marked with dots surrounded by a circle. He ran his fingers over the indented marks, shook the dice to feel the heft of them in his hand. Once in Cambridge he had played with dice of jet, entranced by their dense blackness, their small heaviness. What was it that made ivory, bone and jet feel so different? Something more than their weight. His father had so often spoken about different types of wood. 'Some are heavy, some light, some solid, some smell sweet, but whatever it is, you know a good wood; it feels right in your hand, as if the life of it is still there.'

The memory, the surprising comfort of three small cubes rattling between his palms, drew away the tension in Will's chest and he let the dice tumble onto the table.

In silence, Tom and Benedict watched Will push through the bodies, and the apprentice declared he was off home.

'Oh, stay a while, Ben. Would you keep me company? It's not often I get out.' Tom put his hand on Benedict's arm, much as he had touched Will. 'I don't know much of London. Most nights my Idla and me are working, though of late she's taken to bed even before it's dark. But you, you've lived here all your life, Will says. Londoner born and bred.'

'Born on Candlewick Street, my pa's grocery business. Not far from the wharves.' Benedict's voice was tight, reluctant.

'Mmm, I think I know it. Runs down to Bridge Street. That'd be a place to grow up, watching ships, playing on the bridge, sneaking over to Southwark, hey?' Tom smiled.

'Yeah, though the beadles watch it more closely now. It's not fun like it used to be. And we'd go out on the Moorfields when we could.'

'Mmm, Idla and I walk out there when she's well enough. And if we have time. It's better out there, even when it's freezing, than crowded inside the walls.'

'Then why'd you come if you don't like it? Should've stayed away.'

'Oh, I didn't mean it like that, Ben. I'm just not used to it. I used to dream about living in a big city, but once I had to leave our village, all I wanted was to go back. Seems we always look for what we don't have.'

Benedict frowned, his foot tapping. 'Then why leave?'

'Flooded out. River broke its banks and covered all we had. Our house was all but washed away. Ever seen a place after a flood? Mud and stink ... even more than a London street.' Tom laughed. 'But you, growing up in a business, what made you want to work with books?'

'To spite my pa.' Benedict's voice suggested he would say no more, but Tom laughed.

'Yeah? Seems like it worked. Good on you.'

'Oh, measuring this, measuring that, I hated it. Pa tried to teach me. Showed me how to trade and haggle, argue to get a good price, mix the mouldy food with the good, use false weights, buy food cheap from out-of-town farmers and sell for more. He said everyone did it, that's what business was. I wasn't interested anyway.'

A cheer went up from the dice table and Will shouted in frustration.

Tom waited. After a time, he said, 'But why an illuminator? That's a long way from a grocer's shop.'

'I wanted to make things, not just measure them out. Pa stocked some of the pigments the limners use. I tried mixing some of the powders with water. The colours, that's what it was.' Benedict's sentences were short, his voice a monotone, as if that would reveal less. 'I wanted to paint those colours.' He looked at Tom as if he had forced the words from him.

At the dice table, Will watched the cubes fall from his palms, willing the numbers in his mind to land on the wood. He cursed. 'Again! I don't know what you do, Hugh.'

'My night, 'tis all,' Hugh said as he gathered the coins into his purse. His smile was lopsided, the right side of his mouth caught, as if stitched, by a scar on his cheek. 'A man has to win some time.'

Will was beginning to agree with Adam that Hugh was crooked. He stood, ready to accuse him, but from across the room he caught the sound of sharp words and turned to look.

'Thought I'd seen that ugly face before. You sell on a stall at the end of the Row.'

'We work hard; it's honest labour.'

Taller than most there, Will could see above the thicket of heads that it was Tom speaking, his face tight with stress.

'Yeah, you and your lazy woman. You're in the way there, you know that. You clog up the street, take our business.' Adam had taken his frustration at the dice game somewhere else.

'City says we can sell there. We've nowhere else.' Tom looked away, nodded to Benedict to signal they should leave.

Adam pulled at his arm. 'Freeman are you then?'

'Would be if I could, but I don't have the money yet to buy citizenship.' Tom was clearly nervous now. 'I've only been here a few months.'

'Where you from then?'

'Near Evesham, just a small village.'

'Yeah, a foreign you are, thought so. Born in the country, not one of us. We've too many of your sort round here already. This is our city. You should go back, not come and take our jobs. You foreigns come like dogs to eat our food.' Will watched the pulsing lines on Adam's forehead.

'I can't. We were flooded out. Lost everything. So many children died, some drowned. My sister died and my wife's still ailing.'

Another voice, not as loud. It was Hotch, the tanner's assistant. 'Don't try that as an excuse for coming here. Famine's all but over. So it's been hard, we all know that. D'you think it hasn't been hard here as well? Same freeze, same rain, same prices going up. I know the sheep and cows have been dying, don't I? Where do you think we get skins to tan when stocks are down? Your kind makes it tougher for all of us, coming here.'

'Nothing to go back to, like I said. Every building washed away.'

'Bull's piss, that is,' Adam shouted. 'There's more places than our city. Go scab off another town.'

'We moved to Colchester, tried to get work, but there was nothing. We thought there'd be more here—'

Hotch cut him off. 'All Adam here's saying is there's not

enough to go round as it is. And you foreigns only make it worse.'

'No, that's not all of it, Hotch.' Adam turned on his friend. 'There's some as belong and some as don't. We was born here, raised here and we work hard. God's nails! Why don't those animals, Scrope and Stanton, try getting rid of the foreigns instead of chasing us honest men?' As he spoke the last words he leaned closer, a short, fat finger pointed in Tom's face.

At the mention of the inquisition, anger began to ripple across the room, man by man, like wind in canvas.

'That's right,' Hotch shouted. 'If they won't do it, we will.'

'Come on, Hotch, let us be,' Benedict said.

Will watched the struggle on Benedict's face; only an hour ago he'd said he didn't want newcomers in London, and any other time he would have agreed with Adam and Hotch, but he'd been drinking and chatting with Tom. Strange how a pot of ale could change a man's mind.

'You stay out of it, laddie. Whadda you know?' another man shouted.

Tom held up his hands, palms out and stepped back. 'All I'm saying is that I've a right to be here.'

The few men nearby scuffled forward, poking and prodding at him, men bumping shoulders, hustling one another, building up friction, impelled by no one person. It had been the same in the Cambridge alehouse.

Above the growing murmur, another voice.

'Adam, Hotch, get out!' It was Sabine. 'You know I won't have brawling here.'

'He's a foreign. Shouldn't be here.' Adam was too angry now to be shut down. 'Should be careful who you let in here, Sabine, to drink with us.'

'If I let a man inside my door, whoever he is, he can stay until I tell him to go. You come to my place, you act civil. Now get out.'

Pushing his way through the tight pack of bodies, Will pushed too hard.

A hard hand grabbed at his arm. 'Don't shove me, you!'

Will knocked it off, then staggered under a punch to his head, his ears ringing.

'Will, 's time you went too, by looks,' Sabine shouted. 'You and your friends.'

'Here. Come on.' It was Benedict, helping him stand.

Will forced down the urge to fight, unclenched his fist — those big hands, weapons — and thought about escape. Another punch, and another, this one aimed at his belly, but it landed in his ribs as Benedict and Tom pulled him to the door. Someone grabbed at Will's leg and he kicked out, heard a crunch and a groan as they made it onto the street. Will saw a flash of white, a face with open eyes and mouth, surprised. The snow, the ice, the horse.

'Quick, this way,' Benedict called. 'Down here!'

Shouts, threats, growls behind them, close, as heavy as clubs. A hand reached at Will's tunic, clutched and pulled. He twisted, hit out, heard Adam curse, spit. Will hesitated, wanted to turn and fight, punch instead of fleeing. But it was Tom, he was the one they'd set on, and he was too weak to fight. Best to escape them.

They ran, Benedict leading, down lanes, through narrow alleyways, behind selds, over stable roofs, through back gardens, across churchyards. The curses and footsteps faded, but Will ran on, all thought vanishing, fear taking over, panic gathering in his throat, aching in his chest; in the darkness he could be anywhere, nowhere, running on a Cambridge night, feeling the horse at his heels. When Benedict slowed, he dragged in breath, his thighs burning, his head light.

'Down here,' Benedict said between gasps. 'I know an empty house.'

The alleyway was narrow, dark with more than lack of light. 'They've gone,' Will said. Then rasping, a gurgling breath. Was it Tom, sick from running? No, so close. Something rubbed at his ankle — a cat, or some kind of rubbish, he thought, and he bent to brush it away. It caught at his hand. Hard stone. Cold stabbed all the way up his arm. He looked down, kicked at the big round eyes, the iron grip. Kept walking. But the legs scarpered up the wall above his head, step by step keeping pace with him. He pushed at Tom, tried to get past him, but there was nowhere to go.

'What's the matter? You said they've gone,' Tom panted. 'Will! Stop pushing me. Lane's too narrow.'

'Where's the house, Ben?' Will said. 'You said it was here. By Christ's nails, where is it?'

Benedict didn't answer, peering into doorways, pushing at rough shutters, waiting for one to give way.

'Here, let me.' Will squeezed past Tom. The wooden shutter was so flimsy that it wasn't hard to wrench it away from the window.

'Knew those huge hands had to be good for something,' Benedict muttered to Tom as they climbed inside after Will. Then, 'Leave it, they won't know we're here,' as Will tried to prop the shutter across the frame again.

It wasn't the ugly brutes in the tavern that Will was afraid of, but eventually he gave up and squatted in silence with the others, thinking about escape; for all the walking, Cambridge was only an arm's length away.

For a learned man, he said to Simon later, he was a fool. To think he could speak those ideas aloud outside the university without a bollocking. Simon had seemed unaware of the mob's mind, as if simple reason would be protection enough.

'By Jesus' bones you lads have no idea.' The other man's voice had been low, a growl. 'Come here with your books and fancy ideas, think you can turn Cambridge over like it's a slab of meat.'

Will had seen the pale young student before, but never spoken to him, and though it was no concern of his whether the older men gave him a beating, he was curious.

'I know times are hard,' the student said. 'Worse than hard, as you say. That's why things need to change. We should be able to live without being ruled by the few men who happen to be born into the right families. They won't be suffering from the famine like the rest of us, that's certain. They fill their barns then charge us more for grain. We starve while nobles fill their bellies. We deserve better.'

'Course we want to be treated better, but you'd shake God's order, you would. That's what you'd do.' The red-faced man was nearly shouting now.

'Didn't God create us all equal? All sons of Adam, we are. So why should there be some that get all the money and power, and the rest of us trodden down while they walk over us? The king wants money and he takes it from those who don't have any. Because he can. Because the barons and earls and lords think we're slaves, dogs that don't deserve to live, except to serve them.'

Word against the king was too much. 'It's how we was made to be, like it or not. God's order, it is.' The red-faced man stood and pointed, words spraying. 'You speak blasphemy.'

It seemed strange at first, to hear the working men defending the rule they lived under, defending the nobles especially, but Will understood what they meant. Everyone grumbled and cursed the nobility, but few of them ever imagined they would, or should, change the structure of their world, set in place by God.

The student tried again, but he only made matters worse. The red-faced man leaned closer. 'And you think what you read in books will make it all better?' His spit sprayed in the lamplight. 'Your words are turds, laddie. You've no business shitting them round here.'

Sensing the boiling point of the argument, Will pushed forward and slapped the student on the back. 'Ah, there you are. I've been looking for you,' he said. As he pushed the student away from the gathered men, Will turned back and spoke to them. 'He doesn't mean what he says; he doesn't … you know … know what he's saying at all,' and pointed to his head. 'Come on then, let's go. Stop disturbing the quiet drink of these good men.'

Not waiting to find out if his words had calmed the angry men, Will pushed the student to the door, up the stairs and out into the street.

'This way. Quick.' Will pulled at him and ran, all the way to St John's churchyard, falling to the ground, gasping, under a tree. The mob hadn't followed; the narrow stairs and the pull of ale must have kept them inside.

Will didn't understand why he had bothered with the man; he was a fool, blind beyond his own ideas. 'What were you thinking? What's the point of learning if it doesn't give you sense as well? Couldn't you see those men? So tired and hungry their fists itch at any fool idea.'

By then, the student's breath was even. 'I can look after myself. It was you who upset them, pulling me away like that. They would only have thought of chasing us because you got scared.'

'Is that right? You still can't see how close you were to having your head staved in? Fool!'

Still they didn't move, but leaned back against the trunk of the tree. Will was intrigued; there was sense in the idea that men shouldn't starve while the nobility hoarded grain, but weren't they just words in the air? How could they be anything more, he wondered, though he wouldn't ask. There was a moon in the cloudy sky, and Will could see the gleam of the man's eyes. It wasn't long before he began again, quoting someone called Justinian and more familiar names, too: Gregory the Great and Gratian.

'They tell us we're by nature equal. They all say that. But then, they say, Adam and Eve sinned, so God established orders of men, from the king down to the commoner. In a sinful world, the king rules because of his wisdom and reasoning. And because of his commitment to justice. Ha! Justice. What justice have you seen since Edward took the throne? And the great earls and barons, no better.'

'But if God places the king as leader ...'

'Why would God approve of a man who taxes the people and takes their money for himself, who won't even abide by the laws he's agreed to? What does natural equality mean if it isn't that all men should have justice and a right to the results of their labour?'

At the mention of labour, the young man's words narrowed down to his own family. His mother and sister had died more than two years ago, he said, their land flooded, crops lost. Unable to pay his rent, his father had been forced into Worcester to find labouring work.

'Tell me the men who own the land can't do anything for their tenants. Tell me God intends us to live this way, some just walking bones and others rich as goose fat.' He spat into the night.

Will watched the soft ball of spittle glimmer on the grass and wondered who this man was, with such a way of speaking. What a world he imagined. Was this what Edgar meant when he spoke of the limner painting all that God created, including all that was unseen?

Will, Benedict and Tom sat in the darkness of the deserted house, listening to their own puffing and the scratch of rats running around them, sniffing the air for whatever they might find. After a time they began to whisper in snatches, pausing at the sound of footsteps or voices in the lane.

Eventually Will said, 'Nah, they'll be drinking in some other alehouse, boasting of how they made us quake and run.'

'Yeah,' Tom agreed, but no one moved.

'I thought you were gone, Tom, talking about how you have a right to be here.'

'What else could I do?'

'There's naught to say to men sodden with ale and anger.'

'But why? Why so angry of a sudden?' Tom asked.

'Didn't you hear? The Iter, the famine. And then the dice game set them off. Adam lost all his coin. And me. Hugh was cheating, though I don't know how.' Will shifted, moved a leg that was almost numb.

'His dice,' Benedict said. 'Never trust a man who brings his own dice.'

'Thought you'd have nothing to do with gambling?'

'And I thought after all that happened you'd understand why,' Benedict said.

It was suddenly so obvious to Will that he started to laugh. 'Well, we got our night out, lads. You got some excitement, Ben, and Tom, you met some of the locals.'

'And you lost your money,' Tom said. 'Where are we anyway, Ben?'

'Oh, somewhere in Aldgate. Not far from the Tower.'

It was cold and black, but the three men didn't get up for some time.

II

London
May 1321

Gold Leaf

The gold is melted, beaten and rolled, beaten and rolled again and again until it is fine enough to float on air. How brutal, the search for this fragile radiance.

Cut only as much as is needed, lift it gently, press it lightly. So thin is the gold that it moulds itself to any roughness in the parchment, and any uneven surface in the applied leaf will scatter light in every direction, making it appear pale. To give a stronger, darker sheen, burnish the leaf with a dog's tooth, rubbing again and again until the gold appears like a mirror.

The Art of Illumination

Will had never really stopped walking, even after he'd stepped through Bishopsgate the previous year. Nowadays, he needed to stretch his legs before he settled to work, walk off the night and its dreams of snow. And so, whether it was raining or sleeting or clear and frosty, he walked. It wasn't far from his room on Bread Street to Paternoster Row, so he usually headed in the opposite direction, down Candlewick Street toward the Tower, munching a pie or a bun, veering to his left toward Aldgate, then tracing along the city wall, making a circuit toward the Row.

Usually he woke well before dawn, but this morning he was later than usual, slow to leave his bed. He, Benedict and Tom had walked home slowly, stiff from the cold, Benedict guiding them through back lanes to avoid the beadles. Will had no idea where they were, though now and then he wondered if this doorway, or that corner of a courtyard, was a place he had slept when he'd first arrived in London.

The city was already awake and busy, these days dragging itself from bed in a bad mood that became worse as the hours rang through the day. He stayed away from the Tower, where the justices continued their tedious and vicious examination of the accounts and actions of every guild in London. Apart from the poor and homeless, who had their own endless troubles, every face Will passed seemed to have the marks of the inquisition on it. In lanes, houses, taverns, shops and gutters, Despenser's name was whispered: he was the cause of all this suffering, God curse his bones.

None of this affected Will, and for once he was grateful that the book trade was still a fledgling, too small yet to be organised into a guild. As he walked he studied the long lines of shadow thrown by the rising sun, the soft yellow colour of the air on a clear day, the diffuse greyness when it was cloudy. How might he render that on parchment? In Cornhill Market he would stop to observe the line of a man's back as he bent and straightened, setting out cabbages on his stall, or the way the light shone on the roundness of a pig's back as it nosed through rubbish, or the lopsided curve of a woman carrying chickens, their feet bundled into her hands, and the flap of their feathers; they might, who knows, show him how to draw an angel's wings.

But this morning he shortened his usual route and cut from the wall down St Martin's Lane by St Michael's. As he turned into the Row he looked up. The gargoyles of St Paul's were still in shadow, the rising sun almost reaching them, and all still in place. Of course. What else did he expect?

He pushed inside the shop. Usually, by this time, he was at his desk, more awake than anyone else, inclined to speak too loudly or sing, when all they wanted was to be left in peace. This morning, he said nothing. John was out again, it seemed, so he simply nodded to Gemma and Benedict, though he cuffed Nick around the ears as always, pulled him into a headlock, wrestled him down to his knees.

The lad struggled, laughed and grunted. Looking up from the floor, he gasped, 'You just wait, Will. One day.'

'You're late this morning, Will,' Gemma said, irritated by the disturbance, by the man bundling in so casually, by the illumination she was painting.

'I'm always first here, so—' Will began, immediately angry.

'Rough night?' she goaded.

'No more than usual. Ben and I went for an ale with Tom.' He looked at Benedict, who kept his head down; he was still an apprentice, after all, and in John's care. 'This city doesn't always make a man welcome.' He glared at Gemma and picked up his pages from the storeroom. 'I'd best work, now that I'm late, as you say.'

Gemma was too astonished to notice his anger. 'You went out with Benedict? Where?'

'A drink, a dice game.' Will paused, sullen mood turned to play. 'And a brawl.' He waited for Gemma's exclamation of alarm, but she was almost smiling. 'Ben saved us, didn't you, Ben?'

'Really?'

'Six years here and you don't know he loves a good scrap?'

Benedict sighed. 'Will, don't.'

'He's so humble, Gemma. Knocked out … what, four, was it, Ben? Tom and I couldn't believe it, weedy little fella like Ben being such a brawler.' He slapped Benedict on the back and smiled broadly at Gemma.

He was fooling, she knew, laughing at her, but he had done what she'd long wished for, and taken Benedict out, gambling, drinking. Maybe the stews would be next.

The room settled into silence, and Gemma looked back at her page. The good news about Benedict couldn't change what she had to do. The instruction was simple, one scrawled word, *Annunciation*. No need to say more, it was such a familiar story. The angel Gabriel comes to Mary, a young virgin, and tells her she is with child and will give birth to Jesus. And, as the story is told, Mary replies, quietly accepts the message: 'Be it done to me according to your word.' Immediate, humble acceptance; right or wrong, Gemma couldn't believe it. She had seen the image many times on church walls, in decorated books, on banners in church processions, and she had the model book for the details she was supposed to use. Encounter, attention, the sharing of astounding and intimate news. You, a virgin, will bear the Son of God.

Gemma lightly ran her plummet along the lines of the angel's wings in the model book. When she had first begun helping in her father's workshop, he had sometimes let her watch as he painted, but only if she stayed very still. She had seen him form Gabriel's wings, painting in curve after curve of the downy feathers and then the long pinions.

'But Pa, the angel comes from heaven. He should have more gold on him. Gold in his wings and his robes and his face because he's so holy.'

'No, Gem.' He was shaking his head. 'Gabriel can't be more splendid than Mary because she will bear the Son of God. He is only the messenger. See what he says, here,' and he had pointed to some words painted on a long, curling scroll that seemed to float upwards from the angel's hand: *Ave Maria, gratia plena, Dominus tecum, Ecce ancilla Domini.* 'You know some of those words already. It means, "Hail Mary, full of grace, the Lord is with you. Behold the handmaid of the Lord." I paint Gabriel with only touches of gold to his wings, and I show how special Mary is, perhaps decorated with gold leaf, or wearing a beautiful lapis robe, or with gold rays from heaven shining on her.'

Gemma had stored away her pa's teaching in her mind, because she knew there were many rules about painting illuminations; they came from tradition and theology, he had said, but still, she knew an angel would shine like the sun. Now, painting the same illumination herself, she didn't care as much about the angel; she had other questions. They danced around her head while she worked. She knew what it was like to find out there was a baby coming and to worry about how you'd get by, even with a husband. How many girls had she seen down by the river or in the lanes of Aldgate with bellies bigger than their starved bodies, and no man to be seen? Young Clare, Douse's girl, had died along with the baby only last Yule. Could Mary really have been so ready and willing to accept the angel's words? She knew her pa would have talked of faith and God's grace, and perhaps one of those girls might have slept more easily if an angel had visited, its wings beating loud above her. But she'd still be cold and hungry. And alone.

Plummet in hand, Gemma paused as she drew the curve of Mary's shoulder. A simple girl, that could be our Alice washing the dishes of the Bishop of Llandaff, scrubbing his floors, or pounding his sheets at the river. At the quiet part of the river, that's where Gabriel looks for her, by a tree. She looks around at the sudden breeze and the sound of great wings beating the air. Alice, the angel says. She kneels, our girl — well, who wouldn't? Shields her eyes from the light of heaven, all the time drying her chapped hands on her skirts. An angel is bound to make a soul humble, whether or no she was that way to begin with.

Gemma kept drawing the arch protecting Mary, adding long, sinuous branches, transforming it into a tree that leaned toward the centre, its complement on the opposite side. Tufts of grass, a single rock and the washing, abandoned, collapsed in a heap nearby. Just above Mary's head, the simple outlines of London buildings, the spire of St Paul's.

Gemma thought again of Alice and an angel: you, a virgin, will bear a child. The young girl stands, astonished, aghast, trying to find words for her tangle of emotions. It must be a joke, some troubadour's story. But this is an angel of the Lord. No, a baby can't happen just like this, with no man. Too sudden, these words from heaven as she washes clothes; she wasn't even praying, but thinking about the bishop's long toenails making holes in the sheets. Too much to ask of a simple girl, powerless in the world of men. So much condemnation: the neighbours, the sheriff. The bishop will throw her out. The words are real, but whenever she looks up, the angel seems to pulse with light. Is it anger, glory, comfort, sympathy? She can't tell, but it forces her to bend her head and mumble the words she must say: Be it according to your will.

Gemma dropped the plummet, couldn't sit still, stood up. John was at his desk, head down, close to the page. She hadn't heard him come in. 'Nick. Nick.' The boy never listened. She walked into the storeroom. 'Go and see if old Fred has those vine leaves yet. You know the shop? Down—'

'Not to worry. I'll go,' John cut in. 'You know Fred and his choler, Gem. He's as like to slap the boy as give him the order.'

'It's his job, John. He has to learn.'

'He will in time, love. He'll be right. I need to go out anyway.'

Gemma glanced around. Benedict and Will were hard at work; Nick was by the storeroom door, watching his parents. She walked close to John and whispered in his ear.

'By all that's holy, John, stop pretending. We need to talk about this.'

'Yes, love. I'll remember,' John said as he opened the door. 'Back soon.'

'Ma, shall I go?'

'Go, Nick? You should have gone before now. It's your job to know when orders are due. Can't you do anything without I tell you? Alice—' She stopped herself. 'Alice would have done this by now,' she wanted to say, but she knew it wasn't true. Alice would be here, that was what she wanted. Here, not washing clothes or bowing to an angel by the river.

Will looked up, frowning, but Benedict kept his head down. The silence beat around Gemma's last word.

Gemma turned, walked to her desk, then back into the storeroom. 'Nick, I—'

'It was Pa ordered them,' Nick cut in. 'He said he'd get them.'

'I know Nick,' she said quietly. 'I know he did.' She touched his cheek with her palm. 'I misspoke, is all. You work well. You do.' She smiled. 'And this room is neater than I've ever known it, even when I was a girl.'

Back at her desk, she looked at what she had drawn. A washerwoman, a Thames backwater, St Paul's. She understood the truth of it, but it was not her book; it was for Lady Mathilda. What would a pile of washing and a London view offer to a noblewoman from Hertfordshire? Many things; it would teach her many things she should know. But it wasn't Gemma's place to teach them. Her job was to paint an illumination in which the lady could see herself standing with Mary to receive news of a baby to come, obedient to her duty to produce heirs, maintain the family line. Pumice stone, a light rub, and the story of an angel and the London woman was gone.

When John returned, blustering about the business he'd done, she took no notice. Drawing in part from the model book, and in part from memories of her pa, she began again, outlining two figures tucked inside the *D* as if inside a sheltering arch, the angel kneeling, his wings following the upper curve of the letter. Mary was tall and graceful, her head bent a little in acknowledgement, one hand modestly held in front of her, and in the other ... yes, a book. Lady Mathilda would see Mary reading, perhaps a prayer book, and know she followed the Virgin's example. Would Mary have read stories, perhaps, or poems? A simple girl who worked in the fields, probably she couldn't read at all, but that, Gemma knew, was not the point: this was the Virgin Mary of Lady Mathilda's book of hours.

Two days later, it was time to apply the gold leaf. She'd hoped Will wouldn't see her doing even more of John's work, but she had no choice. Gold leaf made its own small spectacle. The fragile sheet was next to her on the desk, protected under parchment. A puff of air and it would fly away, flutter and disintegrate.

Gemma knew how to use the gold sparingly, and she preferred only a touch here and there, just enough to lift the picture, draw the eye: gold on Mary's hair and halo, touches on her book and on the scalloped edges along the curves of the angel's wings and robes.

'You can watch this,' she said to Nick. 'And if your hands are clean, you can try burnishing the gold yourself. Remember to bring the dog's tooth.'

Will stopped working and watched as well.

The pink tinted gesso she had painted on had dried, so she leaned close to the page, opened her lips and released an even breath over it, here and here and here, just enough to moisten the gesso again. The leaf was like air made of gold, too delicate even for her fingers. She cut a piece from the corner with her knife, though no matter how slow or careful she was, it shifted and wrinkled away from the blade, a tear more than a cut. She rubbed a fine brush through her hair, took it close to the gold and watched the fragment leap toward the bristles. Once it was placed onto the gesso, she covered it with silk and pressed it down firmly with her thumb. Glancing up, she was aware of Will's eyes on her.

Nick handed her the long, curved tooth attached to a handle and she rubbed it over the gold. 'See how the gesso you made is thick enough to raise the gold from the page like a pillow? And the pink gives it that extra colour.' It was always at this stage that she allowed herself to think about the magic of it all, the way the fine leaf, once attached, would transform into something hard enough to be polished. Tooth of a dog, plaster, bole and glue: who would imagine they could persuade gold to shine so?

Nick took over the burnishing, awkwardly at first.

'You can press a little harder, as long as it's a smooth movement. That's it,' Gemma said, thinking of the words she would use to describe this in her book on illumination. 'Now, take this brush and flick away the ragged pieces of gold and we'll collect what we can.'

The fragments that hadn't attached to the gesso lifted from the page, the tiny ones floating in the air, sparkling dust, and slowly settled. Gemma would try to capture them, every last speck, to use again as shell gold. Most limners wouldn't bother, she knew, but would blow away the specks. This beauty could be so wasteful. John called it exuberant, saying that great work always demands loss along the way, but Gemma couldn't believe that. Their lives weren't beautiful, but they survived because nothing was wasted: every scrap of meat, every bone and spoonful of flour was used, and she could not blow away gold dust so carelessly.

She looked up. Will was watching the air glistening between them. He tipped his head a fraction toward her, and bent again to his work.

The gold had taken her away for a time. Whenever she worked with the flimsy leaf, the feeling was there, as if she were still the girl allowed for the first time to press it onto the page, her pa watching, instructing, leaving her to rub and rub at the pillows of gold until they shone. She'd blow away the frilly edges of the leaf and try to catch all the fragments, watch her hands glisten and think of the tall and shining faerie people in stories. It was never quite the same now. Too many years and sadnesses to be thinking of creatures from that other world, but still the gold made her forget.

Until she had seen Will watching. She knew what was coming; the problems with John's work couldn't be hidden. Benedict must suspect as well. Even if she could trust Will, how many people could keep a secret before it bled, spilling its red truth?

'That's enough, Nick,' she said. 'We need to check with your pa before we do any more.'

As Nick walked away, she studied Will bent over his desk, the way his forehead pulled together and creased, then released again, the occasional hint of a smile, the line of dark sweat by his ear. He loved painting, that was easy to tell, and he had skill, even more than she had thought on that first day. Where would his commitment to the work lead him? Was he ambitious enough to tell Southflete of John's absences and her involvement, in the hope of gaining goodwill? He seemed to admire John, bent to his guidance, but disappointment could be a rabid beast.

12

London
May 1321

Words and Pictures

When you paint, be aware that pictures and words are to be read together. As much as the prayers, the illuminations tell the sacred story and help the woman pray by drawing her into the heavenly realm, present to God. But more than this, the woman who prays will use not only her heart but her mind, reading the ways words and illuminations speak to one another.

In a similar way, the pictures in the margins are not simply decoration, like lace on a dress. Whatever you paint — flowers, capering creatures or monsters — be sure the margins listen to the words and respond to them. They might dance or play with the words; they might help to show their meaning; they might even challenge or resist them.

Always it is a conversation, words and pictures together helping the reader to pray.

The Art of Illumination

Jacob is asleep alone at night, his head resting on a stone, when an angel comes to him and wrestles with him.

Will knew the story. It was a mystery to him why an angel would fight with a man. Even if he was powerful, surely the wings would be clumsy behind him. Or perhaps not; the vicious goose his ma kept could near break a man's arm with his mighty wings.

The two fight, on and on, until finally the angel smites Jacob in the thigh, the priest had said when he told the story in church, and those around smirked knowingly at one another. Will had thought it strange, but once he'd met Simon, he understood the story in a way that couldn't be narrowed down to words, or sly looks.

Whatever he understood, it was his job to draw it, the story of Jacob and the angel. Will looked around the shop and wondered if he could pass it on to someone else, though he knew the answer already: he hadn't seen the master at all this morning; Benedict was intent on the borders; and Gemma wouldn't be able, though she seemed to think she was, playing with gold leaf and paint. You know the story, he told himself. Draw the outline and put on some colour.

Across the frame, from the bottom left to the top right, he sketched the waving lines of the river, and on the left side, a gathering of people, Jacob's family asleep where he had left them. On the right side, a few bushes, a single tree and, beneath it, man and angel holding one another in a bear hug, arms wrapped tight, feet spread to brace themselves.

Will tried to keep away the memories, but he couldn't imagine the picture in any other way. Though the sheriff of Cambridge had forbidden wrestling matches after a student had been badly beaten, townsfolk and students still met under the huge oak in the stretch of grass on the Backs of the River Cam. That was where, one moonlit summer night, Will had seen Simon a second time, the student he had rescued from the tavern brawl.

'Come on, Simon, tell us who you'll take on next,' one of the other students called out.

A few years younger than Will, shorter than him by a hand's width, his face pale and his arms those of a scholar, Simon announced to the crowd he would fight any challenger.

'Anyone. As I said.'

Will smiled and stepped forward: the man I saved from a beating wants to wrestle anyone who offers? Perhaps he'll remember my face when I have him on the ground.

The first time Will landed on his back, he was ashamed of himself. As a boy, he had stamped and sulked and tried to hit out whenever his pa forced him to the ground and pinned him there, laughing, and though Will had vowed to grow strong enough to beat him, it never happened. Instead, he would fight his friends; he was taller and generally stronger than them and could get by with grabbing them around the waist and pulling them over. Lying on the damp grass under the Cambridge oak, the pale face smiling down at him and the crowd cheering, he was confused and embarrassed; he may have been working with parchment and brushes for years, but he still played football and scrapped with students and other apprentices often enough to maintain some of the strength he had developed working with his pa.

He scrambled to his feet and the two men locked together in the opening stance, arms clasped around the other's back. Will lunged at his opponent as he had as a child, but Simon stepped, quickly and almost imperceptibly, to the side, leaving Will off balance. Some small effort then, using the momentum of the taller man's attack, and Simon pushed him to the ground. Will lay again on the grass, gasping and confused, as the students laughed and cheered. A third round: this time Simon hooked his foot behind Will's knee and pulled him over.

'Strategy,' Simon said later, as they walked away. 'Strength isn't only in the arms and legs; strength is strategy, speed, technique. You have to know how to use your own weight, and even more than that, how to take advantage of your opponent's weight and heft.'

Will hadn't wanted to hear, wanted to lash out, hook his arm around Simon's neck, pull him into a headlock and punch him in the stomach, though that would have been churlish. Determined to prove him wrong, he had agreed to fight him again, but away from the eyes of others. The next meetings netted the same result, but in time, his face tight with resistance, Will had accepted the lessons, had learned to laugh at his own clumsiness. One night, thrown to the ground, he began to sing where he lay. He watched the surprise on Simon's face, then his sudden smile and laugh as he stretched out beside him and joined in the song. His green eyes seemed always curious and certain.

Will had never really understood how they were friends, so different were they, but he was intrigued by the difference. Simon had learned his world from books; that was clear from the night in the tavern. In a game with rules, and against one man, he was hard to best. But would the rabble have lined up and waited to wrestle him, one by one?

'You need to know what ordinary folk are like before you go spouting your grand ideas,' Will had said.

Simon had remained silent.

In the atelier, Will kept drawing, sketching outlines, filling in details, quick and intent; it was the only way he could manage the memories. Yet again he mulled over the realisation that both he and Simon had spent their time with books, but gleaned so much that was different. Simon had seen glimmers of what might be possible, a world made new, a philosopher's world. Will looked for the beauty in what was around him — tree and face and fall of cloth — yet he too sought, as Edgar taught him, for what more lay beneath the veil of the ordinary.

In time, wrestling with Simon, he had learned to gauge the shifts in balance as if they were a conversation, not simply one man overwhelming the other with strength. He became aware of the tightness or flex of Simon's arms, the clench and release of muscle, the adjustment of his weight in one leg or another, the tilt of his head. Although he still loved to win, when he could, he settled into the fluid shifting of bodies. That was the place where he and Simon were most comfortable together.

The two figures on the page grasp one another, their faces close. There is the wounding in the thigh, that place of a man's strength and weakness. The raspy prickle of Simon's cheek against his own, the sound of his breath, the heat of his body, the occasional groan of effort. Walking back to his room from Simon's Peterhouse lodging, Will would flush at his pleasure in the touch of skin and body, and wonder if, even when he won, he had lost something, given in.

The drawing took shape and detail. The angel's feathered wings spread out behind him, arching strong and tall above his body. It was man and angel — Jacob with his determination, the angel with heaven's power — but the lines were Will and Simon: so much between them had been attraction and resistance.

'Should I mix some colours for that?' It was Nick.

Will pulled himself back to the workshop. His face was hot.

'Will you be painting every single leaf like that? Every single one?' Nick asked.

Will focused on his page. Unseeing, he had drawn the finest detail of branch, twig and leaf on the oak tree. 'Why not, Nick? I'll need green for that, but something different from the grass. I suppose there's no malachite yet?'

Nick shook his head. 'Harry won't even talk about it. Just says no.'

'Well then, mix some verdigris again, but mix it so you get more blue than green. You know how to do that?'

'Course I do. I'll add only a little apple juice so's it don't go far to green.'

'Good lad,' Will said. 'Your ma'll make a limner of you yet.'

The flush in his face was subsiding, but the touch of Simon's arms was still there.

Will picked up his plummet again, protected himself by drawing, but not the scene of man and angel. Something in the margins, perhaps. He noticed a small hole in the parchment of the next page, a slip where the parchmenter had scraped too hard in preparing the hide; it wasn't unusual, and parchment was too valuable to throw away for a small blemish. The hole was small, and Manekyn had arranged the ruling so that the hole was in the lower border of the page, barely noticeable. It was Will's job to decorate it, to make a virtue of the mistake. He carefully drew a hand reaching out from the edge of the hole, angled so that it appeared as if it was reaching through from the next page, fingers stretching upwards.

When Nick came back to the desk, he laughed. 'Will you draw the body on the next sheet, calling, "Pull me out, help me?"?'

Will said nothing, but he could hear the voice, feel his legs running in the dark night. Sticky feet were on his back, his neck. Nick was laughing, saying over and over, 'Will, Will, pull me out. I'm on the next page.'

When Nick eventually wandered back to the storeroom, still chanting, Will reached for a pumice stone. With a shaking hand, he erased the arm and, with it, the invisible floundering body. Instead, he drew a rabbit peering out of its burrow, tufts of grass on the edges of the hole, and on the other side of the parchment, the fluffy tail of the rabbit, snug in its warren.

'I'm off to see Southflete. Some news of pigment, he said.'

Will looked up, surprised to see John. He had not heard him come in. 'I'll walk a way with you,' he said quickly, rubbing at his shoulders.

'No need for that, Will.'

'And Will, I just mixed your paint,' Nick called from the storeroom.

'I know, lad. But my neck won't let me work until I take a rest. I'll walk out the pain, won't be long.' He felt like an apprentice giving his excuses.

'All right. You'll be company for a way.'

The two men set out and turned right into Old Change, Will adjusting his pace for John's shorter, ailing legs, his slight limp. The sounds, the bustle, even the squelch under Will's feet helped him shake off the sound of Simon's voice.

St Paul's sat queenlike on their right, and no matter how many times Will passed it, he couldn't help but look up toward the spire. The gargoyle scampered along the gutter, keeping pace with the pair, its eyes intent on Will. To shake it off, Will studied the simple brick wall bordering the cathedral grounds, punctuated by houses and chapels, a mixture of heights and sizes and widths. The gargoyle leaped down from the cathedral, prowled like a cat along the top of the wall.

'Wat Scrivener will be in there, intent on his business, no doubt,' John said as they passed the porch outside the cathedral's main doors, crowded, as always, with men busy about matters of the law.

Will said nothing, trying to ignore his stone companion.

'You don't look too well, Will.' John peered into his face.

'The shop gets warm. So small, and five bodies.'

'Aye. We've grown used to the freeze. Anything else seems warm. How about an ale to cool us?'

'Why not? The Swan's not far from here.' Will led the way.

They turned into Old Fish, where the tangle of animals, carts and people separated them until they sat in silence either side of a table in the Swan, pots in hand.

Three parts of his ale gone, Will's heart began to settle. 'Difficult business with Southflete?' he asked.

John seemed surprised. 'Southflete? Oh no. Pigments, accounts, the usual.'

Will studied John's face. He seemed thinner, and tired of late, rubbing his eyes, sometimes looking vacantly at his work.

'You seem worried, John.'

The older man laughed sadly. 'My legs ache, is all. The cold hasn't left them.'

'Southflete's content with the book, then? He visits so often, looks for you.'

'Oh yes. He likes to bluster, does Southflete.'

Will wanted to ask more, to find out why John did so little work, why he argued with Gemma about the pages. When John brought back a second pot for each of them, he tried again.

'Gemma must be a help. Training Nick, sketching.' He paused. 'Even some gold leaf. I was surprised.'

'Ah, our Gem. She's been around that atelier longer than me. All her life. Born to it, she is.'

'But a woman. Surely …' Will paused, hunted for the right words. 'Southflete, he's so concerned about quality. He wouldn't be happy about—'

'Why all the questions?' John gazed into his companion's face, his eyes troubled, even if his tone was mild. 'Let me worry about Southflete.'

'I just—'

John's voice changed, found iron. 'Don't be a fool, Will. Gemma is more talented than either of us.'

Mathilda

Wain Wood Manor
May 19, 1322

Maggie is holding onto the curtains around the bed, using them to swing to the floor.

'Maggie, don't do that. I told you. You'll pull the curtains down.'

The little girl flops onto the bed. 'What else can I do then? We've played all our games.'

She has been in trouble with Angmar for getting in the way, and it's still not safe to be outside. 'Come and look at my book,' Mathilda coaxes her. 'We can talk about the pictures.'

Still frowning, Maggie puts the book on her knee and turns the pages. 'No. No. No. Don't like that. Not that one. Nor that one.' Then she pauses. 'Ma, tell me about this one. This one with the angel talking to the lady.'

It's the Annunciation. Mathilda knew it was there, of course, but had turned quickly past the page.

'It's a beautiful angel. But why is the lady reading when he wants to talk to her?'

'Perhaps it's her book of prayers, just like this one,' Mathilda says, straightening the bed.

'No. It's not prayers. It's stories of knights rescuing ladies just like her.'

Mathilda laughs. She'd like a book of those stories, too, but says, 'That's Mary, the mother of our Lord, Maggie. I think we're to imagine Mary praying when the angel comes. Why else would he come to her unless she loved God?'

Mathilda sits next to her daughter and together they study the page. 'When I was a little girl, I thought the angel's wings would sound like a hawk's, as it lands.' She had imagined the dense feathers finally still and raised, a shelter above him and Mary. 'I used to think that if I were Mary, I would bow my head and the angel would make me shine just like in that picture.'

'She's beautiful with all that gold,' Maggie agrees.

Now, Mathilda thinks that those great wings, unfolded, however much they were made of light, would cast a shadow on a young girl without a husband. Baby, scandal, rejection. So many times she has heard of Mary's quiet acceptance of the shame that would be cast on her, but only now does she know what shame is really like, her husband a traitor who saved himself from the executioner only by dying with a sword in his belly. No disgrace in dying on the battlefield, Robert always said, but he will be remembered as the man who died fighting against his king.

She touches her belly in that habit she has now, not sure if she is welcoming the baby or telling it to leave. To be a good woman she should have some of Mary's devotion, but she can't be grateful for her tender breasts or the sickness that ferments and rises into her mouth.

This is what it's like to be a widow. Alone. When she was first with child, twelve years ago, even the sickness had been welcome because it told her, each day, that the baby was growing and demanding; it was her task to bear a child of the Fitzjohn line. Robert had been delighted in his serious way, careful of her and distant. And even though other women had warned her not to expect too much, the child had lived. Her Joan. She was Robert's first disappointment. Not Joan herself, as he pointed out, but it was a shame that she wasn't a boy, an heir. That was all. She was hale and strong; of course he was pleased. There would be more babies, a boy.

Robert's mean commiseration floated past Mathilda, suddenly irrelevant. She could never find words for the ways Joan's arrival had changed her. What it was to know her body could bring another into the world. How, through all the fear and pain, she had felt herself, at last, a being of blood and skin and bone. Power. Perhaps that's the word. She wonders sometimes if that's what battle did for Robert, that travelling to the edge of death and coming back again.

Then the dying. Women, the same ones as before, told her how blessed she was to have Joan; babies don't usually come so easily, they said. Or if they do, they struggle to stay. Gavin, who had been so well, such a promise for the family, was gone before he turned five, Robert pushing him too soon to grow up. He had to learn to ride, of course, but the horse was too strong for him. She had told Robert, and as usual he had shushed away her worries, leaving her to struggle even now with forgiveness. Trying to soothe her grief, some said it was because he was so beautiful, that God wanted him in heaven. Then God is as cruel as my husband, she'd thought. After Gavin, another baby she never saw, barely formed, no way of telling if a boy or girl, the midwife said. Maggie had been the respite, the face of God shining on her, Father Jacobi said. Robert kissed her, a hard, dry kiss, and nodded. Next time, next time surely, an heir.

It was a relief, the very first time she set eyes on Robert Fitzjohn, only weeks before they were married. At least he's not old, she thought. Fifteen years her senior, but not old. She had been terrified at the thought of an old man's skin. It took time to find out how to feel some pleasure with him, and even longer for her to persuade him it was possible. He was a man for getting things done. But his gratitude for Gavin's birth, relief perhaps, seemed to touch something in him. Recognising the moment, Mathilda had coaxed him, taught him to regard her. She was surprised that he could be so tender, and even after Gavin died, he looked to Mathilda for comfort.

Mathilda shakes her shoulders. She's never before thought of her children, dead and alive, lined up like this, like a story in pictures. And now another one. Angmar suspects and has stopped offering tea to help bring on her monthly flowers, but she hasn't said anything. No doubt she and Ysmay have talked it over, how a child will be another burden, there being so little inheritance, but how a boy and heir would be a chance to rebuild position and respect for the Fitzjohn line. How they will need to care for the lady's health after so much shock; how — counting on their fingers — the baby must be due near Michaelmas ... no later, since Sir Robert left before Yule. And how he was away for months before that. Yes, Michaelmas or thereabouts.

Maggie laughs aloud, pulls at Mathilda's sleeve. 'Ma, Ma, look at this! It's a monkey dressed like the bishop and he's talking to those animals.'

Mathilda is glad it's not a holy picture; she doesn't want to think about Mary and obedience and babies. Walls around her, rules for her soul, demands on her body.

'Did Will paint this then? Do you think that's our dove, like in the dovecote?'

Mathilda glances at the picture Maggie is pointing to in the margin, but it's nothing to do with a dovecote. It's a monkey dressed in a bishop's robe and mitre, and holding a staff, preaching to a duck, a dove, a cat and a dog. 'That's funny, isn't it? Do you think the painter was making a joke, Mag?' she says, feigning interest.

'Mmm. But why?'

'Well, in the big picture, the angel, his name is Gabriel, is bringing a message from God to Mary, and Mary is pleased because she wants to obey God.' Ah, the stories we tell children, she thinks. The things we pretend. 'But the bishop isn't really a bishop, he's only a monkey, so he can only talk to silly animals. I don't know why ...' She smiles as she sees the words painted beneath and understands the monkey's babbling prayer is a playful echo of Mary's: *O Lord, open my lips and my mouth shall sing thy praise.*

'The cat and dog are standing on their back legs!'

'They're pretending to be people.'

'Why?'

'Well, I think the limner is saying that people who don't listen to God are as silly as animals.'

'I don't think animals are silly.'

'No. But it's funny, isn't it? It made you laugh.' She pauses; she can't do this right now, be patient with this awkward child. 'Mag, why don't you look for the special rose Master Dancaster always paints?'

'No. Will did this page.'

Mathilda lets out a sigh. 'Just try. Look in the borders, around the edge.'

While Maggie hunts among the foliage, Mathilda gazes at the painting with no real focus. There's something soothing in this one, something that resists her bitterness. She looks closer. Slowly, she realises that the colours are simple: only red, blue and white, but in all shades from the deepest to the palest, with a few touches of gold leaf. She had assumed that any illumination of the Virgin Mary would demand the richness of gold and many colours, but the simplicity of hue in this painting shows humility and grace. How much the limner has managed with such a small palette. Was this indeed painted by Master Dancaster? she wonders.

'There it is,' Maggie says. 'Found it, found it.'

There, by Maggie's finger, is the rose, tucked inside one of the loops of the interlaced knot in the bottom border.

'So it was Master Dancaster after all. Good searching, Maggie.'

For Mathilda, it's a quiet satisfaction, as if it gives her some contact with the man who painted this, a man who seems to understand how to soothe the troubles of shame.

13

London
June 1321

Folium

Folium is the hue drawn from the turnsole, the plant called thus because it turns its face to the sun. In the south of France, the land of St Giles, it grows. Three seeds it has, tiny seeds that will give up their vivid hues for the illuminator. Gather them in summer and squeeze gently, without crushing, to extract their juice. Allow the juice to soak into linen cloth. Such is the nature of this dye that it will vary depending on its treatment. Plain linen cloth will render a red hue, and cloth soaked in lime water, then dried, and soaked with turnsole juice will give violet. For blue, that many call sapphire folium, so clear and strong and jewel-like it is, the violet cloth must be soaked in ammonia; urine is the most easily obtained. Once made, store the linen cloths away from sunlight, for though the plant loves the sun, the colour drawn from it will fade.

The Art of Illumination

On his morning walks, Will gradually noticed that the air no longer had its harsh bite, and the breeze stirred with gentle warmth. Stalls were now selling leafy vegetables, a relief from parsnips and swedes, and flower sellers had some colour to offer. He felt a heavy hand had lifted. The cold that had spurred his memories of snow was passing; perhaps the haunting would cease as well.

But if, walking along Cornhill, sun on his face, he believed that winter's frigid punishment was over, he was

one of the few. The farmers who travelled to the city with
their carts and stock said the sun only shone on devastation
in the countryside: a murrain slayed cattle, and though crops
had been replanted, the scant stores of seed meant it would
be years before supply was properly re-established. And even
if some in London dared to believe that the years of freezing
weather might have passed, they knew the sun shone on their
city seething and fearful of invasion.

Armed men patrolled the streets, quick to arrest anyone
thought to be a troublemaker; workers crawled over the
great wall, building and repairing it; men huddled in groups,
planning, plotting; the sounds of ringing metal from the
smithies seemed somehow urgent; preachers called from street
corners, declaring judgement and the dark reward of sin.
Will saw it all, heard all the warnings, the announcements of
stricter curfews, the demands for workers to help fortify the
city, but everything slid off his sun-warmed back. The fresh
grass by St Michael's and around St Paul's was vivid green
where before there had been mud, and he paused to consider
what pigment would render that hue.

As the muck in Paternoster Row began to dry out, its smell
changed and intensified, as if it had been distilled.

'Have you felt the warmth outside? Gives a man hope,'
Will announced to the shop as he stepped inside. 'Ah, at last.
What a relief to have the shutter open. No lamps today. We
can't stay in despair when the sky is clear. Surely the long
freeze is over.'

'Aye, and we thought that last year,' Benedict said. 'And
look what happened. We saw maybe two days of sun.'

'True, Ben, but it has to change sometime. Summer is
coming.'

'Trouble's coming, that's what. Between the king and the
Marcher barons. They want Despenser gone, and they'll fight
to see it happen,' Benedict said.

'True enough,' John agreed.

'Nothing to do with me,' Will declared, as he walked to the storeroom and picked up his pages. 'I'm a simple limner.'

'Matters to us all, Will,' Gemma said. 'You should know that. What happens to the city hits all of us, one way or another. And we've still the Iter meddling where there's no need; folks are on their knees.'

'Quiet woman!' John warned. 'The shutter be open. You never know who's out there, listening. So far, we've avoided those men. God willing it'll stay that way.' He dropped his voice even lower. 'There's some say the king might close down the inquisition anyway. The barons are demanding an end to it, and now. Say it's evil.'

'It is evil. Did you hear what they've done to Paul, the haberdasher from Westcheap? All but destroyed him, and his business. He's been thrown out of his shop. An honest man, he is, whatever Scrope and Stanton say. They should be strung up.'

'Shush! God's bones, woman! Why don't you declare it at St Paul's Cross? Ask them to come and investigate our shop?'

Gemma glared but said nothing.

'Wat Scrivener says the king's ordered parliament to meet in a few weeks,' John went on. 'To try and put an end to all this trouble in the Marches. Says it's all because of Despenser. Get rid of him, and it'll all sort itself out. The barons say he must leave the country, or else.'

'Or else what?' Nick asked, peering around the storeroom door.

'Who knows, Nick? It's all just rumours, but if Despenser doesn't go, the barons might come to London with their demands and ... who knows what? Get rid of Despenser themselves, I suppose.'

'Here? All the barons and their soldiers? A war, here?'

'Let's hope Lancaster sees us right before then,' John said.

'But the barons would make Despenser leave, you said. And that's what we want, isn't it? So they're not our enemies.'

'Not so simple, lad,' John said.

'Your pa's right, Nick. War is war, whoever's fighting. We don't want a war here,' Will said quietly, his hopeful mood shaken.

'No need to worry yet, Nick. Get on with your cleaning, son,' John said.

Gemma watched Nick walk away. He'd seen death, but not close enough to feel the pain that lodged forever in the body. 'Our Alice needs to come home for a time, until all this is over,' she said.

'You know she won't, love, and asking only makes it worse.'

'She'll be here for St Swithun's Day. I'll try to make her see sense.'

After an hour's work, Will called to Nick for some red paint and walked to the window. He breathed in the air, rancid but warm, and watched the business of Paternoster Row pass by. Stretching out his back, he turned to John, stepped toward his desk. 'What are you painting, John? I've been keen to study your work again.'

John stood up, rubbing at his knees, forcing Will to move back toward the window.

'St Francis, it is. Yesterday a friar in Cheapside, just by Eleanor's Cross, was telling about St Francis preaching to the birds. I stopped to listen. Haven't heard naught but sin and doom from those as preach there. But this friar talked about how Francis gave away all his worldly goods and went out, preaching to the birds. They all gathered around him. I thought Lady Mathilda would enjoy Francis.'

'I saw some birds this morning, perched in the trees by the cathedral. This warm weather's coaxed them out of hiding,' Will said. 'I'll paint some in the margins.'

'Look, there's one now, sitting on the head of a gargoyle.' It was Nick, clam shell of red paint in his hand. 'Look, Will.'

Will hesitated, looked up to where a dove perched between the horns of a gargoyle. His gargoyle. He blanched as it closed one stone eyelid in a slow wink. It had not departed with the cold.

'Look, Pa! And some on the wall there. What sort are they?'

John turned then looked away.

Gemma saw his squint, his unease; he had no idea about the birds. 'Nick, put that paint down on the desk before you spill it,' she cut in.

Will caught her fleeting expression of pain but didn't understand it. So much fear and worry; his morning hopefulness was seeping away. Chafing, he spoke again to John. 'Do you think she'd give away her goods, Lady Mathilda? Throw it all out the window like Francis?'

John smiled. 'Hardest of all for the rich, eh? Born to it, they are. Don't know aught else. Remember what Jesus said about how hard it is for the rich man to give up his belongings?' When Will didn't speak he went on. 'Harder than for a camel to go through the eye of a needle, so this preacher said.'

'Even when those around are starving?'

'Hard, even then.'

'So why paint this for the lady if you think she can't do it?' Will's voice was sharp now.

Gemma glanced across at the two men. She understood what Will meant, had argued with herself over just this, but she knew she would always return to her paints and parchment.

'Same reason we paint anything,' John said. 'Because it's true, and because it's what our Lord taught us. Not for us to say what the nobility should do with their wealth. God's business, it is.'

'Maybe. But Christ tells us that those with money and position have even more reason to look after the poor.'

'I suppose they do,' John said. 'Some pay for hospitals and churches, and they buy things people make or pay for work to be done. Like this book. Where would we be if Sir Robert didn't pay for the book, if his wife didn't want to use it to pray?'

Will shifted his feet and glanced outside. Surprisingly nimble for a stone creature, the gargoyle was climbing down the cathedral wall, its eyes never leaving the workshop window. Will wanted to agree with John, but he needed to argue. Simon was at his back, urging him on. 'But that doesn't make it right.' He could hear how thin his voice sounded. 'They store up what they need against hard times, then make their money from the poor.'

'Why do you paint, Asshe? Why do you want to work on a grand book like this, then? You had a job, after all.' John's voice was mild, curious.

Will raised his head to meet John's eyes. 'Because it's what I've always wanted to do since I was a lad, younger than Nick, and I saw a psalter my ma had hidden away in her kitchen. I'd never seen anything like it before, even in church. Always wanted to paint like that, page after page of it.' He paused. 'And I want to work with you. Edgar showed me an illumination of the Virgin and Child you painted and I thought I'd never seen anything as beautiful. It has always been my hope to work with you.'

Gemma sucked in a breath. So much longing in the young man's words. How cruel would the truth about John be to him? Disappointment could be vicious.

John touched his arm. 'Then we must thank God for Sir Robert and Lady Mathilda, eh?'

Will was silent, confused. He had been so drawn to Simon's desire to defend the poor against the powerful. So often he had listened to his friend talk, painting in his mind Simon's dreams of what might be, giving them shape and colour. They would be all that he imagined John's picture of St Francis to be, the rich man shedding cloak and tunic, shoes and hose, emptying chests of linen, sharing grain and wine, offering blankets, robes and cushions to those who were freezing. So it was a bitter truth to realise that, in Simon's dream, the boundaries were rigid; John's illumination of the saint would have no place. Will felt beaten down, cowed by his friend's words, and wanted to lash out at something, anything.

Somehow, though, John seemed to shuffle those ideas gently around, shake them down like apples in a basket, giving everything room to be there together. Will tried to imagine Simon speaking with the master limner, but he couldn't see it. There wasn't space in his head for the two men together, certainly not with the gargoyle nearby on the shutter, its green tongue hanging out.

He stood for a moment watching John lower himself awkwardly to sit at his desk, his parchment covered. Simon never understood Will's longing to paint, but John did; he shared it, every day. But still, Will couldn't settle; there was more to say. What was it? He couldn't find words. The thick, slimy chuckle of stone was in his ear. His skin crawled. This was the first time the gargoyle had ventured inside the atelier. Would it never leave him alone? What did it want?

Then, as if the gargoyle had whispered in his ear, he recognised it. Like Simon, Will resented the way the nobility treated those beneath them, but what he hated most was the feeling that he gave them power. With the skills he posessed, he could make cart wheels for the man who brought his vegetables to market, or he could copy treatises for students. Men like him. But when he longed to paint illuminations and grand books, he had to court the favour of the rich. There must be a place for beauty itself, he thought. Beauty beyond their power.

Frustrated, he said to John, 'Can I see him? Francis. And the birds?'

'Not finished yet. When I'm done, eh?' John picked up the double page, held it to his chest.

'Just a quick—' Will reached out a hand.

'No, Will. I said, when I'm finished.' John's voice was sharp.

Will stepped back, feeling slapped.

'Eh! Aren't you one of them limners?' The soldier grabbed Will's arm. 'You're one of that soft-skinned lot from those shops down by the cathedral, you are. What game is this, you thinking you can work on the gates? You've no place here. Get down there and dig.' He pointed to a group of men below them, more than their own height below the level of the ground, clearing and widening the ditch that skirted the wall.

'Not me,' Will said. 'I'm to work on the gate. I've some expertise—'

'God's holy bones!' The soldier barked out a laugh. 'These gates have to protect the city in a battle. Important, they are. Why'd we let you work on 'em? You as waste your days with pretty colours and pictures.'

'Nah, he's right,' a second man said. 'I'm Owen, the builder sent to work on this gate. Asshe is to come with me. His pa's a wheelwright, he learned some skills as a boy. That right, Asshe? Look at those hands now. He'll be useful to me.'

Will watched the two men haggle over him. Some in the tavern would laugh, in a careful way, about a man born to a hammer and axe, using tiny brushes to paint fancy loops and intricate pictures. It was an old joke for Will, and he'd end it by wrestling them over a table or barrel.

The first man peered at Will's hands and raised his eyebrows. 'Big enough, that's sure. But soft as a lady's paps is my wager.' He frowned. 'All right, Owen seems to want you, so we'll see what you can do. But I'll have an eye to your work, God's body I will.'

Will was hot and didn't want to be there. 'See these big hands?' He stepped close and held them up in front of the soldier. 'The ones you're so interested in? They do good work, and they'll have something to give you if you don't shut your mouth.'

The soldier didn't move, his fists clenched white. He looked around; no one else seemed to have heard. 'We'll see, won't we?' he growled. 'And who's that?'

'That's Ben Broune. Works with me. More useful than he might look.' Will slapped Benedict on the back to stop him protesting. 'Well Ben, we've a job to do. Tell us what you need from us, Owen.'

The three men walked away.

The king had called, and his people had no choice. Edward had agreed to the demand that he end the Iter inquisition into guilds, but in exchange for London's agreement to help protect him from his enemies, the barons. Cold comfort in that deal, most said: the inner threat exchanged for one coming to the gates. All this brought on by Despenser's greed and the king's collusion.

By the end of the morning, Will's big hands were covered in blisters and scratches from cutting, carving and nailing wood onto the gates guarding the city's Ludgate entrance. It was true that his hands had softened. He sucked at a loose and bloody piece of skin on the heel of his palm, rewrapped the scrap of cloth covering it, and went back to shaping a beam of wood. His life had looped around itself like a vine painted in a margin; he'd been brought up hauling timber heavier than he was, even as a toddler dragging whatever he could manage, learning, as he grew, how to shape and join the wood for cartwheels. It was satisfying enough work, and he had thought it would be his trade. Until he found the burned psalter. His strength still showed.

Despite his curses, he was enjoying the work. It was good to be outside in the warmth of the sun, rediscovering the muscles and skills he hadn't used for years.

'Lift it higher, Ben,' he said. 'Come on, man, higher.'

'Devil take you, Asshe. I am lifting.'

Together they removed all that had rotted and began to prepare new, thicker beams. Benedict rubbed a hand over his face, spreading the sweat and dirt. 'It's too hot to be heaving wood. It's breaking my back. Like the soldier said, we've soft hands. Working with wood might be your trade, but it isn't mine, Asshe.'

'Nor mine, Ben, nor mine. And don't think to insult me or my pa. Shaping wheels is a precise trade, not easy to master. It's not only brawn, you know.'

At the sound of church bells pealing, they paused, looked up. Not the tolling of danger or death, but a surprisingly merry sound. A faint cheer went up. Queen Isabella had been delivered of a baby. A girl, Joan.

'In the Tower, she is. The only place she can be safe,' Benedict said. 'Strange times, these are. The queen imprisoned in her own city. A princess born into captivity.'

'And here we are, strengthening the gates against our allies, fearing the war that might rid us of Despenser. Strange times indeed, Ben.'

Day by day the two men worked together, Will cutting and planing the wood, explaining each step to Benedict. 'Now this wood, Ben …' he would begin, and recount the lessons his pa had taught him. The apprentice stood quietly, and Will knew he wasn't listening.

When the measurement of a beam was inaccurate, or the fit of two corners not snug, he would insist they adjust it. 'Come on, Ben. We have to do this again. "Near isn't good enough, lad," my pa used to say. "If it's not right, stop and fix it."' Will could see his father humming as he shaped the curve of a wheel, pausing now and then to frown, purse his lips, measure and consider. Over and over until it was right. Perhaps that was how Will had learned the importance of even the finest detail in decoration. 'We wouldn't leave a misshapen painting, would we?' he said to Ben.

As the gate took shape, Will felt a hum of pleasure in his work. Not the sense of delight in creation that colour and line gave him, but the kind of satisfaction he saw on his pa's face when a wheel he had made turned strong and true. This gate would hold firm.

At times they climbed up the scaffolding to work. The top of the wall gave them a broad view over the river and the open land surrounding the city, and Benedict pointed out places where he would play as a boy. It was an exchange of childhoods.

Will knew some of the buildings, but others he hadn't noticed before, and as Benedict told stories of houses, docks and churches demolished, built or extended, Will began to see the city in a different way. He had walked its streets, hidden in its lanes, but he didn't understand it the way Benedict did.

'We climbed up here, onto the wall, though the guards would chase us down. Sometimes at night, we crept from shadow to shadow, just so we could look at the sky. Up here, it seemed bigger, like it was everywhere around us. So many stars. We made up stories about them.'

A pain stirred in Will's chest. The wide open skies of Cambridge.

That evening he walked, restless, not sure whether he was chasing or fleeing the memories. At Cripplegate the gates were closed and bolted earlier than usual.

'No one goes in or out. Can't trust no one or his mother in these times,' the guard told him. 'Time to be inside, it is. No saying when the soldiers'll come. Maybe by cover of night.'

Turned away, Will walked instead in the grounds of St Alban's nearby. He shouldn't stay after curfew, he knew, but the night was still and warm, the memories luring him. He looked up. The stars, the clear sky, the soft air on his face; there must be music in the firmament. He could hear Simon's laughter. 'It's not the kind of noise you can hear, Will. It's an idea.'

They had been walking back to Cambridge from a wrestling match at the oak tree, but Simon was so excited that he pulled Will around. The memory came back slowly, in fragments.

'Will, let me show you what we've been learning about the stars.'

Tired but intrigued, Will stopped and, leaning back on the grass, the two men looked up at the cloudless sky.

'There are celestial spheres,' Simon said, 'each one following its course around Earth in the centre. First there are the elements: water, then fire, then air; then the moon; then Mercury and Venus; the Sun; then the rest of the planets, Mars, Jupiter and Saturn; and beyond that, the stars. And further out, the *Primum Mobile*, the first mover.' As he spoke, Simon drew on the grass with his finger, circles inside circles, shapes that vanished as soon as his hand moved on.

Will had begun to see it, the shape of the universe.

'Now ...' Simon said, and Will could sense the shining in his eyes. His invisible picture discarded, Simon opened his arms, shaped globe upon globe in the air, using his whole body to speak. 'Now, think of these circles being not flat, but spheres, each one completely round like a ball. And each planet travels around inside its own crystalline globe, each one tucked inside the one before. Can you see it, Will?'

Will nodded uncertainly. 'I think so.'

'I've seen drawings that show it. So clever, they are, the men that draw them, to show something round on a flat page.'

'I know, Simon.' Will was angry then. 'It's what I do. Not that, exactly, but I put things with shape and depth onto flat parchment. It's my skill. The skill you say is a waste.'

'No, that's not a waste. Of course we need men who can draw such things, help us see ideas. It's the beauty shut up in books for the nobility that's a waste.'

'You say those pictures have value, but they're also shut up in books that only students and teachers can see.'

'That's different. Because ideas are important.'

'And so is beauty. You can't separate them.'

'But I do. I only look at pictures that are useful.'

'To me they are all beautiful. Whatever I decorate, a herbal or a medical treatise or a romance, it's all beauty to me, even the treatise on warfare that Edgar decorated a few years ago. Each page is more than just ideas.' His voice was sharp. 'More than your "useful".'

Now, in the tranquillity of St Alban's churchyard, Will hugged his knees. The anguish was still there.

They'd sat in an uneasy silence, until Simon spoke. 'Yes, I see that, Will. You're right. It is more,' and reached out a hand to him.

The touch of skin, fingers caught into his own, ran along Will's arm. The familiar warmth that drew him in again. They were so different, but the struggle mattered. They had lain back on the grass then, looking into the sky, trying to see it all.

'What about the music?' Will asked.

'Oh, some think it's a real noise, the crystal spheres touching each other as they move, but I don't think so. It's all about mathematics and harmony.' Simon went on to list names and theories, but Will wasn't listening, absorbed in the thought of the sky's music. Of course, those silver stars would jangle as they moved and touched; the moon would make music.

Hunched on the grass of St Alban's, looking up, thoughts shifted around in his mind, each searching for a place. So many questions from the last few days. There were no simple answers. The gargoyle squatted nearby, not moving. So familiar now, it was oddly comforting. Will cocked his head, strained to hear the music of the spheres. There must be such beauty in the heavens. Of that he was sure.

14

London
July 1321

The Master's Example

Draw every day. Do not judge such pictures harshly, but simply continue to practise and in time you will see improvement. You may copy from the masters, for they are the ones who have travelled the road before you and can teach you through their work, but choose one great limner rather than many, so that you are not confused by a variety of styles. In time, you will find your own style.

Above all, copy from Nature. It is she who is your greatest master and teacher.

The Art of Illumination

For the first time in five years the sun shone for St Swithun's Day and though Londoners tried to dance and sing, and watched their children play and bob for the few apples they had saved up, it was as if they were peering over their shoulders, their laughter tight and short, as if any pleasure would leave them unguarded.

Will joined in for a time, spinning Hawisia's tiny Mirabel like a top, as she always asked, carrying Annie's Drew on his shoulders so that he could touch the clouds, and chasing a crowd of little ones who wanted him to be the dragon come to eat the city. He roared and clawed, chased them and ate them, and finally, when required, fell dead with his legs in the air as the children pummelled and roared their victory. Shaking them off, staggering to his feet, he realised that even the games couldn't overcome the fear they all felt. Word travelled through every gate of barons meeting, land and castles taken and then retaken, Despenser's cruelty and the king's determination to bring the barons to heel. The land had turned against itself and war was near upon them.

Will looked up at the sun, a yellow ball that suddenly seemed demonic. If the story of the approaching civil war had been a play performed at Smithfield, the actors would not have thought to include a sun getting hotter as the threat drew closer. They would not have cast a man dressed in yellow with spikes radiating from his hat, loitering silently, then transforming, taking up a spear and dancing like a devil as his gentle smile turned into a leer. But that was how it seemed. Will smiled at the idea, and thought that was how he would paint it — the heat and the threat of war joining hands to squeeze the city.

A week later, the gate repaired and strengthened, Will and Benedict were allowed to return to the atelier.

'A hundred soldiers won't get through it now, thanks to our work, eh, Ben?' He slapped the younger man on the back.

'Hard work it was, but even that grumbling soldier admired our gate,' Benedict said.

'But a trebuchet. Would it keep out a trebuchet?' Nick asked. 'They'll bring trebuchets, won't they?'

'Let's hope not, lad. They're big and clumsy things. I think they just want to scare the king.'

Nick persisted. 'But it's a war, a battle, and that's what they do, break down gates and walls.'

'Even so, Ludgate's now as solid a gate as you'll find in Christendom. My pa would even say so.'

'I've never seen a real trebuchet. Just think what a rock thrown from one could do to the wall. I hope they do bring one and try.'

'No, you don't, lad,' Will said. 'Now, I hope you haven't lost my pages.'

After the days outside, working with wood, the shop seemed quiet, his desk so small, the sheets of parchment so thin, the paint so compliant. For the first time, Will felt his own bulk, his calloused hands rough and clumsy. He looked over the pages he had been working on. In the margin were the birds he had painted after seeing them perched around St Paul's. He smiled at the story they were telling.

Magpie, goldfinch, crested tit. Light as air, only a breath of brush stroke, they perch on even the smallest leaves, the finest curl of vine, the most delicate flower bud. The goldfinch sings high and sweet, fluttering and strong, a knight declaring devotion to his lady. His face is vermilion, as red as blood and crowned with black. The porporina stripe on his wing flashes in the sun. Look, across the page she comes, hopping from word to word, demure and coy, her head down, wings lifted to accept his love. Hopeful now that his quest is not in vain, he sings his love more loudly still, lifting his tail and his wings, the colours he will bear for her.

The scene settled Will's discomfort about being back at his desk and he began to plan the capital.

When Nick announced that he was off to the apothecary to see if the malachite had arrived, John stood and said he would go with him.

'I can do it myself, Pa,' Nick said.

'No, lad, best I go with you, city as it is. No telling what's going to happen out there.'

'But Pa, it's not far. I can—'

'He's right, Nick. It's dangerous times,' Gemma said.

'First the apothecary, then one of Ellyn's sweet buns, I think. Can't work all the time, eh?' John took his pages into the storeroom. A hot breeze blew in as they walked out the door, John with one hand on his son's shoulder.

In here and out there, Will thought. For an hour or two of painting, they could fool themselves they were safe.

The shop fell into silence. Outside, the street shouted and

called and clattered its business as usual, though now at the edge of a screech. St Paul's chimed the hours of prayer and the limners worked on. Will began to sing softly, then to hum as he lost the words, concentrating on his work. Benedict sighed once or twice in his direction, but said nothing.

His sketch outlined in ink, Will put down his quill, squinted a little, and examined the shape of his design. Inside the capital D, an angel lifts his hand in greeting to a shepherd, bringing news: a child is born. Between them, a dog raises its head to the angel, its mouth open, every suggestion of a smile on its face, while beneath, sheep graze contentedly, their coats falling into regular waving folds of wool. At the top of the page, a tiny angel blows a trumpet. Will had drawn shields in the margin because Manekyn's instructions ordered them, but the dog — the dog was for the Fitzjohn children. He hoped they might laugh at it, imagine the angel, come with such grand news of Christ's birth, patting it, calling it a good dog, maybe throwing a stick.

He was ready to add some touches of gold leaf, but Nick still wasn't back from his errand with John. Will walked to the storeroom and stood for a moment, smiling at the neat rows of jars and boxes, the few bladders holding plant juices lying forlornly on their sides, the tidy stacks of clam shells, the mortar and pestle in their place in the centre of the bench, and at one end the bowl of turnsole berries and the block of brazil wood. All very ordinary, keeping their secret of colour locked away. He scanned the shelves for the batch of gesso Nick had promised to make. There it was. As he moved to pick up the pot, he noticed a cloth covering something and, barely thinking, lifted it. John's painting of St Francis was underneath.

Back at his desk, Will struggled to concentrate; his face was hot, as if everyone was looking at him, accusing him. As if he had peered through a crack in the wall onto a naked man.

And found him disfigured. He jiggled his leg, chewed at his lip and glanced around without lifting his head. John Dancaster's reputation had travelled among limners to Cambridge, Oxford, Peterborough and further: the fullness of detail in his pictures, the exquisite layering of colour that created such grades of shade and light, painting that Edgar had described as the work of a man led by genius. What Will had seen made his belly clench.

No, he reasoned with himself. He had simply expected more than was possible; if he looked again, he would see it was good work after all. It was the time working on the gate with wood and hammer. He'd forgotten the process. It was the hot weather making him see things. If there was a problem, Gemma would have said something. Even John himself. The book was so important to him. But he didn't move, didn't want to see.

He looked up. Gemma was watching him as if she knew what was in his mind.

The gesso was good, the right consistency, and he brushed it on, though he saw nothing but John. The days he had gone on messages; the anger in Gemma's replies to him; the times Southflete had come to the shop and John had been out; the times he had walked around the desks, talked to Nick about this and that; his new interest in the garden. Busy, but not painting. And now, he realised, he hadn't seen any of John's recent work. When he was at his desk, he squinted and worked slowly, sometimes bending so close to the parchment he almost brushed it with his nose. Sometimes he passed the pages he'd been working on over to Gemma. Will had thought all that was the method of a great painter. Really, he had refused to see it.

The double page he had peeked at had a small illumination of Christ in the temple, with St Francis along the bottom of the page, and if Will had not seen John painting it, he would have thought it a child's work: the figures were simple, the faces round with barely a detail, the colours strong, without shading, only blended where the brush had slipped across the ink lines.

No. He was being unfair; the page wasn't finished and John would come back, add layers of colour, give detail to the faces, turn the mess into beauty.

Sighing loudly and muttering about having forgotten what he needed, he went back to the storeroom. Turning to check he was unobserved, he took down some of the finished pages stacked on a high shelf out of harm's way. Gemma had worked on the calendar pages, he knew; here they were. He gasped softly; they were not what he'd expected. Beautiful in their simplicity and elegance, each page had a fine sense of balance in the composition and colouring. And the shading was so delicate, the kind of work he expected from John. Surely a woman couldn't have done these. But he had seen her draw, then add gold leaf, then paint, and there it was, on the parchment. He pulled out the next page. It was definitely Ben's work and very different from the rendering of St Francis: he could see the apprentice's neat painting, each flower and leaf carefully coloured and outlined, though the shading had little subtlety. It was precise and correct, but somehow lacking.

He walked back to his desk, careful to avoid Gemma's eyes, though he could feel her looking at him.

'Still no malachite.' Nick returned alone. 'It's been so long now, and Harry doesn't see that it matters.' He walked, muttering, into the storeroom.

When John returned a few hours later, he was red-faced and looked unwell.

'John, sit down,' Gemma said. 'You shouldn't be wandering around in this weather. I'll get you a drink.'

'It's hot out there,' John agreed as he sat down. 'Hotter than you'd think from in here. So many lined up at Sewale's, never thought we'd get served.'

Gemma came back with a cup of water. 'Here, drink this, foolish man.'

'I saw Rowley Buxton down by the Guildhall. Parliament's still meeting, of course. All those powerful men — bishops, earls, barons and their lackeys — every one of them after their own gain.'

Will watched the sweat sitting in the lines of John's forehead, his mouth opening and closing, the dry white spittle in the corners. What was he talking about?

'That's not like you, John, to attack the powerful,' Will said.

Gemma heard scorn in his voice and stepped toward him, her eyes sharp. 'You have a problem, Will?'

He looked away awkwardly.

'So,' John went on more loudly, 'seems it's only days away and it'll all come snarling to our doorstep. Makes my bones shudder to think of the king's army meeting the Marchers only steps away from us. We'll be in the middle of a war.'

Gemma turned so quickly she knocked her brush and plummet onto the floor. 'They're really coming to our gates? I hoped parliament would sort it out.'

'What about Sir Robert? Is he with the lords?' Nick asked.

'Sir Robert?' Gemma broke in. 'You're worrying about Robert Fitzjohn? It's our Alice is the worry. Alice. The barons days away, you say?' She stepped toward John. 'Have you thought about Alice? I told her. I told her at the St Swithun's Day celebrations that she needs to stay with us until the threat's over. No city walls to protect her out there on the Strand. She'll have soldiers all round. They'll want places to stay, and nothing to stop them demanding the bishop play host.'

'But the house is behind St Mary's church, love, and those trees in front. They wouldn't even notice it's there,' John said in his mild way.

'That's what you'd like to think, but all those men, thousands of them, you said, have to stay somewhere.'

'Even so, Alice has the bishop with her. She'll be fine.'

'The Bishop of Llandaff? You know how old he is! He can barely see or hear. And it all depends how the Marcher barons feel about him. He's likely to be a supporter of Despenser. They'll sniff him out if they want to. Who knows what they'll do? What if the soldiers take a dislike to a Cardiff man and his household?' Her voice shook. 'Or a liking to his maid?'

John looked at Gemma as if he had seen her for the first time. 'Hadn't thought of it that way.'

'We have to get to her, bring her home, John. You have to go.'

'Yes. I will. I'll go now.' He turned to the door, an unusual urgency in his movements, and grasped at his knee as he opened the door.

Gemma took a step forward, as if wanting to stop him because he was unwell, but wanting him to go anyway. She turned, looked at Will, but said nothing.

Still thinking about John's pages, he had watched husband and wife talking, their mouths moving, their faces changing with the words, sounds that made no sense. As the door banged behind John, he began to slowly understand what they were saying. The danger coming toward them, the fear for Alice. He should have offered to go with John; there was still time, he could get up now and run after him. Yet he sat frozen, his mind full of borders breached, edges overrun.

15

London
July 1321

Depth

A limner takes what we see around us, people and objects that have substance, and renders their likeness on a flat piece of parchment. This is a skill best developed by close observation. The first step is to recognise when the person or object depicted is inside or outside a structure. Then perceive whether it is in front of or behind another person or object. This gives placement, position on the page. This may sound simple, but many times it is overlooked. A crowd is not a line, but a gathering where people stand behind as well as beside one another.

The greater skill is depicting an object or person so that it appears you might touch or hold it. Begin with the precise and subtle use of white and black to render shadow and light. When you have mastered some of this, begin to consider the face, its contours and colour, and think where a touch of white or grey will show not only its true shape, but its true emotion as well.

The Art of Illumination

Gemma's eyes were scratchy, wanting only to close, her limbs were sluggish, but somehow she was alert, shot through with worry. It was better to have her eyes open; behind her lids it was only soldiers with their boots on the table, slopping wine, demanding food, pulling Alice close to kiss her and lift her skirts, laughing. Even awake, she could almost hear the sounds of their carousing. It wasn't yet dawn and John was still in bed, snoring, though he had lain awake with her for hours, listening to her worries and trying to console her. Nothing helped.

She pulled the small bundle of pages from the bottom of the chest in the hall and lit a lamp at her desk. Her book on illumination was a comfort. In time she'd give it to Nick, show it to John, maybe Alice as well, if she'd look, but now it was hers alone, growing a few lines each turn of the week. At first she'd thought it would be a help to talk over her recipes and instructions with John before she wrote, but he had been bewildered by the idea.

'Why'd you bother with a book like that? There's others already, good ones, written by masters who've worked for years, longer even than me.'

'Longer even than you, John? I played with clam shells on this floor before I could walk. I stood on a stool and washed brushes and shells as soon as I could stand up. A year or two later I was mixing paint with Pa.'

'True enough, Gem. But why write it all again? We'll teach Nick the recipes.'

'I want to write more than the recipes. I want to write about what it means to be a limner, why it matters to work well, how to make the paintings … I don't know, I'll have to find the words. It's not only technique. Who's written about what makes an illumination special or what makes it sing? No one I know of. So I'll do it.'

'As you say, it's so hard to talk about. Why bother? It's simply work we do as best we can.' John smiled; she couldn't tell if it was humour or a fatherly patience. Either way, it was an answer she had no time for.

It was as well. Now, day by day, as she painted in the book of hours, she thought over the words she needed, then added a little more to the pages of her book. She was glad it would be hers alone. Her thoughts, her knowledge, her years of experience.

A knock at the door. She startled, half-asleep with her musing, stood up and knocked some pages to the floor. A constable? News of Alice? A soldier? Had the armies arrived? She bundled through the shop door, then paused, pulled the front door open a crack.

'Come on, Nick. Let me in.' It was Will's voice.

'Will!' She opened the door wider. 'What are you doing here so early? I thought … I didn't know who it was.' Her voice was hard with fright.

'Gemma! Oh, I couldn't sleep, so I thought I'd get to work on that illumination. I didn't think anyone would be up yet, planned to go round the back, see if I could rouse Nick. But I saw the light in the window …'

'Come in. I'll lock the door again.'

She followed him into the shop, and before she could stop him, he'd bent and picked up the pages she'd knocked off her desk.

'Leave them. They're mine.' Gemma pushed forward, reached out a hand.

Will could tell it wasn't the Fitzjohn commission; the pages were bigger, and the skin was rough, thick. Glancing at the sheets as he passed them over, he noticed the headings: *Sketching, Vermilion, Composition.* 'You have a new commission?'

Gemma gathered the other pages on her desk. 'No, not a commission. Something else.' How much had he seen?

'Ah.' Though desperate to know what it was, Will had at least learned enough about Gemma not to press her. He hoped she would explain, but Gemma held the pages to her chest and left the atelier. What were those words? Was she copying instructions of some kind? He hadn't realised she could write, though he knew of nuns who worked as scribes. And his mother knew how to write. But this, sketching, composition, pigments, this wasn't a book of prayers, or even romances. It had to be about illumination.

Hearing Gemma moving about in the hall, Will used the chance to quickly search the storeroom, looking for the St Francis pages he had seen the day before. They were nowhere to be found, had to be hidden. He'd look again later. He picked up his pages, though he knew he wouldn't be able to settle to work.

Plummet in hand, he barely noticed yesterday's small sketch of Samson with a lion inside the letter *S*, but began to draw in the margin, in simple fluid lines. A spiny hand wraps around the *d* at the beginning of *domino*. A body attaches itself, long and thin, hanging onto the word lest it fall off the page.

As Will's leadpoint played, the revelations of the past day, and now this morning, paraded themselves before him. Piece by piece, it seemed the atelier was false, traitorous. Yesterday it was the master's clumsy work, and today it was his wife's meddling with words about the craft. The same woman who behaved as a limner, sketching, applying gold leaf, even painting. It was clear that Southflete, the man who was building the London trade's reputation for quality, was being duped. As was Will. He had thought God was shining his face upon him, blessing him with work on this book, and with such a fine master, but it was all secrets and concealment. He worked long hours, gave his skill and experience to these people who took him for a fool.

The creature in the margin is wearing a shift, surely stolen from another, so short that its rounded, bare arse is hanging out. One leg dangles free, while the other clutches its claw-like toes to the letter *o*. Two horns grow from its head and beneath the rounded nose of a dog, or perhaps a monkey, it smiles, all sweetness. But its eyes tell another story. Will focused on what his hand had drawn. Just who was this Master John Dancaster?

Gemma walked back into the shop expecting more questions from Will, but there was nothing. He was absorbed, apparently unaware of her. She sighed, relieved, but the silence had an edge. She couldn't concentrate any more. Will had seen something; she'd noticed him pause to look. Would he tell John? That wouldn't matter, though if he spread the news elsewhere …

So many times she had seen Will looking across at her desk, peering at her work. He knew she was doing more than touching up the edges of John's illuminations, or painting on gesso. How ambitious was this man? He'd plied John with ale to get work on the book; would he tell Southflete about the meddling woman, working above her position, playing with paint when she should be cleaning? Would he keep quiet, if she asked him?

She wiped the back of her neck; so early and already so hot. Let him wonder. She would say nothing. He had been closed enough about his own past, after all. A man with a secret could be dangerous, though.

She started to work, adding dabs of colour to an illumination she had already finished, wasting time, pretending. Thoughts buzzed in her ear; she swatted them away and they buzzed again. What had Will seen yesterday in the storeroom that had seemed to unsettle him? She wouldn't listen to the answer. Not now. It had been hard enough accepting the truth about John, that truth she had resisted so long. She wouldn't defend him to another.

The gate was shut already, though the bell for Nones had only just finished ringing. She had to bribe her way out. Bart the guard knew her, but still said he needed money. 'The risk,' he said. 'Case I get caught and lose me job.' Gemma paid, as John had paid the night before. What good business war is for some, she thought.

Head bent, sweat trickling down her face, between her breasts, she walked quickly. It's real, she thought. The barons are coming. The city lived right outside the Dancaster door, and they knew most of what went on, but there was something about painting that made the atelier a world apart.

Perhaps John, outside so often and separated from the pages, understood it better than the rest of them.

It wasn't Alice at the door, but an older woman, her words short. She was in a hurry. Alice was occupied, she said; her father had visited yesterday. Was that not sufficient? She kept the door half-closed.

'He didn't understand how serious the situation is,' Gemma said. 'You understand, I'm sure, a mother's fear for her daughter's safety. I'll need only a few moments to talk to her.' She paused. 'Though I wonder, are you not worried yourself about the barons coming? So much work on the wall. It's serious. There's bound to be battle in the streets. And the soldiers, hundreds and hundreds, they say, will be looking for food and a bed somewhere.' She gestured into the hall she could barely see. 'Like here.'

The woman frowned. 'The bishop is praying for protection. I'm sure the Lord will guard us from the godless rabble that threatens our peace. Our Lord protects the just.'

Gemma felt pressure in her chest, but held it there, refused to allow it to become words. 'Of course. No doubt God hears the Bishop of Llandaff and will answer his prayers. But God also bids us act to defend the innocent. Girls like Alice, who might not understand—'

'Are you suggesting that the bishop will not fulfil his duty to his housemaid?'

'No, of course not. I'm asking that you allow Alice to come home until the danger here is passed. One less person for the bishop to worry about.' Gemma smiled weakly. 'Please, just let me speak with her. And the bishop himself, perhaps.'

The woman sighed and crossed her arms.

'Not possible. I told you, Alice is busy.'

'I think I've explained my concern. As a godly woman, I hope you—'

'Hope for nothing but your salvation. I cannot stand at the door arguing.'

'I'm not arguing. I'm asking.'

'And now you need to leave. Alice has no interest in returning home and I will not bandy words any longer. Go back to your husband.' The door closed in Gemma's face.

Without thinking, Gemma banged on the door again. There was no answer, so she kept banging until it opened again. It was the same face, impassive.

'Please, just—' Gemma began.

'Leave! Or I'll call the gardener to haul you away to the constable.' The woman's voice was hard, loud.

The slamming door made Gemma flinch, but she lifted her arm, fist clenched to thump at it again, then let it drop. Tears stung her eyes. The pain of frustration, impotence, stepping day by day around others. She'd stop trying, let them all handle things themselves: John, Alice, Nick, Benedict. She turned from the grand house.

Suddenly exhausted, drained of feeling, she walked to the river's edge, lifted her face to the breeze across the water. Further along the river, the bustle of men crawling over the docks and ships, loading, unloading, wearing themselves out in the business of living. Their shouts drifted toward her, then faded away. Had they brought malachite from some place where people loaded and unloaded ships just like this, wearing themselves out in the same way? Why was she up early and to bed late, worrying for others?

And then, a voice nearby. Alice. That ugly woman had changed her mind, brought Alice to the door. Gemma rushed back, but no, the door was shut. In the lane beside the house, Gemma followed the wall protecting the garden; yes, again, that was Alice speaking. Gemma called out, taking a chance that Alice was in the yard, maybe tending the vegetables and fruit trees, maybe collecting eggs.

'Ma?' the wall said. 'Is that you?'

'Alice. I need to talk to you. Is there a gate, some way we can talk?'

'No. And don't shout. Judith will hear. Go further back, away from the house. There's no gate.'

Gemma walked along the lane looking up at the wall. Here, an apple tree reached over, and here, ivy, dry and brittle in the heat, crawled along the bricks. And here, the wall had begun to crumble, almost enough to allow Gemma to see in. Gathering the fallen bricks into an awkward pile, she climbed onto it, hanging on to the ivy and calling to her daughter.

'What are you doing, Ma? Do you know what trouble you'll give me?' The girl's hair and forehead, then her eyes, appeared in a gap.

'Alice, this is important. Seems that … Judith, is it? Seems Judith and the bishop have no idea what's coming.'

'What? Have you spoken to them? At the door? God's teeth! Pa came last night.'

'Listen. Soldiers, there will be, hundreds of them at our city, but the gates will be locked. There'll be battles, most like. And the soldiers will need places to stay.'

'So? What's that to do with me?'

'Don't play the fool, Alice. I know you understand what it means. Come home, just for a few days, until this is over.'

'I can't do that.'

'The bishop is going to pray for safety, Judith says. What will that do when a soldier takes a fancy to you?'

'Ma, don't—'

'Don't pretend with me, girl. You know what can happen.'

'I'm working for the bishop. I live here, not at your house. Leave me alone for once. Now go.'

Alice disappeared and moments later the door banged. Gemma slipped from her awkward perch and trudged home, tears in the dusty sweat on her face.

16

London
July 1321

Proportion

It is clear that an object in the distance will appear smaller than one that is closer. However, in a decorated book, our interest is not with rendering the world as it appears to the eye, but to show relationships of power, hierarchy and importance. Some figures or buildings will be bigger than others, and Christ and Mary are drawn larger than angels and humans. Where, in real life, a large figure may seem more powerful, on the page its true nature can be shown through the limner's choice of size and position.

The Art of Illumination

It was not quite dawn and already the air was warm and thick, trapped tight between the London houses. The marketplaces were full of people escaping their hot rooms, their restless night. The heat and the threat seemed like one force pressing closer, and there was no sense to the city. Everywhere people were nailing up their shutters, taking inside anything that could be stolen, shushing their children, telling them to stay nearby, warning of the coming danger. And yet there they were, out in the streets, talking and selling and arguing. Too hot to stay indoors, too afraid and frustrated to be civil to their neighbours. In the Poultry, two women were fighting over the price of a cockerel, the buyer trying to snatch its feet from the seller, the bird squawking and snapping between them. Children scratched and bit in the rough queue for water from the Great Conduit. Just past Mercer's Hall, a group of regulars was gathered around Ralph's stall, abusing him for putting up the price of his fish pies. 'Then go somewhere else!' he shouted, trying for bravado, knowing they needed to eat. Cursing him, they handed over their coins.

The Marcher lords had moved closer still, past St Albans, but that wasn't the only threat. Any unease made the fragile order of the city weaker. Though everyone spoke of the danger riding toward them, there was as much, or more, seething inside the city's locked gates. The mayor had appointed extra constables to protect the people, but there were even more men patrolling the streets, self-appointed and dangerous, ready for a fight, using the fear and unrest to their advantage.

Will walked quickly. The weather was different, the tensions were different, the coming crisis so much more dangerous, but the feeling was the same as in Cambridge a year or so earlier. A spark here, Will thought, would set fire to the buildings; a wrong word would set fire to the people. The city's roiling mood seemed at one with his own. Ever since he had seen John's work, and Gemma's hidden commission, he could think of nothing else. The atelier was not the place it pretended to be; John was not the master his fame proclaimed. What had happened? Will had seen his work in Cambridge, studied it.

He looked up. Two men, clubs in hand, were standing on the corner by St Augustine's, watching him approach down Watling Street. As he drew closer, they lifted their clubs just a little, daring him, then eyed him as he passed. He felt their stare on his back until he turned into Old Change and out of sight, hoping they weren't following him. As he passed St Paul's, he couldn't see much in the pre-dawn gloom, but he could hear the scrape of stone legs crawling down the wall, could feel the creep of bulbous eyes on his skin. He hoped the shop was open.

* * *

Gemma let him in without comment and went back to her
desk.

He stood in the doorway of the storeroom, suddenly
awkward. He had been so angry, so determined to confront
her, but the sight of her pale face and red-rimmed eyes made
him hesitate. The woman was exhausted. 'I thought the birds
would have left,' he said, suddenly aware of how foolish he
sounded.

'Birds?' Gemma said, without moving.

'Can't you hear them? Because of the danger. I thought
they'd sense it and fly away. But I just realised they were
singing as I walked here, and now it's getting lighter, they're
even louder.'

Gemma lifted her head to listen. The chirping was strong,
tuneful. She glanced at Will, her eyes questioning, and bent
to the page again.

'Any news of Alice?' Will asked.

Gemma shook her head.

'The bishop will look after her ...' His words collapsed
as the woman looked up at him, challenging him to keep
pretending. 'It must be hard for you. A worry,' he added and
collected his pages.

The capital of Samson and the lion was complete, and the
page needed only some turnsole blue on the shields in the
border. Will sighed. It always made him cross, spending time
and detail on these dull shapes with their marks of privilege.
He looked toward Gemma, tried to discover what she was
working on, but she had turned to one side. Whatever she
was doing, it was probably more than tidying up the edges of
John's work.

It rolled around in his belly again. So much seemed
hidden from him. Why should he be afraid to ask? 'I've been
wondering. John. Is he well?'

Gemma looked up.

'He seems unhappy,' he went on. 'With his work, I mean. He's so often away, as if he doesn't want the work. But I can see how important it is to him, how much he wants the decorations to be beautiful. It makes no sense.'

Gemma examined the tip of her brush. Here it was. 'You see John every day. You can see he's well. He's busy, has people to visit, is all.'

'I've seen some of his work. Before I came here, and it was magnificent. Then, just days past ... by chance, really, I saw his page of St Francis. The difference, Gemma. It's clear there's something wrong.'

Gemma's gaze felt like a slap on his face, then she bent again to her work. An uneasy quiet took over.

Gemma wanted to stand up and scream, throw brushes, knife, parchment and paint onto the floor; she wanted them all to leave her alone. Benedict with his particular ways; Nick with his sacred apprenticeship that Alice couldn't have; Will with his smug skill and his questions about John; Southflete with his talk of quality and his precious plans for a guild. And John, John most of all, with his illness and his pretending everything was fine. John, who expected her to do it all for him. Still. Again. While he was the one praised for his talent. Why couldn't they all leave her alone to get on with the work?

Wasn't it enough that she'd given in, faced the fact of John's illness, even when he wouldn't?

And now, did she have to lie to Will as well? Make up some story? She studied his bent head, the slight wave in his hair, the smooth and careful movements of his hand. She couldn't trust him; he'd walk out, go straight to London Bridge, tell Southflete the alarming news that would win him favour, and who knows what else. But she'd had enough of pretending. He'd seen John's work. He knew he couldn't paint any more. She had to deal with it.

Will startled when she spoke. 'Have a look.' She picked up a parchment sheet from her desk. The page had a wide decorated border and a small capital surrounded by curlicues. As with the painting of St Francis that Will had seen a week ago, paint was smudged beyond the borders and the colours were bold with no shading. Will blanched, felt the shock anew, had nothing to say.

In that moment, exposing John's work to someone who might not understand, Gemma's anger collapsed into a deep sadness. 'He was the best limner I've ever seen. Such a light touch with colour,' she said.

'I know, I've seen. Master Edgar had two of his illuminations, and he showed me often, used them to teach me about detail and shading and such.'

'My pa — John was apprentice with my pa — said it came natural to him. And John always said it was a gift from God. He doesn't say what he thinks about this, though.'

'What should be done, do you think?'

'Nothing. John won't talk about it, so I fix the pages when I get time. When he's not here, of course. That's all that can be done.' She held Will's gaze. 'Say nothing about it. Especially not to Southflete.'

'He doesn't know?'

'Of course not. Him and his chant about quality. He knows that the last year or two John stayed longer in the tavern than in the shop. When Fitzjohn, or Lady Mathilda, in truth, asked for John to decorate the book, said it had to be him and no one else, Southflete made John vow to give up his long hours in the tavern. He thinks that's the problem. Southflete seemed content when John agreed. But he worries that John's hours out of the shop mean he's in the Peter and Paul. That's why he comes here, noses around. I know John hasn't been slipping out of the shop to drink; the commission is too important to him. And if the work's done, Southflete lets us be.'

'And if he looks, he thinks you're tidying over John's minor mistakes.'

'Yes. He'd never believe I could do that kind of work.' She smiled wearily. 'So we must do nothing to make him take notice of us. You understand the commission depends on that. We'd all be out of work.'

Will nodded. The shadow that had hovered for the past days settled over him. It was as bad as he had imagined.

'I've managed it so far,' Gemma said, almost to herself.

'So only you know, Gemma?' Will asked.

'Yes. It's been hardest this year. In the past there was less to do.'

Will felt the ground shift beneath him. Whose work had he and Master Edgar admired back in Cambridge?

'How long, Gemma?'

She said nothing.

'Gemma, how long has there been a problem?'

Eventually she spoke. 'Three, maybe four years. As I say, it wasn't so bad at first. It's been a slow failing. His eyes …'

'And John won't admit it?'

'He must know,' she snapped. 'You've seen it. He stays away from his desk when he can, busies himself so it looks like he's working. In truth, it's a mercy that he doesn't paint more.'

Will lapsed into silence. He wanted to know more, but he didn't know how to find a place for it. He'd been taken for a fool. No longer was he working with master limner John Dancaster, but with his wife. He couldn't sit still, couldn't summon careful words, couldn't stay in the shop. And most of all, he couldn't face Master Dancaster.

Outside, Will blinked in the morning sun. The streets were much the same, but everything had changed. He walked past the cathedral, and didn't even look around when he heard the scurry of stone legs on the cobblestones behind him. Right into Old Change; he looked for the men standing outside

St Augustine's. They were still there. He walked toward them, staring into their faces, his fists clenched. Come on, do it. Give me a reason to punch.

The men raised their clubs. The one on the left, his jaw wide, his eyes close together, stepped forward, tapping his club against his free hand. Will moved closer, chest out.

'Gotta problem?' the man said.

'I do. I don't like you watching me.'

'That right?'

'Aren't you that limner with the big hands?' the second man said. 'Heard talk of you. They say you can best most men at a wrestling match, but in the day you put a tiny paintbrush in those big paws.'

Will stepped his left foot forward, raised his right fist and swung as the second man lunged with his club, hooking it behind his right leg, throwing him off balance. As he fell, the first man punched him, hitting his left temple and bringing him to the ground. Before Will could protect himself, they rolled him onto his stomach, both arms pinned behind his back.

Will struggled, furious, but they held him down. He could be under the oak at Cambridge.

'Look, you're a big ugly churl with something to prove, but you can't prove it here. We're not interested in fighting you. Why don't you go back to your desk and little brushes?' They pulled him to his feet, dusted him down with exaggerated care.

As he walked away, Will could hear their laughter. His face and neck pulsing, he continued down Watling Street, onto Candlewick Street, past St Swithun's and right onto London Bridge. The gargoyle kept him slimy company. The warm breeze blowing through the buildings cooled his sweat and he stopped outside the shop with an elaborate painted sign of a book and pen. He'd tell Southflete; what else could he do? They'd made a fool of him, making him work unknowingly for a woman. With a woman. The stationer would be grateful, the deceit exposed. Probably let him finish the book himself.

He'd be known as the man who painted the glorious Fitzjohn book of hours. The man who found out about Dancaster. Wat, Manekyn, even Rowley and Peter Binder would buy him a drink, tell him … No, whatever he told himself, he knew the fraternity wouldn't slap him on the back. They loved John. He walked on, but soldiers were guarding the Southwark end, so he walked back. Three times he paused outside Southflete's shop; three times he walked away. He'd visit Sabine's instead.

Watling Street was quieter than usual, and wary. Ettie was still taking laundry, but next door, Gaspard the silversmith had his door locked, a bull of a man on guard outside.

Sabine wasn't open yet, and she had no patience with Will's mixture of anger and pleading. She especially had no interest in cleaning the cut over his eye, now covered in dried blood. 'Go back to work, Will, or go home. Else you'll get one to match the other side.'

The workshop that seemed impossible to warm had gradually become unbearably hot. For days the door and front shutter had been closed and bolted — 'for the dust,' John had said, and no one believed him.

Benedict opened the front door. 'Will, you're late. Thought you weren't coming today either.' Then, seeing the man's face, 'What have you been doing, brawling again?'

Will ignored him.

'Will, we missed you yesterday,' John said.

'We were working hard early on, weren't we, Will,' Gemma cut in. 'Did our day's work before anyone else turned up.'

'That's right,' Will said quietly and walked to his desk, through air sticky as treacle.

Suddenly, shouting and swearing, the meaty thud of punches, the scuff of feet and running, pursued and pursuers. Everyone in the shop paused, looked up, waited. But the brawl, whatever it was, passed by.

'Nick, I need some more of that green,' Benedict called.

When there was no answer from the storeroom, John said, 'Perhaps he's out back, cleaning them vine leaves? I'll take a look.' But barely a minute later, he returned. 'He's gone. Out the back and over the wall, little brat.'

'I told him to stay indoors,' Gemma said. 'God's teeth! I told him.'

'As did I, love. But he'll be fine. You know the lad, quick as a squirrel up a tree, he is.'

'The soldiers could be here any time,' she went on, as if John hadn't spoken. 'That's what they're saying. And our boy out there.'

Will worked, distracted, finishing the shields he had abandoned the previous morning. He watched John sit at his desk and squint at a page, pick up his brush and dab at it. How hard it must be for him to paint so badly. He'd thought he could learn so much from this man and his genius, could make a name as one of his atelier, but those hopes had been destroyed. A trickle of sweat ran down the centre of his back and he wiped his face. No whisper of breeze. The hot weather, the arrogant barons keeping them all captive, and now John and Gemma's deceit. Had he walked so far on that frozen road for this? He stood up. 'That's a gathering finished,' he said, and carried a double page to the storeroom. 'Hardly need to hang this; it's so hot, it'll be dry already.'

'Good work, Asshe. Let me have a word about the next one,' John said. 'Just look through those gatherings there and find me the Complaint of Our Lady, will you? The first lines will be something about Mary living for fifteen years after Jesus ascended. It should be easy to find.'

Will pulled out a gathering at random. 'Is it this one?' he asked, holding the bundle of eight folded pages about an arm's length from John's face.

John looked away. 'You should be able to see yourself, Asshe. I told you the first lines.'

'Well, I'm not sure, John. You should check. Have a look.' He was behaving like a stubborn boy, stamping his foot. But so was John, wasn't he?

Gemma shook her head at him. 'Just find the pages, Will,' she said quietly.

'Enough of the foolishness, Asshe. Find the pages,' echoed John.

His voice was no louder, but it reminded Will of his first time in the workshop when John had threatened Benedict with not signing off on his apprenticeship. He found the correct pages and took the gathering to John's desk.

He could feel Gemma watching him as the flush slowly faded from his face, though his whole being still pulsed with anger. Or defiance. Whatever it was. Not pity.

'Ah, good,' John said, as if nothing had happened. 'I want you to decorate this series of pages. They're not prayers. They're devotions called the Complaint of Our Lady. It's the story of Christ's suffering, from his betrayal through to his death on the cross, and all told by his mother, Mary, as if she's talking to Lady Mathilda in person.' He turned the pages as he spoke. 'See? It's a series of twelve. These will be different from most of the other illuminations. You need to keep each one simple. No creatures or flourishes, just one illumination and the border. I want this sequence to be beautiful, full of grace, your very best work. I know Gemma says a lot about the place of the pictures, and she's right, but your pictures here need to make space for the words that Mary speaks. No distractions. Let Lady Mathilda hear Mary's voice.'

'So the words are more important than our work? Is that what you're saying?' Will asked. He knew he sounded sulky, once more the fourteen-year-old being berated in Cambridge, the boy who had wanted, who still wanted, to argue with Edgar's idea that the pictures were handmaids of the words.

'I don't know what you mean, Asshe. Importance? It makes no sense. They're both on the page, aren't they? Both there for the woman to read. They serve each other, surely. Just the way borders and illuminations serve each other, eh Benedict?'

Benedict nodded, then looked at Will and smiled. Will's face blazed.

'So. As I said, keep the paintings simple.'

'But each of those scenes is complex, with lots of people. They're full of—'

'Exactly. Tragedy, emotion, action. That's why you need to do it. You understand so well how to design that kind of picture, how to show the crowd and the atmosphere. I've never been able to do that, not the way you can.'

How do you know? Will thought. You can't see clearly what I paint. Gemma must have told you. It always seemed she thought little of my work.

'But remember,' John went on, 'you need to focus all that feeling and make space for the story itself. Find the main concern of Mary's words and let the picture reflect that. Think of Jesus' entry into Jerusalem. The crowd cheers at Jesus, but Mary knows it will turn against him. So the drawing needs to show both the crowd's adoration and Mary's sense of the danger when that adoration turns sour.'

Gemma looked up suddenly, alarmed. Did John understand what he was saying? And to this dangerous man?

Will nodded and walked to his desk. His thoughts were tangled. He hadn't expected such deep understanding from John, though this was not the first time he'd heard his wisdom. It was almost as if he'd begun to believe that John's failing sight had blighted his brain. But the man was not a buffoon. Master illuminator, he understood so well how the pictures would best serve the words and the reader. But still ... still, he felt stung, betrayed.

The room settled again into its hot, gasping silence.

Will decided it was too hot to paint; the brush would only slip in his sweaty hands. He'd plan the pages, do all the sketches first. Drawing Jesus' entry into Jerusalem surrounded by an excited crowd was the kind of challenge he liked, and the movements of his hands gradually cleared his mind of other thoughts.

In the drawing, Jesus rides into Jerusalem on a donkey. His face is still, passive; but he is aware of the crowd. His head, tipped to one side, is an omen of the Crucifixion to come days later, pages further on. The people cheer him, proclaim his greatness, but there is danger. Such acclamation so easily turns to disappointment, even hatred. Faces are pressed together, those at the front distinct, different from each other; one frowns. Behind them, only foreheads and eyes are visible, straining to see the messiah. Palm leaves wave and curl above the crowd, a sequence of repeated lines bending in the same direction, with here and there a leaf curling the other way.

Will paused to check the effect: yes, it was what he wanted. He couldn't explain exactly why, but the frown among the cheering, the break in the pattern of leaves, suggested unease and threat.

Clattering and shouting. Nick burst through the back door, dirt clinging to his sweaty skin.

'It's the barons from the Marches. Came like they said they would. Hundreds and hundreds of them all around the city walls. There's so many of them, Pa. They're not allowed inside the wall, and our soldiers are everywhere on every gate to keep them out. I went around to all of them. They're all shut.'

Nick's excited chatter seemed to bounce off the walls, fill the air. The four adults kept working as they listened, slowly becoming aware that the looming threat of war was now lodged outside the gates only a street or two away.

'I saw Wat at Holborn. He says there are meetings. The barons are demanding the king gets rid of Despenser. The leaders are Mortimer, Hereford, Audley and another one.'

'Damory, that would be. What about Lancaster?' John said.

'That's it. Damory. Dunno about Lancaster. Do you think Sir Robert would be there?'

'He might be somewhere, but not at the meetings with the barons. Not important enough for that, Nick.'

'So there might be a battle? Here?'

'Don't wish that on us, lad,' John said. 'Never wish for war, especially at our gates. And it's the king they'd be fighting. Their own king, anointed by God. That'd be civil war. Let's hope they'll find a way out of it.'

'And our Alice out there, surrounded by soldiers.'

'I know. But we tried, Gem. We both tried. No more we can do. The girl is headstrong, knows what she wants.'

'Aye, but she doesn't know what soldiers can do to a young girl.' Gemma turned and ran out the door.

John watched her go. 'Now, Nick,' he said roughly, 'get on with your work. That's a day wasted.'

Will watched in silence. Gemma was right, he thought. Bishop or no, the soldiers wouldn't be denied their ease and play. He looked at John, master limner, brush in hand, peering at a page.

How had he not seen it from the beginning? The strain on John's face, his eyes narrowed, the uncertain movements of the paintbrush. Tomorrow, or the next day, or the next, Gemma would unmake all that John was making.

Will wanted to stand up and shout, drag him away from his desk, shake him, make him acknowledge his illness. But he couldn't. How much was the man's reputation worth? What would Southflete say?

He turned to the next page with Manekyn's rushed script in the blank space: *Last Supper*, and next to it, his neat, clear script intended for Lady Mathilda. Mary's words, her memory of Jesus' last evening with his disciples, described how much he had understood of what was to come: *My sweet son said, 'The one who touches my dish with me is the very one.'* The one who would betray Jesus to the men thirsty to kill him.

A rasping sound of grinding stone made him look up. It was in the corner, lifting one stumpy leg and then another, its eyes unblinking, focused on Will. He looked away, then back again. It was crawling across the ceiling now, just above Benedict's head.

'What are you looking at? Inspiration on the ceiling?' Benedict asked with a smile.

Will looked down. There was nothing he could have done that night. The dark, the freezing water, then the snow. To make the stony gaze go away, he picked up the plummet and drew.

Thirteen at the table would be too many. He needed to show that they were close to each other, talking about who would betray Jesus. Lady Mathilda should see their faces, each one different, each worrying about the man they loved. Would he be arrested? Would he die? Who would betray him? He'd include just a few apostles: John closest to Jesus, then two either side, and Judas at the front, slightly apart from the rest. Guilty. Betrayer. With his thirty pieces of silver. A cup fallen, its wine spilt.

Yes, this was what the words needed: the gathering of those who loved each other, the heavy, crowding sense of impending disaster, the grief of what was to come, of all that would be lost. It was Judas who would betray Jesus. Judas, his close friend who admired him, who ate and drank with him, talked and learned from him. Who shared his dream for a time, but would give it up — give his friend up — to the soldiers.

Mathilda

Joan and Maggie are giggling over the book, pointing to the creature with a man's head and chest, the legs and feet of a dragon, and a tail that extends and curls, gradually becoming a stem thick with leaves and fruit.

'Look,' Maggie says, 'that man's picking berries from his own tail and putting them into the basket on his arm. Just think, if we could grow our own food on our tails.'

'I wonder how he waters them,' Joan says. 'I bet he pisses on them,' and the two bend over, limp with laughter.

Mathilda is relieved to see them so merry, forgetting for a while this strange state they're in, hiding from the king's anger. If Robert were still alive, if she still lived in his grand house and helped to manage his land, the label of traitor's wife would make more sense. But so much of that is gone. The king has a bailiff at Aspenhill, and the lands in the Welsh Marches are lost to her.

She knows the girls have heard the talk around the house. How could they not? But the word 'traitor' is a difficult one. She has heard Ysmay explaining to them that a traitor is someone who doesn't play the game properly, like the boy who peeks when playing hoodman blind, but even worse. Like the boy who promises to be on your side and then changes because he thinks the other side has a better chance of winning. Mathilda told Ysmay to be quiet and mind her work, but it was too late; all her explanations to the girls about loyalty and property and rights, about loving the king and fighting for him even if it didn't look like that, even to the king himself — all were wasted after Ysmay's examples.

Oliver sends word from London that the king's retribution against the rebel barons seems to be coming to an end. Some noblewomen are still in the Tower, and likely to stay for a time, but he hasn't heard of any more being hunted down. 'It appears that you and your children will be safe if you remain at Wain Wood, but do not rouse the king's attention.' He goes on to inform her that Edmund Fitzjohn, Robert's nephew, has died of the illness that had weakened him for some time.

Mathilda blanches; she had forgotten about Edmund, the man Robert was fighting for. They had ordered the book on the prospect of Robert inheriting his lands. Now both men are dead.

Days pass, each one the same as the last, though the weather is warming and the sense of threat is beginning to fade; the soldiers in her mind are creatures of frost and ice, so it's difficult to imagine them marching in sunlight. They'd soon soften and melt, become puddles in the road. Thoughts of a madwoman, surely. Danger comes to the door, whatever the weather.

She and the children go outside sometimes, but only into the small kitchen garden, and that is enough for her. The bees fly among the mustard plants, and a few other herbs — fennel, chamomile and mint, she recognises — are putting out delicate tendrils, recovering after being burned by the hoar frost early in the year. Mathilda pulls out weeds and gathers soil to cover the roots of plants exposed by the heavy rains. She will ask Caine, the gardener, to bring some straw and sheep dung to put around them; she can see where he has begun planting the vegetable garden in neat rows, though the shoots are tiny still. Shouts and laughter, the bleats of lambs and the noises of people working drift up to her from the village. Children yell and call, and a flock of crows flies overhead. Mathilda looks up; the birds have been shooed away from feasting on the new seed. It's cloudy, but there are patches of blue, and though she has made a nest of this captivity, she knows it can't remain that way. The baby moves, as if it knows her thoughts.

The girls play a game with sticks and pebbles they've gathered. With passing time, and only whispered mention of Robert, they seem to be slowly understanding that their father isn't coming back. Joan talks about death more often now, her eyes still, her forehead wrinkled, as if she is trying to make herself understand it. When they look at the illumination of the Crucifixion, she and Maggie become sombre. Maggie says 'Dead' as if it now means something to her; Joan thinks Jesus' sad eyes look a bit like Pa's.

'And that lady. That's Mary, isn't it?' Joan says, pointing to a figure in the top left corner, her gown blue, her hands clasped on her chest. The few lines for her mouth and eyes are full of sorrow.

They talk about the angels playing trumpets and lutes painted around the edges of the picture, about Jesus going to heaven. Then they laugh at the funny man in the border, his bearded head on top of an animal's body with big paws and a tail. The girls make up stories about him climbing among the vines and flowers.

Mathilda can't tell them why he is there, gazing on the death and sorrow. 'I suppose the whole world was sad when Jesus died,' she says.

Some of the heaviness in her limbs is lifting. She is easier since Oliver told her the reprisals were ending, but this new feeling is more than the ending of struggle. God knows there's more to come. Is it being with child that is changing her? The baby moves more often now, its flutters turning to stirring and now and then a kick. It's time to tell the girls.

'We will have a new baby some time after Michaelmas. A tiny baby.'

Joan looks serious, but Maggie keeps on playing. She has built a moat around a stack of stones and wants to fill it with water.

'So we'll all be very busy looking after it,' Mathilda says. 'Will you help me, Joanie?'

Joan nods. 'Yes. But it won't like being in this house all the time.'

'I think by then we'll be able to go out. To the market, or to town. I think that soon we might go to the village.'

'The market? Can we go to market? Can we, Ma?' Maggie jumps up.

'There's a baby, Maggie. That's what Ma's saying.'

'Mmm.' Maggie goes back to her moat, scratching in the dirt to make the channel deeper.

'It won't have a father,' Joan says.

'Well, no. But it will have you and Maggie, and Angmar and Ysmay, and Fraden and Cornell and Godwin and Caine.'

'And Matt, the reeve. But Fraden isn't here.'

'No, he's gone to our old house just to see how it is. He'll be back soon. Do you want to feel the baby move?'

Joan shakes her head and Maggie runs to the kitchen for water for her moat. Mathilda hears her telling Ysmay about the baby.

'Yes child, I know,' Ysmay says. 'That babe will be among us by Michaelmas, you see.'

Three days later, Fraden returns from Aspenhill. The news isn't good, but it's what they expected.

'I told the cook I was a traveller and mistook my way to London, asked for ale and bread, a place in the barn for the night. She gave me food, and I looked around outside, but I couldn't see inside the house, except the kitchen. It looked much the same. Dirtier. And the gardens not tended.'

'And the village?'

'Well enough. Better now the weather warms. Some of the men died in the battles. Hugh Penifader, Richard Miller, John Hirdman and his young Richard — remember him, still a lad? They didn't come back. John Golle is home, but can't work.'

'John and Thea Beecroft. How are they?'

'John's gone and Thea gets by, but I don't think she's got long.'

'No, well. Did you meet the bailiff?'

'Nah, stayed well away. Naught to be gained by talking to him. He's fair enough, John Golle says, for a king's man. Though it's early days. There's Harvest and Michaelmas yet. Have to wait and see how much he makes them bleed the little they have. The king ...' He stops, shrugs his shoulders.

Mathilda nods: no point saying again what they already know. King's taxes, Despenser's greed. She shivers.

'And the dovecote?' she asks.

'The dovecote? I didn't look.'

'My father, is all. My father built it,' Mathilda says, feeling herself blush.

'I did bring this, though.' Fraden pulls a spoon from his bag and hands it to Mathilda.

'Ah.' She runs her fingers over the tiny human shape formed at the end of the handle, then the outlines of fish etched into its bowl. 'A wedding present, this was.'

Fraden nods. 'When the cook went out for water I crept into the kitchen. It is yours, after all.' He turns to Joan and Maggie standing nearby. 'And I found this. Dropped in the garden.' He holds out a closed fist, then turns it over and opens his fingers.

'My bird!' Joan takes it, makes its wings and tail move.

'It's my bird,' Maggie says. 'Mine.'

'You lost it in the garden. And it was mine first.'

'Now you have to share it,' Mathilda says, and takes it from Joan, feels the weight of the lead in her hand, the fine ripples of its etched feathers. 'Don't lose it. The baby will love to play with it.' She avoids Fraden's eyes, but she's aware of him looking up quickly.

'But it's mine,' Maggie says, and walks away.

'The girls must find these walls very narrow,' Fraden says. 'It's Rogationtide in two days. Perhaps Godwin and I could take them to the village?'

'Ooh, yes,' Joan says. 'Can we go?'

Mathilda stands by the front gate and watches the little company walk down the track from the manor house to join the line of people trailing around the edges of the village. Snatches of laughter and words float up the hill to her; this is a serious ritual, but a procession of any kind is fun, Mathilda thinks, especially for those near the tail. She is fascinated by the way the long worm of villagers continually changes its shape, but somehow stays together. The priest and those carrying the parish banner and cross lead the way; those just behind them and at the very end of the line carry bells that they shake, some in a rhythm, some in a long rolling peal. The messy centre of the procession bristles with small swaying trees: branches the young boys carry and beat against the stones that mark the boundaries of the village.

They walk around the eastern edge, disappearing from view behind trees or a hillock and reappearing. Every now and then they all stop, and though Mathilda can see only a tangle of bodies, a scuffle, she knows the men will make sure the boys remember the edges of their small world by beating it into their bodies, knocking their heads against stones, dragging them through hedges and streams, emphasising the markers of the village boundaries. It's brutal, and necessary, and it's what they've always done.

'It's the lads' job to remember the village boundaries,' her father had said to her when she was no older than Maggie and argued that it was mean. 'You need to know this for when you're grown and helping look after your husband's estate.'

'That you will,' John Beecroft had added. 'Who's to know when those in Croxton'll shift the stones to steal more land. Ten years or more back, they moved 'em, bit by bit, would've taken all our land if we hadn't stopped 'em. Our lads need to know it in their bones, keep the memory of the land.'

She had shrugged then, but only a year or so later in the procession she had laughed at Hugh Tulke yelling and crying, blood running down his face. She had never liked him.

Will they be beating the bounds at Fordham this year, she wonders? How many men and lads remain? She thinks of the ways men take each other's land: in battle, barons against kings, or little by little, villagers against villagers. Aspenhill Manor, her home since childhood, had seemed part of her body and it was taken.

The bells and shouting stop and she looks up. At the far end of the village, past the mill and the bridge, the priest lifts his arms, a jar in his hands, and prays. Mathilda doesn't need to hear the words: Look down upon your people with mercy, Lord, dispel the evil that brings floods and frost and suffering to our land, bless this earth we plant with seed, give our animals health and multiply their offspring. The bells ring furiously to drive away threats and carry the prayers. Maggie is dancing, she can see, but Joan stops her as the priest casts the jar onto stones, holy water spilling onto the soil. The people cheer, some beginning to dance.

For the first time since she has arrived at Wain Wood, Mathilda begins to think about them as something more than 'the village'. This is her estate, her responsibility now.

London
August 1321

Yellow

Yellow is a symbol of renewal and hope, but use these pigments with care.

Orpiment, dug from the ground as stone, has a sparkle like gold, and has led many an alchemist to spend his days seeking to extract its tiny grains of the precious metal. The limner may also be drawn to its lustre, but like the rich man, orpiment will not mix well with others; it will attack verdigris and white lead, and maybe the glair itself.

In its place, use a colour from the ranks of commoners. Bile yellow, also called the gold of Lombard, is made from the bile of fish or gallstones. Massicot is a yellow that emerges when white lead is prepared by roasting minium or red lead; it is most useful in lightening green without turning the hue toward brown.

Mosaic gold or porporina is formed by the careful and prolonged heating of tin and sulphur until sparkles of gold hue can be seen when an instrument is dipped into the heated mixture. Do not use this near areas where gold leaf has been laid, for it will not mix with the superior material. If, by misfortune, porporina is used near real gold, take a needle and scratch finely to form a small ditch that will keep the troublesome elements of porporina from damaging the gilding.

The Art of Illumination

Paternoster Row had breathed out; Gemma could feel it without even going outside. She opened the window of the solar, trying at the same time to restick the oiled parchment that was coming loose from the top corner of the window frame. Sunlight flowed in, the breeze was warm, but without the oppressive heat of the last weeks.

Down below, people ambled along the street with that sense of release that holiday and procession bring. There was so much to celebrate. After days of circling the city, keeping people trapped and terrified, the barons and their men had left. The king had exiled Despenser.

The news was shouted long and loud. The streets filled with people wanting to eat and drink, the pastries, chicken, fish and ale tasting better than they'd ever known; children burst out of houses still hoping for a sight of battle; the women of Gropecunt Lane walked sore but happy, their purses jingling with coin. Smithfield became a swarm of musicians and dancers, players and troubadours performing again and again the shaming of Despenser, the wounded boar surrounded by hunters, speared and hacked, his guts fed to the dogs. Rumour and fear still roamed. But, like the relief when an aching tooth stops for a time, life without a looming war seemed brighter than ever before, and everyone chose to forget what they all knew: the king was a man who needed his favourites close by. Some said that Despenser hadn't really left the country, and was playing pirate in a boat on the Channel. Wherever he was, most knew he would be back. The tooth would have to be pulled.

Gemma had never been keen on Mayor de Chigwell, but for once she was prepared to watch him strut and cheer him on. It was a fine line he had walked between king and barons, negotiating down the threat of war at the city's gates and ending the Iter's inquisition of the guilds. But Gemma knew a city celebration would do little but offer respite for a few days.

She leaned out the window to look for Alice. During the barons' siege of the city, reports had trickled in from toll keepers and guardsmen of bored soldiers and brawls outside the gates, and in the gaps of their words, Gemma had imagined every kind of violation of her daughter. When a message finally came, it was brief and impatient: Alice was well and unharmed and, yes, she would come to the procession.

A breeze blew between the houses; it delivered to Gemma a waft of odour so strong that it seemed to have shape and weight. She held her breath and turned her head, then looked out again. The street seemed even muckier than usual: food scraps and shit had soaked into the stale rushes that were banked up into a foul-smelling pile, baking in the sun. The muckrakers had been working hard to clear the streets and carry away the filth accumulated over the days of locked gates, but there was so much. Today, of course, they would have been busy making sure Cheap was clean, ready for the procession, leaving the smaller streets to wallow.

Ah, there was Alice. The set of her head and the neat steps were so familiar, almost part of Gemma's own body. She called down and her daughter looked up quickly, though without smiling, and picked her way through the mess.

A short time later, she appeared at the doorway.

'Oh, the muck out there. Deeper than ever,' she said as she glanced around. 'This place seems so small.'

'It's the same as always.'

'Yes, just small is all. Low roof, hardly room to move. After the bishop's house, you know. His hall is four times the size of this. No, more like six times. And grand.'

Gemma smiled.

'And the parchment on the window. Is that still not fixed?'

'You're unharmed then. We were worried about you, Alice.'

'I told you I'd be fine, didn't I?'

'What happened? Did the soldiers come? Did the bishop make them go away?'

Alice looked down, awkward. 'I told you. I'm fine.'

'But did the bishop …?' Something in her daughter's face, and Gemma realised the truth. 'Was the bishop there?'

Alice crossed her arms. 'He had business in Wales, so he had to go. But Judith was there, and Leon, the gardener.'

'The bishop left you? Holy Mary Mother of God, he saved his own miserable skin. I'll go and—'

'No. Leave it. Do you want me to lose my position? Just let me be.'

Gemma was shaking, knew she should leave well enough alone, but she spoke anyway, her voice urgent. 'And the soldiers. Were you harmed?'

'Some stayed, but they were friendly.'

'Friendly. What does that—?'

'Friendly is all. Now leave me be.'

Gemma knew that tone, knew she would learn no more. Still shaking, she said, 'And we're all safe, though your pa isn't well.' She sighed into Alice's silence. 'Well, best we go, girl. If you want a place to see the procession. No point staying any longer than we have to in this small and draughty house.'

'No, I just, I just meant—' Alice stuttered, but her mother cut her off.

'Let's go. I'll just visit Idla before we leave.'

Gemma climbed the stairs next door to Tom and Idla's simple room above the goldsmith's shop, one in a warren of cheap lodgings. They had a bed and a small table in the solar at the front; there wasn't much room for more. Idla was only just visible beneath a pile of thin blankets, but she tried to sit up when Gemma called her name and walked in.

The smell of damp never left these ramshackle rooms, even after the hot summer, but Idla's room had another odour. Sickness, Gemma told herself. It was a fog, invisible but pervasive, that distinguished between the hale and the ill.

'Thought you might be well enough to come out for a bit,' Gemma said. 'The sun might do you good.'

'Ah, I thought that as it's a holiday, I'd stay and sleep. Tom's gone to see if there's food they're giving out.'

Gemma snorted. 'Fountains of wine, they say. But Tom's a fit lad, he'll get you something. And I'll bring some of what we have tonight. Can't get well unless you eat.'

'Don't miss your procession talking to me, Gemma.'

Gemma stroked her bony hand. 'I'll be back with some food and let you know about the procession. Now you rest.'

The bells of St Paul's pealed out loudly. Westcheap was always crowded and noisy, but even before they reached the junction, Gemma could hear a difference. It was the high, excited sound of holiday. She wanted to enjoy the day with her daughter, but instead she was poring over Alice's words, wondering what had happened with the soldiers.

But when they turned the corner, Gemma gasped. The street was transformed. Banners hung from the houses: tapestries, lengths of cloth in red and purple and deep yellow, waving in the wind, billowing like a ship's sails. They could drag the whole street out and into the Thames! She had never seen the like before. All the way down Westcheap, down past the Poultry and into Eastcheap, she watched the street weigh anchor and set sail. She had heard the rumour that Andrew le Gras wanted to entice the rich to buy from him by showing off lengths of his latest shipment. And though Gemma had scoffed like the others at Andrew's play for royal favour, she was mesmerised by the colours, especially the yellow. She loved what gold leaf could do to a page, but this extravagance was another kind of sumptuousness.

She and Alice found a space among the crush of bodies, and Will joined them. Alice turned to Will, pointing at banners, chatting, tugging at his sleeve. Gemma moved closer, but her daughter ignored her. Ah well, she was enjoying herself. Children danced in the centre of the street, arms spread wide, delighting in the space cleared of muck and mud and shit.

Officious men chased them back to stand with their parents in the crowd, the children daring them, darting out again and again, the crowd laughing, enjoying the game. At last, this was a holiday, Gemma thought.

A flash of gold and she looked up. A sudden gust of wind and a yellow banner shivered, loosened and pulled free to float above the street as if it were the opening act. Children lifted their arms, trying to catch the yellow sail, and the sounds of the procession began to filter through from Eastcheap, now louder, now softer as the wind gusted them away or blew them closer. People craned their necks and children ran into the middle of the street to see the parade. Anticipation, sometimes better than the real thing, Gemma thought. Excitement rippled and gathered, swelled and subsided.

Then — ah! — sound and colour filled the street, bounced and echoed between the rows of tall houses. First pipes and timbrels, then fiddles and tabors, their different tunes meeting and tangling. Now jugglers, tumblers, dancers mixing colours and separating again as they crossed and recrossed the street, some retracing their steps to make of the straight street a stage, a fairground, stopping to spin delirious children. Acrobats assembling, tumbling, then running on.

The excitement did nothing to help Will's mood. Ever since the barons had held their siege at the city gates, Will had wrestled with all he knew of the problems in the atelier. At night he woke, hardly breathing, a stone weight on his chest, whispers in his ear; each day he joined in pretending all was well, seeing clearly now what had been before his eyes all along: a master incapable of working, and his wife pretending she was. He would not continue with the joke; when all was revealed, he would be caught as well, his reputation ruined.

Someone pushed him from behind, and he jerked his elbow back, connected with soft flesh, heard the grunt of pain. A man squeezed past, his breath reeking, and a woman coughed thick and loud; maybe Death would come for her in the parade. And in his left ear, Alice. She kept on, chatting like a sparrow, asking about Cambridge, describing the bishop's house, the tapestries and rugs, the silver plate, the nobles who visited. As if he cared. She nudged, pulled at his elbow, nudged again.

Why was he standing there? So that the pompous and powerful could strut their finery and have him watch? We love spectacle, colour, music, he thought; that's what prevents us throwing stones at them. He was tired of the sweaty press of people around him, the cheering and laughing, and most of all, he was tired of his own complaints. Each time he shook them away, they crept back in: a shoddy painting he had scraped off and tried to cover with a new picture, new paint. But it was never enough; the old found its way through. He was about to push his way out of the crowd, when a flash of red and yellow caught his eye.

Gemma watched a man on stilts, his costume red on one side, yellow on the other, his face painted the same, as he stalked across to them and smiled down at Alice. Moving closer, his groin at her face level, he thrust forward and back, his tongue darting in and out in rhythm. The men nearby whistled and cheered. 'Go on, lovely!' Alice looked up, her smile strained, and stepped back awkwardly. But those around her shuffled and shifted, made a space for the stilt walker to pursue her.

Gemma moved in front of her daughter, swore at the leering harlequin face, threatened to push him off his stilts. The crowd jeered: ''Tis playful, that's all'; 'Leave him alone, you dried-up old hag'; 'Can't get enough yourself, eh love?' It was just a game to them, so familiar; Gemma refused to look around.

At last, the stilt walker tired of his antics and moved on. Gemma turned to Alice, put an arm around her, but she shrugged it off, tears rolling quietly down her face, her chin wobbling in that familiar way. Gemma looked away, but kept close, her arm and shoulder warm up against her daughter. Will, she noticed, flanked her other side, his eyes flicking now and then toward her, his shoulders tight and high.

The parade passed before Gemma's eyes but she was aware only of Alice, the girl who would once have bantered with the stilt walker about his tiny prick or his cowardly need to make himself taller than everyone else. The girl who had insisted, shouted, that she would stand up to any soldier. What had happened in those few days under siege from the barons?

The leaders of the London guilds were next: butchers, tanners, cordwainers, cooks, carpenters, stonemasons, apothecaries, weavers, wine merchants, goldsmiths, fishmongers, grocers. It was all a blur until shimmer and colour caught Gemma's eye. As the wind gusted along the street, Southflete's assistant, Ingelram, was struggling to hold straight his banner, one of the most spectacular in the parade. St John the Evangelist, patron saint of the book trade, glittered and shone, resplendent with gold leaf, lapis, carmine and madder. There had been arguments about how much the fraternities should pay for the display, but Southflete had insisted that London, and especially the chancellor and the king, must be made to notice and recognise their significance. 'Our work is mostly closed between two covers, so we must use what we can to show we matter. However else will the king consider granting us status as a guild?' True enough, Gemma thought, though the cost of such magnificence could have bought food, clothes, a physician's aid, for so many in the fraternity. And she knew how much the stationer loved to preen; there he was, with Wat Scrivener and Manekyn following behind.

She glanced at Alice. The girl's face was impassive, sightless; she was standing still but not resisting the touch of Gemma's body beside her. She would no doubt say that none of this — fraternities, painting, an apprenticeship — mattered to her, yet she and her childhood friend Mabel had played with whatever scraps of cloth or parchment they could find, wrapping sticks and painting them to be grand ladies and their gallant knights. Mabel was now working as a silk maker, but would Alice ever be anything more than a housekeeper? Devil take Southflete and his rules.

Will stood by Alice, seeing nothing of the parade. Across the street, one of the terracotta chimney pots had grown a leg, and then two, each with a paw like a lion's. Now two arms and a head. He knew what it would become, but he watched as the eyes formed above a stumpy snout and winked at him. Scampering down a red banner, agile as a squirrel, the creature hung from a corner with one paw and with the other grasped between its legs, rocking back and forward like the stilt walker. Even its long green tongue kept the rhythm.

Will knew it was right; he had stood next to Alice, a dumb man, a fool, doing nothing, while the ugly mouths of men around him smiled and joked. He had even wondered about drawing them, maybe using them in his painting of the Crucifixion. And he had seen Alice's face. She was crying. Silently. That was the most frightening thing. She suddenly seemed so young. He should have done something. He moved closer, stayed with her. That was all he could manage.

Will followed the gargoyle's dance as it leaped into the street, capering between the legs of the guild leaders, ducking below horses' bellies, making its way toward him. Watching, fascinated instead of repulsed, Will saw it as if for the first time, this shadowy creature from the edges, playing, resisting, challenging, neither good nor evil. Alien yet familiar. Didn't he draw such visions every day in the margins of his pages?

Suddenly, it vanished, replaced by a fractious horse and its rider, one of the minions heralding the arrival of the mayor.

'Gerroutavit,' the rider shouted, and Will focused, saw the little girl who had stepped forward, wondering where the procession had moved on to.

'Ma! Where'd the jugglers go?' she asked, not aware of the horse behind her until it reared.

Horse's hooves. At that moment Will could see only Cambridge High Street, Simon face down on the cobblestones; could hear only the thud of wood on flesh, Mayor Hotham's laughing face.

Without thinking, Will lunged forward, pushed aside the bodies in his way. Why was no one else moving? 'Mary, my Mary!' a woman shouted. He grabbed the child around the waist with his left arm just before the hooves landed, bundled her into the arms of others who had only then noticed her peril. The minion spat, jeered, pulled at his horse's mouth to make it rear again. Fury in his arms, Will threw a wild punch that landed on the rider's thigh, not a direct hit, but with Will's strength enough to make the man yell in pain. The crowd cheered. Will's fist wanted more, and he took a step, roaring, arm raised, but the man spurred his horse, cantered away. A few in the crowd shouted along with Will, spat toward the departing rider, knowing they were too late to do any damage.

Suddenly, hands wrenched his arms back, punches set his face afire with pain, then his belly, another and another, forcing out his breath, bending him double, the constables yelling for him to yield. He didn't notice Mary's mother holding her screaming daughter to her breast, wiping away the blood, thanking him; didn't hear the crowd roaring their support for him, a few protesting at the constables as he was dragged away. Will could barely walk, but the memory of the man's yelp and the thought of the knot of purple pain on his thigh were reward enough.

London
Late August 1321

Violet Folium

Violet or purple is often used as the colour of penitence and mourning, hence its use in the seasons of Lent and Advent. Violet folium is made when the clothlets used to absorb the juice of the turnsole plant are soaked in lime water, then dried and soaked again. The colour produced is a reddish violet that may be used to good effect, especially when blended with blue that is added slowly to ensure the hue does not become too dark.

The Art of Illumination

It was dark enough to be a nightmare, but Will's aching belly and swollen knuckles reminded him it was real. His first night in a prison cell was all he had imagined, and more. The damp, the cold, the muck, the groaning prisoners. But the smell he could never have conjured. It was ancient, grown into the rock, coming at him with a force that could almost knock him over. In the corner, an odd gap in the stones looked like a mouth. It moved, gurgled and spewed a thick green stream, then curled into a smile.

He shut his eyes, tried to block it all out, fell into dreams of a long white road and walking, always walking. In this dank place, the ice and snow seemed a comfort. But they wouldn't let him stay in that frozen landscape, these men who pulled him to his feet, punched him — 'Free of charge,' they said — and laughed to see the big man gasp and stagger. They dragged him outside, into the fierce daylight. Will barely saw more than his own feet, felt nothing beyond his raw pain, until he realised he was in the Guildhall to be tried. Causing affray, they said. And at the mayor's own procession. John was there. And Southflete, his face severe.

It was to save the little girl, Will said. The rearing horse, its hooves on the stones. He had intended no disrespect. The punch? The punch was an accident. He mumbled on until they stopped him, pushed him to the side.

A lawyer spoke, then Southflete, calling for mercy. Asshe had rescued the little girl from certain death; he was a man of good character, a limner (yes, despite his bulk, a fine craftsman), a freeman of the city. Will watched their serious eyes, saw their mouths open and shut, but made no sense of their words until that single one, 'pillory', that seemed, for some reason, to make most observers laugh. He was hauled away, confused.

''Tis a fitting punishment,' a constable leaned over to explain. 'For disturbing the celebrations of the good mayor's procession, the custom of the pillory be for trumpets and pipes to process your way to your punishment. Is that not deserved?' He slapped Will around the face. 'Eh? Why're you not laughing?'

And so it was. Will was taken back to Newgate only to be loaded onto a cart and paraded through the Shambles, then past St Michael's and down Cheapside to Cornhill, following much the same route as the mayor's procession, but in the opposite direction. Of all that happened that day, it was the laughter that stung him most, that burrowed beneath his skin and lodged inside. Later he would be angry at the court's injustice, furious at the gaolers' violence, indignant at Southflete's talk of disrepute. But he had no defence against the capering children, the pointing fingers, the mockery of rough music and colourful costumes. And *it* was there as well, leaping from rooftop to rooftop, swinging its stone arms, stretching its stumpy legs out long, grabbing lintel and shutter with its lion paws. At first Will tried defiance and kept his head up, but when he saw a face or two he recognised, he let it slump and wished he could hide.

A crowd gathered at the pillory: the tableau after the procession, Will thought, as the wood closed over his neck and hands.

It was a dark mercy that he couldn't see the onlookers, apart from the children who knelt beneath his face to look up, or flick a finger at his nose. Will reflected bitterly that his anger over the bloodied child was repaid by making him the distraction for every other urchin hereabout. He bent his heart to it.

He studied the pile of rotting food beneath him, identifying where fish tail ended and eggshell began, and wondering whether that clump of tubular shapes was maggots. After a time, when it didn't move, he decided it must be the innards of some bird. A beggar rummaged through it all, grabbed at this and that.

Only an hour, he told himself, but who would have thought a body, even a strong one, could feel pain in so many places? If he looked up, the movement felt like a knife slicing the back of his neck. He'd never known his head was so heavy, but if he let it relax, the wood below his neck rubbed at his skin; it must be almost raw. The ache across his shoulders was a bird with its talons digging deeper each time he breathed. He flexed his wrists and hands, and as a thin wire of fire shot through them he wished once again that they didn't belong to him. He had lost any sense of his legs. They might not be there any more.

When Nick arrived with food and water, he wanted only to drink, but could barely lift or turn his head to take it.

'Stupid lad. What are you doing? Leave it.'

'Some bread, then?'

'Why would I want bread without drink to wash it down? My throat's too parched. Just leave. You shouldn't be here.

You'll anger the beadle and things'll go worse with me. Think for a change, boy.'

Without a word, Nick stepped off the platform, his face tight.

Will wouldn't look up, but could tell that the boy was still there. More quietly he said, 'Go home, Nick. Look what you made me say to you. Leave.'

His hour of shame finished, Will was released. Slowly, his legs remembered how to walk again, and he hobbled off toward the docks — anywhere but Paternoster Row or Bread Street, where everyone knew him — rubbing at his wrists, avoiding the faces of people he passed. He still knew, from his early days in London, the barely used alleys where he could hide and try to sleep.

The night was a delirium of memories emerging from the pain in his body. His ma rubbing away the soreness from carrying wood too heavy for his young body; a cartwheel falling across his legs and pinning him down; Father Matthias slapping his hands for drawing on the church walls; Simon's hands tight around him, legs binding his own, triumphant as they wrestled; the sheriff repeating, over and over, disturbance of peace, of peace, of peace, until they all joined in, even his ma and Gemma. Alice laughing so loud and wide that her face split open and out fell a mass of rotting food. A pig walked by and stopped to sniff at him with its flat, wet nose, saying, *Shameful. Shameful. Give me a bite of that nose.* He fought, tried to pull away, but a creature was holding him down, its talons in his back, its hands holding his wrists, its beak wedging his neck. No one came when he screamed. Or perhaps they did; he could hear them chanting in the darkness: *Shame. Shame. Pig food. William Asshe. Food for pigs.*

The chill deepened just before dawn and, as he expected, from that emptiness it came. The slimy, choking sound of its breath, the grind of stone feet, the sniffing of its dog nose. From the cathedral to Bread Street, all the way down Westcheap, past St Peter at the Cross, dodging the muckrakers, climbing a shopfront, perching on a second-storey shutter to get a better view, then down again and past St Mary Colechurch, faster now that the scent was stronger: Will or rotten food, probably both. It was nearer now. He felt it jump onto his back, its dense weight. *Why do you think of near and far, Will? I've always been as close as your skin. You know that. All the way from Cambridge, your only companion.*

19
London
September 1321

Glair

Glair is a binding medium. Its function is to hold the pigment in place. When used with the benefit of experience, it can have a pleasing effect on the appearance of the pigment. Egg white is made soluble with water by whipping, or by pressing through a sponge, though the latter method may contaminate the glair. Use a clean bowl, set aside for this purpose only, and whip the egg white thoroughly. Anything less will give an inferior finish. Earwax added to the mixture will help remove any bubbles remaining. Well-made glair is retiring and delicate, and ensures the original qualities of the pigment are maintained but, if required, a little egg yolk may be added to provide lustre to the colour.

The Art of Illumination

John's face was worn, as if creatures of the air had spent the night kneading his cheeks, pulling down the fine skin beneath his eyes. He stood in the centre of the shop, murmuring to himself, 'So much to do …' Gemma pushed past him, a sheet of parchment in her hand, and sat at her desk. The night creatures had danced on her face as well.

'John, will you send for Hugh of Oxford now? Now that Will is gone?' Benedict asked. He waited, then said more loudly, 'John, are you ill?'

The older man looked toward him. 'Benedict, ah Benedict. The borders are coming along?'

'I asked if you would send for Hugh of Oxford. Now that Asshe has gone.'

'Gone? Where's he gone?'

'He's gone back to Cambridge, hasn't he? He isn't here and it's been … what, ten days now?'

'Nine.' Nick took a step out of the storeroom. 'He hasn't been in his tenement room.'

'How do you know that, Nicholas?' Gemma looked up. 'Have you been to Bread Street? I told you to stay away.'

'I thought he might be ill after the pillory. I went to see.' Nick stepped back again.

'I warrant he's not gone,' John said. 'The book means too much to the man. He's ashamed, is what it is. Needs some time.'

'Then why isn't he in his room?' Benedict asked. 'I say he's taken his shame back the way he came.'

'That's enough, Benedict,' Gemma cut in. 'Do your work.' She wondered at herself. Benedict was right. Work on the book was piling up with Will's absence, and finding a replacement for him couldn't be delayed any longer.

The pillory was Will's own fault; it had been reckless to punch the mayor's man. But she knew that he was the only one of them, hundreds though they were, prepared to do what they were all thinking. And not one in the crowd had tried to defend him. He had saved the little girl, after all. That must count for something, though she had stayed away from the court and pillory, and had forbidden Nick to visit. Now they had to deal with Southflete's renewed concern about the shop; he was threatening to revoke Will's position, suggesting they send him packing back to Cambridge, if he wasn't there already. He'd appeared in court, appealed for Will to be pardoned, but once the sentence was passed he'd turned heel on his fellow, claiming he shamed the fraternity. John wouldn't see it, but it was clear to Gemma that Southflete had been defending his own reputation in the fraternity as much as Will, and was embarrassed to have his plea overlooked. It would be easy to call on Hugh, let Will go, keep peace with Southflete. But this time, Gemma wasn't prepared to be practical.

'John,' she said, 'do as you said and go looking for him. Why not ask the man he helped with the banners. Osmund, was it? Or ask Jack Tyler, he knows every lowlife in the city. And we'll get to work. Benedict, Nick.' She didn't understand herself. Will knew about John's problems; why not let him go?

She bent again to her sketching. It was to be an illumination of the Nativity, but she didn't have patience just then for the demands of convention. There was space for some pictures at the bottom of the page, so she picked up her plummet and began.

The woman is in a forest, a tree either side of her, and where the ground rises into a small hill with a burrow, a rabbit sits sadly, its long ears drooping, its eyes pleading. For its life. In the woman's hand is a bow and arrow, drawn and pointed at its prey, ready to be released.

Gemma considered her sketch. On a later page, the woman would carry home her brace of rabbits, dripping red — after all, she must eat. But here, the question is not answered: will the woman ignore the animal's sorrow and shoot?

As John told Gemma later, he found Will slumped at the end of an alleyway in Aldgate. It seemed that half the city had seen him, here or there, mostly drunk and always a few days earlier, or a week ago; some had bought him a drink or two, but no one knew or wanted to say where he was when John came searching. John was a boss looking for a scoundrel worker, after all. The strumpets knew Will and smiled at his name, but he hadn't wanted their services lately, they said.

The streets by the wharf were crowded and too busy for a man to sleep off ale and shame, but the end of a lane, or a deep doorway, perhaps, might give shelter. Eventually John found him asleep in the far corner of a dead-end alley that the muckrakers apparently never visited, a large lump among the rubbish.

'William Asshe. You've grown to love this place, eh? Come on, I think you've had enough of the company of pigs by now.' John grabbed him under the shoulders to pull him up, but the bigger man groaned, shook him off and crossed his arms.

'Leave me here. Just leave me here,' Will said. 'It's my place.'

'Aye, and it may be, Asshe, but I need that pair of hands working on my book, though I'm nearly the only one as thinks so. Ten days of work you've missed. And Southflete wants you gone.'

'They're right. You should just take my eyes and leave me, though this one don't open too well.'

'Take your eyes, man? What are you saying?'

'Then you can paint. And I wouldn't have to see it any more, peering at me.'

'It? What's it?'

'Doesn't say much, just creeps up and watches. Sits over there, mostly.'

'You're still drunk.'

'No. Money for ale ran out days ago. Just leave me.'

'I hear talk you've had plenty buy you drinks. Famous you are for what you did.'

'What I did? You'd leave me here if you knew. Just go.' Will hunched his shoulders, bent his head and turned away, but roused at a pain in his thigh. John's boot, he knew.

'Enough, man! Now get up.'

Will had heard that tone from the master twice before. He couldn't remember when, but bleary as his mind was, he understood.

'It's almost curfew. You come now, or you stay here, wallowing in your own shit and pity. Take off those hose and we'll get the worst of it off, at least. Fool of a man.'

In a shop off St Dunstan's Lane, John bought a chicken pie and, though Will said his belly wouldn't bear it, after a mouthful or two he realised how hungry he was. Gradually the world took on a familiar shape, too loud though it was.

'Your room's gone,' John said. 'Only mercy is Nick rescued your clothes before they took 'em all.'

'And my …?'

'Yes. And your master's piece. Nick has it safely tucked away. You can stay with us tonight, but tomorrow it's another room to find. Come on, let's get you home.'

They walked slowly through the streets, the setting sun spreading its gold light between the buildings. People passed by, probably returning home. No one heeded a dirty, beaten man and his companion.

'And the little girl?' Will asked. 'I hear word she's healing.'

'Yes, far as I know. You knew her, did you? Her ma?'

'No. I don't even remember what she looked like.'

'Oh, I figured she was close, like.'

'No. You'd have done the same, John.'

'Maybe. I hope I'd have tried to save her, but to attack the mayor's man? What's the point?'

Will shuffled to a halt. 'The point is, John, that anyone with a say over the rest of us thinks they can do whatever they please. A horse is a weapon. That man had control of it. He let it rear. I think he made it rear. He didn't care what happened to the girl. No one else was going to make him pay.'

'But the mayor's man.'

'If not him, it would have been someone else. I saw it all in Cambridge. The mayor and his violence against the students, horses running them down in the street. Hotham didn't care who was hurt or even killed. He enjoyed watching the chase.'

'Ah,' John said. 'The tragedy?'

Will hesitated, then walked on.

'I understand now.'

'No, you don't, John. Yes, it was a tragedy. My friend drowned in the Cam, and yes, it was Mayor Hotham's horse that pushed him in. It was a dark night, I couldn't see, and I ran. I ran.'

John pushed his hand through the taller man's arm, though it was tense, tight against his side. 'Maybe so, but you saved the little girl.'

Will stopped, turned to John as if it were news to him.

'Come on, let's get you to bed, Will.'

The touch of John's body, the sound of his breath, the rhythm of their slow steps, and Will began to let go, just a little.

He slept on the floor between Nick and Benedict, and when he woke once or twice, bewildered by blankets and warmth, he was surprised that their low snoring was a comfort. Once he settled, he slept long and late, then washed his face and walked carefully down the stairs and into the hall. Gemma had left some bread, cheese and ale on the table for him, and again he discovered how hungry he was. Murmurs came from the shop. That was the sound of Nick's eager questions, and Gemma's answers, though he couldn't decipher the words. Then a lull, and in his mind he could see them all, bent to their work. Benedict would be frowning, no doubt; John would be squinting at his page, uncertain; Gemma would be tired but brisk; and Nick, as always, would be eager and cheerful. The shop he had thought was gone from him. He felt received, gathered in.

But he still had to face them. He opened the door, feeling sheepish. Nick ran out of the storeroom and bumped into his chest. 'Will, I thought you'd never wake up! You were snoring when I got up. And when I nudged you with my foot, you muttered and grunted, just like a pig, and rolled over.' He laughed. 'I have your master's piece in there. I went and looked for it, in case a thief broke in. There's been so much thieving. Since the siege, you know.'

'Thank you, lad,' Will said and patted Nick's back. The touch, like John's last night, was recovery. He looked at Benedict, who nodded and went back to his work.

'We've missed you, Asshe,' Gemma said. It was an accusation, not a lament. You're needed here.'

Will flinched, avoided her eyes.

After a pause, her voice gentler, 'And the little girl, Mary, is recovered. Thanks to you. Are you feeling stronger?'

Will nodded. 'Thank you for the food. And the bed.'

'You ready to start work then?' John said. 'Nick has your pages.' He turned to Gemma. 'I'll go now, see Southflete about Will, so you'll need to get on with the rest of that gathering, love. Here it is.' He held out the pages, carefully covered. 'I've started it for you.'

'And Will,' John went on, 'wait till I've had words with Southflete before you look for lodging. I'm sure I'll talk him round, but no point getting ahead of ourselves, eh? Gemma agrees you can stay here until you find a room.'

As the door closed behind John, Benedict spoke. 'It was kind to save the child. But punching the mayor's man? What could you gain?'

'A little girl and a thug on a horse. Gain was not something I considered.'

'Ah,' Benedict said. 'Of course. I'm sure the little girl's mother was grateful.'

Will looked at him, strangely comforted by his words. For a moment, it seemed his breath settled, his struggle subsided.

His sense of ease slowly drained away as the old tensions returned and he understood his part in them. John was still going blind, Gemma was still doing the work of a man, the book still had to be finished, and he was once more a player in the Dancasters' game. His chest ached and he could only see well through one eye. Nick brought him the pages for the Complaint of Our Lady and he looked back on some of the sketches he had finished: Jesus' entry into Jerusalem; the last supper; Judas handing Jesus over to the soldiers, misery and confusion on his face. It felt as if he had painted them in another year, the procession and the pillory an abyss between.

He touched the page, ran his finger gently over the bare, smooth animal skin. It felt like a homecoming.

Yet he wasn't capable of planning more illuminations that day, nor steady enough to paint. Instead, he would begin the borders. The pages were to be full of grace, John had said. They were the words. He drew some designs but, unsatisfied, rubbed over them with pumice stone.

'Gemma,' he said, 'I wonder if I might look at the calendar pages you decorated.'

The hesitation in his voice made her look up quickly.

'John wants these pages for the Complaint of Our Lady to be beautiful. Simple and full of grace. They were the words he used. And your calendar pages, though I only saw one or two, were beautiful.' They were the most elegant borders Will had ever seen, but he wasn't able to say that. 'I thought they might help, if I looked.'

'Yes. I'll get them. I'm keeping them safe, away from harm.'

Side by side in the storeroom, they leafed through the pages. Strong though the memory was, Will was surprised once more at the pages. Some would overlook them, miss the beauty of the simple lines, believing that more decoration was more effective. Master Edgar, perhaps, though not Claude, who understood the effect a single line could have. Will felt suddenly foolish, bumbling, his hands too big and awkward as they held the pages.

'And you were the one …?'

Gemma nodded. 'Yes, I designed them. My father taught me how to be sure each part of the page worked together. "It's not St Bart's wool market," he'd say. "Don't crowd it. Give each part room to move and breathe."'

They both laughed.

20

London
October 1321

Patience

One of the first lessons an apprentice must learn is patience. If you have waited for years to dip a brush into colour, you must learn to wait longer. If you think the world has been holding an indrawn breath just to see the treasures of your skill, you are mistaken, and you will not learn. A child begins by crawling; an apprentice begins by cleaning and grinding and mixing. There is an art and skill in the making of every colour. Attend to all that you are taught. But remember that your talents will be as chaff in the wind if you do not learn the humble art of patience.

The Art of Illumination

The shopkeepers of Paternoster Row, living and working only paces from one another, argued and bargained and cajoled their way through the days, with customers and with each other. But they would always come together for a celebration, of whatever kind. And an apprentice becoming a journeyman was an event worth marking, the making of a freeman and a citizen, perhaps a potential employer.

As soon as John, Southflete and Benedict returned from the official signing at the Guildhall, a throng gathered in the fraternity undercroft of St Michael's to wish the new journeyman well. Seven years Benedict Broune had lived and worked in Paternoster Row, and had done his share of buying stores and sending messages, though he rarely stopped to speak of more than business. And even if some, not members of the fraternity, weren't quite sure who he was, they came along, specially as there was ale to be had. Manekyn the scribe, Wat Scrivener, Peter Binder, Rowley Buxton the parchmenter, Henry and Hawisia Archer, Luanda de Biville — all shook his hand. Benedict's mother, Joan, and his father, Galfrith, watched proudly, even if still not convinced of their son's decision. Jack Tyler felt like he knew Benedict from John's stories about the workshop over ales in the tavern; Sewale the apothecary nodded to him; Harry the assistant slapped him on the back; and Gocelin the goldsmith wandered in for a short time to see what was happening.

Even though it was the final moment of his seven years as an apprentice, cleaning and mixing and learning to paint, it was clear to Will that Benedict would rather have let the milestone slip by unannounced, without the praise and jokes that speeches would bring. But there was no escape. Southflete, dressed in splendid velvet and his shoes longer than ever, with strings attached to keep them from drooping, insisted that any opportunity for recognition of the growing community of London scribes, illuminators, bookmakers and stationers should be taken. He made a speech about the strength of the book trade in London, soon to rival that of Paris, he claimed, and praised John Dancaster as an illuminator whose skill was unrivalled.

'You are blessed, Benedict, to have received training from an artisan of John's talent and commitment. His work is known both here and across the water for its fine detail and subtlety of colour and shade. If it weren't to blaspheme our Lord and creator, I would suggest that he breathes life into his figures on the page. It is a privilege to have learned from this master, who in turn learned from the masters who came before him, carrying on the tradition of illumination. Mark well your training and do not wander down paths of invention, imagining your thoughts more important than those of the men who have come before us. Benedict, we welcome you as journeyman.'

Will, standing against the far wall, hoped Southflete wouldn't notice him above the crowd. He was pleased for Benedict, yet he shuffled his feet, struggled to concentrate. He watched John smile and shake his head at the praise, then looked across at Gemma, the woman who had trained Benedict in all the skills he would need, who had coaxed him through his nervous desire for perfection. It was she who corrected John's work each day. And, it seemed, the one with the skills the stationer had praised. As always when Southflete was around, her face was still, a blank page.

Benedict nodded and shook the stationer's hand, tried a smile that seemed more a grimace, and refused to make a speech, saying little more than a quick thank you to John and Gemma Dancaster. He nodded at Will, looked pleased to see Tom, with Idla holding onto his arm, and resisted the drinks that were slopped and pushed into his hands.

Gemma watched Nick chattering to Benedict and smiled at her son's excitement; no doubt he saw himself in six years, the centre of attention and officially a limner. His feet danced as he spoke, his arms never still, his voice teasing as he coaxed a laugh from Benedict. It would soon be a turn of the year since the lad began as an apprentice, and his curiosity and interest hadn't faded. She had been wrong to resist him beginning, and John was right, even if she didn't agree with his reasons. It was clear Alice had no interest in the skill. Her son, on the other hand, wanted to learn; he would value 'The Art of Illumination'.

Nick stepped back, guffawed and stretched his arms wide as Benedict dipped his head, bent his knee and bowed in mock salutation to the lad. Gemma laughed, though she had no idea of the joke between them. It was a relief to see the new journeyman and limner finish his seven years. He would be capable, if not inspired.

He hadn't ever ventured a dream of what he would paint for his master's piece, the way John had done when he was her pa's apprentice. John had talked for hours of how he would paint the Trinity: Father blessing the Son while the Holy Spirit as a dove flew above them. The background would be a host of angels with their wings outstretched, each rendered in a delicate shading of colour and shell gold. It was, as he had said it would be, a magnificent piece.

And since she was fifteen, Gemma had thought about the illumination she would paint for her master's piece if the veil were ever torn and the fraternities allowed women to qualify. Not the Virgin Mary, not Christ enthroned, nor the Crucifixion or King David. It was the story of Susanna, which her mother had often told her, that Gemma longed to paint.

The garden and orchard are surrounded by a wall that forms an arc from the house so that no one can enter except by the gate or by the kitchen door. In its centre is a pool bordered with roses, oregano and rosemary. The beautiful Susanna bathes there in warm weather, when the sun has begun to ripen the fruit, coaxing the scent from the plants, and although the women who attend her want to fuss and stay, Susanna tells them to leave her to her solitude. Captivated by her beauty and wanting more of it, two elders of the town have plotted to spy on Susanna, and pay the stable boy to unlock the gate and let them sneak into the garden where the old olive trees and overgrown apple trees hide them while they watch her bathe. As Susanna steps from the pool and picks up her robe, the two men come out from their hiding place and stand each side of the frightened woman. She pulls her robe tight to cover her nakedness as the men look on, arms reaching out to her, eyes threatening. They insist that she lie with them. If not, they say, they will tell the town leaders that she has arranged to meet a young man in the garden and has lain with him. Remember our position as elders, they say. Our words will not be doubted. When she refuses their demands, they accuse her before the town authorities. She is dragged to gaol and found guilty as an adulteress, unfaithful to her husband.

Yet Daniel, the wise elder, calls a halt to proceedings and insists the men be questioned separately about all that they have seen. We saw her meet her lover under a mastic tree, one says. We saw her kissing a young man under an oak tree, the second man says. Thus their deceit is exposed, a mastic and an oak being so different in size and shape. Daniel declares Susanna innocent and free.

That story was not often told, though Gemma's ma said it was from the Bible, and that it told of the wisdom of Daniel. Gemma had questions, though. What had Susanna's husband done to save her? Were the elders who had accused her punished? And, above all, had Susanna been allowed to speak? The answers weren't in the story that Gemma's ma had been told, so Gemma tried making up the ending herself, though she knew she wasn't supposed to do that. She spent long hours devising punishments for the men: dragons eating their toes, one by one, then starting on their fingers; muckrakers throwing them onto their cart and carrying them off with the city rubbish; Hew the tanner slowly flaying their skin so it could be turned into parchment for her to decorate. She had especially liked that last one.

Gemma smiled at her gruesome imagination. What a strange child she had been. How ready to demand justice. She took another gulp of ale and walked up the stone stairs, back to the workshop.

21

London
November 1321

Blue

Azure, the colour of the skies, is used to signify heavenly grace.

The finest blue, a hue that surpasses all others, is ultramarine azure, extracted from lapis lazuli stone. It is rare and expensive and, as its name tells us, must be brought from across the sea. Ultramarine is the most illustrious and perfect of all blues; for its beauty and its value, it is most appropriate for painting the Virgin Mary's gown.

Azurite, though not as sumptuous as ultramarine azure, also has a fine colour and may be used when the superior pigment is not available. The stone is crushed, but not too finely, or it becomes pale.

Folium blue [see Folium entry] may also be used, and woad, although its process is long, gives a strong, if less refined, colour.

The Art of Illumination

Gemma's book, 'The Art of Illumination', was growing only slowly. She had known from the beginning of Lady Mathilda's commission that she would have to correct John's pages, but in a book of hours there were so many decorations, and all had to be perfect. With her daily chores of buying supplies, visiting the baker, cooking, cleaning and tending to the chickens and the garden, as well as working in the shop, there was so little time for her own writing. She had tried getting up even earlier to work on her book, but all that meant was that she would later wake with a start, head on the desk, sometimes ink on her forehead. All she could do, she thought, was to add a little more whenever there was time. It was dark, well before dawn, when she crept down the stairs and retrieved her parchments from the chest. Since his absence from the shop, Will had begun arriving early for work once again, even though the weather was cooling, so Gemma unlocked the front door and sat to her task.

After the brief introduction for *Blue*, she began a new section: *Ultramarine Azure*. Nick wouldn't need to make the pigment himself because they bought it already prepared from Sewale, but an apprentice should appreciate the long, slow steps involved in extracting the colour of heaven from rock. Word by word she set down the process, drawing on the mixture of childhood memories: her own wonder, and her pa's precise instructions, watching her, helping her when needed, the rock too precious to risk a mistake. Whatever she wrote, she knew her words would be but shadows of a colour so beautiful.

The first steps were familiar from the process of making many pigments. She had crushed the rock, a mottled mixture of grey and blue, then milled it to fine powder on a slab. Next, in a porringer, she had melted arabic and mastic gums with yellow beeswax, tipped in the lapis powder and watched it turn a disappointing grey-blue. On and on she stirred, feeling the mixture begin to resist the spoon and thicken. When it was time to pour it out onto the slab, her pa said he would do it because it was so hot and the porringer heavy. As it cooled, she had watched it turn from a thick liquid into something like dark blue dough, and her pa had left her alone to knead it; it was just like blue bread, she had thought. When her pa wasn't looking she'd pulled off lumps to make animals and people or the strange creatures she had seen in the margins of her pa's pages, then squashed them down and kneaded them back into the lump. 'Now roll it into long sausage shapes and leave them to rest and turn hard,' her pa said. 'No creeping back to play with them, mind. They need to rest.' He hadn't known why they had to do this, but said, 'Our Lord rested for three days in the tomb, and so we must wait three days for the colour of heaven to be ready to emerge.'

Each day Gemma had uncovered the lengths of dull blue and touched them gently, feeling each time that they were harder. On the third day, they were solid. Her pa told her to bang one on the bench; it was like hitting it with wood. She thought that meant he would be ready to perform whatever magic would transform those ugly lumps into pigment, but it turned out there were yet more steps: heating them in water to soften, then kneading and stretching, leaving them to rest again. It was more and more of a mystery. Somewhere, some time, someone must have discovered that the blue needed patience, that the process had to be repeated.

Absorbed in the past, Gemma wasn't aware that Will had come in, until he was standing near her desk. The early mornings were colder as winter approached, and he rubbed his hands together to find some feeling in the fingers. He watched her gather the pages together.

'More work on the mystery commission?' he asked.

'Nothing to do with you, Will. I've told you that.'

'You're right.' He went into the storeroom.

Gemma decided to keep writing. She put down the pages. This had been her time to work; she was tired of so much hiding.

'You write with ease, Gemma,' Will said in the doorway. 'And from this distance, it seems you write well.'

'My pa taught me.'

'Ah. You were fortunate.'

'I wanted to know what the words said on the pages he decorated, so perhaps he thought it was quicker to teach me to read than to be forever explaining them. Romances, recipes, herbals — I'd read whatever he showed me. And then

I wanted the letters to write my own stories.' She laughed. 'An annoying child, no doubt, but my pa was patient.'

'I learned only when our priest saw I had a skill with line. He was the one who arranged my apprenticeship with Master Edgar.'

'Seems you were fortunate as well,' Gemma said. She wasn't really listening, didn't want to be talking to Will, but back at a desk with her pa, learning to form letters on a wax tablet. Over and over she'd repeat them, feeling the wax give way beneath her stylus. Then clear the wax and begin again.

Will sat down, picked up his plummet and drew in the margin of his page a young woman seated by a window, a book in her hands. Eventually he spoke.

'I've been thinking, Gemma, about John. You've so much to do correcting John's pages, and with only this hour or so in the morning before the others arrive. Maybe I could help you.' He could hear the hesitation in his voice. Journeyman, employee, newcomer. Would she tell him to mind his own business? But Gemma was not the master, not even a journeyman, and he, Will, would become a master soon, once his Beatus piece was finished.

'You understand this cannot be spoken of. To anyone,' Gemma said.

Anger flared in Will's chest. He was offering help, and she spoke like this.

'Southflete sniffs like a hound after rabbits. If we stay quiet and do the work, he's no cause to accuse us. As long as we keep our heads in the burrow.'

Will wanted to argue, remind her that he would be giving up his time, but he bit down on the words.

When Gemma spoke again, her voice was gentler. 'Thank you, Will. That would help. I know you understand John's style.' She sighed. 'So that the book looks like his work, I mean.'

Will studied John's latest work, a small illuminated capital of King David with his harp. The balance of colours was right, he could see all that John had intended, but it was clear that John's brush wouldn't paint what was in his mind. Will was surprised at himself; after all his disappointment and anger at John, what he felt most keenly was the trespass in removing John's brush strokes. His jaw ached with the effort of it. This isn't the work of the master, he told himself as a thick flake of paint flicked against his face; it was John's illness that he was painting over. Though the sense of remorse was difficult to shake.

'Master Edgar, who taught me illumination, showed me John's work as the best example of shading and colour that he had seen,' he told Gemma. 'Even the French, he said, didn't understand colour like John Dancaster. "Look how he shows where the light falls," he'd say. "See how well Dancaster uses white blended and layered to create a sense of light and shadow." Claude, the French master, admired his work, even though it was by an Englishman.' Will laughed and bent to the work, but looked up again; he was chattering, he knew, anxious about what he was doing.

'Claude taught me about form, about rendering movement in the body and between bodies. Master Edgar didn't agree with trying to take illuminations beyond convention, changing them from what has already been handed down, but Claude told me that we must always be thinking past what we know. "God does not keep still," he used to say. "Why should we?"'

Gemma was writing the instruction for kneading the lapis dough, and caught somewhere between her father's careful teaching and the Frenchman's words; the room seemed bathed in the past. She had dropped the thin log of hard dough into water and begun kneading, feeling it melt beneath her fingers, watching as it bled heaven into the water.

222 Robyn Cadwallader

'I couldn't believe it when John agreed to take me on,' Will continued. 'Such a chance to learn, to watch his work.'

And then, the moment of magic, when her pa had pushed her hand deep into the water almost to the bottom of the pot, then pulled it out, her fingers covered in vivid blue sediment. This the reward for their days of work and waiting.

'Now I can't believe I'm correcting his work. It doesn't make sense.'

Gemma was gazing at her fingers. Such beauty she had never seen; Will's words wrenched her away. 'Has to happen some way. It's what we are. Born to fail,' she said, without looking up.

'That's a cruel way to think of life.'

'It's how things are. *Sunt lacrimae rerum*. It's outside the door, down the end of the street, in the hospitals, the grand houses.' Her father had died, her baby daughters had died, John was losing his sight. Idla was upstairs in bed, barely alive. Did Tom, lying next to her, know she was dying?

'But of all things for John to lose. His legs, perhaps, or even his ears, but his eyes … For a painter to lose his eyes *is* cruel, Gemma. You must feel that.'

'It's hard for all of us. Why else would I be keeping his secret and correcting his work?' She looked up, paused until he met her eyes. 'You don't need to remind me that life is hard, Will.'

All that was true, but he'd expected something more from Gemma. He could see she was concerned for John, but where was the grief for his loss? Something softer than what he knew already: *There are tears*? They went back to work in silence.

Gemma finished writing the instructions for making lapis lazuli, her mouth dry and bitter. This man with his questions, his demands that she say what he wanted to hear. Gentle words that would wrap around him and John, save him from facing what he feared the most: his own frailty. She had seen his ambition, imagining the future offered to one who had worked with the fine craftsman, Dancaster. John had offered Will so much, and now, in these very pages, he was showing him how easily it could all come undone.

She read over the words she had written. Lapis lazuli. Blue. The colour of heaven. 'You've heaven on your fingers,' her father had said.

Mathilda

Wain Wood Manor
June 1322

There isn't much to harvest, but the smell of cut hay travels on the warm air. Mathilda is outside more often now, usually with her book of hours. She feels she has emerged from a long sickness, and the sun seems brighter than it ever was. Sometimes she walks with Fraden down the hill among the fields. Her legs aren't as strong as they were, and Fraden walks slowly, asks if she wants to rest. She snaps at him; she doesn't want to be this pale form, unfit for anything but hiding. She hates what grief and guilt and fear have done to her.

Matt, the reeve, meets them near the demesne fields, and they look across the yellow landscape scattered with workers, some swaying back and forward with the action of their scythes, some bent to wrap the bundles. Some look up and nod or bob, then keep working. Matt talks quickly about the number of new lambs, his plans for ploughing and sowing, and asks Mathilda questions she doesn't want to answer. She knows that Matt worries for his position; an estate this size doesn't need two men running it. But he has been elected by the village, and after so much suffering, they need a man they can trust.

'Let's wait and see to the harvest and the next seeding. We need you here, Matt.' She turns and walks away so that they can't see her crying, suddenly missing Aspenhill and Fordham village. She knows how strange she must be to others, how strange she is to herself.

In the garden she turns the pages of the book, thinking of the village she left behind. Will had visited it to make sketches, though he came back with only a few and said it was such a dismal sight that he would draw his imagining of what it had been like before the famine and frost. Still, she looks for her past, for some connection. In the margin of Psalm 23 are sheep in a willow pen, all standing side on, one behind the other, each an echo of the one before and behind, their fleece painted in waving folded lines, just like the sheep in the capital for the Annunciation to the Shepherds. There are only ten, she counts them, but they stand so close together, their bodies rounded, that they speak of plenty.

At the bottom of the page, a man ploughs in long, neat furrows, his horse glossy, and on the facing page another man scatters seed. Two pages further on, there's the scything and the binding, and the workers are dressed in colourful clothes with no patches. Nearby, they stack the hay, so much and so high that there's barely room for more. It's what she and Robert asked from the limners, and there is no truth in it, though she recognises some of the buildings as brighter forms of what they really are.

The memories of Fordham come back to her as if through fog from the other side of a river she crossed after Robert's death, and with them all the hopes she and Robert had for advancement. The buildings and the people of the village, even Aspenhill Manor itself, will remain in one way or another, for a time at least, but her plans are now no more than spirits of the substance they wanted them to be. She and Robert had believed they could make them real, solid enough to touch, a place to live in. But they are no more. This book, too, is a ghost.

She looks down at the small object that she carries everywhere now. She had thought it a failure, but it offers her something. She can't quite say what, though it's more than prayers, and even more than beauty. In time, she thinks, it will show her.

22

London
November 1321

Red

Red is the colour used at Pentecost celebration. It represents the Holy Spirit. A deeper, crimson red represents blood, suffering and the atonement.

There are many red pigments, but be aware that they do not always produce what you may expect, and a bright rock will often, when ground, give a dull or weak result. The red ochres are drawn from deposits in the earth, and produce a wide range of colours from pink to purple, though many are not bright enough for our needs. Red lead is a vibrant colour and can be obtained by roasting white lead in the open air.

Vermilion, the most beautiful of the reds, is made from grinding the mineral cinnabar. Be sure to grind it well, for the longer and more finely it is ground, the purer the colour. Though it is a brilliant and gem-like hue, made even more lustrous with the addition of egg yolk, or by blending with minium or red lead, it can sometimes turn black. Consider well when using this hue that its richness and brightness demand other strong colours be used with it, for many hues will pale alongside it.

The Art of Illumination

The door flew open and the boy pushed his head inside. Still panting, he spoke in bursts. 'Master Southflete, stationer. Says he'll see you. John Dancaster, limner. At London Bridge. Now, he says. You won't be busy, he says.'

'Thank you, Ingelram,' John said.

The face disappeared and the door slammed.

'Ingelram?' Will said.

'Yes. Too much name for one small boy, isn't it?'

'Ah.' Will tried it out again. 'Ingelram. With a name like that, the boy needs a horse and a sword, not a stationer's shop.'

'Ingelram the Great, Ingelram the Valiant, Ingelram the Ready.' Nick's voice came from the storeroom.

John stood up, laughing. 'Nicholas the Poet, teller of tales, grinder of pigment. I'd best do as the great knight Ingelram says and head for London Bridge.'

The chiming for None slipped through the door as John opened it.

'Long meeting,' Gemma said.

'Mmm. Payment arrived.'

Will and Benedict looked up; Nick rushed out of the storeroom. 'Payment?'

'Not before time,' Gemma said.

'It's here in time for Yule. Lady Mathilda's Yule gift.'

'Gift? We've worked for that.'

'All right. It's timely then,' John snapped back.

'What else did Southflete tell you?' Gemma asked. 'Took long enough.'

'The barons are heading north. Crops dying from no rain, though we knew that already. News of murrain up north, cows and sheep collapsing in the fields, price of parchment going up even more. Pigment as well.'

'For a man with coin in his purse, you don't look pleased. All is well with Southflete?'

'Yes, fine.' John undid his purse. 'He says Lady Mathilda wants me to visit before Yule to paint the chapel.'

'Now? But why? It's coming on winter.'

'Sir Robert's back, so it seems a good time. Though it won't be for long. Whatever unrest we've seen already, there's more to come.'

'But you can't, John. You can't.' Gemma's voice was strained. 'It's ... it's too hasty. Why does she decide when you should go?'

'We'll sort it out. Don't fret like that.'

'Fret? I'm worried.' Gemma was twisting the brush in her hand.

'Leave it, Gemma. She's paid us, hasn't she? All of you. Let me be.' John slammed the door.

Gemma and Will looked at each other, both aware that their struggle was different, yet somehow the same.

It wasn't a surprise, really, the thumping on the door. Gemma told Nick to go downstairs and answer it. She'd have nothing to do with their drunkenness, even if they thought they were helping by dragging John home.

'Tell them not to come upstairs,' she shouted. 'Leave your pa at the door; inside or outside, I don't care.'

From the solar, she could hear grunts, gasps and words, then the sound of scuffles, dragging wood. She opened the shutters and called down as quietly as she could, trying not to wake the neighbours: 'I said, don't bring—'

'Ma, he's hurt. Bleeding,' Nick shouted through a sob. 'It's Jack brought him home.'

Gemma ran to the stairs, stumbled on the first step as her knees gave way, but it was only a moment's weakening. As she took the next steps, she realised that she had been expecting this. John was slumped at one of the desks.

'Move him back here, into the hall. The blood, Nick. Think. Come on, through here. Get a cloth and water.'

'A fight it was,' Jack Tyler said quickly as he pulled John out of the narrow desk and wrapped his friend's good arm around his own neck. 'Come on, John. Help me out, try to stand.'

As they shifted John through the door into the hall, Jack kept up his chatter, alarmed, guilty, afraid. 'Some fellow just come to London. Small, ugly, he was, looking for a fight. You could tell. Seemed John was up for it.'

Gemma looked into his face. 'Up for it?'

'I know he's not one for his fists. Not even one to brawl with words, usually, though these last weeks he has ... Not as I see him often, mind, at the tavern,' he added quickly. 'But since the commission, it's odd to say, but since the grand book he's been, well, not the same John as usual. Bone weary, I thought, all that work and for gentry like, but ...' He paused.

Gemma unwrapped the dirty cloth the men had wrapped around John's arm.

Jack went on. 'I shouldn't say it, but I thought he wanted to fight almost more'n the ugly churl.'

John stirred, looked up. 'Leave it, Jack.'

But the tiler had a story to tell, excuses to make to Gemma. 'I didn't hear how it started but there was shouting, and even when the stranger backed away, John walked toward him. We didn't believe it at first. Then we saw the knife, too late, and the stranger lashed out, just once. I pulled John away, I did, so it wasn't worse. Then I saw the blood.'

Gemma didn't speak as she cleaned John's arm, revealing the long slice just below his elbow. She held back a gasp and bound it. Nick stepped back, pale. Awkward now, his story told, Jack stumbled on his way to the door, and Gemma looked up.

'Thank you, Jack.'

He nodded as he closed the door.

Gemma knew better than anyone that John was a peaceable man, not usually one to be entangled in an argument. But she wasn't surprised by the injury; she'd known there would be something, though she hadn't known exactly what. The drink, and then the cut on his right arm, they were as an order he'd placed at the apothecary's: *Carmine, lapis, brazil wood and a wound to stop me painting, please, Sewale. Soon as you can, eh.*

The next morning, after barely any sleep, she felt an odd mixture of anxiety and relief. Piers Stratton, the barber, told her the cut was long but not deep. 'Let him rest all he needs, give him plain food and clear wine. I've bandaged the wound and left another jar of the ointment for his sore joints. I see he's trembling, but that's the effect of the wound and the fight, no doubt. Be on guard against fever.' He smiled weakly. 'Look after him as best you can.'

Gemma was silent as she sat on the bed, John watching her face. She could feel his plea for comfort, but she had none to give.

'We won't give up the commission,' she said eventually.

'Course not, love. I'll be well again, as he says. We can finish.'

Gemma stood and kicked one of John's boots across the room. Her voice was quiet, even. 'Stop it, John. If this isn't enough, still you pretend. God's holy nails. I pretended along with you, for the sake of the shop, not to upset the others — all those messages, meetings, leaving me to paint. I've been making excuses for you. And to Southflete.' She walked to the chest and sat down, leaned against the wall. 'The breviary for Father Theobald three years ago, wasn't it? It was a small enough commission, so I didn't say anything when you left it all to me. I thought perhaps it would pass, the problem would pass. Even did the rose, your signature, waiting for you to get better.' Her voice was louder. 'But now, with this book, it's too big, too important to go on like this. I see your work, I correct it, day after day. You must know that. No more pretending as if you're three years old and the world will be the way you want it.' After a pause, and more quietly, with as much gentleness as she could find, she said, 'I know it's your eyes. You can't see to paint. And it's not going to get better, is it?'

She pulled back at the look on his face, but even so, relief swept over her. The words had been said.

'And more than your eyes. Show me your left hand. Show me, John.'

John pulled his hand from the blankets and briefly held it out. It was the tremor she had recently noticed, and tried to ignore.

'It's just the shock of it all, Gemma. Now leave me be.'

'Leave you be? I'm doing the work, pretending it's yours. How can I leave you be?'

'Wait until I'm better, woman. Did he not say to rest? Let me rest.'

Gemma walked out, slammed the door and stopped at the top of the stairs. She felt caught once again. John always found a way to step around the words. Illness, blindness, the end of painting. She understood why; it was all he had done since he was younger than Nick, hanging around her father's shop, asking to help clean the pots and scrape off the carbon black, offering to piss for the turnsole blue or in the pots for making lead white. She smiled. 'Never seen a lad with so much piss in him,' her father would say. John had worked and watched and copied until her father took him on as an apprentice, and though at night he had diced and brawled and run the gauntlet of beadles, he was always at work and willing the next day. She had thought then that he was unassailable.

The book, and now this fight, had made her look back along the road and admit how much had changed. The only trade they knew, and John no longer fit. Either they continued the playacting that John still painted, or they tried to build a business on her skill, and eventually Nick's. Step by step down the stairs, she tried to imagine what might be in a year, two years, but she could see nothing. At the bottom of the stairs she stopped and stared into the garden.

* * *

Gemma was on a stool next to the bed, coaxing John to eat, when she heard the door to the solar quietly close.

'It's me. Came to see Pa.'

'Alice, I'm so glad you came.' Gemma stood, hugged her daughter, tried not to cry.

'Ma, don't fuss.' Alice pulled free of her mother's arms and walked to the bed.

'Alice, love,' John said. 'You needn't have come.'

Wiping her eyes, Gemma watched her daughter examine John's bandage, gently adjust the knots, put a hand to his forehead. It was no use; the tears insisted. 'I'll be in the kitchen,' she said, and went downstairs.

She sent Nick out to buy fish, cleaned the kitchen and the hall, moved pots and baskets, then shifted them back again. Alice had left her with nowhere — no way — to be. She could see the tension in her daughter's mouth, the hunch of her shoulders, but, most of all, the shift of her eyes, down and away, as if she wanted no one to see her. What had happened to her during those long days of the siege? What memories did that young body carry, unable to speak them aloud? Whatever Gemma imagined, she would never know.

In the garden she threw a few scraps to the chickens. 'Here we are, just you and me,' she said to them. She felt so weary, she could have lain down right there and slept. She wanted her own mother. No, it was her pa she wanted, to be back in the shop with him looking at a book of romances, learning to shape the letters, understand the words. She wanted Clarissa on her knee, or running around her feet, chasing the chickens. The need was suddenly overwhelming. She longed for the chance again to make Ella breathe. Had she not loved her enough, pulled her into her arms soon enough to make her keep living? So much lost. And now more.

'He's pale,' Alice said behind her. 'Is it a bad cut, did the barber say?'

Gemma pulled in a breath, and turned around. Alice, arms crossed, was standing in the doorway. She looked tired, Gemma thought. Older. 'Long, but not deep. As long as he doesn't get too bad a fever, seems he'll recover.' She wiped her hands on her kirtle.

'Your message frightened me.'

'Aye, and it frightened me, and our Nick, to see him like that. Bleeding. I've scarce had any sleep.'

'He says he'll paint again, that it'll all—'

'Oh, he says that because he can't think of it else. Piers the barber told me there's no saying yet if he'll use that hand for something as fine as painting.'

'He has the other hand still.'

Gemma kicked a chicken away from pecking at her shoe. 'That's foolish talk. Painting's not so easy, as if you can change hands like that. You've seen how much skill it needs, Alice.'

'Then he can do something else.'

'What? What would he do?'

'I don't know. But there's more jobs in the world beside illuminating, Ma.'

'Not for your pa. It's been his whole life. He can't just give it up.'

'That's the problem. You won't see that there's anything else but painting.'

'Cleaning the floors for a bishop who won't even keep you safe, is it?'

'Your work, that's all it is, Ma. You want to be a limner. I have my work, and it's enough. At least it's not here.' Alice turned, took a step to the kitchen and paused. 'I'll be back to visit Pa,' she said, and kept walking.

Gemma watched her daughter's back disappear and wept.

* * *

'Despenser's back. Did you hear?' Will said to Gemma. 'The king's brought his man back to his side.'

Gemma, her face pale and drawn, simply shook her head.

'Wat says they're already arming to travel north. The king was brutal, but with that man by his side, who's to say? What's happening to us?' When Gemma still didn't speak he understood. 'Sorry, Gemma. You've enough worry, without me adding to it. How's John today?'

'You'll have to paint the Fitzjohn chapel, Will: the lady at prayer that John was to do. It has to be done.'

'Of course. I can start in a few days. I only need to finish the last page on this quire.'

'Good. Stay for Yule before you go. Lady Mathilda has no right to demand you travel at Yule.'

'Travel? What do you mean?' Will paused a moment and then understood. 'You want me to go there in John's place? To the estate? No, I can't do that. Send a letter. John can tell me … or you … and I'll write it down. Surely he'll be well enough soon.'

'You know he won't. Even if he was well, he couldn't do it. He can't go and pretend to sketch the patrons at prayer. Why do you think he got into a fight?'

'Yes, but I've been thinking,' Will said. 'What about spectacles? Why doesn't he buy spectacles? I've heard—'

'He tried that, even before I knew what the problem was. They can't help. All he'll say is that it started as dullness, like it's a cloudy day, so he could still work. As it gets worse, it's as if the cloud is there, in his eyes, gradually getting greyer. He loves painting, so he'd use them if he could.'

'But surely there's something.'

'Will, he's already delayed going. They're paying for the book.'

'Then tell the lady that her book will have to be like

every other book, painted here, from the model book and our imaginations. It was only the fancy of the rich to get John there, and nothing more. I'm surprised John agreed. Even more that Southflete allowed it. Will she pay more for a personal visit, wasting our time?'

'Fancy or not, it was the agreement. Southflete told John we have to do it. You have to.' Gemma's voice had that familiar edge: she would not be denied.

'She'll understand, I'm sure, that John is ill. And if she wants Dancaster in particular, she won't welcome me into her precious chapel.'

'We'll have John write a letter about his injury and testify to your standing. She'll have to understand. And if she doesn't, we'll have done all we can.'

'Gemma, I'm sorry John is ill, but I won't stay in the house of a nobleman.'

'You think you get to choose, do you, Asshe? Who gave you such rights suddenly?'

Will took a step back, but wouldn't give in. He could hear Simon's voice, the late-night debates. *What I'm saying is, there shouldn't be some that get all the money and power, and the rest of us trodden down while they walk over us. The barons and earls and lords think we only live to serve them, that they can tell us to come running and we have to.* He took a breath, spoke Simon's words: 'I've the rights of a man who's as equal as any other man. They don't have to be given to me.'

'So that's what you discovered in the pillory, is it? Found your rights buried in the rotten food they threw at you?'

Gemma looked down at the floor, wishing she could swallow those words that Will had received as a physical blow. This big, swaggering man.

'All I mean, Will, is that there's no book without a patron. And no patron without we do as they ask. We can't afford to refuse what's been agreed. We paint because it puts food in our mouths. If painting's also something we really want to do, so much better; we could be like poor Tom, making belts and freezing himself in the street trying to sell them. Lady Mathilda makes our work possible. Whatever you know of rights and God, money and position is the order of things.' Gemma looked away. She didn't usually make this kind of speech. She added quietly, 'However much we want to, we can't change that.'

Will said nothing. The memory of the pillory was caught in the bones of his neck and back, the ache of his knees and wrists. He tipped his head once and walked out the door to visit John.

London
December 1321

The Invisible Realm

The book of hours is a world: words and pictures, heaven and earth, prayer and play. The pictures reach for inner meaning, extending the real world into another realm. They reveal the truth of that invisible realm by giving it form in line and colour. Do not simply seek to show what the words say, but use the strength of your brush and your imagination to enlighten the woman who prays.

The Art of Illumination

In the days before Yule, Will and Gemma continued to work early in the morning. A few times, she looked over the changes he was making to John's sketches and paintings. When he'd first arrived, Will had seemed so arrogant, so certain of his own skills, that she was afraid he'd use this chance to show off his own work, overpaint John's style entirely. But she was wrong. It was still possible to see John's particular use of line and form, which was more conventional than Will's; less French, Gemma thought with a smile. And though Will's work didn't have the quality of John's fine shading, she wouldn't have expected such a young man to have that delicacy of touch.

There was a new ease between them.

'There's less to correct now that John isn't painting,' Will said to Gemma. 'It should be easier. But somehow it isn't.'

'The shop isn't working as well, you mean?' Gemma said. 'I've noticed that. I always thought John was never here, that he did nothing, but whenever he was in the shop he was planning; he understood what should be done next, how the book should take shape. He didn't say much, but he made it seem we were doing well.'

Will nodded, remembering John's moments of quiet instruction and encouragement. 'He'll be back. That's John. His eyes might not heal, but as soon as he's well you won't keep him in his bed.'

If it were that simple, Gemma thought. She knew now that John's illness was more than his failing eyes, or a wounded arm. Last year on May Day when he'd danced and stumbled, they had all blamed the drink, but since then his legs had become weaker, and she had seen him rubbing his knees, had lately seen his hands tremble. What would happen when it was clear he couldn't work and she could no longer pretend her work was his? Southflete wouldn't offer commissions to a woman.

Gemma ran her fingers along the margin of her page, added a fine, ornate curl that ran from the heading down the left side and beneath the words. Into the silence, she said, 'It's notes, a guide for Nick. What he needs to know about being a limner.'

Will looked up.

'These pages. They're to help Nick. A guide for the apprentice. Pigments, colours, illumination. The familiar and basic.'

'Notes? He's fortunate.' Will spoke quietly.

'No, not just notes. A small book, it will be.'

Will nodded, unsure what to say. A woman writing a book?

'It's about more than what to grind and mix and for how long,' Gemma said. It was almost anger, a challenge, her words fast. 'He needs to understand how pictures work, what a book is for, how its parts are like parts of a body. He should learn how to think about its shape, how it grows, so its limbs and its head are pleasing, well proportioned. If I'm to train Nick, I'll tell him what I think he needs.'

Will studied her tight jaw, the furrows above her eyes. A woman writing a treatise? He had thought she was copying, perhaps some work for Manekyn, but choosing the words herself? And not simple recipes, but philosophy, the art of beauty and proportion. No wonder she was secretive. He bent to his work.

Adding white to the folds in St Christopher's robes, he thought about the Dancaster pages Master Edgar had used to teach the techniques of fine shading; they were most likely Gemma's work. Even the Dancaster rose. The delicate lines of the calendar pages.

After a time he said, 'I think it's a good idea, the book for Nick.'

Gemma looked up. 'You do?'

'Yes, I think it is.'

'Should I be pleased about that? Grateful?'

Not understanding, Will replied, 'Just thought I'd say. Helpful. To have a book made for you.'

Gemma put down her quill. 'Yes, I know it's a good idea, Will. And I knew that before you told me. Helpful, yes, that's why I'm doing it.' She knew, though, that there was more to it than being helpful. How could she explain to him, a man who was so easily accepted into the guild? Why should she try? So much of her knowledge and skill was hidden. But words on parchment, her own words, her own thoughts, all that she had learned — it would be there, written down, the pages bound, able to be picked up and held, even if the guild would not recognise it. 'It was to be for Alice, for when she became an apprentice.'

'An apprentice limner?'

'It was a fancy of mine, that she would be the first in London. With John and me to teach her, help her. We could have shown Southflete that a woman could do the work, could have made

him accept Alice into the guild, when it's finally formed.'
Gemma laughed awkwardly. 'But she didn't want that.'

Will listened, nodded, kept his silence.

'I do the work,' Gemma said quietly, 'but Southflete
won't see it.' She wondered why she had told Will, given
away the secret she had kept for herself. The early morning
was no longer her own, but the words on the page were. Her
choice, her script, her quill. Perhaps it was that John was ill,
that she was weary of doing so much on her own. Perhaps it
was her dawn companion going away.

Will stood and stretched. 'That's St Christopher finished.
Where are the other pages?' He walked to the storeroom. 'In
here?'

Gemma joined him. 'I've put them away here.'

She leaned across the bench in front of him and Will put
a hand on her back. For a moment neither of them moved.
Gemma felt the warmth of his touch, his shoulder against
her hair, his hip and legs brushing hers. Limner and mistress.
Will sensed Gemma leaning toward him. He knew that if he
pulled her closer, she wouldn't resist. They faced each other,
not speaking, barely breathing.

'Here they are.' Gemma pulled a pile of pages from beneath
the finished quires and stepped away.

The silence shattered as Nick rushed down the stairs
looking for food. St Paul's rang the hours, and Nick needed to
eat: the markers of another ordinary day.

It was dark in the shop, only one man at his desk in a pool of
lamplight. Will had stayed late to work on the illumination
of the Crucifixion, but even so, it wouldn't be done before
he left the city the next morning. It was taking longer than
he'd hoped, planning the figures beneath the cross, showing
a mother's grief as she watched her son die. He was slow to
paint the women's faces, Mary and Mary Magdalene's, the

simple lines that would be their cries of anguish. Outside, in the churches and streets, London prepared to celebrate Jesus' birth, but he could feel only unease, as if nothing was certain. He had thought he was painting the opposite of Yule, the bleak end to a man's thirty-three years, but slowly, without realising it, Will felt time folding: birth and death touching. Hadn't he painted one of the wise kings bringing myrrh as a gift to the newborn Christ? Myrrh to scent his lifeless and bloodied body. Was it winter's chill, or the renewed threat of war, or the sense of uncertainty that John's knife wound had brought? Death only an arm's length away. Had Simon been marked for death that frozen night?

It hadn't yet snowed, but the white road had returned, threading through his dreams. Rustling in hedges, twigs snapping behind him. And always the empty road. Tomorrow morning, he would take it again, leaving behind this place that had been so welcoming and so cruel.

A few cold pies as his offering, he walked down the steps to the undercroft for the fraternity's Yule celebration. John was still in bed, healing slowly. His absence was a hole in the gathering; it was only with him away that Will noticed how essential he was to the fraternity. Idla wasn't there either, too sick to leave her bed. Tom had no smile but Benedict stood with him, their shoulders touching in a silent conversation. Some of the faces Will recognised only slowly; they were the poor from the streets thereabout, invited in to share some warmth and food.

Henry Archer greeted Will, clothes hanging from his shoulders, his face a grey that smudged into black beneath his eyes. Illness and no job left their marks on the body. Will imagined the quick, feathery brush strokes, the gradual blending of grey into black.

Hawisia, Henry's wife, looked no better, but she smiled and said, 'Our little Mirabel's been waiting to see you. Big Will, she calls you.'

The little girl ran to Will and grabbed his leg, so he lifted her up, held onto her waist and spun her over and over, her hair flying out like streamers.

'It's not Mirabel at all. It's a spinning top,' he said.

The little girl staggered away, giggling.

'We need a song, Will,' Hawisia said. 'Haven't heard you sing for a while.'

'We've all had it rough, haven't we?' Henry said.

'Any work yet?' Will asked, veering away from memories of his hour in the pillory.

Henry shook his head and frowned across the room at the parchmenter whose shop was a few up the Row from the Dancaster workshop. 'Rowley says there's no way he can take me on again. Price for skins is so high since the murrain got worse. Years I worked for him, years. And the son of a whore puts me off, just like that. How are we to live? If I was stronger, I'd try for work as a gong farmer, but even that's hard to get. Who'd have thought, men fighting one another to shovel shit?'

'Manekyn says the fraternity has some money set aside that we can have to see us through,' Hawisia said. 'For a little while, anyway.' She pulled at her husband's arm. 'Let it go for now, Henry. It's Yule. Let's have a song. What about "Welcome, Yule", Will?'

Will looked at the two faces; what could he say? It was easier to sing.

'Welcome, Yule, Welcome are you, Heavenly King, Welcome …' The undercroft took his voice, rolled it between the arches, the stone adding warmth to its depth. Voices began to join in until the space was filled with song, a claim on life, however thin it might be. For a moment, the gloom faded. Whatever had happened yesterday, and whatever would happen tomorrow, there was this gathering and this time that whispered that all might be restored. Death's presence made life more precious. Perhaps myrrh at birth is not entirely grim, Will thought.

Mirabel stretched up her arms and Will picked her up, sat her in the crook of his elbow. Her hand on his chest to feel its vibration, she watched his face. When the song finished, Henry began another: 'A beautiful woman, white as ivory ...', and though Hawisia frowned that it wasn't a song for Yule, she joined in.

Will sang along, but he was elsewhere. Students roaming stupidly drunk by the Cam, singing in the cold, their breath white. Simon's hand locked into Will's elbow.

The sound, the grip-grap of the gargoyle's feet on stone, somehow made its way through the singing, and though Will braced himself, he realised there was an odd comfort in it. That familiar pain that said he was still alive. Then a movement, a glimpse from the corner of his eye. He sang on, looking away. It moved again, creeping now, leg by leg up the brick frame of the arch, each step delicate, deliberate, its eyes never leaving Will. All the way to the peak of the arch, an arm's length above Wat's swaying head, but the scrivener saw nothing. Mirabel, feeling the tension in Will's arms, watching his eyes, looked up to where he was staring, and giggled. Will's singing stumbled and he lost the words, looking from Mirabel's face to the gargoyle and back, confused. But the singing had caught, the arches embraced its sound, and the song flowed on.

London
January 1322

Black

Black symbolises death and fear, hence its use on Good Friday.

The very best black is vine-charcoal black. Use only the youngest shoots from the grape vine, form them into a tight bundle and place them in a covered terracotta porringer so that no air can reach them, otherwise the leaves will become ashes instead of the carbon required. At a low temperature, bake the leaves and wait patiently until they are completely burned, for if you do not, the colour will be spoiled and produce an inferior brownish hue.

Although not as fine a colour as vine-charcoal black, lampblack may be easily obtained by burning a flame beneath an earthenware or metal vessel or plate. The carbon that gathers may be scraped away and used without grinding. Even in this simple process, the fuel for the flame will affect the quality of the carbon that results. Olive oil or hempseed will produce a fine and pure hue.

The Art of Illumination

The shop was quiet: just Gemma and Benedict at their desks, and Nick moving between storeroom and limners. Gemma began a new page: *Hail and rejoice most holy mother and ever virgin Mary, you who clearly opened to us the gate of paradise, which had been shut by Eve.* The scrawled instruction was to paint Mary opening the doors of paradise to Eve. This is the sacred history of women complete, Gemma thought: Eve eats the apple, and she and Adam are forced from paradise. We are all Eve, at fault even when we're not. But Mary, who is pure, ushers Eve back through the gate, and with her, all of us.

Gemma knew that when she planned the picture, she was to consider ways to help Lady Mathilda pray, but she had no patience any more with the woman in her manor house, no doubt leaving her tenants to starve while she celebrated her Yule feast, complaining that the master limner from London hadn't yet arrived to entertain her. Gemma felt as if no amount of candlelight could quench the darkness creeping toward her, and across the land. After years of numbing cold, the warmth of summer had seemed like a new beginning, as if the poets were right and the wheel of fortune was finally turning from its sojourn in hell. But, like a bad joke, summer had been so hot and dry that cattle dropped dead and crops shrivelled in the fields. Father Paul, who for five years had preached that the freeze and famine were God's punishment for mankind's sins, now had a waver in his voice. It almost seemed as if the man of God had given up. Even contrition wore itself out, a rag beaten so often that there was nothing left but threads. People barely prayed for mercy to a cruel God, and clung to each other instead.

And now the familiar winter cold was exacting its annual toll. The dead and dying were legion. Gemma knew that she needed the reassurance of paradise, even if she doubted it existed. Stories we tell ourselves, she thought, to ease the pain; we need them, whatever the truth of God and heaven. She had drawn the two main figures and the tall crenellated tower that would be paradise. There would be gold leaf in each corner, so she painted on the gesso.

The shop felt empty, almost hollowed out. Will had left, and John was asleep upstairs. The day before, she had called a physician, Richard Cambor, without telling John; she knew he would argue at the cost. She was worried that even though his hand was no longer red, and the fever not so fierce, he seemed no better.

'The hand is healing,' he'd said to Gemma downstairs in the hall. 'No saying how it will mend; it might be little use to him when it heals completely. For his craft, I mean.' He'd looked back toward the solar where John still languished. 'It's melancholy is my worry. No surprise, if he fears he'll never paint again. Melancholy is slower, harder to discern than fever, but I've seen men die of less than this. Give him milk and eggs, poached is best. And give him some green ginger. It's not easy to find in this weather, but do what you can, search around the stalls. Allow company that will cheer him. Laughter, he needs. And ensure he has no worries, no more than he has.' He glanced around the cramped dark hall. 'Be sure the rooms are clean and light, full of odours that will bring pleasure to him.'

Gemma had thanked him, paid what she owed, and swallowed the words she wanted to say: wouldn't we all like soft food, exotic ginger, pleasant rooms and company? And a woman to provide them all. After she has finished his work in the shop.

Her face burned now as she remembered. She had sent Nick to search for the precious green ginger, and though he relished the chance to be out of the silent shop and hunting around the markets, it was nowhere to be found. But he had bought a sweet cake for Idla from Ellyn's stall as Gemma had asked. Perhaps it would give the poor woman a moment of pleasure. She had the look of death.

In the window of the tower, Gemma drew three women, the dead now alive in paradise. She would use light colours for the ladies' clothing, perhaps a touch of gold leaf. What would Idla think of it? Would there be comfort in the thought of following Eve, ushered in by Mary's touch?

Cold air sliced across her thoughts, and she looked up. Southflete, again. She stood and smiled.

'Morning, Gemma. I thought by now John would be pleased of a visitor.'

'Very kind, I'm sure, but his fever returned last night,' she lied. 'The physician says it's only rest will help.' She moved just enough to block the way to the door into the hall. Rest. John didn't need the stationer asking about the book's progress, pressuring him to return to work.

'I won't bother him. Just want to wish him well, that's all.' Southflete stepped forward.

Gemma didn't move. They were so close that she could see the pores on his face, the black hairs in his nose. It helped. 'In a few days, of course. Come and see him then. I'll pass on your good wishes.'

The stationer stepped to the side. His nostrils flared and his hands tapped against his thighs, but he said nothing. Looking across the room to Benedict, head buried in his work, and the other two desks empty, he asked, 'Where's Asshe today?'

'Not here,' Gemma said.

Southflete turned on her. 'I can see that, Gemma. Being difficult only makes matters worse for all of us.'

Realising she had pushed her game too far, Gemma flushed. 'He's on his way to the Fitzjohn estate. To paint the chapel and sketch Lady Mathilda at prayer. As you agreed on our behalf. He'll be gone some days, of course.'

'But she asked specifically for Dancaster himself. What's Asshe doing?'

'We ... John decided it best not to keep Lady Mathilda waiting any longer. He wrote a letter. Well, Will wrote down John's words to introduce him. And she'll see his skill soon enough. I'm sure she'll be happy with his work.'

'I'm worried about this, about all of this. Look at this workshop now. All you have is two apprentices to do the work. It's not what we agreed.'

Benedict looked up and Gemma said quickly, 'Benedict is a journeyman, qualified. Remember?'

'Ah yes,' Southflete said, uninterested.

As he glanced at the page on Gemma's desk, she realised she hadn't covered it.

'Is this your work?' he asked. 'Are you helping out? Adding a little to John's sketch?'

'I am,' Gemma said, and bit down on the temptation to say more. I'm doing it, as I've painted the rest of the book, she wanted to add.

'There are a few questions about this workshop that we need to deal with once John is well. Your fraternity might not care, but there are others in the book trade who would be unhappy. Quality, as I keep saying. We need trained and experienced men working on a commission like this.' He looked more closely at the page. 'This. What is this?'

Gemma tried to loosen her jaw, willed her anger to subside. 'My sketches for the Salutation of the Virgin.' She took a breath. 'John and I discussed it, and I'm making a beginning, as he is unable. It's Our Lady opening the gates of paradise for Eve.'

'I can see that, woman, but why three figures?' Southflete said. 'Who is this behind Mary?'

'The figure isn't finished yet, but it's to be Lady Mathilda, echoing the gesture of the Virgin.'

'Lady Mathilda as the Virgin? That's inappropriate. It's not theologically sound, surely.'

Gemma felt her years of learning and longing banking up like a wave behind her. She had to show the stationer that she understood how pictures could speak beyond words; it was a language she had learned as a little girl, and it was as familiar to her as speaking.

'You were the one who first told us that one of the aims of this book is to help Lady Mathilda see both her past and her future as part of the story of a family with great aspirations.'

Southflete shuffled his feet, stamped lightly. 'Yes, yes. The coats of arms of their past lineage, their neighbours, those they influence. The pictures of them, their children, the continuing line. So?'

'We want to show their greatness not simply as nobility who gather land and power, but as godly people who use it in the service of the Church.' Gemma swallowed. 'Eve's story is woman's story ... or so the Church tells us. Both sinners. But Mary bears Jesus and overturns that story. She ushers Eve into paradise.'

Southflete crossed his arms.

Pointing to the sketches she had made, Gemma was absorbed in her ideas. 'See here, the way Lady Mathilda echoes the Virgin's gesture? That's the picture showing the way Mary gathers the lady into her own story. She becomes as Mary. I want Lady Mathilda to see that as a woman from a great family, as a mother, she follows in Mary's line. That's how pictures work, telling stories.'

Gemma was excited and looked up; perhaps she had gone too far. 'Of course,' she added quickly, 'Lady Mathilda might not understand all of those ideas, but she can feel them when she sees herself there, in the picture.'

Suddenly aware of the shop again, Gemma looked around. Benedict was bent to his work, though she could tell he was listening; Nick was peering round the storeroom door; Southflete was frowning.

'These are conversations I'd best have with John. I'll need to see it when it's finished, to see whether you've given the Virgin due honour. Tell John to use gold leaf here.' He pointed to the corners of the frame already painted pale pink with gesso. 'And lapis on the Virgin's robe, nothing less. I won't have woad or anything inferior. And when John is recovered, we will discuss the atelier and its practice.'

As Southflete closed the door, Gemma walked the few steps across the room and back again; she wasn't sure what had just happened. Southflete had seen her page. They had both called it John's work, yet it was clear Gemma was involved in the sketches. And even more, in the ideas behind them. She turned, continued pacing. And even though the stationer had blustered, tried to keep the upper hand, he had discussed theology with her. She had enjoyed the chance to speak of what she knew, and he had listened, at least for a moment. She stopped and smiled. What a strange dance she had just performed.

But the quiet flutters of excitement in her belly gradually subsided as a familiar wariness took over. She was like a dog sniffing the air: the meat might smell good, but it could be a trap. What was the stationer thinking as he walked back to London Bridge? She had discussed design with him, even dared to contradict him, however mildly. Surely he wouldn't let that pass without an answering slap. And however much he understood the need for an extra hand, would he accept a woman doing the work? Perhaps on his way down Old Change he'd meet a friend and stop in a winehouse for a warming drop or two, or perhaps the sun would shine on the Thames and he would be mollified, see the sense in Gemma making use of her talent. She could hope, but still the dog growled its low warning, hackles up, as usual.

She walked into the back yard, letting the cold air bite at her face. The apple tree was bare sticks, John's vegetable patch a few sad tufts of green. Idla. In the buttery she looked at the sweet cake. Why had she even dreamed that Idla could eat one?

As Gemma climbed the stairs to Idla's room, heaviness dragged at her feet with each step, and by the time she reached the top one, she knew what it was. It nailed her in place. Her hand at the door refused to push it open. She'd seen enough of death, she wanted no more. Death gathers, she thought — threads spun between every one. Every other grief would gather in Idla's room as well. John was in his bed in the solar, trembling and still pale. That was her main concern. She couldn't deal with it all.

She tapped on the door, pushed it open and stepped through in one movement, before she could hesitate or run. Idla hadn't fought, Gemma could tell from her face, but there was no sense of peace, either. Exhausted, ravaged. Eyes glassy, her mouth hanging open. They said that an open mouth allowed the soul to depart the body, but it made her undignified, a leering, sightless fool.

Gemma touched the woman's cold face, pressed her mouth shut and ran her hand softly over her eyes, let her sleep. Idla's mouth gaped open again, insistent, so Gemma rummaged for a rag, eventually tore a piece from the thin bedsheet and wrapped it around her head. She noticed, then, Idla's white kerchief neatly folded on the pillow next to her head, and remembered.

'When I die … No Gemma, listen, when I die, take my kerchief and give it to St Michael's to use as a corporal. It's a comfort to think of it, as small as it is, covering the chalice, so close to Christ's body. I know I won't be here, but it's the one thing I have as remembrance.'

Gemma took the kerchief and set it on the table; she would tell Tom.

Gently straightening Idla's body and crossing her hands over her chest, Gemma placed the half-finished basket near her feet. Idla, Basketmaker. She opened the window, as much to clear the thickening stench as to allow the soul to escape, as they said. Were they the souls of her own dead that gathered around, or just the revisiting of so much pain and helplessness? The room was almost bare, but on a small ledge near the window Gemma noticed Idla's comb, simple and carved from bone; it was, apart from the white kerchief and the clothes she was wearing, probably the only object she owned. Gemma placed it gently on Idla's breast, a piece of this world to take with her. The doing helped, the business of death — some of it necessary and some of it arranged to keep the living moving. She would send Benedict to fetch Tom home.

A short time later Gemma returned from errands to find Tom sitting on the side of the bed, his face no different colour from his wife's, and Benedict with him, both silent but companionable. She smiled weakly at Benedict and he nodded back.

'Annie will come, help me wash the body,' she said. 'And I've told Father Paul.'

Tom looked at her, his eyes wide with horror. 'Unconfessed. She's unconfessed. She'll—'

'No, no. Father Paul came yesterday. She begged me to call him. She knew, Tom.'

'You did what?' He stood up. 'You called the priest and didn't tell me my wife was about to die? You let me leave her, not be with her? Were you here?'

'No. I …' Gemma stepped back, nothing to say. She could have stayed.

'She was alone, and you could have told me so I knew not to leave her.'

'They did. She did tell you, Tom,' Benedict said quietly. 'You didn't want to know, that's all. 'Course you didn't.'

Gemma looked on as Tom ranted his anger at London, at its people that didn't care, at God, at Gemma, at Benedict and finally at Idla for leaving him. He grabbed the basket at Idla's feet and tore at it, breaking what he could, pulling out strands of wicker, shaking them loose, until the effort collapsed into sobs and he sat, cradling the basket in his arms. Finally, exhausted, he sat still looking at nothing, and then, perhaps worst of all, he noticed the basket on his knee, a tangle of canes, and seemed to really see it for the first time. 'The last thing she made,' he said, and with shaking fingers, began to weave the bent and twisted canes together, but it was impossible. Finally, he tried to push what was left into its round shape. 'The last thing she made,' he said over and over. 'The last thing.'

Gemma watched, knowing there was nothing she could do. The man's nose was red and swollen, his eyes staring, his mouth the shape she'd seen on her mother just before her pa died. How ugly it all is, she thought.

London
January 1322

Burnishing

Rubbing the gold leaf to a consistently smooth surface will make it like a mirror, but think carefully on what this means. Whereas before the burnishing the gold is light and scattered, burnished gold invites the shadows, reflecting them back, and can appear quite dark.

The Art of Illumination

It was good to begin painting again, good to be back at her desk. With Benedict, Gemma had helped Tom step by step through the rituals of death, and she turned to the parchment with relief. The gold leaf she had just finished burnishing seemed brighter than ever before, and the azurite in its clam shell, always beautiful, was a blue so rich that the back of her tongue tingled. It was only a week or so since she had planned the illumination of Eve entering paradise, but the business of death had swallowed time into its dark struggle. She began the background, measuring and ruling tiny squares for a diaper pattern. Nick brought more clam shells of paint — woad, white lead and vermilion — and looked at the page. 'How do you do that?' he asked. 'All those tiny squares and lines.'

'I like this fine work, building an effect with detail,' Gemma said, and normally would have told him to stay and learn, but she needed to be quiet, without his questions. 'Come back and see when you've mixed the shell gold.'

Painting alternate squares of red and blue — a chessboard of colour — she then added to each one a white crescent on its four sides, with a white dot in the centre. When Nick came over to peek, he laughed at what he saw: paint and parchment with the appearance of plush fabric, each square pressed in the centre with a button.

As she thought about how to paint the figures, she remembered her conversation with Southflete, then her slow steps up the stairs, but she brushed it all away — all apart from Idla. The only solace she could offer Tom, and even more, Idla herself, was to paint her face on one of the women at the window in paradise. She had been alone when she died, but there she would be, in paradise, radiant with the light of heaven, shell gold in touches on her hair, standing between two welcoming women.

She was at rest now. The fraternity paid fees for the funeral and held a simple wake. Many in the street had no interest in Idla's death, and Gemma knew some felt there was a certain justice, or at least a cruel satisfaction, in the grief of a foreign. Bound inside his own pain, Tom spoke very little, and then only to Benedict.

For Gemma it was a confusing time. Idla's death had shifted her world, as if a sketch had been outlined clearly in black. She was thankful for what now seemed the extravagance of her life: a son, a daughter and a husband. Riches, compared with Tom's sadness. However hard things were, there was hope. John was alive, and even if he couldn't paint, his work would be remembered, handed on in bound books. And Alice visited more often since John's illness, sat with him while he slept, chatted a little, or not at all, both content with quietness, it seemed. Like Gemma, she had always been most happy when she could be with her pa. Gemma was pleased that they had each other's company.

And yet she was bereft. At night, their solar seemed colder than ever, refusing to warm up, and though John slept next to her, and Nick and Benedict slept only paces away, she felt forlorn. John asked often about Will, but she had no news to tell him; the man simply wasn't there. In the atelier before dawn, usually her favourite time of day, the walls echoed every movement, gave back to her every murmur she made. She felt herself a body alone. Even her work on 'The Art of Illumination' felt without purpose.

Once John was well enough to be out of bed, he became the ghost of the workshop, unable to stay away for long, but restless when he was there, finding fault with insignificant mistakes, warning them all how much more work there was to do. Gemma looked up from her sketch of women hunting in the lower borders of the page and watched him pace around the desks, peer into the storeroom, nod at Nick, then sit at his empty desk. At times it seemed that he was more outline than body. The shop had seemed empty without him, but since his illness he unsettled them all with his melancholy.

If John stopped moping over his fate, he could take charge again of the atelier — he had so much wisdom to impart — but right now, without a brush in his hand, he seemed useless. Sometimes he went out; once or twice he had visited the apothecary and the goldsmith for supplies, even found reason to visit Manekyn, though most of the time it seemed that he wandered the streets, gleaning whatever news he could. Of late, he was obsessed with talk of yet more strife between the nobles and the king and Despenser.

With Will gone, Nick spent more time near Benedict's desk, and Gemma was surprised that he didn't send the boy away. No longer an apprentice, perhaps he felt some duty to teach what he knew, though it seemed to be more than that. Benedict spent most of his evenings in Tom's room or going out with him to an alehouse, walking against the cold; he was giving Tom what no one else could.

This particular afternoon, Nick was leaning over Benedict's work, laughing but uneasy, as if blustering in the face of fear.

Benedict smiled up at him and said quietly, 'It comes to us all, Nick. But look, they're smiling.'

'So who are they?' Nick asked.

'I don't know. It's a bit hard to tell when they're skeletons, isn't it?'

Nick spluttered a laugh. 'That's what I mean! How can a skeleton smile? I like this one at the back with the really big smile. He looks like he's just told a joke. And they've got such big feet, too. And big hands.'

'Well, this one has his hand out to the men on the other side of the picture, see? The skeletons are people who've risen from their graves and the men there are welcoming them to Jerusalem. That's what I've written here, around the edge of the picture: *Les mots resusciterent et alerent en iherusalem et temoygnerent la mort de ihesu le fiz deu*. God opens the graves of the saints and they go into Jerusalem to see the Crucifixion. I've written that so that Lady Mathilda can understand what the picture's about. So I'll need vermilion and blue and some turnsole violet for the robes of the men, please.'

'And what about the skeletons?' Nick asked. 'I can grind some bone white,' he laughed. 'Yes! That's what I'll do. Perfect.'

'Just a little then,' Benedict said and smiled.

'Did you hear, Ma? I'm making bone white for the skeletons. Bone white!' Nick rushed to his bench, still laughing at his own joke.

Gemma smiled at his pleasure. She wouldn't have chosen bone white for that picture, but Benedict was right to let the lad make a decision. It wouldn't make much difference. Perhaps in a few months he would have the book to help him. It was easier to think about that now. Whatever Gemma wanted for her, Alice would not work in the trade.

Mathilda

Wain Wood Manor
July 1322

Mathilda closes the door of her chamber, hoping to rest. The baby, now kicking and strong, makes sleep uncomfortable; her back aches, and when she stands thin pains shoot down her legs. She smiles; nothing about her makes sense. After all the fear and frustration of hiding from the king, now the urge to retreat into the cocoon of mother and baby is equally as strong. And yet she is restless. She tries to pray but she can't settle, even to the psalms she loves so well.

She turns to the illumination of the Annunciation. Despite what she felt when she first saw it, her stomach turning at the announcement of a baby born into shame, she is beginning to look forward to the next few months, a sense of anticipation threaded through her day. The baby and the warmer weather feel like a reprieve. Oliver says they will likely be safe now, though they must wait on the king's mood.

This morning she looked down the valley. The villagers have planted the spring crop and now they are bent-backed, crawling along the rows, weeding thistles and dock. There's a nervous hope among everyone, though Fraden, especially, will not speak it aloud.

A year ago at Aspenhill they had done the same, planted their hopeful seed only to watch it sprout, and then shrivel in hot, dry weather, the parched corn like scarecrows rustling in the wind. Fraden replenished the stocks of sheep and watched, helpless, as they sickened with murrain and died. 'Don't the preachers say God knows our hearts?' he had said. 'What are we to do? Must we explain our prayers now? No floods, Lord, but some rain for the crops, please.' The turning of the seasons could not be trusted; as winter returned, cold and harsh, everyone was fearful that this time it might not end.

Mathilda shudders at the memory. Into the gloom, she thinks, the Marchers' victory at the gates of London had seemed a brief and mocking moment of light.

Robert and his men returned home exhausted for a brief respite, but with news of death, treachery and battles. When Mathilda questioned him about rumours of the Marcher barons plundering starving villages for food and arms, he scoffed and told her she knew nothing of the ways of war. When she pressed, he said, 'Why don't you call for Dancaster to paint me with the family arms in your little book. I can't stay for long, but there should be time enough for that.'

It was a distraction, Mathilda knew, a sop to his guilt. But as soon as the message was despatched, another one arrived: King Edward had recalled Despenser to his side and was determined to tame the Marcher barons, once and for all. It was no surprise. 'By God's nails,' Robert said. 'He might be our king, but he never keeps his word. There's no room for negotiation any more.' The next battle would be the country at arms against itself.

More painful yet, the king would call upon men from the villages to fight for him; this time their own tenants, some of them only lads, would be caught up in a smaller, more reluctant civil war. Mathilda's chest had ached when she heard the news. So, while Robert rode west and then north to battle with the king, his tenants would join the king's forces in a war against their own lord. How simple it would be if it were only good against bad, the way the romances described.

The manor house bristled with fear and panicked work. All the gear the men had unpacked had to be cleaned, polished and repacked. Robert was busy and distracted, even in bed, and Mathilda resented his rushed, almost angry love-making. But afterwards he held on to her, as if the release had left him exposed and afraid. He had been to battle before, but the coming one, he knew, would decide his fate.

Drawing him aside from the bustle, Mathilda asked him what they should do about the village men forced to fight, but he told her only what she already knew: 'Nothing we can do. I won't punish them, if that's what you mean, and we have to hope we defeat the king.' Mathilda wanted more, wanted him to think about more than the horses' fittings and his own armour, to think about all he would be leaving her with — struggling tenants, dying crops, a failing estate — but he insisted there was nothing to be done, and no time. 'No point having crops if Despenser takes away our land,' he said. 'Use Yuletide to pray God defend us.' She walked away from his pious words; as if God would take more notice of men with swords than starving children. But perhaps that's how it was.

She insisted the Yule feast for the village take place in the manor as usual, even without its lord, and with as much meat as they could manage, though she knew full bellies were a fleeting comfort. The gathered company sang while the Yule log was carried into the hall, seeking some comfort in the rituals they knew so well, their cry to whatever god might govern the seasons. Gathered around the fire, they told again the stories everyone knew but had to tell again. Stories of children dying, of crops flooded or frost-burnt, of starving animals wallowing in sodden earth. An end of days, some said, the death of the Earth; the pouring out of God's wrath, Father Jacobi said. Others suggested sacrifices, a return to the old ways and the ancient gods of sun and earth and rain. Some blamed the king and his taxes that sucked villages dry.

Mathilda watched on, saw their fear, heard the quiet terror in their words. She wanted Robert to push open the door, announce that they had won, that Despenser was dead. Surely that would help the land recover. Instead, days later, William walked in.

The man was not John Dancaster. Silly to point it out to him, but she did. Fright had made her angry. Tall, his clothes filthy with mud, the man looked as if he could hardly stand. She thought he was a messenger, come to tell her that Robert was wounded — or worse, killed by axe gouge, sword cut, spear thrust. Those men came often to her dreams, each one with a slightly different story, though always with the same ending.

The man before her curled his mouth in acknowledgement of who he was not. 'I'm William Asshe,' he said, and explained that Master Dancaster was ill and wouldn't be fit for painting for some time yet. As she wanted the book to be finished quickly, the master had sent him in his stead. He handed her a letter.

The pounding in her head slowed as she read: an apology, Dancaster's unfortunate accident, long recovery. *I commend to you my fellow illuminator, William Asshe. He is a man of considerable skill and his work is of the highest quality. I am confident he will fulfil your needs.* Mathilda lowered the letter. Who was this man who strolled in, later than planned, exhausted and rough looking? She had no time to worry about some apprentice illuminator. He would have to leave. She told him that when he was strong enough, he could go.

'Yes, my lady,' he said without concern. She had expected a protest.

'I don't know you, your work. Do you have experience? You are a master limner, I presume?' She looked at him then, but there was no sign of unease on his face, and so she studied the piece of parchment, as if that might have the answer.

He claimed to be almost a master, having studied with Edgar Gerard in Cambridge. She had heard talk of that man's skill. Then he had moved to London and found work with Dancaster.

'You left your master, and in such uncertain times?' she said.

'I was forced to leave.'

She remembers that word, *forced,* but even more, what he said next.

'A death, my lady.'

Her belly dropped, clenched. It seemed he was that night-time messenger. Robert? Was he telling her Robert was dead?

'A close friend, it was. A student,' he said, almost as if she had spoken the question. 'I felt I couldn't stay there. It forced me to leave.'

They surprised her, those words; not what she expected. 'Whatever may be of your feelings …' she paused to look again at the letter, 'William Asshe, I am paying for a master illuminator to paint my portrait. Not an almost master. You'll have to leave.' Why was she being so difficult?

'Certainly, Lady Mathilda, though I assure you I paint well. I was also trained by Claude of Paris, a student of Jean de Floret, the French master. Perhaps you've seen his work? It's very beautiful. Sinuous lines, graceful figures.'

'Sinuous?' She pounced on the word. 'Mary save us, this is a book of prayers. I do not want it to be sinuous.'

'No, my lady.' He tipped his head. 'I misspoke. Elegant is more my meaning, giving figures life and grace, as if they might live on the page.'

The limner's voice had gathered a fullness now and Mathilda hesitated before she spoke. But whatever it was that had taken control of her would not give in. 'And I tell you that I chose Dancaster because I know he can paint. I won't trade words with you about your skill. I am paying and I will pay for John Dancaster, when he is recovered. I can see you're tired, but you must leave as soon as you are rested.'

'My lady. I wonder, then, if I might spend that time sketching — your tapestries, the chapel, the gardens, perhaps the workers in the fields — for the book, that is.'

Confused, Mathilda thought that her face must appear blank, stupid.

He added, 'To make this trip worth the time it took.'

Now she thinks about that moment, all she can remember is the hole in the side of his right boot. 'Have the stable boy fix that before you leave,' she said.

Mathilda flinches when she thinks he could have obeyed her and walked out the door. She still doesn't understand that rejection of him; they were such strange days with the young limner.

She was too busy with matters on the estate to think about him at first, though she would come across him in the garden or tucked up in the corner of the hall, sometimes sketching but most often simply looking. Looking at one place or thing. Had he stayed only to do nothing? She ignored him, or merely nodded.

The girls were intrigued by this visitor all the way from London, and though Mathilda told them to leave him alone, she saw them both peering at whatever he was sketching. Maggie spoke to him and then laughed at the next thing he drew.

'Joan, Maggie, you have lessons,' she called.

'Oh, but William is showing us—' Maggie began.

'Lessons!' Mathilda said.

William spoke to them, something Mathilda couldn't hear, and the girls ran off. He glanced at her, then bent his head to his work again.

Head bent over papers, Mathilda was checking the buttery accounts when Maggie ran to her and pulled at her arm.

'Maggie, stop it. I'm working, you can see that.' Fraden usually tallied the records, but he was dealing with tenants, struggling since so many men had gone to battle. Mathilda wished away the columns of words and numbers, but work like this kept her imagination from creating scenes of horror, men and swords and horses.

Maggie stood close by and tapped her foot until Mathilda gave in. 'Will's been showing us how to draw, with a stick in the dirt. I drew a tree and one of the ducks on the pond and then a dove sitting on top of the dovecote. Come and look.'

'I'm busy.'

'He even went into the dovecote. I told him not to because it smells, but he went anyway. He says it's beautiful.'

The words caught Mathilda's attention. 'It was my favourite place of all when I was your age,' she said. 'I'd be in trouble all the time for going there and upsetting the birds.'

'Did you? But—'

'Now go. I must finish these accounts.'

Mathilda kept working, but the memories floated before her eyes. Opening the door and creeping into the close gloom, hearing the birds flutter and coo, the muffled sound floating on the air like feathers, the warmth making the place feel as if it was lined with cushions and tapestries.

Later, Mathilda noticed the girls standing either side of the limner in the hall. He was giving them turns with his stylus to draw on his wax tablet. Maggie was chattering, hopping from foot to foot, impatient for her turn, while Joan was frowning with concentration. Mathilda smiled. As a girl, only a little older than Maggie, she had loved to draw on wax, a cat or a mouse or a monster in the corners, flowers along the edges. How she would have enjoyed the chance to meet a limner. She let them be. No doubt Maggie would tell her about it later.

After mass the next morning, Fraden asked to speak with Mathilda as she walked from the chapel. John Beecroft, one of the tenants, was unable to pay his rent. 'I told him he could work on the demesne lands to make it up, but he's some problem with his legs and can barely walk.'

'Does he have any crops planted?' Mathilda asked, though she knew what the answer would be.

'His corn failed last season, like everyone else's, so there's scant seed. He has one strip of rye sown, but that's all.'

'What does he want me to do? Find seed, then plough and sow for him?' she asked, her voice sharp.

'His wife Thea's not strong enough to plough the rest, but she spins. He's hoping we might take some wool, or that she can work in the kitchen here, to make up for the rent.'

Mathilda took in a shaky breath and tried to wrap her cape more tightly around herself. 'It's so cold,' she said. There were no ways to work this out.

Fraden seemed to know what she was thinking. 'It's hard, but if we excuse his rent, they'll all ask for the same.'

'I know. Tell Thea we'll take some wool for the rent, but not so much that they freeze. Or starve. Let her work here two days a week until John's better.'

'I don't think he'll—'

Mathilda shook her head. 'Don't tell me that. Not now.'

She walked on, leaving Fraden to deal with it.

In the hall, the limner was seated in front of her favourite tapestry, humming quietly and sketching its garden scene. Without thought, she stopped to look over his shoulder. There were the graceful lines of the orange tree, the curl of its leaves, the simple, round globes of the fruit. Even his simple sketch was beautiful. She looked up to the tapestry, felt again that hum of pleasure in the richness of its colours, the warmth of the wool.

'Sir Robert gave me the tapestry when we were first married,' she said. Robert, fifteen years ago, so pleased that she loved his present.

William nodded. 'It's very fine. And the thread, the stitches. You can't create that texture with paint.'

With no answer to that, Mathilda walked on, then turned to it again. How long since she had really looked at the tapestry? So much worry in each day, so many things to manage, it had seemed to have no place.

The next day she carried in her purse the breviary her mother had left to her, and when she saw William working at the hall table, stopped to show him the simple decoration on the first page. He looked up from his work, surprise on his face. Mathilda suddenly felt foolish, like Maggie wanting his attention. But he immediately took the book from her and studied the illumination. It was Christ enthroned, and behind him a diaper pattern, giving the effect of the padded fabric often used on grand chairs.

'It might not be what you meant about texture, but I've so often looked at this picture and thought how clever the artisan was,' she said.

She watched William's face as he held the page up to the light. He frowned, his forehead creasing, his eyes intent, and just the slightest tightening of his mouth.

'You're right, it's well done,' he said and leafed through the breviary, stopping now and then. 'Not many decorations, but each one drawn well. A fine artist. It's beautiful,' he said as he handed it back.

'Yes, I've always thought so,' she said quietly and turned the pages of the book.

'You appreciate paintings, tapestries. The detail.'

Mathilda looked up, surprised.

'I do,' she said, feeling that she had exposed more than she realised. This wasn't something she often talked about. She had always loved church, as much, perhaps more, for the stained-glass windows and the paintings on the walls as the worship. But that had not been something to speak aloud.

She stopped at the page she was looking for, and held the book open. 'I did this when I was eight,' she said.

Halfway down the right margin was a small crowd of faces drawn in ink: one with a huge nose, one with eyes like marbles, one poking out its tongue, one with curly hair like a lion, one with long, flapping ears.

William laughed, turning on the bench to look into her face. 'I see. Anyone in particular?'

Mathilda spoke quickly, excited by his interest. 'Oh yes, all of them.' She pointed as she spoke. 'My teacher, the priest, my father's friend — I can't remember his name — the maid Juliana, and that's someone who worked in the garden. I used to study their faces and all I could think about was how one part stuck out more than others.' She paused. 'I wanted to keep my drawings, not just have them scraped away on a wax tablet, so I did this. It was my mother's breviary, but worth getting into trouble.'

William looked at the page again, but Mathilda could see that his mind was somewhere else. She stretched out to reclaim the book just as he spoke. 'Yes, I wanted that too, so I scratched mine onto the church wall. A dragon it was. Got a boot up— A boot from Father Michael, when he found me scraping away. But he let me finish it when I told him I still had to draw St George with his spear above it.'

'The church wall? That was brave,' Mathilda laughed.

'Or foolish. But I was so taken by it all. Line, colour, story.'

'So, you grew up to paint in fine books and I grew up to enjoy them. To commission one.' She realised then that she hadn't laughed for days. And with this man?

She looks again at the page, from the procession of hybrids in the margin to the illumination in the centre. She turns it over, finds the Virgin and Child. There is the elegant drapery that William does so well, Mary's blue outer gown covering a soft grey shift that falls in folds and gathers around her feet. She thinks about the shape of the picture, the 'composition', as he called it. Mary has Jesus on one knee, one arm around him, and in her other hand an apple that she holds up to her son's gaze. The bend of her head is gentle, attentive, a slight smile on her lips, her eyebrows raised just enough to suggest she has said something to him. Teaching her son, Mathilda thinks. Surely God as a baby needed to learn how to live in this world. Tucked inside the letter *D*, they are in their own world: mother and baby.

But, for all that, the young Jesus sits tall, one hand raised in blessing as he looks across at the apple. Always God and always man, Mathilda thinks. On either side an angel hangs in the air, wings outstretched, one plucking the strings of a vielle, the other a citole. The sounds of heaven. She smiles and remembers now that William had sat in a corner sketching as she listened to her daughters' music lesson. Will they notice this, be excited to think of themselves as angels attending upon the Virgin? Her gaze drifts to the woman kneeling at the bottom left of the illumination. Herself. The first time she has allowed herself to see it. The woman has her face raised toward the Holy Mother and Child, her mouth open in song.

As her eyes move around the illumination, she notices that her own gown, the colour of a grey dove, is the same hue as Mary's shift, and that the red trimming on her sleeve echoes the fruit Mary holds. Once she would have thought this was because the artist had few colours, or to give pleasing shape to the picture. But now she understands that William has drawn her from the Earth into the heavenly circle of mother and child.

26

Aspenhill Manor,
Fordham, Hertfordshire

January 1322

Perception

Each time you make pigment, whether you are mixing a fine powder the apothecary has provided, or one you have ground yourself, or yet one that you have made through its long and necessary process, each time the pigment will differ in some way. Do not presume carbon black is always the same quality, or that malachite will grind to always give a particular green. Turnsole, of its very nature, is always changeable. You must perceive the differences conveyed through the touch of the pestle or through the muller as you mix; you must learn to see the very slight distinctions in thickness or hue, how dense or vivid or opaque the paint may be. This you cannot be taught. This you must learn as each day you discover what the pigments show you.

The Art of Illumination

At first, nothing about the manor and its lady surprised Will; he had expected little else but the high-handed ways of the nobility, though the lady's fluster at his arrival was almost payment enough for the long walk. He had enjoyed it until she called him an apprentice. He could have left then, and perhaps she would have waved him off at the door, but he was exhausted, too tired and cold to do anything more than accept her offer of food and a bed.

Later, in the barn, as he drifted off to sleep in a pile of

hay, he wondered why he should even care about the lady's opinion of him. A few sketches on the scraps of parchment Gemma had given him, and he could be gone.

But his body was bone-weary, the miles he had walked demanding their payment. He slept, then woke when his belly clenched with hunger, wandered into the kitchen to beg some bread or pottage, then slept again. He dreamed of a black night, a silent river, something lost. He wasn't sure how many days passed.

One morning, sun in his eyes, he woke feeling stronger, and as if he hadn't eaten for days. He wandered in search of food and company. Godwin, the young lad who worked in the stables, ran into the yard and asked for his boots to repair. 'I nearly came and took 'em while you rested, but these cold nights, I thought you'd be wearing 'em the whole time.'

Will sat on a stool, his feet wrapped in some old cloth, and chewed on bread, taking note of the bend of the boy's back, his wide, flat nose, the frame of the doorway behind him. He might never be able to see the chapel, or draw the lady, but these pictures would go into the margins.

As he worked, Godwin talked about his fear for Cornell, Sir Robert's page. 'He's not even as old as me, and he's out there in a war against the king. He said he wanted to go. It's what he's been trained for, so he can be a knight one day.'

Will nodded and listened. London had felt the threat of civil war at her walls, and the workshop had felt it only paces away, but this was different again. It took him a time to recognise it, but the manor was filled with Robert's absence: the men who had gone with him leaving extra work for those on the estate, and above all, the fear of what would happen to the men who fought. Beneath it all, the mutterings that defending the Fitzjohn lands was treason, and even victory, if it came, would be sour.

His boots mended, his belly full, Will explored the gardens and its outbuildings. Two little girls were squatting to play with knucklebones on the cobblestones in the courtyard and when she saw him, the youngest ran to him.

'You the man from London then? You come to draw pictures like my ma says?'

'I have. I'm Will. What's your name?'

'I'm Maggie and this is Joan. We can show you round,' Maggie said, pulling at Will's arm.

'Maggie, come away,' Joan said, but Will smiled that all was well.

'I'd like to see the dovecote. I noticed it when I walked in a few days ago. It's very fine.'

'The dovecote? But it's dirty and nasty in there,' Maggie said.

'Don't go on like that, Maggie,' Joan said. 'Caine cleaned it out yesterday, remember? Fraden said they want the bird shit to mix into soil, ready for planting.'

'Ergh,' Maggie said, but she led the way.

The dovecote was round, built of stone and tapering to a soft point at the top, with a line of gaps for the doves to enter and leave. Will had seen others that were round, but with straight sides and a separate roof, and he admired the way the stonework gradually curved with the height of the structure.

'Our grandpa built this,' Joan said.

'It's very fine. The man who cut and placed those stones so carefully must have loved his craft,' Will said. 'So much work and patience to make it taper the way it does.'

'But our grandpa built it, like I said.'

'Built it? With his own hands? I thought you meant he had it built.'

'Ma says he wanted it here, by the front gate, so everyone who passed could see it.'

'I'm sure he would. Something like this.'

They opened the door carefully and peeked in, though Maggie covered her nose and walked away. It was gloomy inside, the dull light filtering through the gaps in the stone, but Will could see the walls were lined with rows and rows of strips of wood and, behind them, spaces for the doves to nest. Some of the birds cooed and stirred, but they were familiar with sounds from below.

Outside Will said, 'I would have enjoyed meeting your grandpa.'

'And now you can't even meet our pa. He's off to war,' Maggie said. 'He might even die. That's what Ysmay said.'

Will startled for a moment. How old was she? Six, perhaps. 'Oh, I'm sure he'll come home to you,' he said. 'Now, what else will you show me?'

Maggie took his hand and led him into the hall, chatting without pause.

The house was very fine, though not as grand as Will had imagined of gentry who had ordered an expensive book, but he remembered what John had said about Sir Robert's expectations of inheriting land. No doubt the estate in the Marches would be magnificent. The surrounds of the large fireplace were painted with black and white diamonds, and the wooden beams in the walls and ceiling were finely decorated with red curls and twists. Simple, but effective, he thought, and both designs he could copy for the book of hours.

Whenever he sat to his work, the girls would appear, intrigued and asking questions, Maggie wanting to try copying his sketches, Joan standing back a little but readily taking the plummet from him. Once or twice, Lady Mathilda called the girls away to their lessons, or to help Ysmay, the cook, but as the days passed, she let them be. As Will took turns to draw with the girls, he thought it seemed a conversation between them, their thoughts put down in lines and curves. They all chuckled quietly over Maggie's picture of Ysmay with a huge nose, and Will drew a cat with a snail's body that made the girls giggle. He felt the tightness in his face and shoulders begin to release. Children, he thought; children are the same everywhere, London or Fordham.

Feeling stronger, and restless to explore further, Will walked down to the village. He was surprised to see women and lads driving the ox and plough, until he remembered Godwin's lament about the men pressed into fighting for the king. He sketched some scenes, knowing he would need to change them at the workshop: paint burly men at the plough; add sheep to the few mangy ones in their pen; plump up both the woman scattering seed and the hens she fed; put red cheeks on the little girl braiding her sister's hair. It was a sad, muddy place, and he hadn't stayed long.

He wondered why he didn't simply pack his bag and leave. The lady showed no signs of relenting and asking for him to sketch her in the chapel; he hadn't even seen the chapel. Noblewomen are all alike, after all, he thought; hair, gown, shoes and jewels. The journey was a waste.

Still, he stayed. Lady Mathilda seemed too busy to take much notice of him, though at times, his head bent to his work, Will could sense her watching him as she passed, or turning to look now and then when she sat over accounts at the table. Most part of her day seemed taken up with figures and lists, ordering servants, discussing with the steward some matter of the estate or teaching Maggie and Joan their lessons. Will had expected her to spend her time praying, or gossiping with neighbouring women; isn't that what the stories recited at Smithfield said about such women?

He noticed she was a little taller than most women he knew, with a slight hunch in her shoulders, and the way her gown flowed out from a fitting bodice revealed how slight she was. Her face was round, her eyes almond-shaped, and when she frowned, two dimples formed above her eyes. Drawing a sketch of her one day, Will smiled at himself and his limner's eye for detail that made him look, even when he wasn't interested. He'd leave tomorrow. He paused. There it was again, the lady brushing away what seemed to be stray hair from her forehead. He'd seen her do it before, many times; it seemed more a habit, perhaps a sign of worry.

Later that day, she looked over his shoulder at his sketches of the very fine garden tapestry. He waited for her words. She expected him gone, no doubt; there was a famine, hadn't he noticed, and no food to spare for an almost-master. Her brief hospitality was at an end. His jaw clenched, but he kept on drawing.

So he was surprised when she spoke, her voice lighter than he had heard before. It was something that he didn't quite hear, about her husband and a gift, the oranges and leaves. He mumbled something in reply, commented about the wool or the stitches, and watched her walk away. Then she turned back and looked again at the tapestry. For just a moment, he saw something new in her face. Was she remembering the man who had given it to her, the man she might not see again? Or perhaps it was simply his imagining, his confusion at her civil words.

The next day, almost as if the tapestry had been their introduction, Lady Mathilda — hesitant, shy — offered him her breviary. The work was simple, but he could see the book had been well used, clearly of value to the lady. Cautious, he was polite, kept his comments short and waited for her to dismiss him. But she stayed, turned the pages, studied the pictures. Her lips opened a little as if she would speak, though she said nothing; it was memory, he thought, longing perhaps. The slight curl of her mouth, the bright movement in her eyes, the gathering pink in her cheeks, they gave her a beauty he hadn't seen before. For all his observation and sketches, he hadn't really seen her.

Holding the book out again, she showed him her childhood drawings, listed off each character and name, pointed out their exaggerated features and laughed. As she spoke, his own childish scratching on the church wall was there in his mind, clear and shining, then the story pouring out between them. Childhood and trespass, pictures and delight.

When she left, he was restless, couldn't settle again to his work. There was still the question of the portrait, but perhaps he could wait a day or so. Wait? A day or so? He didn't know himself, so happy to slowly court a noblewoman's good will, entertain her children and eat at her table. Enough; he would sketch the chapel tonight and leave in the morning.

How had it happened, then, that he came to tell them about his ma's psalter?

'You've been showing the girls how to draw?' Mathilda asked him that evening.

'They remind me of when I was their age,' he said. 'So keen to find out.'

'Will's been showing us how to make it look like one person is standing behind another one. Depth, he calls it,' Joan said.

'And about doing a face,' Maggie said. 'Eyes and nose and mouth. I could draw you, Ma, couldn't I, Will?'

'Why not?' Will said. 'If your mother agrees.'

Lady Mathilda smiled and nodded.

'Did you always draw?' Joan asked him.

'Not always, but once I started, I drew wherever I could. I found a book my ma kept hidden in our house. A psalter, it was. It didn't have decorations on every page, but I thought it was the most beautiful thing I'd ever seen. And from that day, I knew I wanted to do that.'

'Hidden?'

'Under the floor, it was.'

'Did she paint it then? Your ma?' Joan asked.

'No. There's a long story about where it came from, and she only told me a little of it.'

'Oh, tell us, tell us! We won't tell anyone else, will we?' Maggie said, pulling at Will's arm.

'Maggie! Stop that,' Lady Mathilda said. 'Off now, both of you. Go with Angmar.'

Once Angmar had shooed them upstairs, the lady turned to Will. 'Was that why you drew St George on the church wall? After you had seen the psalter?'

'Yes. And because of that day, even though I was in big trouble, Father Michael arranged for me to become an apprentice.' Will knew he wanted to stop, but out the words came, with a life of their own. 'He said God had given me a talent.'

'It seems such a strange thing, to find a beautiful book hidden like that.'

'Yes, my ma slapped me over the head when she found me with it.'

'There were no illuminators in your family? It wasn't something handed down from a craftsman relative?'

Will felt a prickle of irritation at her questions. 'My father's a wheelwright like his pa before him. Everyday work, but skilled. My mother works with him.'

'Wife of a wheelwright. And yet she owns a book such as that,' Lady Mathilda mused, and might have kept talking, but Will abruptly stood up.

'Even we working folk know beauty when we see it, Lady Mathilda.' Will's voice was low, but sharp. He nodded. 'I'll leave you now. I return to London in the morning.' He bumped a cup that clattered to the floor, and as he walked away, he could feel the eyes of the room on his back.

He should have seen it: the lady intrigued and amused by him, by a wheelwright's wife who might appreciate a fine book. As if the love of beauty was bestowed by God only on those with wealth and position. He had seen how much she liked art and had thought she would understand, but that didn't stop her looking down on him. He hadn't wanted to come, had he not made that clear?

Mathilda

Wain Wood Manor
July 1322

Sitting alone in her closet, Mathilda looks down at the book, at the portrait. No Mary, no Jesus; only the hand of God reaching down to her as she kneels before the carved grapes and arches on the walls of the chapel she loved, but is now lost to her. A pink gown pools around her knees, the lines fluid, shadowed with grey paint, the light from the candles shown in soft, graded white. She hasn't realised before that William painted her as she was that particular night, in her own dress, not the stiff cote-hardie usual in a portrait. She looks up, away from the picture; the memories are pressing in and she's not sure if she's ready for them, but her eyes move back to the page, insistent. In another detail she hadn't expected, her hair is braided around her face, marked in a criss-cross of black lines on pale brown. She touches it gently and sees her mouth, the single black line shaped with red, a sweet almost-smile. Is that how William saw her?

That night in the chapel she was both: woman looking, and woman looked at.

Compline had finished. There was no fresh news from Robert, but the clash of metal and thud of bodies followed her about the manor house, especially in their chamber at night. It was only in the chapel, small enough to make her feel protected, that her mind quietened.

As she opened the door she saw him. It was dark apart from one glowing sphere of light, its reflections flickering in the wooden panelling of the walls. All was still except for the movements of his hand over the parchment. Head bowed, sitting near the altar, he could have been saying his prayers, his fingers moving along his paternoster, bead by bead.

She took a step back, as if she was the one who intruded. But he must have heard the door creak and turned. He seemed ... not dazed, but uncomprehending, and she felt compelled to speak.

'I thought you would be sleeping.'

William stood. 'I thought I'd sketch the chapel. As you said John was to do. I didn't realise anyone would come here. It's so late. My pardon.'

They were awkward, remembering what had happened at the table, his sharp words.

'I couldn't sleep ...'

'Still no news from Sir Robert?'

'Nothing, save that they are headed further north, seeking support from Lancaster.' She glanced at the parchment. 'May I see?'

Without looking at her, William passed over his work.

The page was covered with small sketches: the barn, the manor house, tapestries, musical instruments and, in the bottom corner, the chapel. The simple lines were ... what were the words he had used? Fluid, sinuous, as if liquid themselves. The cloth from the altar draped so that she could feel the weight of the pleats in the fabric and the vines were not as carved in the wood of the panelling, solid and still, but shifting, curling as if a breeze had just blown through them.

'The vines are different.'

William shrugged. 'That's how they are to me, and what I would draw in the book. Your book. Elegance.' He paused, but Mathilda could see he had more to say. 'I misspoke earlier tonight. And it was rude to walk away as I did.'

Mathilda looked away. 'Yes, it was rude. To me, your host, in my house. And in front of the servants. But I think we didn't understand each other.'

'What I meant was simple enough. Even a beggar knows beauty when he sees it.'

'William, enough of your anger. We're born into the position God gives us, that's all there is.'

'What's that to do with beauty? God gives *that* to all of us.'

Mathilda flinched, as if her mother had slapped her for being rude. Is that what he had heard? This man who spent his days making such beauty, the kind she so longed for. Had she wanted to diminish him because of it? 'Yes, you're right. To all of us.' She paused, searching for the right words this time. 'I only wondered how God had given that beauty to your mother. It's the story of the book I was curious about. How she came to have it, why she hides it.'

William was twisting the plummet in his fingers, and she thought at first he would say nothing.

'She hides it from my pa, though she'll never say why. "That's matters for us," she says. It was her ma gave it to her.'

'So your grandmother had it? Was she …?' Mathilda sank onto a chair, hesitating over the question in case William stopped telling his story again.

'Eleanor, her name was. She lived in a village in the Midlands and found the book in the ashes when the manor house burned down. The pages are all burned on the edges, but the words and pictures are mostly clear.'

'A burned book,' Mathilda murmured to herself.

'Eleanor was a little girl then.' Will sat down as he spoke. 'Ma says the village holy woman looked after it for her, and this woman taught her to read and write. There's a list of names on the fly leaf. I wonder if Eleanor wrote the names of her family and friends, so she could practise.' He glanced up at Mathilda. 'And there's a story on the last two pages about a holy woman and a bishop. A cruel story it is, but whoever wrote it swears by Our Lady that it tells fairly and true. Ma says she doesn't know who wrote it, but perhaps it was Eleanor. Who else could it be, if not her?'

William paused, and went back to his sketching, adding lines here and there, apparently without purpose. Mathilda thought he had finished his story, but she waited. The candles glimmered, the chapel was silent.

'When Eleanor left the village she took the book with her, then she handed it to her only child, my ma. Eleanor wrote in the front of the book that it was to be handed down to the first daughter, and if there was no daughter, the son was to take it and hand it to his daughters. And the girls were to be taught to read and write.'

'So, your mother, she can read and write?'

'She can, though she only uses her knowledge for my pa's accounts. And for reading the psalter, when she can. Pa can't read and I sometimes wonder if that's why she hides the book, so he doesn't feel it as shame.'

There were many questions Mathilda wanted to ask, but William seemed to carry the story so tenderly that she was wary. 'Thank you for telling me. Do you have a sister? Will the book be given to her?'

'Nerida. It will be hers, Ma says, to hand on to her daughter, as Eleanor wanted.'

He fell silent and Mathilda watched as he drew in the lines of the small prayer desk with its simple trefoil carving on the sides.

'You said the book was burned. I can't imagine how it must look.'

William stopped drawing but didn't look at Mathilda. 'There are signs there was a clasp on the cover when the book was first made, though it's gone, perhaps weakened in the fire. Being shut tight would have protected the pages a little, so you can still read the words and see most of the pictures. But the edges of the pages are black, so wrinkled that they fan out and the book won't close any more. I thought they were like the feathers of some magical black bird. It's strange, but being burned like that is one of the things I most like about it. At first, it was the decorations; they're so beautiful. I still wonder about the man who painted them.' He looked up. 'But after a time I began to think about the little girl digging the book out of the ashes and opening it, seeing it for the first time like I did. It's as if she rescued it, that damaged book.'

In her closet, Mathilda hears William's words again as if he were there with her. She had soaked up, longed for, more of his story of the book made for one person, a nobleman or his wife, but lost to them. And though she would have denied it that night in the chapel, she knows she was curious about an expensive book, damaged though it was, being in the hands of a little village girl, then a craftsman's wife and son. She runs her hands over her own book — not damaged, but not all that she had hoped for. She hadn't known then, two seasons ago, how grateful she would be for Will's story of all that the burned book had offered.

They sat for some time, William working, Mathilda watching his hands as much as the sketches that flowed from them. When she asked how he would go about painting the chapel, he explained that he would set it inside the arch of a letter A, with the lady kneeling in the centre, holding her book, and the hand of God's blessing reaching down from a cloud above. 'With some gold leaf,' he smiled. 'Though not too much.' The colours, he said, would be reds, pinks and blues, with some touches of purple.

Looking up, he said, 'Would you kneel for your portrait, my lady? This is what you want? To be painted here, and in prayer?'

'Yes, yes it is. In prayer.' She stood, uncertain what to do.

'If you would kneel here …' William moved to the front corner of the altar. 'I know it isn't where you would usually pray, but for the portrait, it means we can see both you and the altar.' He turned to light some more candles.

Mathilda felt suddenly flustered, unprepared. She had not expected this, had almost forgotten about the portrait. As she knelt, William asked her to stretch her arms out, hands away from her body.

'But that's not how I pray. I couldn't hold my arms there for so long. And I couldn't read my prayers if I needed them. This isn't what I want.'

William seemed not to hear; he was sitting again, parchment and stylus in his hands. 'Just a little higher, if you would.'

And so Mathilda held that unnatural pose until her arms began to burn and she had to let them drop. She wondered if William would react, but he said nothing. How dare he ignore her, as if she were some kind of bear on a chain? What was she doing, kneeling for this man? He was here at her bidding! She turned her head to him, determined to unsettle him, make him look up. But he was looking already, absorbed in putting her onto parchment.

She was surprised at the shock of William's eyes upon her. She had been regarded before, many times, for the neatness of her clothes, the depth of her brow, the whiteness of her face, but this was different. Being seen, taken to the page, wasn't the simple thing she had thought. Names and positions faded, their narrowness suddenly apparent; no longer were they lady and limner.

The conversations of the past days, the glimpses of beauty she had forgotten, the strange story of the wounded book, and now this, being drawn — they were gathering in a way she could not have expected. She watched his face, his eyes on her body.

The moment slowed. Her skin tightened as if a finger slowly followed her shape, over her face, hesitating at the swell of her lips, along the rise of her breasts, the dip and arch of her belly, the roundness of her thighs, gently around the pressure of her knees on the cushion. Then from the top of her head over her hair, stroking down her back, through hollow and curve to the back of her legs. A kind of touching, without hands. Her body formed itself anew. Once, then again, she saw the flicker in his eyes as they met hers, noted the slight hesitation in his hand. Mathilda was content to stay this way, watching him, being seen, but William put down the plummet, nodded and said he was finished. He stepped forward and helped her stand, held her elbow in his cupped palm.

'May I see the sketch?' she said.

'Yes, of course.' His hand still on her arm, he offered her the parchment, but she didn't take it.

Though he didn't move, warmth spread through her flesh as though his fingers touched where his eyes had traced her body. This familiar longing, this unknown man. She looked at his face, then down again. He stepped closer, leaned toward her, his hips against hers. The sound of his breath so near, shifting strands of her hair. Her body reaching toward his, she murmured simply, 'Not in here.'

With the two girls in her bed, the hall full of sleeping bodies, and others in the barn and stables, there was only one place to go. She wonders now why the slap of cold from the heavy frost didn't shake her, remind her who she was, leading this man to share the dark night with her. But she knew only his eyes on her. Without words she led him into the cold, through the courtyard to the dovecote near the front gate. William behind her, she pushed the door open onto the sharp smell, the close darkness and the sound of birds disturbed in their sleep, murmurs that rose and settled.

'We need to move these,' Mathilda whispered.

Feeling their way, they pushed aside baskets and a tool of some kind, heavy and iron, bumping against each other as they fumbled to find a clear space beneath the tiers of pigeonholes. The air trembled between them, laden with hesitation and desire. Mathilda wanted him to hold her, now, afraid that in these moments one of them would see clearly what waited outside the door: noblewoman and artisan. Something hard knocked against her shoulder. 'My pardon,' William said, but she found his arm, reached up to touch his face. In the dark, his mouth found hers.

Their clothes were awkward. William pulled up her kirtle and she was afraid he would rush when she needed him to touch her skin, lingering the same way his gaze had when he sketched her. But he tugged at her sleeves, laughed and mumbled, asking how the thing came off. She fumbled with the laces at her side, felt him pulling off his own clothes, reaching back to her. Finally free of cloth, shivering, Mathilda pulled him to lie down with her, only the soil beneath them. Their bodies took over. She gasped when he kissed the curve of her neck. His lips on her breasts, her belly, her thighs. Even the dark space between her legs became sweet. She was shaped anew with every touch. Her fingers traced his back and chest, the soft skin of his belly, the heat of his cock, feeling him rise and gather toward her, inside her, his groans echoing her own. Her body restored.

Later, when she stepped into her chamber, she found Maggie sleeping sideways across her bed. As she moved her and settled in next to her, her own limbs felt as soft and new as her daughter's.

The next morning was the remembrance of Angmar's husband, Arthur, who had died three years earlier, after he had fallen while repairing the roof of the barn. Angmar was already in the chapel, and though Mathilda went to comfort her, her mind was full of the portrait and the dovecote, her skin flaring again.

She didn't see William and had little time to look for him. Lady Margaret visited, asking after Robert, then Fraden needed to speak with her. A group of village women had come to see him; their men had been conscripted into the king's forces, and they were left alone.

'They can't work the land without their men,' Fraden told her. 'They say their children are starving.'

Mathilda sighed. 'Give them enough grain to see them through the month. If the weather improves, I'll see if we can help them work their fields.'

By evening, she was tired and angry. William had been at the edges of her mind all day, was there in particular places of her body — yes, the lingering wetness at the top of her thighs, but more so in that place at the back of her neck she had never known about, and the hidden, inner part of her arms. When she spoke, she was sure her lips must look different, and was glad that the rest of her new skin was covered. When they gathered to eat, William looked at her and nodded, but sat at the far end of the table, laughing with Godwin and Caine. Mathilda was relieved; she didn't want to speak to him, wasn't sure what she might reveal. She went to her chamber later and watched her girls sleeping, the small twitches of their eyes, the steady rhythm of their breath, the flush on their cheeks. Her skin, she thought, must look like theirs now.

Too agitated to sleep, she walked through the courtyard to the chapel; it was dark, but for one candle. William stood up as soon as the door opened; he had no parchment or tools and walked toward her.

Their space on the floor of the dovecote was covered in hay. William said simply, 'For you, my lady,' and she could hear his smile. The doves stirred and took their time to settle again; every night of those six nights, they fluttered and cooed before judging it safe to sleep. In the darkness, Mathilda felt that with every touch of her skin, William was seeing her, outlining her, filling her in with colour. With gold leaf. When she told him, he laughed and said that he would use the precious delicacy of shell gold for her, not the glare of the leaf.

Aspenhill Manor
January 1322

Lead White

From the vintner, access a supply of marc, the waste from the wine-press, and use it to cover strips of lead. Fill vases no more than half-full with an acidic liquid such as vinegar or urine, and suspend the wrapped lead above it inside the neck of the vessel, ensuring that the wrapped metal and the liquid do not touch. Heat the vases by burying them in dung that is fermenting. Kept in such proximity for several days, the two elements will interact, the acid from the vinegar and the fermenting marc working upon the lead so that it produces a white crust.

Harsh though the process is, the resulting white pigment is so strong and dense that only a single brush stroke is needed to create the effect of light.

The Art of Illumination

Will slung his bag across his shoulder and headed toward the gate. The dovecote looked even more beautiful in the mist, now white with the hint of dawn light. In the manor behind him, Mathilda would be asleep with Maggie and Joan. He could have stayed for days yet, chanced fortune a little longer, but however much Mathilda reassured him in those quiet moments in the dovecote, he knew that strange time was ending. How much longer would loneliness and fear make her need him? Terrors of the long war, exhaustion from the freeze and famine, the burdens of the estate; she looked for comfort, but in time he would fail her.

For six nights the dovecote had taken them in. No, it was Mathilda; she had taken him in, without resistance and without demands. It was so different from the satisfaction of knowing his own strength, the release of winning at wrestling or a few quick moments with a strumpet. He couldn't find the words for the feeling, could only see the flowing lines of Claude's work.

As those six nights passed, the darkness inside the dovecote had lessened. Just last night, the full moon in a clear sky had filtered its white light through the gaps high in the walls, making the doves restless. Whenever a feather dropped, it shone for a moment in the beams of light, then faded into the dark. Mathilda had pointed at one, saying how beautiful it was, but Will could think only of the fall of angels, thrown from heaven. He didn't believe in signs from God, but he knew it was time to leave. He wouldn't tell Mathilda; she could so easily persuade him to stay.

He had arrived as a man with a simple duty: he was to draw some sketches, be polite to the patron and leave. That he would have fulfilled if Mathilda had remained as she was at their first meeting, resentful and rude, treating him as one of her menials. It was what he had expected, had wanted, even. But the girls and the woman herself hadn't allowed that, had disturbed his simple view of the nobility and met him with friendliness and their own love of pictures. For that, he had no defence. He felt himself revealed.

He touched the stone of the dovecote as he passed, felt the pull of it. Turn back, Will, risk what will come.

The sun was almost risen, the sky clear, and he breathed in deeply, turned from the grand gates of Aspenhill. It was good to be on the road again after so many days inside or wandering only the grounds of the estate. He thought how easy it was to leave: stand, pack some bread along with his few belongings, and begin to walk. His legs were strong; he could walk away. That's what he had always believed.

At first the lanes were quiet and he began to whistle. It was near on two days' journey from the manor to the main London road, the lanes winding around and over hills dotted with small settlements. Will took the time to look around, noticing things he hadn't seen on his way to Aspenhill, when he had been too absorbed in his frustration at the pointless journey to bother much with the landscape. How could he have not seen this? Some fields were only a tumble of stone and sticks, grey tree trunks and dried traces of bog. Here and there, abandoned buildings still had a coating of the mud that had crept up their walls with the flood waters, some collapsing gradually into piles of wood and thatch. Grass grew through the ribcages of dead animals; in months, Will thought, they would be gone, the earth sucking them in. His mood darkened; he stopped whistling.

The second night, as he ate a bland vegetable pottage, the innkeeper warned him of freezing weather on the way. Two days ago, at the manor, Fraden too had announced it was coming, had read it in the birds wheeling away south. Will realised then that he had seen none all day, the sky a blank. The talk by the fire was of sin, the end of days, the pouring out of God's wrath. It had seemed the worst was over, but now the frigid weather had returned, there was little hope. Most of the drinkers were locals, and they scoffed when Will told them his plan. Why didn't he turn back? Walking to London in the coming chill, they said, was the dream of a madman. But he shook his head, said he had to go on. There was no explaining it; he had never spent much time worrying over the pains of hell, but he knew the freeze was coming for him.

Will set off early the next day, moving quickly as if he might outrun the blast from the north, but the cold seemed to descend from the sky like a shroud dropped onto the earth. It had its own beauty, especially to a limner's eye, but Will felt the cold as a battle, too fierce for him to spend time admiring the enemy. He saw only a few people on the road, most of them huddled into hoods and coats. As the land levelled out, he knew the Cambridge to London road was ahead. Past another bend and he could see it. He wished there was another route he could take, but he couldn't risk getting lost in byways or travelling through forests; anyone desperate enough to hide there in this weather would be ready to kill for food or money. The Cambridge road again it would have to be.

As if she'd known he would soon be walking this road, Mathilda had asked him about Cambridge. Their bodies tired, still close, the occasional murmur of doves above, she had wondered afresh at how they had found themselves together in their rough bed.

'No point in asking. It's how things have turned,' he'd said.

'My life was arranged. Strategies, it was: lineage and land. No question why I married Robert.'

Will had flinched. Robert. 'Let's not—'

'But you. Why did you travel to London when you did? Such hard times, so much fighting. A friend you said, the day you arrived, a death …'

'Yes, a close friend. He drowned.' No more. Why draw their bodies out of this darkness?

But Mathilda had touched his mouth the way she had that first night, and just as with the burned psalter, slowly the story of Simon's death told itself: the mayor's stockpiling of grain, the dark night by the river, Simon's 'Oh!' of surprise and then the splash. He hadn't told her about his running, only the nobleman's horse, his frantic searching and the loss. Gall rising in his throat, he had sat up. Then her hand on his cheek. It was a grace he hadn't expected, didn't deserve.

28

Cambridge–London Road
January 1322

Bone White

There are times when an inert white is needed. Lead white, a dense and useful hue though it be, reacts with orpiment and verdigris and another must be sought. At table, when the meal of fowl is finished and the bones thrown to the floor, collect them and toss them into the flames of a fire, waiting until they become white and brittle, able to be easily ground until fine. Bone white does not give the same satisfying effect as lead white, nor is it as pleasurable to paint with, but it finds its uses in the limner's store of pigments. It has an important use when drawing with silverpoint, for its marks are not readily accepted by parchment. A wash or tint mixed with bone white gives parchment an abrasive nature, a roughness that is barely perceived but will allow it to receive the marks of a silverpoint stylus.

The Art of Illumination

'Ah, the old road,' a voice said.

Will looked around but could see no one. Then a familiar laugh, wet and thick. He stopped, his throat suddenly tight. There, that rock close by the hedge, he could see it now: the mossy bumps of knees on either side; the lion paws splayed in the grass; the round head; the slash of a mouth coated in green.

This road, this weather, this company; it was more than he was ready to face. Will made himself take a step, told himself to ignore it, outwalk it. The gargoyle perched on his shoulder, its feet heavy, cold as a fall of ice shards. He walked on, tried singing into the clear air to block the sound, but the gargoyle blew into his ear, then his mouth, until his throat seized and he coughed in harsh, racking spasms.

'Remember this road, Will? You're so good at walking. Away, away.'

For over a year he had lived with this creature, cowered from it, tried to ignore it, then grown to accept its presence — even, at times, welcomed it. His own creature of the margins: as solid as stone and as fluid as a shape-shifter; carping, playful, resistant. But here, on the road from Cambridge, he knew it was dangerous.

'What have you done, Will? First you paint a book for a lady, and then you let her bed you. Will you give up all you believe in for your paint and parchment?'

Will walked on; he knew it all, knew all he had done. And he knew the touch of Mathilda's skin had healed some of his grief over Simon, had helped him begin to forget.

Refusing to heed him, the voice went on. 'Why are you travelling so far from the river, so far from that night? You must know you can't escape it.'

The gargoyle capered about him, shifting and changing, sometimes clear as the chill air, sometimes rubbing catlike against his legs, sometimes snapping like a ravenous dog. There was no brush or parchment to keep it away; it had him in its jaws, its teeth sharp, and would not let go.

Will bent his head to it all: the guilt, the voice, the cold. There was nothing else but to go on, to step out this journey with his rough companion, to weather its onslaught as best he could.

That night, Will stopped at a small, dirty tavern, exhausted. The gargoyle wanted a bed as well, no matter that the blankets were stiff with grease. In the dark, it seemed no longer made of stone or air but had a body almost human.

Will remembered stories of St Antony beaten by devils, St Guthlac carried through the air by black creatures that faded into hell, leaving him near death. Will and his demon wrestled all night, tangled in blankets and clothes, and though he used every feint and lunge Simon had taught him, Will could not prevail. Well before dawn, shivering and spent, he gave up, leaving the warmth to the creature that lay shapeless beneath the coverings.

The next morning, the freeze had settled in. It occupied the earth and sky the way an army takes over a city. Hoar frost coated trees and rocks, ice forming on ice, building into lacy spikes; muddy ruts and mounds hardened, some as sharp as knives; roadside brooks froze solid. The road went on, white and still. No snow to soften the air, no wind to make a sound, only bone-deep chill. Will hoped for villages ahead, listened for the sound of a smithy, though most people would be sheltering indoors with their animals. Even so, they might keep him safe. The gargoyle chuckled, as if reading his thoughts.

Will shook his hands, rubbed his fingers through their layers of wrapping, but they had no feeling. His feet were solid blocks and the hair on his face hard white icicles. Frozen puddles glimmered, taunting him. The creature nudged his arm; perhaps Simon was under one of these, his eyes wide, his mouth round with shock. Perpetually surprised. Though Will tried to focus on the snake of road ahead, he had to look. It was his fault; he had run, abandoned his friend. Puddle after puddle, he tried not to look, had to look, until finally he stamped on each one, over and over, watching shards and splinters fly into the air.

With each step, each stamp, Will became weaker. Does guilt ever wear out? he wondered. The biting at his heels, the aching grip on his hands, the sticky feet in his back, and always the whispered word.

Finally, he stopped in the middle of the deserted road and wailed. The hedges, white walls either side of him, sent back his cries. He waited, slapping his hands against his sides, turning to look at the road behind and in front as if the thing he needed — whatever it was — would come walking toward him. He shouted again and again until his throat was hoarse. Nothing. The silence was worse than the whispering; he couldn't bear it.

'What more do you want? You accuse me every moment. You knew I didn't want to go that night. It was your foolish idea, not mine. Scare the mayor, you said. Ha!' He scrubbed at his face with the backs of his hands. 'All right for you, it was. If you were caught, there'd be no trouble. No trial for you, Mother Church would look after her student, whatever law he broke. Did you think about me? If I was caught, I'd be sent to prison. Edgar would have thrown me out. I told you all that. But still you asked, and I couldn't say no.' He wept, wrenching sobs deep from his gut, his eyes and nose streaming. 'I went because I needed you.'

The night was dense, black, the ground soggy underfoot, water trickling into his boots, Simon whispering about the grain Hotham stored, the high price of bread. Will knew it, all of Cambridge knew it. They'd tried protests, meetings, submissions to the mayor and court, but it was all washed away with the endless rain. He wanted to leave, began to whisper a farewell — but horse's hooves crunching on gravel, Hotham on his way home. The stone, the heft of its weight felt cold in his hand. Simon took a step forward. Will felt him throw, heard Hotham's curse, tried to move but slipped, fell to his knees, heard the thick sound of iron on flesh. A faint 'Oh!' and a splash. That was all it took for a man to die. A curse from the dark, the horse rearing again.

Will ran. It seemed he'd never stop running. The panic in his arms and legs had set them moving before he even knew it. The running took over, became a force of its own, and it seemed there was nothing else but his legs pushing on. And

then, like a slap, he saw All Saints and the castle where he and
Simon had often met and walked. He remembered what he
was running from. The horse, the dull thud, the splash that
must have been Simon falling into the water. Simon, sinking.

The thought stopped his legs and he bent over, gasping for
breath, suddenly aware of how far he had run. He'd go back.
Hotham would be gone, home to his tapestries and servants; it
would be safe now to go back.

He turned, tried to run, but his legs shook, their panic
gone. A grey sense of dread all that remained. Simon in the
water. Go back, drag him out. But walking was toil, like
heaving wood for his father. The darkness of the night closed
in, and he wondered if it was all a dream: that sense of urgency
and horror, the desperate need to run. Surely, yes; it must be
so. Too awful to be real.

Still, he hauled his legs on and on and the dream wouldn't
end, even when he reached the river. No sign of Simon. He
felt the torn grass and the shape of a hoof deep in the soil. And
another one. All the way to the bridge he followed the river,
searching.

He wanted to be frantic, to call out to Simon, to shout
for help, but instead he settled into his dream. Heavy legs,
underwater breath, the night a blanket round him. In
the morning, Simon would laugh at him: another foolish
nightmare.

Back in his room he pulled off his boots and sank onto the
bed. All night long in his strange sleep he walked the river,
searching for something. But he had forgotten what it was.

The next morning it was snowing; the world had changed,
the night's black confusion replaced by quiet falling white. His
decorations for the treatise on herbs were overdue, so he wasn't
able to leave his desk until late in the afternoon. He wandered
first around Peterhouse, waiting for Simon, expecting to see
him and to laugh when he complained how cold it had been
when he'd climbed from the water and wandered home to dry

off; he'd make an excuse about losing sight of him in the dark, tell him how he'd searched all the way to the bridge. He'd admire the cut on Simon's forehead, describe it as a battle wound, slap him on the back, a bit too hard, his arm suddenly full of the energy of relief.

But there was no sign of him, and three or four students asked Will if he'd seen Simon. He'd missed a lecture, not like him. At the river, the hoofmarks had become small white craters. The snowflakes dissolved into the water, but ice would form soon. The quietness of the place hung heavy around him and he understood, for the first time, the danger he was in. Hotham wasn't a man to leave an attack unpunished, and as soon as Simon's body was found — downstream, trapped under a thin sheet of ice, most like — he would be known as the second man: he and Simon were always together.

Before dawn the next day he packed his unfinished master's piece, his brushes and knives, and ran from Hotham and his men. It seemed he had evaded them. But it was only in London that he saw what he was really running from: Simon's white face, his eyes and mouth wide in alarm and shock, caught forever in that moment. Waiting for his friend, Will, to reach in and catch his hand, to pull him out. Still waiting.

Will fell onto the road, not feeling the ice beneath his knees, and pulled off his hood and cap, leaving his head bare. It wasn't prayer, and it wasn't quite penance; all Will knew was a year or more of carrying those few moments on the banks of the river.

'Yes, I did it,' he shouted, and turned, looking for Simon, for the gargoyle, for God. For anyone to hear him. Then, barely more than a whisper: 'I'm sorry. I ran, I left you in the river. And then I ran again.'

He waited, expecting nothing. His breath was white mist.

Then there was warmth; was it the fever of his anguish or the tears on his face? No, it was a hand, sure and soft, touching his cheek. He could let go. His sobs echoed between the hedgerows until all he knew was the sound spiralling upward. The white sky received it all.

It was there before him, and he was surprised to see it: not Cambridge, but London, its towering walls, its wide gate open but guarded.

'We're here,' Will said to his companion, but there was no answer.

'You've walked a way, I'll warrant,' one of the guards said to him.

'Came from Fordham,' Will said. 'Days and days it's been. I survived because God walked with me.'

'Ah, you're as mad as you look then. Not even the Almighty'd walk in this freeze. Maybe 'twas the devil.' He crossed himself quickly against the words.

'Could be. It's sometimes hard to tell the difference,' Will said.

His feet and hands had been numb for days, and he had learned to walk without flexing his feet. He hardly knew the feel of his own body.

The starving and homeless were such a common sight that most of the people he passed barely noticed him, but some hesitated, peered at the thin face, the matted hair and beard, as if the man was familiar. Will walked on, seeing little but somehow knowing which way to go. The journey seemed a dream: the whiteness, the flaying on the road, the fear he'd perish and, in time, when the ice thawed, sink into the mud. Above all, the whiteness, the quiet embrace.

In his room he dropped his bag. An ache spread from the base of his back up to his shoulders. His legs were tender, as if they had been beaten raw. The skin on his feet was mottled purple-blue, so he clumsily wrapped an old pair of breeches around them.

He slept long and deep, waking to eat the little he could manage, then slept again. All he could remember was the pain as warmth kneaded blood back into his hands and feet. Each toe, each finger. They throbbed, the skin tight over the swelling. Slowly he discovered how much like a wild man he had become. It took days to restore his appearance to that of William Asshe, limner. As for the rest ... he wasn't sure. So much had changed, he knew, though it was fragile, new-budded.

Mathilda

Wain Wood Manor
July 1322

Mary's face and hair are edged with the softest sheen of gold. Mathilda brings the page closer to study the tiny flecks of light that gently shift as she moves it. This must be the shell gold William said he would use to paint her. She remembers his words, his quiet laugh in the darkness, the vibrations from his chest against her cheek.

It was Maggie who discovered William had left, running out to the barn to tell him he should draw the sparkly frost on the trees around the house. When she saw his bag was gone, she asked Godwin, then Caine, Ysmay, Angmar, Fraden and finally Father Jacobi, working her way through the hierarchy of those who would listen and answer a little girl.

'He's gone, Ma. William's gone,' she said. 'He didn't even say goodbye and now he's gone.'

Mathilda felt the sudden pain and tried to shake it away. 'Today?' was all she said. She'd known that William would have to leave soon, but she'd been sure that Fraden's warning of another freeze would keep him with her a little longer.

'Why didn't he say goodbye?' Maggie wailed.

'He has work to do, Maggie. He can't be waiting around to say goodbye. Now stop that noise and come with me to mass.' Mathilda knew she was talking to herself.

In the chapel, she bent her head, but didn't hear the prayers. Into the quietness behind her closed eyes, the gulf of William's absence opened up. Already her body missed him. She wanted to wail; she wanted to send Fraden out to bring him back, tell him it was too cold, too dangerous to travel; she wanted him sitting in the hall, drawing, chatting with the girls; she wanted his skin against hers. Now there was no one to talk to about line and colour, the way one hue or shape might sit well against another, quite different, one. No one who would understand why she really wanted the book.

Feeling suddenly alone, she became aware of God watching her, waiting; she would have to confess it all to Father Jacobi. But guilt was black and her skin was still bright, newly made. Perhaps the words of penitence would be enough, whatever the truth of her heart. If she could find them, if her mouth would let her say them.

After chapel, she went to the dovecote. Each night they had tossed away the signs of their bodies in the hay, and now she lay down in the little that was left. The ground was cold beneath her. Curled on her side, she remembered, gathered all that she could; she knew there would be no more William Asshe for her.

The air seemed full of the story William had told her about Simon the previous night. She had watched it emerge into the darkness, piece by piece, feeling William's body tense and move away, then drawing it back to her. She had seen the river and the bush, the two men crouching and Hotham on his horse.

Simon was right, William had said: it was illegal for the mayor to hoard grain until prices went up. The king had forbidden it. The burghers of Cambridge knew what he was doing, but they were content with a reward for their silence; money stolen from the starving. Mathilda thought of Thea and John Beecroft, wanted to explain to William, excuse herself, say there was nothing more she could do for them, but he was deep in his story, hiding behind the bush on the sodden ground. She wondered if the hole in his boot that Godwin had mended had been leaking back then. It was a foolish game to attack Hotham, William said: he could have lost his position with Edgar, but he had stayed. 'I don't know why.'

Mathilda had asked whether Simon liked books and illuminations too. William had sighed and sat up. 'If Simon was here, he would tell me my work is a waste. He would tell you your book of hours is a sinful luxury, that you should use the money for the poor wretches you take rent from. Pay someone to paint the walls of the village church if you must have pictures, but don't close them up inside a book.' His voice was hard.

Mathilda was cold. She wanted him to lie down, to hold her, but those words, that anger.

'He was right,' William said. 'I couldn't argue with him. But I wanted to paint illuminations. I couldn't make him understand.'

Mathilda had felt herself accused; she was the book's patron, after all. She thought of the tapestry of the orange tree that William had helped her to see anew, of her breviary, of her girls learning to draw. They had all helped to bring her back from that shadowed place of fear and worry about Robert and the village. Was that enough? It wasn't an argument she would offer Thea Beecroft, but it was real.

There was nothing she could say to William, but when she reached up and touched his face, he relaxed, lay down, and came back to her.

A fluttering above. The memory receding, Mathilda looked up, surprised to see a dove flying into one of the holes; it must have ventured out in the harsh weather. She stood up and went back to the manor house; Fraden needed to speak with her.

Now, in her closet at Welwyn, she turns to the painting of the dovecote with each stone so carefully drawn, fine tufts of grass at its base, a bird flying toward it. So much of her life is in these pages. They came to her in a rich bundle, just like Robert's body, mocking her, reminding her of how much had been lost. But living through this season of grieving with the book, with its prayers and decorated pages, has changed all that her pain once was. With so much lost and yet a baby kicking inside her, she sees that Simon's simple borders of right and wrong won't hold. They leave no space to breathe.

The baby moves, perhaps it is stretching, pushes up under her chest. She puts a hand on it, thinks it might be waking from sleep or testing the edges of its small space. Who are you, child? What mouth and eyes and hands will you have?

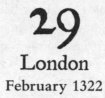

29
London
February 1322

The Patron

You cannot work as a limner without a patron, be that a bishop or a church or a member of the nobility or aristocracy. Perhaps one day the king may commission work from you. It is those who have wealth and a desire to please God that ask for beautiful work. Remember, however, that it is God himself, and not the status of your patron, who demands that your work must always be the very finest you can manage.

The Art of Illumination

At last, with no idea how long it was since he had returned, Will walked along Bread Street, into Old Change and past St Paul's. The gargoyle was there, in its place, neck stretched long, its horns tipped with a touch of morning sun. Without turning its head, it closed and opened one round eye. Will nodded briefly. My companion of the margins, he thought, and turned into the workshop. Gemma and Benedict looked up, Nick peeped out of the storeroom then ran to him and punched him on the arm. Will touched the boy's head but didn't cuff him or wrestle him to the ground.

Gemma smiled and looked him up and down, even more delighted to see him than she had anticipated. 'You're back, Will! You're thin. Are you well? Did you walk through that freeze? Surely not. You should have stayed at Aspenhill Manor until it passed.'

'Couldn't, could I?'

'Surely Lady Mathilda wouldn't have made you leave in that weather. It's enough to kill a man.'

'Oh, I had some company on the way. Rough at times, but company enough to see me right.' It was strange, this need to shape words.

Gemma peered at him. He had that look she knew. What was it? His eyes, something in his voice. Idla, was it? Her own Clarissa, so young but seeing death all the same. A chill ran through her. Had they sent Will out, so stupidly determined to hide their secret, that they'd put him in the way to sicken and die? All for John's pride and reputation. All for an income, and the right to boast of a great book.

'What was the house like?' Nick asked. 'Was it grand? Were there servants and great halls and rich food? Did you dine with them? Did you go riding on the estate?'

'Let the man sit down, Nick. Can't you see he's not well? What do you do for thinking, boy?' Gemma snapped. 'Will, sit down. Now.' Her voice was still a scold, scared.

'Here, Will,' Benedict said, shepherding the tall man to his desk. 'Sit here.'

Will sat at his desk and felt it take him in. When Nick moved closer, Will thought about his questions and couldn't answer them. House? Estate? Halls? All he could remember was a visit to Simon in Cambridge, dreamlike; he'd thought him gone. 'The house was the house of a nobleman: too big, too cold, too extravagant. I ate in the kitchen. I sketched and I came home. That's all.'

Nick sighed.

'You should go home, Will. Get some rest,' Gemma urged him.

'I've slept for days. I think I need to paint or else … I might go mad.' He smiled; they wouldn't understand how serious he was. The shop settled again to work. There was no singing, not even humming, and the room seemed filled with the strangeness Will had brought with him. Even Benedict shifted uneasily at his silence.

'Will!' John's shout was a relief. He closed the door. 'We've missed you here. You look miserable, man. What have you done to yourself? You should be in your bed.' He shook Will's hand with his left, then changed to his right. 'Ah, it's habit now, using me left.' His arm was healed well enough, he said, though he couldn't flex all his fingers any more.

Will noticed he hadn't regained the weight he had lost; even his jowls were missing their flesh.

'So, the lady was happy with your work? I knew she would be,' John said. When Will didn't reply, he patted him on the shoulder and let him be.

Nick brought Will the pages he had been working on before Yule. 'I've done some painting while you were away. Ma let me. Ben drew the flowers and vines and I added the colour inside. Seven borders I painted, didn't I Ben?' He didn't wait for a reply. 'And then Ben showed me how to paint over them with bits of white, just a spot here and there, or a wavy line on the vine. It's all about how you hold the brush, Ben said.'

'Good lad,' Will said and took the pages.

The touch of the parchment was like skin, the inside of an arm or thigh, a woman's face. The dark night and the sound of doves.

He hadn't yet finished the pictures for the Complaint of Our Lady, though he had planned and sketched them all, today he would paint Christ being lifted down from the cross. Now and then he called to Nick for more paint, or told him to mix it differently, but beyond that he had nothing to say.

As he waited for the paint to dry, he dwelt on the other pages, feeling the comfort of completed work, adding some white or grey, aware that if he added too much he would ruin all that he had done. Still he kept on, fussing with a delicate cross-hatching of white to give the effect of torchlight in the

Betrayal of Christ, though he had done it well the first time, and knew it was all better left alone, that tomorrow he would need to scrape some away. It was the brush, the paint, the parchment that he wanted, the company of the workshop, the reassurance that he could do the work well. From time to time he felt Gemma's eyes on him, but she said nothing.

One morning, a few days after he returned to work, Will woke before daylight, walked around the city and then to the shop, slipping back into the habit like an old coat. Gemma looked up and smiled, but said nothing. Even though there were fewer pages to correct since John had stopped painting, only Gemma and Benedict working of late meant that progress on the book had been slow. He collected a new quire and worked without thought; he wasn't aware of planning anything, but the drawings took form. He outlined in black, found the right hue, mixing it on the edge of the clam shell, adding layers of paint. He was surprised how much each new stroke of the brush settled him, brought him back to himself.

He began to look forward to those early hours with only Gemma's firm company. For days they said little beyond what was necessary, and he was grateful for that. Slowly, he began to talk again. About Cambridge and Claude's night-time lessons; his ability with line; his pictures in shades of black and grey, touched with colour only in some small areas; his long fingers; the way he teased Edgar and laughed quietly. He told Gemma about Simon and the first time he met him, rescuing him from the brawl in the tavern; his late-night conversations about the power of the court and nobility; Simon's determination to win every argument; his annoying habit of flicking his nails when he talked; his lessons in wrestling. Into the space Gemma's quietness opened, he told her more than he had told anyone. How Simon's attention, on a person or a book or an idea, seemed to make that thing sharper than all else. 'Almost like we'd outline a picture in ink. Then when he looked somewhere else, it all faded.' As he spoke, it was as if he could see Simon again, his white skin, his thin arms lined with muscle, his green eyes. He didn't tell her about the pleasure of their wrestling matches, or how much he had needed him. And finally, one word taking him on to the next one, Will told her the story of the night at the river and his grief at abandoning his drowning friend. It was easier to tell now, he realised. Since those days on the road, it had lost its accusation. He stopped and looked up, expecting Gemma to excuse him, tell him there was nothing he could have done, but she stayed silent. She understood: death is so hard and final that it always asks if we could have, should have, done more.

Aware of a movement, Will looked up. Simon stood at the open doorway. He looked around the shop, briefly at Gemma, then into Will's eyes. Will watched the slight dip of his friend's head, the curl of his lips in a sad smile, the slow turn. He was gone. For the first time, he left a gentle quietness in his place.

When Will fell silent, Gemma told him about working with her pa in the shop, about learning to read and then to write; her childhood dreams of becoming a limner, and how they had never left her, even when John swore that Southflete would never allow it. Alice had been her hope, she said: perhaps she could fight for Alice to be made apprentice — fight for her daughter the way John had never done for his wife. But Alice would never paint, that was clear. And John would never understand his wife's longing to be recognised. She didn't say how furious she was with John and still how much she loved him; how terrified she had been that he would die from his wound.

The conversation and the painting shaped into rhythms: the brush and the words, the colour and the silences. They sighed when they heard Nick running down the stairs, or Benedict pushing open the door.

* * *

On Will's page, there was only one picture in the right margin, arresting in its simplicity.

A man in profile, tall and thin, formed only of ink. One arm, outstretched, presses against the right border of the block of words. His head is bent. He might be leaning his ale-soaked frame against the solid house of words, trusting it to hold him up. It's been a long night at the market, the brothel, the cock fight and then the tavern, until he was thrown out: not enough coin for all he wanted to drink.

A likely story, but consider this. Perhaps he is a man of principle and learning, a scholar. His long gown, his simple clothes, his fine, learned nose, the slight frown that is not anger or headache, but thought. This man ponders the atonement of Christ, the ways and nature of angels, Pythagorean angles, the movements of feathers and stones, the hierarchy of man, the nature of truth. All these questions and more buzz and nest inside his head. His hand rests on the lines of words as he communes with God, listening to his voice, discerning the harmony of the spheres. He holds up the words. Without him, they would fall, brick by brick and word by word.

And so, the picture says, the next time you see a figure slumped against a doorway, consider carefully what he might be. Today's prison fodder, or tomorrow's genius?

'And Lady Mathilda,' Gemma said one morning. 'Was she …?'

'She told me I wasn't John.' Will looked up briefly. 'Told me she didn't want an almost-master to paint her portrait.'

'Really? You walked all that way and—'

'She was scared, I realised. Lonely, afraid for Sir Robert, wishing she hadn't called John there in the middle of battles and all her tenants so desperate for food.'

'Ah. And did you sketch her, after all?'

'I did.' Will tried to veer away. 'She has two girls, Joan and Maggie. I drew with them. The younger, Maggie, has her mother's keen interest in line and composition.'

'Her mother's? So Lady Mathilda appreciates what we do?'

'Yes, she does. I was surprised too. Mathilda wanted to talk about it all: her tapestries, our sketches, our painting.'

Will stopped. The air shifted. They had both heard it: Mathilda, plain and simple.

30
London
March 1322

Planning

It is most important to plan the commission before you begin work, taking into account both the patron's wishes and the budget available. Do not rush headlong into a few sumptuous pages, only to discover there is scant money, and therefore pigment, for the remaining pages. In large projects, such as a book of hours, the scribe will most times plan the schema of decoration. Heed his directions.

In a similar manner, plan carefully each page of decoration, and then each individual illumination or picture. Mistakes of paint may be scraped away and corrected, but rushing ahead, being too eager to put paint to parchment, can create serious problems.

The Art of Illumination

John spent most of his day on the streets, then carried news into the shop, much as he would bring supplies of gold leaf or vine leaves, as if it was now his job. News spread as it always did in London, like wind blowing through the lanes and into houses, changing shape as it went: battles, skirmishes, barons defeated and killed or arrested, the rest forced to flee north. The king was determined to trounce his enemies, most especially their leader, his cousin, Thomas of Lancaster.

One cloudy March day, messengers reached London, exhausted, desperate, terrified. The rebel troops had been defeated at Boroughbridge. Men killed, barons arrested, Lancaster gone, running for his life.

Then, worse news tumbling upon bad. 'Lancaster's dead,' John announced just inside the door. A chill wind.

They all looked up. Lancaster? The only man who'd had any chance of controlling the king's tyranny.

'At Pontefract, it was. They caught him fleeing on foot and …' He paused for effect. 'And they threw him into the tower of his own castle. The tower he'd built special, at Pontefract, to keep the king prisoner. Can you believe it?'

'Dead?' Gemma said.

'Dead. It's all over, far as I can tell. And Lancaster, forbidden to speak at his trial, he was. Guilty of treason, straight. But even then, the king had to give way on the torture meant for a traitor on account of his royal blood. He was the king's cousin, after all. So he was beheaded.'

'The troubadours will tell all sorts of tales about it at Smithfield, you wait,' Benedict said.

'They'll be too late, Ben. You should hear the stories. All kinds. Rowley says he's heard it took more'n a dozen blows to chop off his head, such was his strength. But Jack, he swears Lancaster's not dead at all. God wouldn't allow such injustice. Says he lives still in the Scottish highlands, biding his time to invade.'

The room was silent. Will thought again how much John changed when he was out of the shop: his words, his manner, his love of carrying news as if he were a troubadour himself.

'Mortimer surrendered some time ago, Will. Did you know that? He's in prison. Don't know aught of Fitzjohn, though.'

Later that day, as if in response, there was news of Sir Robert.

'Died in battle, they say. Sword it was. Lingered a short time but naught to be done,' John said. 'Poor man. But it's as well for him, I say. Otherwise he'd be hung, drawn and quartered like the rest of 'em. All over the country they've taken 'em, put their heads on stakes to remind us. Gloucester, Bristol, Winchelsea, Canterbury. Just like nailing up a public notice for all to see. Henry Tyeys is next.' A dramatic pause. 'Here, it'll be.'

'In London? Where?' Nick said.

'Smithfield, I'd say. Or maybe Cornhill, by the stocks.'

'When? Can I go and see?'

Nick looked at Gemma, waiting for her to forbid him from watching a man be stretched, disembowelled and cut into pieces, but she said nothing, seemed not to have heard him. She had thought she didn't have pity to spare for a woman like Lady Mathilda. But as she'd learned with Idla, death gathers, and however much she turned away from it, the sheaves of grief were gathered in again. So much of her anger at John of late was a way to cope with her fear of him dying. Did gentry women love their husbands in the same way, days and nights forming shelter that now, for Lady Mathilda, was lost? 'It was as well for the lady that Sir Robert died in battle,' she said. 'If not, it could be her and her daughters in prison.'

'What's to say they won't drag her there anyways?' John said. 'It's treason to fight against the king. Bart, you know the guard at Ludgate, he says there's many a lady taken to the Tower.'

'They wouldn't. Do you think so? Isn't his death enough?'

'Death wasn't enough for some of those that dangled in chains before they finally put them out of their pain. They want to show they can make the rebels suffer. Why not their families as well? This isn't just the rule of law, it's revenge, wiping out any trace of insult to the king. Despenser's behind it all, I'll warrant. They've been taking all their property, from the buildings to the chattels. Along with that go the women and the children.'

Will watched John's face, the gleam in his eyes, the excitement at such news that made the men and their women no more than names, characters in a tale told by a man with a lute, as Benedict had said. But Sir Robert wasn't a player in a tale, he was a man. Will had been there, had sat at Sir Robert's high table, played with his children, walked in his field. He caught at his memories, stopped them short.

'What about the book? Does a woman in prison pay for a decorated book of hours?' Gemma asked.

'Nothing we can do but wait and see. And keep working.'

The room fell silent at the prospect of the book being stopped.

That night, Will emptied his bag onto the bed: a few clothes, breadcrumbs and a scattering of parchment scraps covered with sketches, some of them simple, some more detailed, and some with strong, childish lines. He sifted through them, turning the pages at all angles, finding pictures tucked into tiny spaces in the corners. This one, of a face with big eyes and a toothy mouth — he remembered Maggie's laugh as she drew it. And this, of a scythe and fork in a barn, of diamond patterns around a fireplace, a tree laden with oranges. Sketch by sketch, the manor house took on detail and colour, but he went no further, content to leave the gaps in his memory. The next day he took the collection to the workshop to begin copying them. The one of Mathilda praying he left behind.

'Who's that?' Nick asked when he saw the sketch of a boy about his own age bending over a bench, the frame of a door behind him.

'That's Godwin, the stable boy at the manor. He mended my boot.'

Nick's face brightened: the manor house. 'Did you tell him about me? Did you say how much you were missing the London apprentice with so much talent?'

Will smiled. 'No, we talked about his friend Cornell, Sir Robert's page. He was worried about him going off to battle. Now let me work.'

But Nick stayed, keen to find out more. 'Is this a dovecote then? Is that at the manor?'

Will pulled the sketch away from Nick and glanced at it. 'Did I tell you to let me work, boy?'

Benedict looked up at the sharp words and Nick stalked away, muttering something under his breath about 'boy'.

Will looked down at the parchment, at the curved sides of the dovecote, its carefully hewn stone. He had taken time filling in the details. It was as beautiful as he remembered. An ache in his chest, he tucked it under the other sketches.

Mathilda

Wain Wood Manor
July 1322

Mathilda turns another page, knowing it's dangerous, that she's getting close; she can tell the next pages in the book are different. You have to see it some time, she reasons with herself. And still the page remains unturned; instead, she studies one of its pictures, though looking at it only makes the memory more painful.

What was in Will's mind as he painted it? She touches the picture of the limner working inside the bottom loop of a letter *R*, painting the letter around him as if it is a room he is creating. It must be Will: the face has his straight eyebrows, the wide nose, the curved dimple in his chin. Although the picture is small, she touches each feature as if it might really be him. There is the flex of his fingers around the brush, the way he held the plummet when he drew.

She wants to cry but she can't, as if that would be too easy. How angry was he? What curses did he spit against her as he sent her this simple image? She wants him here so she can explain. She wants to go to London, visit the workshop, tell them how sorry she is. She wants to touch Will again, have him hold her. But it's all fancy: with the baby coming soon, and the king's pardon not yet certain, she can go nowhere.

She looks at the faces in the top loop of the letter and puts a finger on each one, as if she knows them. Nick, Benedict, John and Gemma. Will didn't say much about them except that Nick was so much like he had been, as a lad, and Ben was serious about his work. He told her about the time he took Ben out and they were nearly caught in a tavern brawl. And Gemma? Mathilda wondered what Gemma did in the shop, but Will would only say that she was skilled. And Dancaster, the master illuminator — she's surprised he isn't the one drawn largest, but there he is with the other three faces. What book are they working on now? Did they understand she had no choice?

It seems so long ago, but it was months only. Of all days, Easter Sunday. A day of resurrection, and she had agreed to write the letter that killed hope. She didn't need to write it herself, of course. Oliver had been insisting for days, weeks actually.

'You need to cut back all you can, anything that isn't essential.'

She looked at his face, its quiet order, and wondered what it was like to divide the days into accounts and numbers, laws and documents. 'Anything not essential. How would you define that, Oliver?'

His eyes narrowed. He was deciding whether to bother answering, Mathilda thought. It was for him always a dilemma: whether to accept the intelligence behind his mistress's fine gown and braided hair, she knew. And the last weeks had been even more difficult because she hadn't understood how she felt or what she wanted. Feeding the stock, paying wages, providing food — perhaps Oliver could tell her that none of it was essential.

What of her prayers? A book to guide her? She wasn't cruel enough to ask the lawyer if her religious devotions were essential.

'Of course, I understand what you mean. There are some things that must go, though there is the issue of the agreement we made with the stationer. Will you deal with that, Oliver?'

'A verbal agreement only, my lady. And though that has some force in law, I believe we can claim that the time taken … how long is it now? Well over a year since Sir Robert's request? The work has been slow and—'

'No. A book like that takes time. It's not simply a matter

of a picture here or there. We insult them as it is. We won't insult them further with talk of tardiness. Tell them the truth. There is no money.'

'I'll find words more suited to your position, my lady.'

It was an ending as clear as when they lowered Robert into the ground.

Mathilda sighs at the memory. How certain she was that the need to stop the book was punishment, a judgement on her desire. For all her bluster and snapping at Oliver, in truth she was bending her knee to the punishment. Half a book. Her penance was to pray from a book without the beauty she had longed for. Coveted.

She hadn't understood then. How could she, Robert dead less than a month? Everything seemed a loss.

Mathilda takes a breath and turns a page. The emptiness clutches at her like a crying child. This one, this particular rectangle of cured and scraped pigskin, has an air about it, gives off a thin wail. Traces of fear, loss of nerve, as if the shadow world of lead is all it will know. Words without decoration; a head without a body. Then another page just the same, and another. Half the book is naked. Lame, unfinished.

One by one she turns the pages. Not every page is without drawings; here and there she sees ghosts of ideas, sketches in the margins. A leadpoint swan swimming across the page; a griffin, roaring, claws in the air. Perhaps they are reminders for what to paint when the limner reaches that page. Or perhaps the young apprentice was allowed to practice.

How much like her life this is. So much unknown, only occasional hints of what the next years might be. Leadpoint in the air. It's painful, but instead of shutting it away, she is learning to live through the loss.

31
London
April 1322

The Patron Portrait

A portrait of the patron in a book of hours should not attempt her physical likeness; instead, allow signs to represent the woman. This is not because the limner is unable to draw a fair semblance of a face, but because the figure of the patron is set within the page's world of meaning. The masters of illumination teach that architecture, heraldic devices, words and the woman's physical stance in the portrait are all important signs of her life and position. As the woman reads them, she learns who she is and what her duties are as a child of God, a wife, a mother — the one whose duty it is to bear children and continue the great family line.

This is the tradition and I will not dispute what has been handed down. But remember that the patron is always more than the signs that represent her.

The Art of Illumination

Southflete seemed to make more noise than anyone else when he pushed open the door of the workshop. John was in the storeroom teaching Nick about the variations in red hues and when he looked out the door, the stationer moved quickly toward him and gripped his shoulders in greeting. That's when the group of limners knew there was trouble.

'I trust your Eastertide celebrations have given you hope,' he said. 'I won't delay with telling you the news.'

Gemma felt a chill run through her chest down to her belly and into her arms and legs, then, just as quickly, her face flushed hot.

'Lady Mathilda has written a letter to me regarding the commission. You've all heard that Sir Robert died some weeks back at Boroughbridge. Lady Mathilda explains that, as a widow, she does not have access to the funds she had expected. What it means is that the book must stop.' He looked around the shop. 'The book was ordered on the expectation of Sir Robert inheriting lands in the Marches. Those lands can't be passed to Lady Mathilda. And from what I've heard, as the wife of a man who fought against the king, nothing is certain for her, not even her life.'

The room was silent; Southflete's words seemed to remove any chance of sound and movement. Gemma looked from John and then to Nick, who was on the floor in the storeroom doorway, blue staining his fingers, smudges on his jaw.

Will brought his hand down hard on his desk. 'So we're to stop, just like that?'

Southflete winced and looked down at the letter. '*All work on the book must cease*, are her words. She'll pay us what's due and we're to have the book bound.'

'Bound? God's blood, what does that mean? It's not finished, nowhere near. And the pages we haven't done? Bind what? Half a book?'

'Manekyn and his scribes have finished it all, the prayers are complete. There's no reason it can't be bound,' Southflete said simply.

Gemma stood up. 'Does the lady read Latin?' she asked. 'She needs the pictures to read the prayers, to understand them. The prayers aren't complete without them. Else what are we doing? Adding lace to a dress, is all.'

'What are we to do, love? Work for no pay?' John said, his voice weak.

Gemma sat down heavily. 'No. She made an agreement with us,' she said. 'An agreement for the work. For all of it. That has to stand, whatever her so-called circumstances. Nobility crying poor is what it is. She has to pay for all she agreed to.'

'It was her husband made the agreement. Whatever we want, that agreement has to die with him,' John said.

'But she'd still have lands, wouldn't she?' Nick said. 'And that grand manor that you went to, Will. And you said she had others, too. Even if Sir Robert's dead, doesn't she get some of it?'

'You need to learn the ways of the world, boy. What hopeful fancies they are.' Southflete's voice was tense. 'Sir Robert was a Contrarian, as they call his sort. He fought the king. He's a traitor, even though he's dead. If the king, and especially Despenser, decides the wife should pay for Sir Robert's rebellion, her inheritance will be attainted. Gone. Payment for Robert's bad choice in alliances.' He paused, as if to allow them time to absorb the meaning. 'Her messenger said she's moved her household to the small estate she owns at Welwyn. She hopes to be well out of notice. They left in haste, he says, even decided to leave behind their valuables in the hope of satisfying the soldiers.'

For a moment, Gemma caught a glimpse of a woman bundling together a dress or two, shouting at her children to hurry, looking around the room one last time.

A tapestry of an orange tree with rabbits beneath it. The image stayed in Will's mind for only a moment, pushed away by the news.

'So we need to have the book bound and away as soon as possible. It's wise business to finish quickly any connection with the wife of a traitor,' Southflete said.

'Wife of a traitor?' Gemma's voice was loud. 'The king might brand her so, but that doesn't make it so. Can we at least call her Lady Mathilda?'

Southflete's eyelids had the slow movement of an owl's as they dismissed her words. 'As I said, have the book bound quickly.' He walked to the door, making as much noise leaving as when he'd entered.

'Can't expect sympathy from that man. Not for anyone,' Gemma said. 'Imagine running from the soldiers. And with children. In the weather we've had of late. We were afraid of the barons and their men at our gates, but running, and thinking all the time of prison. God's blood, Southflete cares for no one.'

'And how does he do that?' Nick said. 'How does one man make so much noise opening and closing a door? It's an ordinary door, after all.'

As if in response, Will stood up and walked to the door, opened it quietly.

'Where are you going?' John asked. 'Have you finished the portraits of Lady Mathilda in her chapel? Those have to go in after you walked all that way in that weather and …' He stopped when he saw the look on Will's face.

'What does it matter to you now?' Will slammed the door behind him.

'We have pigments and gold leaf,' Gemma said. 'And nothing to do with them. Will the lady pay us for those? That was to be part of the final payment.'

'Well, she has no money,' John said. 'We can use them on other work. Something will come.'

'Aye, on the back of a half-finished book. The nobles will be impressed.'

'But they'll see—' Nick began.

'That's what I mean, Nick. Who will she show off her book to now? Come see my book, just don't look past this page.' She pushed the parchment off her desk and onto the floor.

Without looking at her face, Nick scrambled across the room and picked it up, shook it gently and set it down in the storeroom.

'And we thought it'd be a new start,' Gemma went on. 'That's aristocracy and their ways. Only care about themselves and what they want.' She tried to spit, but her mouth was so dry she managed only an awkward pout. Nothing made sense. She knew her words wouldn't hold, that Lady Mathilda would be terrified and alone. Gemma was angry most of all that there seemed to be no single place to stand any more. Pity, resentment, frustration, sadness, she felt them all — and each one seemed wrong. But how could the gentry demand understanding as they broke their agreements, took away the shop's business?

'Now love, we'll work something out,' John said, but without energy.

'Work something out! That's your proverb for life, Dancaster. Why don't you get angry for once? Tell Southflete what you think instead of bowing to whatever he says. We made an agreement. Does it count for nothing?'

'It's tough news, but we've had tough news before and we've got by.'

'We're always scraping by and naught beyond it, even though we do fine work. I've a mind to change every calendar page. Didn't want to paint those lies, the pictures of bonny villagers, in the first place. Let her look on the skinny faces of those on her land that have to scrape by in the freezing weather, and no help from her.'

'But we don't know that she doesn't care for them.'

Three heads turned toward Benedict as if they were surprised he was still there.

'Just because she's noble doesn't mean that's what she's like. We've never met her,' Benedict said quietly. 'She wanted the book, didn't she? It must be hard on her too.'

'Leave it now,' John said. 'Truth is, we're all upset. Let's just—'

'Go to the tavern? There, I've said it for you.' She stood up. 'Nick, take care of this paint and the brushes.' She looked at John. 'In case we ever need them again.'

* * *

Outside, the sun was shining. The roof of St Paul's glittered colour, its spire flashed light and winked at Will. He walked without noticing: Cheapside, Cornhill, Gracechurch Street, Bridge Street, turning away from the river at Oyster Hill and into Candlewick Street. People nodded and spoke; he nodded back absently.

Mathilda, terrified, running from soldiers, leaving the door open. Mathilda, the two lines in her forehead that dipped when she frowned.

More than a year on a book, the work that would have been recommendation for any workshop anywhere — Paris, even Genoa. Work with masters and not this collection of fools: a blind man, a woman, a tight-arse and a boy.

Joan and Maggie running to the stables. Scared, tugging at Mathilda, asking what was wrong, where they were going.

He should have known in the Peter and Paul all that time ago, the first sight of Dancaster boasting and drinking like a sop. Should have turned and walked away then and there.

Walking. That was his life. All the way from Cambridge, all the way to Fordham. A waste. He should have kept on walking.

32

London
April 1322

Green

Green earth, or terre-verte, is made from mineral deposits found in northern Italy, and though it is dull and inconstant in colour, it will improve in hue the more it is ground and washed in clear water. Verdigris is the most vibrant green and can be made easily by hanging copper plates over vinegar, or by covering the plates in wine marc. In both cases, the blue-green crust that forms can be easily scraped away. Mix it with vinegar and temper with egg yolk, but remember it cannot be used next to orpiment or lead white. Instead, you might use sap green, made from buckthorn juice, or iris green, from the sap of iris flowers. Malachite is a stone very similar to precious azurite and the pigment is obtained similarly, through the long process of separating out dull and coarse stone. It can, at times, be difficult to obtain. Grind with care, for too fine a pigment will become pale.

The Art of Illumination

The street wasn't yet awake, the night lingering, and it was good to take long strides, outwalk the brew in his belly. Will had hoped to sleep the day away, but here he was, awake and unwell. All he could do was keep painting, though he wanted to be angry with Mathilda. He wanted the simplicity of it, the single straight line of it. Last night, in any alehouse that was open, he'd tried to drink himself into rage enough to argue or shout or, better still, punch someone. He longed for the purity of anger's redness, not this greyness. She had stopped the book, hadn't she? Mathilda with her tapestries and cushions and position. She had gathered them into the shop for only one thing, taken their time and labour, then walked away from them. He'd tried describing it all to strangers in exchange for the ale he bought them, but they only slapped him on the back and thanked him again, just to shut him up. And it always, always, came back to a dead husband and wrathful king, both too far away to hear him.

And Mathilda. Mathilda running from her house, terrified but refusing to show it. Mathilda, Maggie clinging to her hand. Mathilda. Her green eyes.

He had only a short time before Gemma would come downstairs; it was difficult to know how she would be after a night thinking over the news. A wounded book. John would accept the situation, as he always did; perhaps he'd be relieved that there'd be no book to scold him, day after day, for his lost abilities.

He took out the sketches he'd made at the manor and began with the chapel: the crucifix that had made him uncomfortable because the proportions of Christ's body were unbalanced; the heavy drape of the brocade altar cloth; the wooden arches decorated with carved grapes. He looked closer, surprised. The grapes and leaves were beautiful. He'd forgotten that he had spent so long on them, adding metalpoint to the curves to intensify the shading and create movement, as Claude had taught him. 'This is grisaille. If you draw this way, you do not need all your colours. This is enough. Let the black and the greys do the work.' Mathilda had come into the chapel then and surprised him. He had let her see the parchment, heard her indrawn breath. It had been awkward, though, the argument at dinner lingering. He had apologised, and later asked her to pose.

Sitting at his desk, he was ashamed to remember what he had done, but at the time it had seemed a defence, the kind Simon had taught him: using your opponent's weakness to topple them. He had asked Mathilda to hold her arms in that awkward way as she knelt. She was right, it wasn't how she would pray, but it suited the angles of the composition and, more than that, it would be hard, her arms would begin to burn. Petty, and all he could manage. His only way of countering her position and rank.

But then, just as if Simon had tucked his foot behind Will's to unbalance him, she had let her arms drop and turned to him, watched him look at her, study her, put her shape on parchment. Sitting in the workshop, he smiled. It was what he had been afraid of as he grew to know her: remove the title 'Lady' and he could not hide behind resentment of the nobility. She became a woman, no longer a noblewoman or patron, each line and curve from his plummet a way of seeing her anew.

He shook his head — all that was gone — and began the portrait. It would be as he had drawn her that night, though looking closely now he saw that the sketch was simple, not much help at all, except for the braids in her hair, the lines drawn over and over again as if he had been afraid to move on to the rest of her body. The face was barely a sketch; he would have to recall the details. But memories of Mathilda were seeded in his hands, his arms, his chest and legs. His mouth. His eyes.

He knew the creases that formed and faded on her forehead and around the bridge of her nose. Her laugh that changed everything, her features softening, her frown lifting. Her nose, he remembered, was slightly flattened at the very end. Not enough to make it square, but enough to create two points where the skin was tight over the soft gristle beneath. A portrait of a woman at prayer, though, needed more than simple details. He thought some more. When Maggie had run to her mother with his drawing of the dovecote, telling her that Will had promised to teach her to draw it too, Mathilda had taken the parchment and — yes, that was the expression he needed. Not a smile exactly, but a slight movement in her lips, and in her eyes. Recognition, perhaps it was, as though she had just opened a book for the first time.

As he drew, filling in the details of her face, the time between now and then, between this shop and her manor house, drifted away and his sketch gathered all in.

A short while later, as if there had been no catastrophe, Gemma, Benedict, Nick and John clattered down the stairs. They stood at the door for a moment and watched Will painting, intent, refusing to look up.

Gemma walked across to him and sighed. 'Such a shame,' she said. 'This is beautiful work, and all for a ruined book.'

'We've all done good work,' Benedict said. 'The lady can't ask for more.'

Gemma smiled. 'Well, I wish she would ask for more. And pay for it. But a book is a whole thing; that's why we plan it as we do. It's not just this beautiful page or that not-so-beautiful page. It's the arrangement of the decorations that tells a story, you know that. All the images need to be read together, like words in a sentence. That won't work now the book's half-done.'

'A book half-done is hardly one to help you settle into prayer,' Benedict agreed. He shrugged, then added, 'We've just got to finish the pages we're painting now, and Southflete says he'll see us into more work.'

John sighed. 'That's true. We'll be back to treatises and breviaries if we can get 'em. Ha! Maybe young Hugh Despenser himself will be looking for a book to celebrate his victory.' He took a slow breath and went to the storeroom. 'Whatever the fortunes of Lady Mathilda, we need to have these pages ready to bind.' He was holding the pile of quires, the same ones that he had touched so gently a year or so ago, only now half of them were fat with paint. 'God's bones, it's a pity to see it crippled the way it is, but it's what the times bring. I'll ask Peter Binder when he can do it.'

'It all makes no sense.' Gemma's voice was low. 'It's like some foolish story told on a street corner.'

'A tragedy,' Benedict said quietly.

'Finish the pages you were working on.' John sounded weary, but his old air of command was there. 'Nothing grand, but finish it off. And no gold leaf, mind. No point giving that away now.'

The shop settled to work. Will had not paused from the moment they arrived.

When the door pushed open, Gemma braced, expecting to see Southflete, but it was a different voice: Harry, the apothecary's assistant.

'Thought you should know, ships's come in from Venice and they say there's malachite. Your lad here seemed to think you'd be needing it. They're unloading it now.' The door shut behind him.

'Now?' Nick burst from the storeroom. 'It's here now? What are we to do with it now? I told 'em we needed it months ago. I went and asked most weeks. They always said there was no sign.' He looked to John, then to Gemma, to Will and finally to Ben. No one moved. 'It's the malachite, Harry said. The malachite. We've had none, and it's no use now.'

Will looked up and smiled. 'Go and get it, mix a little. I promise I'll paint everything shades of green.'

The atelier worked in silence, as if the air was too heavy with sadness to allow more, but Nick seemed to feel the urgency in Will and was at his shoulder, offering paint, occasionally commenting, mostly asking what he needed. Will answered only in brief words: 'lead white', 'turnsole blue', 'carbon black'. Nick rushed from desk to storeroom and back again. When he tripped, Will threw a protective hand over his work, watched the lad rescue the clam shell of malachite before it fell. Their eyes met, a brief smile. Will paused in his painting to look around.

The early evening sun gave the room a diffuse light, picking out motes of dust floating in the air. Ben and Gemma were bent to their work, head and back curving into arm and hand. John was at his desk gently turning pages and peering at each one. Nick was roaming from one to the other, anticipating what might be needed next. For a moment, Will saw not the people who had irritated and challenged him, not the makers of a failed book, but limners, skilled and committed to their craft; they could have been edged in shell gold. And there, suddenly, was the sense of their calling that he had lost in Mathilda's letter, her short dismissal of their work.

St Paul's rang the bells for Vespers and John stood at his desk. 'Time to finish,' he said quietly.

33
London
April 1322

The Work

A limner works on commission, and fulfils that commission to his utmost ability. It may be that the patron praises the work to the limner and it may be that the limner never knows of the patron's opinion. Do not expect to be praised. It is not always in the nature of the patron to consider too carefully the man who painted for him. Remember, too, that you do the work for God, by which I mean that in doing the work well, you honour the ability you have.

The Art of Illumination

It was early morning in Will's tenement room, light peering through the window onto the table below it. As he became aware of it, Will leaned forward and blew out his lamp, continued painting. Piled on the bed were pages, some decorated, some with illuminations and no border decoration, some with writing only. Will worked steadily, pausing occasionally to straighten his back and neck, or to mix more pigment.

Peter Binder had resisted Will's suggestion at first, afraid to cross Southflete's order to finish the book and send it away as soon as possible, but it was only a matter of finding the right kind of persuasion: a down payment and the promise of more with each extra day.

'Why spend your money on a few pages, Asshe?' Peter had asked. 'You can't finish it, you must know that.'

'I need to do what I can, is all. I owe it to the book.'

Peter had shrugged. 'Well, I'll take your money and hope the stationer doesn't come nosing around, but you're a fool. The lady won't pay you for it, and probably won't thank you.'

Mathilda wouldn't even know he was doing this, but he couldn't leave it, that's all he knew. His book, his first book of hours.

His stomach grumbled, almost plaintively, but there was no time to get more food. The loaf broken on the table would have to do. He hadn't left the room for three days, except to visit the privy, and he'd learned not to move too quickly, or the room would spin. He'd finished the Complaint of Our Lady, and the next pages needed no large illumination: he had only to decorate the capitals at the beginning of the prayers. Will created an ornate frame for each letter, and a face inside it. Slowly, he realised that though he hadn't planned it, the faces were familiar: Ysmay the cook with her turned-up lips and red cheeks; Fraden with his thick beard and lined face; Joan with her slight frown and crescent eyebrows; Father Jacobi with his hollow cheeks.

He kept painting, filling in memories of the house and people, trying to stay away from Mathilda. But finally, he had to paint the dovecote. The sketch he had made at the manor house was beautiful, and as he painted in his room it was there before his eyes: its gradual curve, the snug-fitting stone, the warmth of doves inside.

He discovered that lack of sleep and food made painting easier, not harder; tiredness and hunger released ideas from somewhere he didn't understand. He worked carefully, as usual, still finding the elegance of line that was his talent, but the creatures in the borders were those of dream and fantasy, crowding and crawling around the central blocks of words, almost overwhelming them. A cat's face peers from its snail-shell body; a bird with a cow's head and scales for feathers flies past; a man with a blue face charges toward a dragon with red wings and a tail made of vines. Squirrels caper suggestively around a young woman's close-fitting gown; a dog sits inside the curve of a vine, writing on a long scroll of parchment. Rabbits play on every page, a furry, fecund mass: the older ones flirting; the young ones chewing at letters or peering around their edges, nibbling at vines and flowers. Across the bottom of six pages, scene by scene, a group of rabbits track a hunter and bring him down, truss him onto a pole with rope, carry him off to their forest court and condemn him for persecution of the weak. In the last scene, they turn him over an open fire: human stew. On another page, a rabbit stands above a captive bishop, its axe ready to descend.

The bells chimed the day away. Peter had sent his boy to remind Will that he needed to deliver the pages by Vespers, so he had only a short time left. This would be his last picture. He chewed the dry skin on his lip, jiggled his right leg.

With metalpoint he sketched the shape of the letter *R*. Manekyn's scrawl said *Cap R, Tower of Babel*. The tower the people built, believing they could climb to heaven; he knew the story, but he wasn't interested. Instead, he drew inside the top circle of the letter lines that curled and interlaced, and in the spaces between them hair and eyes, noses and mouths, small faces peering out. The people he worked with. Others might not recognise them, but there was Nick's slightly askew nose and the mole near it, Benedict's wide jaw and tight mouth, Gemma's round eyes that he'd paint blue, and John's cheeks and nose that would have a red, ale-fed blush.

Outside, clouds covered the sun; there was still time. The top circle finished, he moved to the arch formed by the bottom half of the letter and continued sketching. An illuminator's desk with clam shells set out neatly, a man seated awkwardly next to it: a big man, almost too big for the work, squeezed into the small space, almost imprisoned. A brush in his large hands, arm extended, he paints the letter *R* surrounding him. Will smiled, drew in his own broad nose, his thick hair. Bells rang the hours and he didn't hear them.

He jumped, almost spilled paint on the page, looked toward the door, the banging. John Dancaster walked in, not waiting for a reply.

'What in God's holy name are you doing, Asshe? Setting out to destroy us completely?'

'John! I was just about to finish, take all this to Peter. We agreed—'

'No, Peter and I agreed, binder and master limner, that the book would be bound days ago. Then I hear from his boy that you've been making deals, working on the book when I told you to stop. Using our paints to no purpose, risking Southflete finding out, disobeying my orders.'

'John, I wanted to finish. I had some ideas and—'

'What in Mary's holy name makes your ideas so important? A journeyman, a boy from Cambridge with a bit of talent, that's all you are. Nothing more.'

Will balanced his wet brush on its clam shell and sat back. 'Careful what you call me, John. I've worked hard for you and your little shop. Without me you'd—'

'Without you, Hugh of Oxford would be working for me, and doing what I say.'

'And would Hugh keep your secret? Would Hugh creep into the shop early every day to correct your pages? Would he pretend that nothing was amiss when Southflete came to visit?' The words flew, slicing the air.

John blanched, stepped back. 'All right, Asshe,' he said quietly. 'Give me the pages and I'll take them to Peter.' He gathered the quires from the bed, assembled the newly painted pages and looked at the parchment on the table.

'This one is wet still,' Will said. 'I'll come with you and carry it while it dries.'

John paused a moment, squinted at the parchment. 'Mother Mary, what is that?'

'A final portrait. The atelier and its workers. A signature, I suppose.'

'You know that limners don't sign their work, that's the tradition.'

'What is your famous rose then?'

'It's different from this. It's tucked into the painting, almost hidden, a mark of my work that I earned from years of serving a master, learning from him, painting and painting again, understanding my faults, being humble enough to admit them. A mark like that has to be earned, not taken.'

'I did my time in Cambridge, I—'

'No. You did your apprenticeship, that's all. Now you begin to learn. Whatever talent you might have, you still have to learn. Like I said, you're a boy, Will.'

'A boy who saved your skin, Dancaster.'

'And you think that gives you the right to this? Pride, Asshe, it's pride, nothing more. Give me the page, I'll take them all to Peter. And make sure you return the clam shells to my shop.'

John slammed the door behind him. Will gathered the clam shells, still wet with paint, and threw them at the door, watching the colours splatter and drip, the shells shatter into splinters.

He paced the tiny room, punched at the door, swept the tools off the table. Some were his, some belonged to the workshop. He sat on the bed, but he was too agitated to sleep, too angry to close his eyes and let go. Head between his hands, he wondered what to do next. Tell Southflete? Yes, tell the stationer everything about John going blind, about how much time he'd spent fixing his mistakes, about Gemma painting the Dancaster rose, Gemma painting so much, Gemma being as good as John.

* * *

A knock on the door, uncertain. Will stirred, opened his eyes, rolled off the bed. It was dark, but only two or three paces to the door.

'Ben? Is that you?' Will turned and fell back onto the bed, left the door open.

'Will? You all right? You look ill. Were you asleep?'

'Just a nap is all. What're you doing here?'

'Came to see how you are. And just as well, it seems. Have you eaten? Have you even drunk anything lately?' When Will didn't answer, he said, 'Come on then. Meat and ale is what you need. And now. Come on. Now, Will.'

Will rubbed at his eyes, scratched his head and pulled on a hood. Ben had never ordered him to do anything. He stood, did as he was told.

The noise in the tavern hit Will like a blow to the head and he hesitated in the doorway until Ben shepherded him to a table in a small room.

'Stay there,' Ben said, and walked away to order food and drink.

Will sat, head slumped.

'Here, take this,' Ben said a short time later, pushing ale toward him. 'Drink just a bit and wait for the food to come, or you'll be drunk.'

Will took a swig, felt his body draw in the liquid like a sponge, his knees beginning to soften. 'What're you doing here, Ben?'

'Like I said, came to see you. John came back from Peter Binder's shouting and cursing about you painting pages, delaying the binding, and something about adding your mark. Never in all my years in the workshop seen him in that state before. Thought I'd better see how you were faring.'

It took the stew and two more pots of ale before Will began to speak, and then it came tumbling out, the man half-dead coming to life, painting with his words the things he had seen and heard: creatures crowding to be put down on the parchment, the illuminations, the drawings, the feeling that his brush knew the way, almost without him. And then John bursting in, breaking it apart with his rules, demanding he be obeyed as master.

'Master,' Will spat. 'Blind, he is. Useless as a limner, and he thinks to order me around.' On he rambled again: the to-and-fro of their words, the threats, the insults, the smashed clam shells, the visit to Southflete, telling him everything about John's blindness, his own repair of the paintings, Gemma's work, even painting the Dancaster rose.

'You what?' Benedict shouted. 'You told him?'

Will took another drink, peered into his face.

'Will, did you tell Southflete? Did you tell him John's sight is failing? Did you?'

Will scratched a crescent moon into the tabletop with his fingernail. It felt so real, but he wasn't sure now. It was what he had planned; he could see it all, how he told the whole story and the stationer listened, frowning.

'And what did Southflete say, Will?'

'He was pleased I told him, of course. And angry, yes, angry at John for hiding it from him. He told me he'd make sure I got work now, the best work, especially since I was so badly treated.'

'God's nails, that's a relief,' Ben said and began to laugh. 'For a moment I thought you'd actually told him.'

'Well, I—'

'Course he wouldn't say that, specially that part about giving you the best work.'

Will felt foolish. Had he dreamed it? Maybe he had slept, after all. 'Well, maybe I didn't talk to him. But tomorrow I will. Tomorrow I'll go there and explain it all.'

Ben leaned across the table and grabbed Will's arm. 'No, you won't.'

Will shook away the hand and stood, but shakily, so sat down again. 'Don't tell me what I can't do, Broune. I'll go first thing.'

'Think, Asshe. I thought you were smarter than this. If you ruin Dancaster, you bring down the workshop, and that means Gemma, Nick, me. And you. What do you think Southflete will do to a limner disloyal to his master? It might be a tough business, but the fraternity, and the guild Southflete hopes to set up, are meant to build the trade. He won't tell the country that London can't be trusted.'

Will spoke slowly, determined not to be out-argued by this stripling. 'But Southflete is only concerned about his reputation.'

'And if he is? He wants to be the man in charge of the London guild of stationers and illuminators, known for its quality. Not the man who gave the commission for a grand book of hours to a man losing his sight.'

'So, wait. Wait, Ben. Did you know about John? All the time?'

'Of course I knew. I offered to help Gemma fix the pages, but she said that you were already helping, and best not to have too many hands showing. Poor man. It's all he's ever wanted to do. Think of it.'

'I know,' Will said, the swell of his indignation collapsing under Ben's quiet understanding.

Mathilda

Wain Wood Manor
July 1322

The page seems to leap out from the book: all the class of the Southwark stews combined with the Bishop of Winchester's palace next door. The capital *D* is small and simply decorated with gold leaf, tiny blue and red flowers winding around the opening words. *Deus qui respiciens humilitatem ancille tue* ... Mathilda knows what they mean and begins to pray: *God, who seeing the humility of your handmaiden made fertile her virginal womb through the Holy Spirit, and filled her soul with ineffable joy* ... The words sit neatly as they should, but their painted companions have other business. Made of earth and whimsy, they roil around the margins that seem to over-burden the text, look as if they will breach the edges of the page, spill out into the world.

The girls like this page; they often look for it, to laugh and make up stories about the images, not yet aware that the squirrel in the lap of the young woman is much more than an innocent furry creature; on the next page, the woman's gown stretches tight over her round bulge. Rabbits leap through and around foliage that carries buds ready to burst; in some of them petals already break through. At the top, a pot hangs over a fire, its stew bubbling, gravy dripping fat and thick down the side; Mathilda can almost hear the fire hissing with the grease. Nearby, a gryllus, no more than a shaggy head and two legs, plays bowls with the eggs he has stolen from a bird's nest.

The baby kicks in Mathilda's belly and she touches the place with her hand. What child will you be? she asks. She can guess that William painted these margins. What was in his mind as he drew? Her eyes go back to the prayer, and the words that linger: *made fertile her virginal womb*. It is only God that makes such things possible, she knows, and yet those words push against each other, refuse to make sense. She should confess her sin with William. Surely that is why she feels confused about Mary's chaste conception. Until William's visit, she had accepted it as the model for her own obedience to God: pray, give birth to heirs of the Fitzjohn line, teach her children of God. Now, the lines of purity and duty are blurred.

The margins dance and leer. She doesn't know what to feel about them. Are they mocking Mary? As always, her gaze is drawn to the gryllus, but she looks away from him, wishes he wasn't there with his huge nose and ugly naked legs, demanding he be seen, asking too much of ... what? She doesn't know. If the angel announced that Mary had conceived without touch and by the word of God, Mathilda thinks, this gryllus must be its contrary. Rabbits and squirrels and eggs — they make the swelling beneath her gown seem raw, the result of an animal's rutting. If all this is in William's mind, it is as well he left when he did. She looks down the margin; she doesn't like the way the young woman gazes at the man nearby, her face and body suggesting she wants to swyve with him.

She looks away, wants to pull away from all she knows is there. Her skin prickles and she flushes. Admit it, Mathilda, she thinks. You know the edges of this. You felt it those nights with William, that heat in the belly that priests warn against. It was not an angel's holy blessing, and it was not the mere rough mating of two animals. But life is not made without whatever it was they shared. Desire, perhaps? She feels the warmth run from her belly, down between her legs and along her thighs. It's more than desire, though she has no word for it. She can't confess, because she can't repent those nights, sinful as they must be. Baby or no, they were the beginning of something new in her.

34
London
April 1322

Binding

When the pages are finished, the binder will sew them together into leather-clad covers. His skills are particular and learned through years of practice. Therefore, if your book is a grand one, be sure to give the work to a very fine binder. Consider that these pages are the final product of many skills gathered into one object, each one necessary and important. And consider further the work you may have contributed, be it grinding and mixing, or adding colour to a master's sketches, or drawing and painting yourself. All of this is shut up between two covers, waiting for a reader to undo the clasp and allow the various splendours to enter into her eyes and her soul.

The Art of Illumination

At the atelier, it felt like there had been a death. Nick packed away the pigments, tools and clam shells, rearranged and scrubbed for a few days, and John and Gemma found things to do while they waited for the book to be bound.

When Peter Binder arrived with it, Gemma reached for the bundle, so small now that their months of work were assembled, rubbed her hand over the cover, turned the pages. Each one was caught in time for her: the arguments with John when she began the calendar; the worries about Benedict's commitment to perfection; the shock that ran through her when she saw Will's first illumination. She paused briefly at one of the pages she and Will had corrected before dawn, scraping away and repainting the confusion of John's attempts, remembering the soft circle their lamps had made. And here, halfway through the book, the last pages: borders where Nick had added colour to Benedict's outlines, other pictures unfinished and still in lead — the ghost of a griffin along the top of one page, a pale swan swimming an invisible sea on another.

'Why didn't we finish these?' she said. 'We should at least have completed all those that we started. It looks as if we never really cared, as if we just gave up and walked away.' Her voice wavered.

She turned the page, expecting to see the very last image she had painted stark in its solitude, but instead the borders were crawling with creatures and plants: three men rowing a boat suspended in the cloudy sky; a man whose body twists into a tail that becomes the curling stem of a vine laden with berries, the man gathering his own fruit into a basket; another man squatting, bare-arsed while his companion collects the round coin of his turds into a bowl. She understood enough Latin to know that the pictures, random though they seemed at first, picked up ideas in the prayers and turned them into small stories, exempla, jokes to make a lady pause and think. And on the last painted page, the limners of the atelier gathered inside a letter *R*: John's face round and ruddy, Benedict's serious but gentle, Nick's with eagerness somehow drawn in the line of his eyebrows, and her own, eyes large and blue. No, not just blue, but ultramarine, painted with lapis, the colour of heaven. Her chest warmed and her face burned.

Then there was nothing but to turn the leaf; the naked borders made her gasp, the emptiness trimmed and bound along with the rest. She wondered at her pain. When had she lost the strength to cope with whatever came along? It was as if the freeze and famine had burned off a layer of skin. She closed the book.

'You did a good job,' John said. 'No need to look further and upset yourself.'

She had no time for this soft way of talking, so she waved a hand and passed the book to him. 'The next one will be better,' she said, and then wished the words away for John's sake.

Peter Binder's assistant pushed through the door, ready to take the book to Southflete.

'Wait,' Gemma called. She ran upstairs and returned a few moments later with a piece of cloth. 'We should at least ...' she said, wrapping the book into a neat yellow bundle.

The young lad nodded and left.

Gemma felt as if a leprous lover had finally died. She sighed, relieved to be free of it because she loved it so much.

At night Will walks the streets. He doesn't want to drink, trapped inside with bodies and noise, the demand he speak to others. London seethes quietly in the dark, erupts here and there like a lanced boil: a fight over a card game that spills onto the street; a starving man chased for the bread he's stolen; a drunken joke turned nasty; a bawd screaming, bleeding from a customer's punches. Will slows his steps and watches, fists tight, letting the anger and pain soak in, feed his own.

One night he joins in when a group of apprentices starts a football game on Smithfield by the light of an almost-full moon. The tanners begin it, the ball a stuffed pig's bladder, the goals marked with tanning frames taken from work; they know they risk losing their positions with their masters, but tedious hours over stinking tubs of hide make them reckless. More men gather, declare themselves on a side, and chase the ball. Bodies collide, scratch and fight for the ball, barely knowing who is on their own or the other team. Most of them lose any sense of where the goals are. The chance to pummel and be pummelled is what Will needs: the meaty sound of punched flesh; the slip against a bloodied chin or arm; the measured violence of an unknown body against his own. At times it flares into something more, but the chance to fight always slips away with the ball.

When the constables arrive with clubs, the players scatter into trees and bushes, into dark alleyways, losing themselves in the blackness. Will runs with them, feeling as if he has drunk his fill after a long hot day, every limb restored, even though they sting and throb.

There is no need any more to be up before dawn to work on her book on illumination, but even though Gemma's body is exhausted, the routine is settled into every cell. The mornings are still cold, but the sharp edge of frost has gone and the light now creeps earlier along Cheapside and into the shop. Gemma keeps writing, but slowly, pausing to think of the book of hours, a child left home, now with Lady Mathilda. A child with a limp. What does the lady think of it? Do the illuminations and borders help her understand the words she prays? What of the pages with nothing but words?

Gemma considers the parchment before her. It seems to her the way of the world that she has been given the time to work on Nick's book only when he has no need to make pigments. She rolls the thought around her mind like a rough piece of rock in her hands, that familiar feeling of its edges tearing at her skin. Don't dwell on that, girl. Mill it down, grind it fine, understand how to draw out its secret colour.

She dips her quill into the ink pot, but her mind won't settle on words. Lady Mathilda's pages without decoration hang like demons around her, tugging at her hair and clothes, squatting on the front of her desk, playing with her feet beneath it. They won't leave; there is more they want her to hear.

She writes the next sentences.

The limner must accept that he makes mistakes, that he cannot create perfection; that is for God alone. Do not succumb to pride with its serpentine whispers, suggesting that you alone can be above all others in the beauty of your work. Allow the mistakes to teach you.

And yet, knowing that it will never be yours, you must still strive for perfection. Let your painting be more than artistry, skill and technique. Alone, they are empty. Understand that an inspired illumination does more than bless the woman who views it; it must change and bless the limner himself. Look for it, humbly and quietly.

All day Gemma works. Then, as the light shifts and fades, she looks back over the pages. 'The Art of Illumination' is almost finished; she doesn't have much left to tell Nick. Anything more he will have to discover himself. Still, she reads through all her sentences, looking for what she has missed, hoping there is something else to write. She adds some curlicues to a capital, but any more would be too much, would unbalance the shape of the letter. There is nothing left to do. Finish it, Gemma. Let it be bound.

She gathers together the three quires: all she can tell Nick gathered into that small space. The writing is small, but she has left room on the first page to add the name of the author. Now the work is finished, she wonders if it has been vanity to think she might write like a master. Who is this Gemma Dancaster, too afraid even to give her own name to the words she writes? Perhaps John's name would give it authority; no one would doubt his experience and skill. Lady Mathilda might curse the book of hours for being unfinished, but she will praise the illuminations, run her fingers over the Dancaster rose, imagine his brush making each fine stroke, with no idea that a woman's hand has painted it all.

It's the order of things, that's what she always tells herself, but it has become a threadbare comfort. Why worry what a noblewoman thinks of a half-drawn book when it was she who made it so? Gemma strides across the shop, its few paces.

This is John's fault for going blind, not doing his work; or no, Southflete's fault for not allowing her to be recognised as a limner. If only they had done that, she would be able. She would write her name. Gemma Dancaster, Limner.

She walks back to her desk, pushes the pages into their rough cover, tucks it under her desk and leaves, slamming the door. Paternoster Row will have someone she can shout at, surely.

Walking helps a little. There is Annie with her laugh, her questions, that keen inability to understand another person's mood. Weeks ago, Gemma drew a tiny face in the margin next to the line from a psalm about the foolish man; no one else would know it was Annie, but Gemma smiled. Now, she nods at her across the street and rushes on, feigning busyness. There is Manekyn in his shop, bent over his desk. Always work for a scribe. There is Drew with another boy, digging a moat of muddy water around their castle made of old wood, sticks and leaves. And there is Tom on the corner of Ivy Lane with his sad display; the belts are sturdy, but he still shows the last few of Idla's baskets, tattered from the damp and being daily packed and unpacked, only good for throwing out. But he will never get rid of them, even when they keep people away from his stall. Gemma understands how he feels, but it is a simple man who lets feelings take over when he's starving. It's time, nearly half a year since Idla's death, that someone tells him.

'Tom, it's time you let go of the baskets,' she begins

He smiles. 'You're right. I will, with the new work.'

'Work?'

'With Owen in his ropery. I've saved enough, bought my freedom, got work. I start with the new week. I can leave the baskets on the shelf at home.'

'Your freedom, Tom? How did you?'

'Truth is, only one mouth to feed, no cane to buy, a few favours here and there.'

'Favours?'

'Not the sort I'd mention. Nothing really bad, mind, but not the sort I'd want to do again. And not the kind I want the sheriff to know of.' He smiles. 'Grand men only look grand because they find others to do what they won't admit to.'

A sad smile, Gemma thinks, but he is pleased as well. 'Men here in London?'

'Well, all grand men make their way to London some time, don't they? All this unrest: the king, the barons, the bishops — so many buying advantage.'

'But you're not … you don't mix with those people.'

Tom looks surprised. 'Here on the street, right by St Paul's, I mix with everyone, Gemma. We all do. Difference between you and me is I look thin and wretched enough to be the sort to do anything an earl or a bishop might want done. I've always cursed the way people don't buy from me, pass by like I'm not even here, but I've found it can be useful, too, blending in, slipping past unseen.'

'I'm glad for you, Tom. That you have work. I'll tell Benedict.'

'Oh, Ben knows already. It was he pointed out the man who would pay for the help of someone like me.'

'Benedict?'

'Oh, I've misspoke, saying his name. He did nothing but show me the man walking past. The rest was up to me. Ben was being a friend, is all. I shouldn't have told you if you'll be angry at him, but you know London, Gemma, better than any of us. You know how it works.'

Gemma nods, wishes him well and keeps walking. Past the pepperer's, past Peter Binder's, then right, away from the bulk of St Paul's, through Old Dean's Lane and past the grand house of the Earl of Warwick. Was he the one who paid Tom? *Blending in, slipping past unseen.* She turns away from the Shambles, the street thick with blood and the carcasses and guts of dead animals, the bellows of live ones sensing what is to come. Before her is Greyfriars Convent, then it's left out of Newgate, past the dark, windowless prison and the Abbot of Leicester's Inn. It could be someone in any of these buildings who needed the favour.

She walks on, past the high walls of St Bart's Priory. The monks there have a scriptorium and word is they're decorating a huge book of canon law. What would a monastery do with a blind limner? Tell him to pray more, no doubt. She smiles; John's more pious than she is, but all he knows is painting. Would prayer answer that need?

Blending in, slipping past unseen. The words fall into the rhythm of her steps and she keeps walking, out through Smithfield, down Chick Lane, over the Holborn river toward Clerkenwell, not noticing the carts and horses, the scraggy cows and sheep, the travellers on foot, the children, all busy with something. *Slipping past unseen, slipping past unseen.* Her litany goes on and Tom's voice fades, becomes her own. She heads toward the open expanse of the Moorfields, turning her back to the sinking sun so that she stays within reach of the city, watching, with her limner's eye, the light soften and deepen, noticing how she can tell the shape and depth of a tree by the touches of light and shadow. She wonders if she might try some of the French style Will talks about.

Blending in, slipping past unseen. The words are still there, a steady beat beneath her thoughts. Along the high city walls and in through Bishopsgate, the light almost gone. Painting the shadows, blending in, the touches of white on the Dancaster rose, finding the master's technique, slipping by unseen. Grand men appear as they are, with others to do the work they won't admit to.

A man bumps her, three squawking chickens dangling from his hand. Gemma startles, suddenly angry, turns and swears, lashes out at the thrashing bundle of feathers, crouches as the man spits at her, catches the warm, wet blob on her forehead, scrubs at it, curses some more and rushes on. The streets are suddenly too narrow, too crowded, the people ugly and dirty, pompous and weak, the muck on her feet more rank than usual. Lady Mathilda's unfinished book is not to be accepted, just as her paintings of fat and happy peasants are not to be accepted. They are not simply the way of the world, a sign of God's order. The book is lopsided, incomplete; it is all lopsided. John's refusal to acknowledge his blindness is a weight she has carried, blending in, slipping past unseen. Bishopsgate Street, on to Cheapside, she walks faster, seeing nothing, hearing only the beat, the beat of her feet, the words.

The shop is dark, so she lights a lamp and pulls out her book, opens the pot of ink, picks up a quill.

On the first page, in the space near the bottom, before the moment passes: *Gemma Dancaster, Limner. Paternoster Row, London.* She sits back, exhausted, feeling as if she has travelled miles, as if her encounter with Tom was days earlier. She looks again at the page and the words look back at her, unblinking. She wants them to look away, past her, like Will's painting of Christ enthroned, but they are steady, refuse to be anything but her name.

35
London
May–July 1322

Tradition

The tradition of illumination is an old and a fine one. In the past, masters have looked to God, to scripture and to nature for inspiration. They have sought ways to mix pigments to produce the very best hues. They have considered what is the most pleasing combination of colour, and how to render light and shade most effectively. In telling the sacred story through picture, they have honoured the symbols and conventions passed down through generations. Revere those who have gone before and learn from them.

Do not, however, believe that their work, great though it be, is the world of illumination entire. The order of things is not fixed. Day turns to night and seasons turn their way through the year so that our world may die and be renewed. Without such changes we would die. So it is with the craft you have chosen. Be wise and thoughtful in your work. Look to past masters, but also to the time in which you live. Perceive what change is necessary for the craft of the limner to flourish, to serve God and his people.

The Art of Illumination

The Dancaster atelier is dark and silent. People walk past the shop, and some pause to wonder what has happened, though among those in the book trade word of the half-finished book has spread quickly and is now old news. In the storeroom, dust collects on the rough pieces of cloth Nick has thrown over the pots and tools and brushes. Mice run around the desks, look for crumbs, mistake the occasional fragment of gold leaf for bread. The sun squeezes through the cracks at the front of the building and settles on the floor. It looks a deserted place, but it's not completely empty. The years of painting and talking and laughing have soaked into the wood.

In Cheapside, only a short walk from the Dancaster workshop, London repeats, performs and embellishes the death of Sir Tyeys; he hangs, still, in chains, his eyes and tongue pecked out, his skin turning to leather. The Peter and Paul tavern is soon to have a cellar built; Gocelin the goldsmith has a commission from the king and is to buy a new house on the Strand; Rayner the pepperer thinks business might improve with the weather.

One night in the tavern Wat Scrivener says that Lady Mathilda, the widow of Robert Fitzjohn, will not be imprisoned. Reports are that the king did not consider Sir Robert significant enough a figure to warrant pursuing his widow, though he has not yet decided whether his lands are attainted. Somewhere in Hertfordshire, Lady Mathilda has her crippled book and there are rumours she is with child.

Southflete has found work for Benedict Broune, journeyman and limner, with a small workshop on London Bridge, though Benedict finds it is too quiet. He shares a room with Tom Herfelde so they can both save money, and they enjoy the company. Tom works hard at the ropery and at night plays dice at Sabine's, though Benedict won't join in. Because he is an apprentice to Dancaster, Nicholas can't work at another limner's, so until more work comes, he scuffs around the streets and moors, sometimes helping at Tom's ropery, learning another skill. Alice has met a young man, and though the Bishop of Llandaff warns her of sin, she goes out with Hugh whenever she can. John Dancaster continues to develop the art of making himself busy doing very little. Gemma Dancaster works in Manekyn's shop doing simple decorations, enough to earn some money but simple enough to not threaten Southflete's concerns about women and quality. She still worries for her daughter, but Hugh seems a good man, and she hopes Alice will be content. William Asshe has persuaded Osmund the panel painter to take him on again, still doing the work of an apprentice.

Sometimes at night, when Gemma comes downstairs, she hears scuffling in the atelier. It's probably rats. There are no ghosts, but when she opens the door, there is an unmistakable presence. All that might have been painted remains — all the plans and ideas the limners left behind when they cleaned their brushes, wiped their hands and shut the door. Christ, the Virgin Mary and a company of saints wait patiently for vermilion, ultramarine and gold leaf. Here and there a sprig of vine still grows and curls, seeking the border it should have decorated. All manner of creatures emerge in search of paint and parchment: squirrels and apes, lions and knights, rabbits and cats, gryllus and dragons, foxes dressed as preachers. Gemma smiles and closes the door.

Mathilda

Wain Wood Manor
July 1322

Oliver advises against it, but she is past taking advice that is always about caution.

'Write the letter, please, Oliver. I'd do it myself, but you know I can't. All you need do is copy down the words I say. I've thought about this for some time now and I'm certain.'

The lawyer says nothing as he picks up his quill and looks at Mathilda, waiting.

It is a brief letter, a simple request, she thinks, but as she tries to find words the idea seems to shrink away from her. And Oliver's tapping foot isn't helping. She wants another picture. Perhaps another two or three, enough to make the book complete.

Unfinished though it is, the book has become so much more than a collection of prayers and psalms. It is a story, the sacred story she has always known, but with her own life gathered into it — not only her old life with Robert, but this new one that she can only glimpse. That is the gift she never expected. For all her instructions to the limners to stop painting, for all its blank pages, the book keeps growing. Is it some kind of magic in the pictures?

Over the past months, the book has begun to heal her grief, but not in the simple way she had expected. She had assumed the book of hours would give her the prayers and lessons Father Jacobi has always taught, firm and unchanging. But the illuminations of the sacred story have shifted, gathering her in where she had expected them to scold her.

With her old world in place, the world for which she had planned the book, when she looked on the Annunciation she would have seen, depicted in colour and symbol, the glory of the Virgin Mary's obedience and humility, and understood her own duty as wife and mother. But every time she looks she sees something different. Now, the same illumination helps her to recognise the burden of Mary's shame, her loneliness and longing, her worry for her child. This is the revelation Mathilda had never imagined: that here, hiding in fear, the widow of a traitor, about to bear another man's child, and looking to an uncertain future, Mathilda is like Mary. In everything she thought was failure, she is nonetheless like Mary.

She had no idea that pictures could shift like that, as if the light had changed and the figures had moved, rearranged themselves like water with its fluid reflections.

Sometimes, she thinks it's the creatures in tangled procession around the edges of the pages that speak to her more than any other figure in the book. She had thought life would be ordered, but it is, like them, both beauty and chaos. That is what the creatures in the margins have been telling her, in all their delicate, bawdy and capering life — decorating, and at the same time disrupting, the ordered authority of the words.

They seem content with their strange bodies and their home in the margins, and she too is learning to accept her new situation. She has been forced beyond the edges of the aspiring woman of the gentry into some new place she does not yet fully understand, a place for a woman with new skin. She cannot afford to ask for the book to be finished, but perhaps, with pictures that speak of her new position, it can become complete.

'Say, I wish to commission a further three pages for the book.' Mathilda speaks slowly, waiting for Oliver to catch up. 'Say, each one is to show my lineage and my status as a widow with two daughters, and a third child to be born near Michaelmas, God willing. Write that I trust their experience to choose fitting pictures. They are to give no more reference to my late husband.'

As she says this, Oliver looks up and frowns.

'Have I spoken too quickly, Oliver? Add some assurance of payment; you will know the right way to say it. And send it to the Dancaster workshop, not to the stationer Southflete. There's no need for him to be involved.'

She trusts that William will understand what she has not said.

36
London
July 1322

Light and Shadow

We have seen that a quality of life and depth is created by developing shadow and highlight. To understand how to do this, there is no better teacher than your own eyes. Learn to observe where light falls and where shadow forms. Be aware that as the source of light moves, the object itself will change.

After the base colour is applied, shadow is first formed by using either a darker shade of the base hue or, with darker colours, by applying black. In small images such as leaves, simple lines may be applied; in larger areas, use many fine lines. Be sure they are very fine and cross one another in the technique called cross-hatching. Once the black has dried, take a clean, damp brush and lightly brush over it in such a way that the shadow is darker on one edge, and lighter on the other. Again, observe, and nature itself will show you how to proceed.

For highlights, add white or a very light shade of the base hue, in a similar manner to shadowing, and blend it in with a soft brush. For leaves and border decoration, fine lines and dots may be added in white to enhance elegance and detail.

The Art of Illumination

John is waiting for him, letter in hand, as Will steps out of Osmund's workshop.

'Will, good to see you have work. Osmund's a good man. I came to find you because I have a letter. For you and me, the messenger said. From Lady Mathilda. You'll need to read it to me.'

He hands over the parchment and they walk without speaking, the past suddenly before them. Will runs his fingers over the bumps and dips of Mathilda's family seal pressed into the wax. Mathilda's face often comes to his mind, and usually when he is unprepared, grinding paint or washing brushes for Osmund. But he knows how to cover over the past. Like a fall of snow. He and John haven't spoken since the night the pages went to Peter Binder; such vicious words, it had seemed a gulf too large to cross.

In a tavern just down from Skinner's Hall, each with an ale, they sit across a table. Will holds the letter but doesn't open it. It has been a long, hot day, mixing and cleaning up.

'I hear word that Lady Mathilda won't be thrown into prison,' John says, though that news is old now. 'I've heard nothing more of her, so a letter was a surprise.'

Will nods and takes a swig.

'It's good to see you, Will,' John says. 'That last day, we were tired, angry at seeing the book go.'

Will still says nothing.

'Gemma and I miss you in the shop. Well, we miss the shop. No business now.'

Will is wary, but he's surprised at how glad he is to be with John, his face so familiar, as if he's always known him; being with him is like slipping on old boots. 'Yes. I hadn't slept for days. I was a madman. What was I trying to do?'

'We both misspoke that night. Neither of us wanted to let go of the book, that's all.'

Will is confused: that night, surely, all John wanted was to send the book away. 'But I thought you were in a hurry to …'

'Ah, Will, I'd tried to make myself let go of the book long before that night.' He smiles sadly. 'Seems it didn't work.'

Will looks at the man opposite him, his brown eyes focused on nothing in particular, no sign of what he can or cannot see. Perfectly good eyes, for all anyone could tell.

'Gemma said the work was good, Will. Those pages were very fine, some of the best you'd done, madman or no.' He laughs. 'I wouldn't have told you that back then. Your mark at the end, the drawing of us all, though, that was …' He stops himself. 'No, it's all done and gone. You did good work, and now it's in the lady's fine hands. I hope it gives her comfort. So, what does she say?'

Will feels the gall of that last meeting, the scouring shame of Ben's lesson. Does John know he visited? He drinks what's left of his ale and opens the letter.

Mathilda. It won't be her writing, and probably not her exact words; it's business, nothing more. But he knows it can never be just that. As he reads the few sentences, it's as if the rough walls become, for a moment, the wood panelling of the manor house; the ale-soaked table shifts to mahogany, and even his bench has the padding of a cushion. He imagines Mathilda speaking the words, the dip in the line of her frown, the tilt of her head when she is giving instruction. He reads quickly, the manor house appearing and disappearing again.

'So she's happy with the book … what we've done,' John says. 'And she understands how the book can help her now to establish her position. She might be sullied by her husband's opposition to the king, but she still has her own lineage. A clever woman, Will. She understands how the book can help her.'

The younger man says nothing, feeling as if a closed box has been opened.

'And a child to come,' John goes on. 'The poor woman. Any other time, a child would be a blessing from God, a noblewoman doing her duty, bearing an heir to the name. And now, well, I could never call a child a curse, but it's hard.'

Will looks up. 'A child? What child?'

'You read it out. Let's hope it's a boy and an heir. Still, there'll probably be nothing to inherit from Sir Robert. All gone. It'd be a hard road for a boy, finding a way to advance, attainted as they are.'

Will isn't listening. He opens the parchment again, scans the words. *The book has been a blessing for me and has sustained my faith through these last difficult months. I hope soon to have a new name added to the calendar. I am expecting a child, to be born near Michaelmas, God willing.* The sounds of the room dim, he counts back the months to his visit, to what Mathilda said of Robert leaving, something about it being before Yule. Counts months again, knowing only little of what they mean for a woman with child, realises John is speaking.

'And she offers payment.'

'I can't.'

'Does Osmund keep you so busy? We could make a time, maybe early in the morning.'

'I can't go back.'

'No need for that, Will. We paint the pages in the shop, she sends us the book to have them pasted in, and we send it off again. Peter Binder's lad could take it next time he's on his way to Cambridge. Should only be—'

'I have to go.'

Will pushes open the door into the glare of the setting sun, and as he steps away the London streets are dimmed, shadows walking, shadows he bumps into. A face in the darkness, skin, a mouth.

He can't go back. Why turn around, go back along that frozen road? Look at the snow now, how gently it falls, stilling thought and movement, covering everything. Why scrape away to what lies underneath?

He wanders along the Vintry and past the wharves, stumbling around piles of baskets, flagons and sacks, pushed and shoved by dock men, traders, sailors and customs officials.

The smells of fish, wine, garlic and spices mingle in the air, and he imagines he can see them, their odours turned to colour, hues of red, green and white blending and separating. And then the men begin unloading oysters and the colours collapse, overwhelmed by the grey-green of their smell. He turns up the next lane, away from it.

The sun has gone, the shadows it threw dissolving into darkness. There's a trace of burning in the air, or not quite; grey floats in the air. He passes a woman tipping out the ash from her fire onto the street, dust winding away like smoke. In his nose, on his face and clothes. He remembers the burned and crinkled pages of his mother's psalter, the way the book no longer closes, pushes itself open like a fan. Who painted those pages? He had so wanted to do that. Determined he would do that. He smiles. Perhaps he has: two wounded books — one burned, one unfinished.

He walks on. Nothing at Smithfield suits his mood. Not jugglers or troubadours or dice games or football. He jeers when a juggler drops one of his flaming torches. He sings along with the troubadour, though he doesn't know the words, and is forced to move on. He finds a game of dice at a tavern and has to escape out a window when someone accuses him of cheating. He scrambles back inside the city walls before curfew, wanders the laneways.

As far as he can tell, she isn't pretty, not that he is interested. The steamy smells of Gropecunt Lane suit his mood and he takes the first one who offers. Here, in the dark, he can be unknown, to himself as much as to this woman. Before he can think too much, she takes over, his cock (and a few of his coins) in her warm, rough hands.

'There he is, me lovely fellow. Out you come, that's a way, come to Cecily.'

He leans against the wall, closes his eyes and keeps his face turned away from her, saving himself from the stink of her breath: rotten teeth and stale sex. The thick blackness of the lane, its fetid brick walls.

For a few burning moments the world retreats and all he knows is the efficient rhythm, the familiar gathering warmth, the mounting pressure.

'Come on lovely,' Cecily is saying as she works.

Will shakes away the thought, the memory of a white face and braided hair. He looks down at the woman kneeling in front of him — Cecily she said — but all he feels is the dampness of the wall at his back. What is he doing here?

'This one's lost his fight, he has,' Cecily says, hands slapping at the shrivelled flesh. Her voice hardens as she stands up: 'I'll keep me coins in any case. These hands and mouth'll bring off any, 'cept those as aren't willing.' She throws in a few more slaps as if to scold a naughty child. 'And this fella's not up to it.' She laughs without humour, and disappears into the darkness.

Will buttons his breeches as he steps away. Punishment enough for both of us, he thinks, cupping his hands gently over the chafed burning in his groin.

He turns down Cheap and wanders for a time. Something is wearing away in him, bright paint scraped off to the animal hide beneath. He does the only thing left to him: he runs along streets, through marketplaces, down lanes, through churchyards and along the docks. Running until his chest burns.

When he stops running: Mathilda.

He spends the night with memories he had put away: the fine dovecote and its sleepy birds, the feel of skin beneath his hands, the tangle of bodies, the sense of his own muscle taut against another's, the sigh that is skin meeting skin, the smoothness of Mathilda's neck, the struggle and the letting go, giving in, gasping, lying exhausted. She gathered him in, restored his body, made sense of his longing, the time he spent putting paint on parchment.

In the early morning he opens his shutter, breathes in the cold light, tells himself these things are of no consequence: he will never see her again. Her words come to him, then, and he has to admit it: his seed could be, probably is, the child of a noblewoman.

37
London
July 1322

Shell Gold

One of the richest and most expensive pigments is shell gold. Gold is a metal that tends to stick together, and when ground will re-form into clumps, but if the gold has been already beaten to fine sheets for gold leaf, it will crumble into a powder. Take the sheets and grind them on your slab, mixing with gum arabic until you have a golden paint, very precious.

Gold leaf gives a bright, strong shine, while shell gold gives a softer, more shimmering finish. It is especially effective for creating a sense of heavenly radiance in haloes and shimmering beams of divine light. You may also use it to create golden highlights on a special object, where in more ordinary scenes you might use white highlight. It can also be mixed in small amounts with another hue. The trees of paradise can be rendered in all their beauty by using shell gold mixed with green.

I have found that when gold leaf is applied to a page, the excess that is not needed can be carefully blown and brushed away into a pot and reserved for use as shell gold. Remember that your master will be pleased if you take such economies.

The Art of Illumination

'I can't believe she's asked this.' Gemma's voice is high. 'Stops the book, just like that, then asks for more — just a little bit more, that is. Does she think we're so desperate we'll leave our other work and paint her extra pages?'

'What other work, Ma?' Nick asks.

'No need to be clever, Nicholas. You know what I mean. For all she knows of us, we might be working day and night on commissions. The Dancaster workshop has a reputation, as she well knows.'

'She's not making demands. The lady's been brought down, remember, love,' John says. 'I don't think she expects us to do them right away. The letter says that she'll send the book to us whenever we have time to paint the pages. And only if we agree to do them.'

John is right, but as usual his mildness makes Gemma furious. 'Us, John? Why us? You mean Will and me, don't you? Or me.' She looks down at her hands, regrets the words as soon as she speaks. It's the pain of remembering all that's lost that makes her angry. 'We can't ask Benedict to come back,' she says more quietly.

'I'll help,' Nick says. 'At least with mixing and grinding and basic colouring. Maybe even more, now I have my book.' He takes it from the purse where he keeps it, wrapped in cloth, runs his hand over the simple binding and turns to the first page. *The Art of Illumination.*

Gemma can't help smiling. Nick has pored over its pages, asked questions, shown it to anyone who will pause to look, pointing out the title page and his mother's signature. Beyond the words, he has examined the simple decorations in the borders, the tracery of line and curl that Gemma loves to create. John can't see the detail, but he has been impressed, and nods each time Nick reads something from it. 'A wiser book than I could have written,' he told Gemma. 'Nick, mind you care for this. It's a book that will be copied again and again.'

John and Gemma watch Nick leaf through some pages, pause again at the front page.

'Yes, Nick. You and your ma,' John says. He rubs his thumb across a knot in the tabletop. 'You're right, Gem. I can't do the work.'

Gemma looks up. This is the first time he has said the words.

'It will all be up to you now,' he goes on, and it's clear he means more than the extra pages.

For all the worry and hardship that will come, it's only sadness that hangs in the air.

John, Gemma and Nick are at the table in the hall, cups, scraps of cheese and bread in front of them.

'Will. Sit down,' John says. 'We still have some ale. I gather you've changed your mind about the lady's extra pages?'

Will sits and speaks slowly, keeping his voice flat, holding down everything that threatens to erupt. 'I can see that her own family seal on the pages might help Lady Mathilda now that she's a widow. Help her claim the family lineage, regain position.'

Gemma wipes crumbs off the table onto the floor. 'But you were so certain when you spoke to John.'

'It was so sudden, Gemma. We hadn't heard word from her for months. Now, a baby on the way … we should help her if we can.'

'Took us all by surprise,' John says. 'That's true enough.'

They sit around the table in silence, not sure where to go from there. Every word threatens to mean more than is intended.

'So, Will, have you decided what we should paint, you and I?' Gemma says at last. Will doesn't deserve her sniping, but she can't get beyond it. So much that was good is gone.

'Love, come on,' John says. 'Will's agreed—'

'Oh, no,' Will says quickly. 'You and John will know what's best to paint. To finish the story, isn't it? You understand best how to do that.'

And they are surprised, all four of them, that Will seems to mean it.

* * *

Will's work with Osmund on a panel for the Bishop of London's palace will keep him busy for two weeks, and Gemma is doing some simple decorations on a manuscript for Manekyn, so they meet in the early morning to discuss what they might do. It is familiar ground. Even though the work is no longer secret, they are both aware of John: his presence, his interest, his failing sight, and ask for his thoughts on what they should paint. Perhaps he senses their pity, because he says little.

'You know most about this, Gemma. The language of pictures, you say. The book is Lady Mathilda's story, or it was, until her husband died in the wrong battle. She needs the book to tell her story as it is now.'

'A beginning and an end,' Will says.

'Maybe not,' says Gemma. 'We have to add pages that show there's now a different story for the lady. When we paint the Resurrection, we change the meaning of the pictures of the Crucifixion, don't we? The death is cruel and agonising, and we show all that, but what comes next gives it meaning. Life after death, and so death means something more. The book shows Lady Mathilda as the wife of Sir Robert, and the extra pages will show her as a widow, but also more than that.'

'But Gem, she's still a traitor's widow,' John says.

'John Dancaster, you sound like Southflete! Is that all you men see? She's an heiress, a de Saunford, so she's right to ask us to include her family arms, or the family seal, on the pages. And we need to choose pictures that show who she is now. She might remarry, she might have a son and heir, even if there's little to inherit.' She pauses and the men wait. 'She might decide not to marry again. It's not an end of the story, but a way of showing that it goes on.' Gemma hasn't understood this until she hears her own words. Traitor's widow, blind limner's wife — what comes next?

The book, its simple cover, sits on John's desk. It's strange to see it again, a pain Gemma thought was over. No one has picked it up yet, apart from John when he first unwrapped it. He has collected two bi-folium of parchment from Rowley and cut them in half; they'll only need three pages, so John puts the fourth sheet in the storeroom; it might be needed later.

Gemma and Will begin work, only the whisper of leadpoint on parchment as they sketch. John lingers in the storeroom, trying at first to help, telling Nick what he knows already about the pigments. When Nick goes into the shop, John rearranges pots and parchment, wipes the bench again.

Nick stands close to Will as he takes the compasses and draws a series of circles, always keeping the compass point in one place, gradually opening the legs until he has thirteen concentric circles, twelve nesting inside the largest one. A memory flickers. He had watched Edgar as he drew pictures for a copy of Sacrobosco's treatise on the spheres, explaining as he worked the arrangement of the heavens. Will was enthralled by the way such huge thoughts were captured in ink and colour. He already knew from Simon about the shape of the universe, but to a limner's eye, the theory of the spheres became more real on parchment than in words.

Across the top of the page will be heaven with Christ enthroned and flanked by angels, and at the bottom, squeezed under the lower curve of the spheres, the sharp outlines of the battlements of hell, here and there a demon with bat wings torturing a damned soul. Perhaps Nick could help him with the dark, misshapen demonic bodies. He sits back and squints at the shapes, the proportions on the page, and imagines the spheres coloured brightly, hell dark and heaven dusted with shell gold. The universe and the Christian world gathered together.

Inside the tiny centre circle he draws a grand manor house, marked by its turrets and a tower: not Aspenhill Manor, and different, no doubt, from the small house at Welwyn, but that's not the point. And close by, the tiniest of dovecotes in the garden. On either side are the arms of the Fitzjohn and de Saunford families; whatever the king might call Sir Robert now he's dead, Mathilda is connected to his family.

Will has been pondering this page for days, ever since Gemma suggested the importance of representing Mathilda's property and her family lineage in a way that draws them into the sacred story of the book. It seems such a grand statement, the house at the centre of the whole universe.

With his finger he traces the spheres from centre to rim, thinks of the crystalline sphere surrounding it all. He thinks of Simon lying on the grass not far from the great oak, looking up, trying to find a way to comprehend the planets, each travelling inside its globe, each larger than the one before, all the way out to the stars.

His voice low, Simon said simply, 'It makes me feel so small.' But when Will agreed with him, he went on, 'No, not only the stars and the spheres, but all of it. Great ideas, clever theories, mathematics, theology, rhetoric. I think I've learned so much, but there's always so much more. It makes me feel small, incapable.'

Will was startled by the words, finding it difficult to believe that his friend, so sure and confident, could feel that way.

Thinking on it now in the workshop, there is a glimmer in front of his eyes, almost a light. For a moment, he sees it: so many ideas that had to find a place within the small streets and houses of a scholar's Cambridge life. Simon's learning must have been a weight on his shoulders as well as the pleasure he always said it was. Perhaps that was why he argued so hard, would allow no other way. And Mathilda, too; for all that her position and her name have brought her and might bring her still, she is caught inside them as surely as the planets within their spheres.

* * *

John walks through the shop and out into the street. Gemma stares at the door as it closes behind him, and hugs herself for the cold she suddenly feels. So much has changed. All that time ago when the book began, the moonlight on her skin, she and John making love, she felt that sharing the work held them together. She hadn't realised how badly John's eyes were failing, how much could be lost. To Paternoster Row, they are still John and Gemma, but inside the shop, the house, the bed, they don't know who they are. Are there other ways to be limner and wife? Limner and husband?

She watches Will sketching, humming to himself. The two creases in his forehead that tighten and then let go; the occasional sigh of frustration, or perhaps pleasure; the slight pursing of his lips; the clean movement of his hand over the parchment that causes a quiver in the muscle near his shoulder. Gemma wishes away the warmth in her chest. It's not the same as with John. And yet sharing the work, this work now, is a matter of bodies as well as skill. They'll finish the pages, Peter will paste them into the book and John will send it away. It will be an ending, as it was last time, yet different.

In the evening, Gemma lights another lamp and stays at her desk. She was so keen to begin, knew what picture she would paint. It won't be her master's piece, recognised by the fraternity, but it will be her piece, the one she has imagined in her mind for so long. But now, the design feels awkward.

'Gemma, you right, love?' John asks.

She hasn't heard him come in from the hall.

'Yes, thinking is all. The sketch for this page.' She laughs. 'I was so pleased to decide on the subject myself, not just obey Manekyn's instructions, you know? But if I do it the way I want, the picture is unbalanced, the crowd on one side, the

woman in the middle, and only the king on the other side. I
don't know ...'

'So what is it that matters? What's most important about the
story?'

'The woman. She speaks.'

John smiles. 'Well then. Paint that, love. You'll do it.'

Gemma looks at him, this man she has known for so long.
His face is thinner and he's more stooped, but even if his eyes
don't work well, the gentleness is still there.

'I will. Tomorrow. I'm too tired now to lift a brush.' She
stands up. 'Are you coming? I'll douse the lights.'

'No, I'll do it. I'll just sit here for a moment or two and
remember.'

Gemma hesitates, then nods and turns. Her knees give way
briefly.

As her footsteps fade, the shop stills. Memories pour from the
shadows, flickering in the lamplight, curling around John's
head. Two days ago, ten years ago, thirty years ago. A man
moves among them: apprentice, journeyman, master. He's
slower now, collecting a fresh page and paint, red and carbon
black, from the storeroom. Sitting at his desk, picking up his
brush, adjusting the lamp. He begins.

All is lost and nothing is lost.

Mathilda

Mathilda goes to her chamber with the yellow bundle, closes the door and sits on the edge of her bed. For a time, she simply holds it, remembering the first time she saw it, thinking it was so much like Robert's dead body, a monster wrapped in soft fabric. When she thinks of all that's happened, the two bundles sit together in her mind. Even so, it is the first delivery of the book that feels like the centre of the wheel on which her life turns. It should be the moment when the blade struck through Robert's soft organs, she knows, but it seems life after Robert's death only became possible when she opened the book's covers.

The baby rolls and she watches the lemon-like shape of a knee, or perhaps it's an elbow, beneath her skin, moving across the dome of her belly. To those who know her story, it will be her shame, a traitor's baby. She puts a hand over the movement and thinks of Will. Does he understand what she told him in the letter? Is he wondering what his child will be?

She unwraps the book and searches for the new pages. There they are; one by one she finds them. Though she didn't know what to expect, they are beyond what she could have imagined. What worlds these pages make.

The first of the extra leaves has been pasted into the beginning of the book, an illumination of spheres with a manor house in the centre. The spheres, each one a different colour, seem to shift before her eyes as if they might actually be spinning, and heaven shimmers with a soft golden light. The manor house with its turrets is not like Aspenhill, and certainly too large for Wain Wood, but it is the story she needs to tell. She smiles. This house that she ran to seemed so small, but it has been a hole to hide in; it's now the centre of her world. And there … She sees a tiny dovecote. The memory hurts, and she wonders how William felt as he painted it.

Hours pass; she can't stop looking at the pages, wondering at the puzzle they are. The one pasted in after the illumination of the Annunciation and before the Virgin and Child she knows William painted. It's a picture of her doing what she is doing right now, looking at her book of hours. She's wearing her pink gown, the one from the night in the chapel, but now it falls in elegant folds from her belly swollen with child. On her hair, and in tiny touches on her face and arms, gold gleams gently: shell gold, not the leaf, as William promised in the dovecote. Mathilda gasps in a breath, sobs.

Behind her is the lost tapestry, the gift from Robert, the one she loves so much and left behind in the old house. There is the tree in the centre, its graceful trunk and wide canopy that shelters the man and woman beneath, one on either side, and near their feet rabbits, foxes and dogs playing happily together. The tree bears oranges among its curling leaves. She touches an orange and smiles. William has tried to create the texture of tapestry stitches, each one a brush stroke, but so very tiny.

On the page of the book that the painted Mathilda is reading is a woman in a pink dress reading a book. If Mathilda looks very carefully, she can see in that tiny book a line or two in pink, another woman with another book. It's not very clear or detailed, but it's enough to show that this could go on forever, a book inside a book inside a book; a woman seeing herself seeing herself: ever smaller, but never finishing.

She places a finger on the woman in the first tiny book. What is the story of your picture? she wonders. Are you a widow as well? Perhaps you pray more than I do, forever caught at your devotions. Or is your husband alive and loyal to the king? Will he go to battle and survive, come home and run his estate, be promoted to parliament? Are there visits to court, the king's invitation extended to both of you? Are you married to another man, one I don't know? Or are you unmarried still, busy running your small estate?

What did Will intend? Is this Mathilda the woman from seasons ago, the one who knelt in the chapel for him, not knowing what was to come? Is she with child? A child who will be born with the features and skills of an artisan?

The puzzle of this picture stays with her all night. In her half-dreaming, how many women she becomes.

The next day she studies the third picture, shining in shades of yellow and green. These new pages are like a whole new book to study, each one with a story she has to understand. Will painted the other two, she knows, so this one should be John Dancaster's work. There it is, the Dancaster rose, tucked among some lavender. But this rose is different. It takes her some moments to recognise the changes: the petals closer together, less even, with the slightest curl at the edges where there is more still to unfurl. It's more like a bud that has recently opened. Mathilda compares it with a rose on another page; yes, the colour is paler, more pink than red. She might not have noticed except that she has studied the familiar rose so closely, trying to understand how the master has created shape through shade and light. Perhaps the atelier had no more pigment for the deep red colour. But why the change in shape? She will never know.

In the top half of the page a woman crouches by a pool, her yellow robe clutched to her nakedness, scant protection from two men who stand over her, leering. Blonde hair hangs over her bare shoulders. A yellow-brown wall curves around the garden, a tree on either side frames the figures, and small bushes of rosemary and lavender send fragrance across the water from their vivid tufts of purple flowers. The men threaten, speak of power, and the woman is afraid. Yet there is something in the shape of her shoulders and the strength of her neck that says she will not give in. *Say what you will*, she says, *but I will not give myself to you.*

Mathilda looks for words to explain the picture, but there are none. She can't remember this story from sermons.

In the lower half of the page, the woman stands in the centre, alone. Mathilda looks at her first, her yellow gown, her stance. Scanning the rest of the picture to find out who she might be, Mathilda sees the crowd of men at the left, frowning at the woman, as if waiting for a spectacle of some kind. The two accusing men, the ones who leer in the picture above, stand with them, fingers pointing at the woman. On the right sits a king with a kindly face. Not Edward. Perhaps he will use his power, speak against the men and save the woman.

Or he might be silent. It doesn't matter. It's the woman. Mathilda has never seen a woman like this one. Her yellow gown is simple and hangs loosely, but her body is there too, as if it was painted before the gown. The length of her thighs and the curve of her hips shape the fabric; her shoulders are square; one hand rests on her hip, the other gestures eloquently. Mathilda feels her own arms and shoulders, feels what she must do to stand like this woman. She speaks, and though her words aren't written, what words she must say. What declarations she must make. Mathilda can hear them, can almost hear her own voice.

'I will not be shamed by you men. I will not heed your accusations. I will stand.'

38

London
September 1322

The Book

A book is shaped so that it may be picked up and carried, held onto as a baby might clutch a blanket, pondered in the quiet or lonely hours of the night, visited like a friend. You decorate the book for another, for it to be passed on from owner to daughter or son and from them to their children. Once you finish it, you cannot say where it will go and how it will be used. It might sit for years on a shelf, or stay wrapped in a cloth, forgotten. It might be a grieving woman's companion for the rest of her life, or a child's first sight of words, open at a page that carries the marks of much use. Perhaps it will go across the sea in a boat. Perhaps it will crumble or burn. It might be passed from hand to hand, through years, for longer than you can dream of. You cannot know. All you can do is paint faithfully and well, then let the book go.

The Art of Illumination

It is harder than Gemma imagined, saying goodbye to Will. She stands by her desk and watches as he wrestles with Nick, remembering that first meeting in the shop. How tall he was, how deep his voice, how sure of himself. How much she wanted him gone. And now, how much has changed. It is the cruel way of things that it was John's failing sight that gave her and Will those quiet mornings together. Sometimes they spoke, and often they were silent, but so much passed between them; it might have been years ago with John. This work that is both mind and body.

'I win!' Nick yells as Will lets the lad push him to the floor.

'It had to happen,' the big man says, flat on his back. 'All my lessons, all that practice you've had.'

'That your master's piece in there?' John asks, pointing to a bag in the corner. 'Still not finished?'

Will smiles. 'Yes, and my brushes.' He pushes Nick off his chest and stands up. 'London hasn't been what I expected, John. But I'll finish it now. For a time, when the book was stopped, I didn't care to see it, much less work on it. Then something changed. I painted two pages, broke the rules a little.' He glances at Gemma. 'Seems it suits me. And God knows the world needs beauty.'

'True enough,' John says. 'And where are you headed?'

'I'm taking the Cambridge road, so I'll go back, see if it has a place for me. Who's to say? We might not suit each other any more. But first, I'll go to my parents, see how they're faring. And the burned psalter — I'd like to look at it again after all these years. Lady Mathilda reminded ... Lady Mathilda's book has me in mind of it once more.' He smiles. 'It was the first decorated book I ever saw, so of course it was special. But I've been thinking of late that there was something about the burned pages as well, the way they flared out like a bird's tail. The book wouldn't be the same without them.'

'Aye, we think beauty must be perfect, but we miss the rest,' John says quietly.

Will looks at Gemma, her arms crossed, the glimmer of tears in her eyes.

'And who will you wrestle now, Will? What will you do without me?' Nick says.

'I wonder, lad.'

'Come on, Nick, say goodbye now,' John says. 'You can help me mend the parchment on the window in the solar. Been meaning to fix that for a time now.'

'But Pa, I—'

'Find the hide glue and come with me. Now, Nick.' The tone is enough, and Nick punches Will on the arm in farewell.

'I'll be in London soon enough, Nick. And when I am, Paternoster Row is the first place I'll visit.'

Gemma thinks she might leave too. There's nothing more to say. Instead, she walks across to Will and looks into his face. 'How would you show sadness with only a few lines?' she asks.

Will smiles and steps closer. 'Many things in London I hadn't expected,' he says, and takes her hand.

They stand for some moments in that familiar quiet space. Lapis, heaven on her fingertips, Gemma thinks.

As he reaches Bishopsgate, Will feels the familiar squish beneath his feet, frowns at the stench that rises. Without looking down to investigate, he walks to the side of the gate and scrapes the sole clean.

'Gerroutavit,' a voice shouts. It's one of the guards. 'Take your own turds with you.'

Will keeps dragging the sole of his boot against the stone, over and over until it seems clean. 'These are good London turds. You can keep 'em,' he says, then looks toward the guard and bows deeply. 'With me or without me, you'll shovel up your shit and start again tomorrow.'

'Get away with you, cur. And stay away.'

'Can't get rid of me that easily,' Will says. He hoists higher onto his shoulder his small bag of brushes and knives, a few clothes and a roll of parchment, and walks out the gate. He begins to whistle.

Mathilda

Mathilda is resting, the baby big and ready to be born. She is studying the new pages still, and what they might mean for her. It's warm enough to leave her small window open and the sounds of the estate's work — the shouting and banging and animal noises — are fine company. The newly weaned lambs bleat for their mothers, and Mathilda looks up, waits until they stop; Joan and Maggie have asked to help feed them.

Mathilda turns to the calendar page for September near the front of her book, and sees the plump man working with his flail at a big yellow pile of stalks. The colours are beautiful, as she had requested. Down in the village, and in her barn, they are threshing wheat, though the small crop means it will soon be finished, and none of the men have the red cheeks and warm clothes of the painting. As she ponders, she loosens her grip on the book and it begins to close in her hand. It's only a glimpse, but she startles, sees a flicker of colour where there should be none. She pulls open the back cover and gasps.

The page is completely covered in black, a deep, thick black, and marked in places with a scattering of red drops. That's all there is, just black and red; no words, no borders, no creatures in the margins, no illumination, no gold leaf. She has seen one of these paintings in another book; it is nothing but sorrow. The black of Christ's death when the whole earth was darkened, and the red of his blood, the drops of anguish that fell from him on the cross. She's had enough of suffering; she doesn't want more blood, more reminders of her duty to be grateful and humble, even to God. And this image is ugly and crude. She touches the page to feel the thickness of the paint, the way it stiffens the parchment.

She can see it has been pasted in like the three extra pages she asked for, but after the last leaf. Who did this? This rough ending? She's angry now at this ugliness added to her book, this final insult, this jeer to a book some might say has failed. She clasps the cover, puts the book away on the shelf, leaves it alone.

Only hours later, it pulls her back again, this strange and awkward page. This time she closes her eyes and touches the drops, feels their bumps and ridges, the fatness of the paint, as if tears have thickened the parchment. It's grief she can feel.

When she opens her eyes, she sees for the first time the red shape in the bottom corner: a misshapen bloom, a failed attempt at the Dancaster rose. A signature among all this suffering.

Her hand on the flower, Mathilda lets her own tears come at last, grateful for this companion who understands. Seasons of fear and grief and loss.

Through the open window, Maggie's voice floats up, calling to Fraden for a ride in the cart. More words, her daughter's quick laugh. Mathilda wipes her face, walks to the window and watches Maggie climb up next to Fraden, take the reins out of his hand and flick them. She puts her palm on the roundness of her belly, feels the baby stretch, push. Insistent.

Author's Note

Many of us will have seen photos, and perhaps even exhibitions, of sumptuously decorated books from the Middle Ages. My attention, though, has always been drawn to the margins of books of hours, as they are known, where birds, animals, funny and fantastical creatures and even scenes of sin and bawd are often depicted — all alongside prayers and illuminations of Christ and the Virgin Mary. Just what was going on here? How was it the church allowed and encouraged women to view such pictures as part of their devotions? It was in that surprising space — what seemed disjuncture to a modern mind — that I began to explore. Who were the people who created these books? Who were the patrons who ordered them? Once I began to research and imagine, the questions took me far and wide, from details of daily life in London through to the machinations of English politics. And, most profoundly, it took me to the British Library Manuscript Room, and one particular book of hours, the Neville of Hornby Hours. In awe of being allowed to handle a book seven centuries old, I carefully turned the pages, and as I studied the differences of style in the pictures, the personalities of my four limners began to emerge. The decorations they paint were inspired by several other books, including the Smithfield Decretals and the Luttrell Psalter. Wandering around the streets of London, along Paternoster Row, past St Paul's, to the Thames, along what remains of the London Wall, I began to imagine my way into my story of the creation of a book of hours.

In England, the first decades of the fourteenth century were a dark time. For seven years from 1315 to 1322, heavy and prolonged rain brought floods, crop failure and stock losses, resulting in severe food shortage, illness and death across Europe. It is estimated that the period, known as the Great Famine, killed at least 25 per cent of the population.

The political realm was no less troubled. King Edward II's failure to deal with ongoing conflict with France, his losses of land to the Scots and his imposition of burdensome taxes to fund his wars brought him into conflict with powerbrokers of the church and the peerage. Their attempts to control and limit the king's power were blindsided when he accepted and then revoked a range of reforms, the Ordinances of 1311.

Tension increased even further over Edward's close relationship with the ruthless Hugh Despenser the Younger, whose campaign of accumulating land in the Welsh Marches incensed the Marcher barons. As demands for Despenser's exile mounted, the barons marched to London's gates, threatening war. That conflict was temporarily resolved with Despenser's exile, but his return to England brought the country once more to the point of civil war. In 1322 the Marcher barons joined with Lancaster, the king's onetime supporter and the most powerful peer in the land, in battle against the crown's forces at Boroughbridge; their defeat was followed by spectacular and pitiless revenge.

Against this backdrop of deprivation, violence and fear, townsfolk and villagers alike got by as well as they could. In London, trades and services continued, from prostitutes through to goldsmiths, and people bought, or didn't, according to their means. Only the rich and aspiring could afford to commission a book of hours.

The book trade in early fourteenth-century London centred on Paternoster Row and London Bridge. Mentions in the historical record of individuals identified as limners are scarce and incidental, usually just brief notices in court and administrative documents. In the first decades of the fourteenth century, fewer than ten limners are recorded in London, though it's likely there were more.

My characters are all fictional, though I have named many of them from records of book artisans throughout the century. While specific written details are limited, the paintings in decorated books provide more subtle but nonetheless telling information. Close examination of styles and remarkable advances in the analysis of parchment, paints and even the worms that infest some bindings have enabled scholars to locate the geographical origins of many books. Elements of the painting style, including the minutiae of brushstrokes and the choice of decorative motifs and repeated images, can also help identify the work of a particular limner.

From relatively small beginnings, as the creation of books moved beyond monasteries and convents into the secular world, the London book trade grew. By the end of the century, the city recognised its importance and agreed to the establishment of a Mistery [Guild] of Stationers (1403), to oversee and support the work of all book artisans.

No women are listed as limners in the early decades of the fourteenth century in London, though this may be more a reflection of the general attitude to women and their status than a true indication of their involvement in the book trade. Women played a significant and vital role in the labour force of London, and worked in a wide range of trades, from ale-making to cobbling to all aspects of construction work. Often they worked alongside their husbands in their businesses. Nonetheless, however great or necessary their skill, they were considered to be second-tier workers. A wife or daughter might be accepted as an apprentice, but she could not gain full membership of a guild, and would often be restricted to a role that prevented her from marketing the product she made, thus being confined to work in the home or shop; it was often women who trained apprentices. Even in crafts where 'women's skills' predominated, such as silkworking, no officially organised guild existed in the medieval period. Many other women worked in occupations considered to be unskilled, such as domestic service and midwifery, for which no guild was created.

Within this context, a woman working in illumination could not be recognised for her skill and be described as 'limner', so the absence of any mention of female limners does not mean there were none. Manuscripts across Europe show that nuns were skilled as scribes and illuminators, but beyond the convent, there is only scattered mention of women in the trade. Jeanne de Montbaston worked alongside her husband in fourteenth-century Paris, having taken the oath of the booksellers as 'illuminatrix' and 'libraria' in 1353.

Given the fledgling state of the secular book trade in London and the status of women, I have imagined inside the space that the scaffolding of information provides. How might the book artisans have organised their fraternities? How would the leadership have structured and maintained the kind of quality, order and support the Stationers' Guild would come to offer? How would women with talent and a love of paint have managed to be recognised within the strictures of the time?

Noble women were important patrons of the arts, from silkwork through to textiles and book production. The popularity of books of hours grew throughout the fourteenth century; some were commissioned by women while others were ordered as gifts for a wife or daughter. Women of the upper classes were often taught to read in Anglo-Norman, the vernacular of the elite. But there was a distinction between the skills of reading and writing, and even those who could read in the vernacular, and had perhaps learned a little Latin through the repetition and familiarity of prayers, were seldom able to write. Although letter writing was popular among noble women, they usually required the services of a scribe.

The decorations in books of hours were considered an integral part of a woman's devotions, drawing her into the presence of God, and she was taught to understand the 'language' of the images as much as the words. The illuminations — sacred images of Christ, the Virgin Mary and the saints — generally followed convention, but some of the marginal images reference ideas that are hard for us to understand. Vines, flowers and birds appear beautiful and simply decorative, but monsters and figures defecating, or even inviting or indulging in sex, would seem to disrupt and distract devotion. The purpose and significance of these pictures has been long debated. Some scholars have considered them evidence of deranged minds; others see them as aids to memory. Some suggest they are sites of resistance and commentary on the prayers and illuminations; some argue that they are precise and clever plays on words, and even syllables, in the Latin text. Yet others suggest that they reflect the medieval view of life that all of God's creation is suitable for contemplation.

We may never know the real inspiration for these marginal images. But whatever it might have been, one thing is true: all of life is there, in the book.

Further Reading

On the Great Famine, William Chester Gordon's study is wide-ranging and thorough: *The Great Famine: Northern Europe in the Early Fourteenth Century* (Princeton: Princeton University Press, 1997).

There are many studies of Edward's reign, and some well-researched blogs on the topic; a good place to begin is Seymour Phillips, *Edward II* (New Haven: Yale University Press, 2010).

On medieval life in fourteenth-century England, Ian Mortimer's study is entertaining and well-researched: *The Time Traveller's Guide to Medieval England: A Handbook for Visitors to the Fourteenth Century* (London: Vintage Books, 2009).

For medieval life in general, a fascinating study with illustrations of archaeological finds is Roberta Gilchrist's *Medieval Life: Archaeology and the Life Course* (Woodbridge: Boydell Press, 2012).

For details of the early book trade, see C. Paul Christianson, *A Directory of London Stationers and Book Artisans 1300–1500* (New York: Bibliographical Society of America, 1990); and *The Production of Books in England 1350–1500*, edited by Alexandra Gillespie and Daniel Wakelin (Cambridge: Cambridge University Press, 2011).

For a discussion of the shifting situation of working women across Europe in the Middle Ages, see the essays in *Sisters and Workers in the Middle Ages*, edited by Judith M. Bennett et al (Chicago: University of Chicago Press, 1989). The introduction and first chapter are excellent.

Kathryn A. Smith provides a remarkable, detailed study of the significance and contents of three books of hours produced for three noble women in *Art, Identity and Devotion in Fourteenth-Century England: Three Women and Their Books of Hours* (London: The British Library, 2003).

A fascinating study of women's relationships with their books of hours, and especially the self-reflexivity of the woman viewing her own portrait, is Alexa Sand, *Vision, Devotion, and Self-Representation in Late Medieval Art* (Cambridge: Cambridge University Press, 2014).

For those interested in further commentary on the marginal images, Michael Camille, *Image on the Edge: the Margins of Medieval Art* (London: Reaktion Books, 1992) is accessible and well illustrated.

Accounts of the methods of creating and decorating manuscripts have proliferated in recent years, especially online, and a good place to begin is the John Paul Getty Museum's 'Making Manuscripts' web page. An online search will easily find more, including film of various stages of the process.

A brief but thorough and accessible book on scribes and illuminators is Christopher de Hamel, *Scribes and Illuminators* (London: The British Museum Press, 1992).

For more details on pigments, see Daniel V. Thompson, *The Materials and Techniques of Medieval Painting* (New York: Dover Publications, 1956).

Erik Kwakkel's blog, *medievalbooks*, has wonderful content, demonstrating the continuity of our relationship with books from their earliest production until today.

For an example of an early guide for the painter and illuminator, see Cennino d'Andrea Cennini, *The Craftsman's Handbook: The Italian 'Il Libro dell'Arte'*, translated by Daniel V. Thompson, Jr (New York: Dover Publications, 1960).

Randy Asplund decorates magnificent manuscripts with pigments he has researched and made himself, using as close to the medieval method as possible. He has a website and is currently writing a book on the subject.

An online search, using words such as 'illuminated manuscripts', 'medieval marginal images', 'medieval books' and so on, will open an online world of images and enthusiasts!

Many of the libraries that have illuminated books in their collection have begun digitising them and have provided a great service to us in making them freely available online. You could spend many a happy hour browsing through them. There are many available; the following are manuscripts produced in England in the early fourteenth century and are available on the British Library website: Neville of Hornby Hours, London, BL Egerton MS 2781; Smithfield Decretals, London, BL Royal 10 E IV; Taymouth Hours, London, BL Yates Thompson 13 and The Luttrell Psalter, London, BL Add MS 42130.

Happy viewing!

Acknowledgements

I am grateful for the ongoing support of Flinders University, South Australia, where my continuing academic status has given me access to invaluable research materials; my thanks especially to the Off Campus Library Service. The British Library, London, is a remarkable place and a wonderful resource. There, the staff of the Maps Section provided information and leads about fourteenth-century London; the Manuscript Room delivered to me many a box containing a precious medieval book, and one in particular that helped my limners come to life.

I am enormously grateful once again to that special place, Gladstone's Library, and especially to Peter Francis, for giving me four glorious weeks as Writer-in-Residence, offering bed, board, wonderful conversation and remarkable hospitality. Randy Asplund, artist, generously gave me advice on medieval pigments; any mistakes are mine.

As always, my deepest thanks to my remarkable agent, Gaby Naher, who has helped me hang in through the tough bits and continued to support, defend and encourage me. Huge thanks and love to Catherine Milne, my publisher at HarperCollins, who has believed in me once again. Her enthusiasm, insight and love of story have helped me find my way through the maze of my imagined world to shape the story I was looking for. To Amanda O'Connell (once again), Scott Forbes and Bronwyn Sweeney my huge thanks for their patience with me and their precision with my words, saving me from blunders and refining my manuscript; they are the hidden gems of publishing. And to James Kellow, Sarah Barrett and many others behind the scenes at HarperCollins, thank you for helping bring this book into being.

In the process of writing this novel I have proven, as many before me, that second novels have their own particular difficulty. I owe a debt of thanks to all my readers of *The Anchoress* and especially those who took the time to review the novel or to speak or write to me. And, in particular, to those who shared their personal stories. I cannot say how deeply their words touched me, and gave me momentum to stay at the desk, push through the doubt, and write the next scene.

One of the precious gifts of writing is my discovery of a welcoming and supportive writing community, both 'in the flesh' in Canberra and elsewhere, and on social media. I am grateful and privileged to have its encouragement.

My thanks to Greg Johnston, who cheered me on, generously read a draft, gave me detailed feedback and time to talk it over.

As always, the women of my writing group have given me the very best combination of companionship, honest and insightful feedback, and unwavering acceptance and love; my love and thanks to Biff Ward, Di Lucas, Jenni Savigny and Di Martin. Nigel Featherstone, my dear friend, has offered gentle support and understanding, and shared the love and angst of writing, over great vegan food. He continues to remind me that the work is worth it.

Again, huge thanks and love to Judy King, whose delight in investigating the details of language, grammar and culture has been a wonderful, living resource. Above all, she has listened, laughed and believed in me.

And once more, and always, to Alan for giving me space, love and more belief in me than I knew was possible.

The very best creations I have been privileged to share are the births of my four children. From their earliest years, they showed me new ways of perceiving the world and portrayed it, then as now, each in their own particular and spectacular style — word and movement, line and colour.

Jessica, Myfanwy, Daniel and Demelza, this book is for you, with my love and gratitude.

Finally, I am enormously grateful to the limners from so many centuries ago, whose imagination, skill and humour inspired me to begin this novel, and whose glorious pictures maintained my fascination even when the going was tough.